A row of impenetrable iron bars stood between Logan and the woman he loved.

He balled his shooting hand into a tight fist. The urge to hit something, or someone, came fast, but he reminded himself he'd taken a different path than his brother. Still, a low growl of frustration rumbled deep in his throat.

At the sound, Megan looked up and slowly turned her head.

Their gazes met.

Logan's heart pummeled his rib cage. The brutal assault made each intake of air a struggle.

Lost in her eyes, a compelling tapestry of silver over blue, he experienced a deep sensation of completion. The emotion was so simple, so pure, he wondered how he'd been able to walk away before.

Well, he was home now.

"Logan?" A little sigh slipped from her lips. "Is it really you?"

"Yes, Megan." He forced his words around the breath clogging in his throat. "I've come for you, just like I promised."

Renee Ryan
and
Catherine Palmer

The Lawman
Claims His Bride
&
The Gunman's Bride

LOVE INSPIRED
INSPIRATIONAL ROMANCE

LOVE INSPIRED®

INSPIRATIONAL ROMANCE

Recycling programs for this product may not exist in your area.

ISBN-13: 978-1-335-45472-0

The Lawman Claims His Bride & The Gunman's Bride

Copyright © 2020 by Harlequin Books S.A.

The Lawman Claims His Bride
First published in 2011. This edition published in 2020.
Copyright © 2011 by Renee Ryan

The Gunman's Bride
First published in 2011. This edition published in 2020.
Copyright © 2011 by Catherine Palmer

This edition published by arrangement with Harlequin Books S.A.

For questions and comments about the quality of this book, please contact us at CustomerService@Harlequin.com.

Love Inspired
22 Adelaide St. West, 40th Floor
Toronto, Ontario M5H 4E3, Canada
www.Harlequin.com

Printed in U.S.A.

CONTENTS

Renee Ryan grew up in a Florida beach town where she learned to surf, sort of. With a degree from FSU, she explored career opportunities at a Florida theme park and a modeling agency and even taught high school economics. She currently lives with her husband in Nebraska, and many have mistaken their overweight cat for a small bear. You may contact Renee at reneeryan.com, on Facebook or on Twitter, @reneeryanbooks.

THE LAWMAN
CLAIMS HIS BRIDE

Renee Ryan

Many are the plans in a man's heart,
but it is the Lord's purpose that prevails.
—*Proverbs* 19:21

To Donnell Ann Bell, my favorite pair of fresh eyes.
Thank you, my friend, for all the times
you answered the call for a "quick" favor.
I owe you more than words can express.

Chapter One

Denver, Colorado, 1888.

Megan Goodwin had not intended to die today. But as she stared at the knife inches from her throat, she feared her plans were about to change.

Yet to face her end in a brothel, the same one where her mother had died five years before, was simply unacceptable.

Frozen in terror, she watched the knife's deadly point creep closer.

Megan prayed for courage to face the next few minutes. *Oh, Lord. Oh, God, please help me.*

She lifted the silent appeal to the God she'd counted on her whole life.

Where was Mattie? The madam had promised to return shortly. She'd left Megan here in the safety of her private boudoir, out of sight and hidden from Cole Kincaid.

He'd found her anyway.

Gritting her teeth, Megan forced her gaze to stay on

his face, if only to prove to herself she still had some control of the situation.

He was big, just over six feet. His face was hideous, all flat planes, sallow skin and dark, dirty beard. He had small, black eyes. Mean eyes. The eyes of a killer. The—

He yanked her head back with a hard tug, cutting off the rest of her thoughts. Small white dots of light burst in front of her eyes.

She'd done nothing to warrant this savage attack. Nothing, except put herself in the wrong place at the wrong time for what she thought was the right reason. The act of kindness might be her last.

Cole eased his grip from her hair and lowered the knife, shoving her back against the divan. "Let's have us some fun, shall we?" His voice had a soft note to it, as though he were suggesting they share a cup of tea.

The man was a monster.

Megan pulled her gaze from him and focused instead on the room that had been intentionally decorated for sin. Beneath the expensive silk and garish furnishings hung a decadence that spoke of the ugly work performed here.

So this was it, then? This chamber of wickedness was where she would die? No matter that she'd lived a pure life, no matter that she'd been raised in a Christian orphanage across town, she'd failed to escape her mother's vile world after all.

"Look at me," Cole snarled.

When she kept her gaze averted, he muttered a curse and clutched her jaw, forcing her head around. "Mattie shouldn't keep a pretty thing like you hidden from her paying customers."

The smell of whiskey and week-old sweat trailed in the wake of his words. He swayed, just a little, but enough to tell Megan he'd consumed quite a bit.

"I… I'm not one of her girls."

He laughed at her, an easy sound full of heartless pleasure. "All the better. I like 'em innocent."

Panic clawed for release, but Megan refused to give in to the emotion. She pressed her eyes tightly shut.

She would think of Logan. Only Logan, the good, solid man she'd promised to love the rest of her life. He would be home soon, any day now. Then they would be married.

The thought brought sorrow, not peace. Megan should have never set foot in Mattie's brothel today. She'd only come to read to Suzanne, a young prostitute dying of the same disease that had claimed Megan's mother.

What had she been thinking? That she'd be safe simply because her motives were pure?

Well, it was too late for regrets, too late to scold herself for coming here at all. She'd thought her midafternoon arrival would get her in and out before customers started arriving. Normally, she would have been right. Today, she'd woefully miscalculated and Cole Kincaid had been here, a man known for his cruelty to women.

And now Megan was snared in his trap.

He placed his lips close to her ear. "I promise you one thing, my little beauty." He wrapped velvet around his words. "This *will* hurt."

Something dark inside Megan snapped at the threat.

Cold, ruthless rage took hold of her.

She forgot about the knife at her throat. Forgot about

the menace in her attacker's eyes. And only focused on the black emotion spiraling through her.

Fury controlled her now. She allowed the power of it to spread, allowed her hands to act without permission from her brain. Slowly, resolutely, her palms snaked up her attacker's arms and latched onto his shoulders.

Cole grinned and lowered his head toward hers. His eyes were a bit unfocused, as though the whiskey had dulled his thinking.

Megan shoved him with all her might.

Unprepared for the attack, Cole staggered back a step. The knife dropped from his hand. It hit the floor with a loud crack. Roaring a curse at her, he caught his balance and lunged for her again.

This time, murder glittered in his eyes.

Everything Megan wanted in life flashed through her mind. Logan. Children. A home of her own. "No!" Using her nails as talons she rushed at the man. *"No."*

Trying to cover his face, he fumbled back a step. He began to fall but he grabbed her arm for support. They lurched backward, together, heading straight for the stone fireplace.

Megan fought to free herself, pulling her weight in the opposite direction. Another yank on her arm carried her straight into him.

Tangled together, they stumbled two steps back. Three. His head slammed against the mantle.

The hand on her arm went limp and he slid to the floor like a bundle of discarded rags.

Megan fell to the ground a second later, struggling for air. Now on her hands and knees, she blinked in horror at the man beside her. As quickly as they had come, all the dangerous emotions inside her disappeared. In the next instant, tears welled. Tears of frustration, of fear, of...

Why wasn't he moving?

Hands shaking, Megan reached out. Attacking an innocent woman, indeed. She poked his cowardly shoulder.

He didn't respond, didn't budge.

Heart hammering in her throat, she glanced at the clock above her head, the one sitting on the center of the stone mantle. Megan was shocked to discover that no more than five minutes had passed since the outlaw had entered the parlor.

Feeling as though she was looking at him from a very far distance, she forced herself to study his face. His mouth hung open, slack at the jaw. And with each tick of the clock, he turned deathly pale.

Thou shalt not kill.

What if he was dead?

Thou shalt not kill.

What if he wasn't?

She had to know for sure.

For several heartbeats Megan watched him closely. His chest rose and fell in an unsteady rhythm.

He was alive. But injured.

Megan tried to force up some regret, but she felt no remorse. Cole had attacked her. Given a few more minutes he'd have forced himself on her. Or worse yet, killed her.

Bile rose in her throat. Covering her mouth, she rushed into the bathroom. At the same moment, the door in the outer room opened and closed with a bang. She heard a man's voice.

The sound brought with it a terrible thought. Men

like Cole Kincaid ran in packs. Had one of his gang come to check on him?

No. No one could know he was here. He'd slipped out of one of the upstairs rooms when he'd seen the owner of the brothel rushing Megan down the back stairwell. He'd told her that himself, right before he'd pulled the knife.

Then who could be sneaking into the madam's private parlor?

Megan took a tentative step toward the door and listened. She heard a muffled, "Get on your feet, Kincaid. Now."

A nasty oath came in response to the demand.

"I said get up. I want you standing when you face the devil."

Megan couldn't identify the newcomer's next words, precisely, yet the husky baritone sparked a feeling of relief. She knew that voice, knew it well.

What was he doing here tonight, in Mattie's brothel, at this hour?

Bewildered, she edged forward and peered into the parlor. The man's back was to her so she couldn't see his face. But she recognized that powerful build. Except...

The way he held his shoulders wasn't quite right.

Her thoughts knotted together in her mind, blurring like a distant dream just out of reach.

The man suddenly turned to face her. Their gazes met for only a brief moment before Megan's vision grayed, darkened. And then her world went black.

Winter clung to the damp March air, refusing to relinquish its frigid grip on Denver. In an attempt to calm his raging emotions, U.S. Marshal Logan Mitchell filled his lungs with the biting cold. Eyes narrowed, temper hot, his thoughts pinpointed to one impossible reality.

Megan had been arrested. *His* Megan.

The churning in his gut formed into a tight, angry spasm. He could easily allow the dark emotion to take hold, but that would unleash a part of him he'd held tightly controlled since childhood.

Rubbing at the tension at the back of his neck, Logan studied the unassuming brick building directly across the street. He didn't need perfect vision to read the words embossed on the plaque nailed to the door. *Sheriff's Office and Jailhouse.*

This had to be a mistake. His future wife should not be locked up. She should be back at Charity House, the orphanage where she lived and worked, helping settle the younger children into bed for the night.

Logan lifted his eyes to the dark heavens, tried to formulate a prayer, but words escaped him. How did he turn to God for guidance when he had yet to discover what Megan had done, or why Trey Scott had locked her up like a common criminal?

No one at Charity House had given him a direct answer as to Megan's whereabouts this evening. Instead, they'd given him some cryptic explanation about her reading to a sick woman living in Mattie Silks's brothel. *Mattie Silks's brothel!*

When Logan had questioned the ornery madam, she'd been the difficult, condescending woman he remembered all too well. She'd circled him like a rat sizing up a meaty piece of garbage, all the while talking to him in half sentences and irrelevant facts.

But Logan had been on to her game of distraction. He hadn't missed her covert glances toward the back of the house, where her private suite of rooms was located. The woman had been hiding something. Or someone. Only when he'd started toward her boudoir did she direct him to the county jail. *The county jail!*

He sucked in another hard breath. The dark, damp air magnified the stench of stale liquor, cloying perfume and the polluted smells of Denver's underbelly.

Nothing had changed on Market Street in the last five years. One glance at the bustling sidewalks told him that gambling, prostitution and saloons still flourished. Men of various sizes and economic situations spilled out of buildings only to stumble into others. Some moved in packs, others sought their pleasure alone. Raucous music mingled with shouts, cursing and laughter.

Bringing order and redemption to these streets would not come easy or fast. Logan would attempt to do so anyway.

But first, he had to free Megan.

Jamming his hat onto his head, he trekked across the planked sidewalk and wove through the labyrinth of activity on the street.

The moment he entered the jailhouse his heart beat a single, heavy kick against his ribs. The room held little light and the air shimmered with a cold, gray foreboding. Closing the door with a firm click, Logan forced his vision to adjust. He dropped a cursory glance at the desk cluttered with piles of forgotten reports before focusing his attention on the lone occupant in the middle cell.

Megan.

With a fierce mental shake, he slammed shut the part of him that wanted to beat down the bars between them. He willed her to look at him but she didn't acknowledge his presence.

She appeared lost in thought, so small, so fragile. So...*alone.* Guilt pushed at him, mocking his attempt to think rationally. He'd waited five years to ask this woman to become his wife. He'd remained loyal to her in the face of every temptation San Francisco had to offer, and he'd done it without an ounce of regret.

Until now. *Now,* as he stared at Megan's bent head, he knew nothing but regret. Regret that he'd put off coming home for too long.

For one brief moment, he savored the soft lines of her shoulders, the elegant tilt of her head and the wheat-colored curls spilling down her back. She held her shoulders stiff as she twisted her hands in her lap, rubbing them over one another again and again and again.

Logan frowned.

He'd seen her like this only one time before. The day Pastor Beau had told her of her mother's death. Logan had fought the urge to steal her away back then, to rescue her from her grief.

She'd been too young at the time. That's what they'd said. Pastor Beau and her guardian, Marc Dupree, had insisted Logan step back and assess the situation like a man and not a "boy in love." When he hadn't backed off, Marc had threatened him, resorting to brute force to make his point. In the end, Logan had relented. For Megan's sake, he'd allowed the others to sway his better judgment.

A mistake.

Now a row of impenetrable iron bars stood between him and the woman he loved.

Logan balled his shooting hand into a tight fist. The urge to hit something, or someone, came fast, but he reminded himself he'd taken a different path than his brother. Still, a low growl of frustration rumbled deep in his throat.

At the sound, Megan looked up and slowly turned her head.

Their gazes melded.

Logan's heart pummeled his rib cage. The brutal assault made each intake of air a struggle.

Lost in her eyes, a compelling tapestry of silver over blue, he experienced a deep sensation of completion. The emotion was so simple, so pure he wondered how he'd been able to walk away before.

Well, he was home now.

"Logan?" A little sigh slipped from her lips. "Is it really you?"

"Yes, Megan." He forced his words around the breath clogging in his throat. "I've come for you, just like I promised."

But had he returned too late?

Chapter Two

After two endless seconds Megan finally jumped up and hurried across the cell toward Logan.

Hungry for this closer view, he clutched at the bars and strained forward. Just like it had five years ago, her beauty made his throat ache. Her hair still tumbled down her shoulders in golden waves, and her skin was as luminous as he remembered.

But there were differences, too. Her features had become more mature, less rounded by youth. But her eyes—her glorious, sparkling eyes—were haunted now. Deep purple smudges shadowed the skin beneath. It was clear she needed food, sleep and tender care.

A possessive urgency to see to those needs had him curling his fingers in a white-knuckle grip around the bars. Inhaling slowly, he forced his hands to relax and then reached for her.

She smiled at him, shyly at first. Then, with growing confidence, she took a step closer and placed her fingers in his. Gripping his wrist with her other hand, she brought his open palm to her face.

He cupped her cheek as gently as the barrier between them would allow. The contact eased the furious knot of tension in his stomach. But only for a moment. Old guilt warred with a new sense of regret, and Logan couldn't say which hurt more to suppress. He clenched his teeth so hard a muscle jumped at his jaw.

Suddenly, she staggered back a step. "Oh, Logan, I have to tell you—"

The outer door burst open, cutting off her words.

Heavy, purposeful footsteps approached from behind. Logan's shoulders stiffened at the familiar sound. He'd know that clipped, efficient cadence anywhere.

Frustrated at the interruption, he turned on his heel and came face-to-face with his former mentor. Trey Scott. The man who had trained Logan to think before shooting. The man who had recommended him for the U.S. Marshal position.

The man who had locked Megan in a cold, dark cage.

"Give me the key... *Sheriff.*"

"Ah." Trey hitched his hip against the desk and crossed his arms over his chest. "I see we're dispensing with the pleasantries. Nevertheless, welcome home, Logan."

Logan swallowed back an angry response and forced out his words with precision. "As the newly appointed U.S. Marshal I have a duty to—"

"I know your job description." He gave Logan a meaningful look, reminding them both who'd held the position first. "But this is my jail now. And you'll play by my rules."

Out of respect for all this man had done for him, Logan relented. For now.

Changing tactics, he appealed to their history as partners and friends. "I saved your life when Ike Hayes was bent on destroying you. You owe me this one request."

"Logan," Trey began, unfolding his arms and pushing to a standing position. "You need to understand the situation. You won't be so ready to release her once you know the truth."

The truth? There was only one truth. Megan didn't belong in a cold, impersonal jail cell.

Logan had failed her once, by leaving town when he should have married her. He wouldn't walk away again. Nor would he allow her to rot in a cage another hour, much less another day.

"One thing in particular you should know." Trey cast a look over Logan's shoulder, sighed. "She—"

"Explanations can wait. I want to speak with her first. Alone."

Trey's lips compressed into a thin line. Logan knew the look well. Trey Scott was in an unrelenting mood.

Well, so was Logan. He needed to be near Megan, needed to know she was truly safe. "You can lock me in with her."

Clearing his features of all expression, Trey glanced over Logan's shoulder again. For a moment, he simply stared at Megan. A silent message seemed to pass between them before he focused on Logan once more.

"All right." He retrieved an iron key from his vest pocket. "You can have a few minutes with her. But then you'll listen to what I have to say." The last was not a request but an order.

Unwilling to battle his longtime friend—yet—Logan nodded his agreement.

"Now that we understand one another…" Trey lifted his hand.

Logan snatched the key then turned toward the cell door. Before releasing the lock he glared at the other man. "Don't you have something to do? Outside?"

Unmoving, Trey lifted a single eyebrow. The gesture made him look like a protective father.

Logan remembered the other men with that same look in their eyes. He remembered their resolve as they told him to stay away from Megan. She was too young, they'd claimed a hundred times over. He was too old. She was grieving her mother's death. He needed to make a secure future for her before whisking her off in marriage. On and on they'd argued against him.

If he had ignored them, if he'd taken Megan as his wife when he'd had the chance, she wouldn't be in jail now.

Logan had to make this right.

Some of his torment must have shown in his eyes because Trey patted him on the back in a fatherly gesture. "I'll be just outside, my friend. You have five minutes, no more."

Logan nodded.

Trey left the jailhouse without another word.

Pivoting, Logan kept his gaze on Megan as he unlocked the door. The grind of metal hinges filled the silence between them. Taking a step into the cell, a sudden wave of helplessness enveloped him. What if he couldn't save her?

No. Whatever had warranted Megan's imprisonment Logan would find a way to fix the problem, but for now…

He opened his arms wide.

She hesitated only a second, then a swift smile flashed across her face and she rushed into his embrace.

"Logan," she whispered, wrapping her fingers around the lapels of his jacket with a fierce grip.

He folded her tightly against him, breathing the scent he remembered well. Clean and fresh, like soap mixed with spring flowers. A pleasant calm descended over him, smoothing the jagged edges of his embittered soul.

So many mistakes to regret.

Exhaling, he dropped his chin on the top of her head. So many choices he should have made differently.

But he was home now. They were together. Everything would be all right. Except...

Everything wasn't all right.

Megan held her shoulders stiff, as though she intentionally kept a part of herself back from him. In all the times he'd dreamed of this moment, in all the ways he'd expected their reunion to go, none of them included her unyielding in his arms.

He tried not to feel disappointed by her reaction and focused on calming her. After all, she'd been through an ordeal. That alone explained her reticence now.

With a gentle stroke, he smoothed his hand down her hair. One time. Two times. Three.

At last, she relaxed against him. "I knew you would come home to me," she said in a soft voice.

His heart twisted in his chest. Despite her confidence in him, Logan could see where he'd gone wrong. He'd not tried hard enough to come back for her sooner.

Easing her head back, he touched the side of her face, his thumb brushing her cheek.

God had brought him home at last. Logan had to make this right. For Megan, if not for himself.

Lord, may I not be too late to undo whatever dam-

age has been done. I pray You give me the courage needed to save this woman.

Just as she rested her face into his hand, just as everything felt right between them she pulled back and shuffled out of reach. Tugging her bottom lip between her teeth, she lowered her gaze to the floor. But not before he saw the flash of guilt in her eyes. Not regret. Not pain. Guilt. Unmistakable guilt.

What had she done?

Trouble rode the uncomfortable silence that spread between them. But a deeper, more disturbing current of secrets ran below the surface.

"We'll figure this out," he promised. "And then we'll be together, like we planned."

She lifted her head, gave him the sweet smile he remembered so well, the one he'd recalled on his darkest and loneliest nights.

"I missed you, Megan." It was the simple truth.

As though his words gave her strength, she lifted her chin a fraction higher. Logan's gaze connected with a long, jagged slash starting just below her jaw and running down the smooth column of her neck. He knew a knife cut when he saw one. It wasn't deep and it had been cleaned, but someone had held a knife against Megan's throat.

A violence he hadn't known possible roared past the regret in his mind, past the anger and morphed itself into blinding fury. "Who did this to you?"

She raised her hand to her neck and covered the wound with trembling fingers. Logan caught sight of the dried blood on her sleeve. Sucking in a hard breath, he lowered his gaze and noted similar stains on her dress.

"Megan, please." The control required to keep his

voice soft brought a physical pain to his chest. "Tell me who hurt you."

She blinked in an absent manner, and then looked around the cell as though she was searching the room for her answer. "Co… Cole Kincaid."

Kincaid. The name meant nothing to him. But Logan would find him. And when he did…

"I'll kill him."

She gasped. "No. You don't understand." Her eyes filled with desperation. "He's already dead."

At the catch in her voice, the remorse in her gaze, Logan shut his mind to the truth staring back at him. It couldn't be. Not Megan. *Never Megan.* Nevertheless, he pushed for an answer. "Who killed him?"

Taking a deep breath, she clasped her hands behind her back and lifted her shoulders. She stood in the posture of the condemned walking to the hangman's noose. "I did." She cocked her head at a defiant angle. "*I* killed Cole Kincaid."

There. Megan had made her confession. Even if she couldn't remember any of the details of her time in Mattie's brothel after her initial arrival, even if Sheriff Scott wasn't convinced she had the strength to shove a knife into Cole's chest, the possibility was there. After all, she'd been found in Mattie's private rooms. Alone with the dead outlaw. His blood literally on her hands.

What other explanation could there be than the obvious one?

She would lose Logan now. Maybe not today. Maybe not tomorrow. But soon. He was a U.S. Marshal, sworn to uphold the law. And she was a suspect in a brutal murder.

Elevating her chin a fraction higher, Megan gripped

her hands tighter behind her back and willed Logan to say something. *Anything.* But he didn't speak. Instead, a frown wove across his forehead and he cocked his head to the left.

The ripple of a memory slithered through her mind. She'd seen him look like this before, as though he couldn't reconcile her presence in this wicked, dangerous place.

She tugged at the shadowy thought. Tugged and tugged. Just when she almost captured the elusive memory, her mind filled with a void as black and unreachable as her time with Cole Kincaid.

Logan focused on her again. But, *still,* he didn't break the uncomfortable silence that stretched between them. He kept blinking at her, his chest rising and falling in an uneasy rhythm. She understood his struggle. She was having difficulty finding words herself.

With a slight tremble in his hand, he ran a finger down her throat. She gave an involuntary shake. The cut was still sore from the knife's jagged edge and the skin was probably starting to bruise.

What must he think? "Logan, did you hear me? I killed—"

"You didn't kill anyone."

How could he be so sure? "You don't know that."

"I know you." The certainty in his voice made her want to weep with relief.

But what if he was wrong? What if she was capable of far more evil than anyone realized? Perhaps that was the reason she couldn't remember what happened at Mattie's brothel. Or why she'd been found alone with Cole.

"People change," she reminded him.

"Not that much." He stroked her hair. *"Not that much."*

His conviction staggered her. She hadn't expected his unwavering defense of her character. It was disheartening to think she might not be able to live up to his expectations.

"Oh, Logan." She sagged back a step and lowered her gaze. "What if you never really knew me?" *What if I never really knew myself?*

"I know you, Megan." He gripped her shoulders with gentle hands and pulled her toward him again. "I've seen you with the younger Charity House orphans. I've watched you hug away a hurt. You're a fine, godly woman with compassion in your heart. You are not capable of cold-blooded murder."

But what if it hadn't been cold-blooded? What if she'd been defending herself? What if it was something in between the two?

Why, *why* couldn't she remember?

As though sensing her panic, Logan kept his hands on her shoulders, his gaze stark and measuring but not condemning.

Her reeling senses couldn't take all that intensity, all that confidence. Why wasn't he judging her? Unable to withstand the strain, she pulled free from his touch.

Raking his fingers through his hair, he paced through the cell with hard, clipped steps. Back and forth he went, moving with the lethal grace of a large mountain lion. Every few steps he'd toss her a frustrated glare. His hands were clenched into tight fists, as though he was trying to control his pent-up emotions.

Letting him walk uninterrupted, she followed his progress, greedy for this first opportunity to watch him move in five long years. The sight of him was so familiar, so dear.

Time had changed nothing. Time had changed *everything*.

He was as tall as she remembered, six feet at least, but there was no boy left in him now. His lean, rangy body had filled out with the muscles of a man and his hair had darkened to a rich sandy-blond. Dressed in a simple black coat and pants, his white shirt stood in stark contrast against his tanned skin. Even without the tin star pinned to his shirt, he had lawman written all over him, with his square jaw, defined features and the shadow of a beard just starting.

Remorse crawled over her, around her, sucking out what little hope she'd held on to since Sheriff Scott had locked her in this jail cell.

If she hadn't tangled with Cole Kincaid, she might have become this man's wife in a matter of days. One unfortunate incident and she stood to lose everything important to her. She stood to lose Logan.

Her life was collapsing around her, her dreams crumbling like a house with no foundation. All because she'd set out to show mercy to a woman who had reminded her of her dead mother.

Regret congealed in her throat.

Is this what comes of kindness, Lord? Is the inevitable loss of the only man I've ever loved to be my reward?

The question was a betrayal to everything she'd been raised to believe about Christian charity.

Logan returned to her, thankfully cutting off the rest of her troubled thoughts. His expression softening, he took her hand into his, then twined their fingers together in the same way he had years ago. She looked down at their palms pressed tightly against one another. Her hand was so small in his.

"Megan, my sweet, look at me."

The genuine affection in his voice compelled her to do as he requested.

He smiled, but he didn't try to pull her into his arms again. She was thankful for that, at least. She barely had power over her emotions as it was. She would probably collapse into uncontrollable sobs if he offered her any more kindness. Tears would do neither of them any good.

"Start at the beginning," he said. "Tell me everything that happened."

She saw the many questions in his eyes, the frustration underneath, but he held to his silence as he waited for her to begin.

He was so patient, so willing to think the best of her. How could she not love such a man?

"Logan, I... I..." Her throat cinched around a breath. "I can't tell you what happened because I—" She broke off, unable to push the words past her lips.

"Because?" he urged, using the same patient tone as before.

"Because..." She broke eye contact and focused on a spot just over his left shoulder. "I don't remember."

Chapter Three

Megan waited for Logan to respond to her stunning declaration. But he didn't move, didn't blink. In fact, he didn't react at all.

Perhaps he hadn't heard her.

Just as she opened her mouth to repeat herself, the outer door swung open with a rattle. She jumped away from Logan like a guilty child.

Sheriff Scott had returned. And he was looking directly at her as he entered the cell. The fierce angles of his face coupled with the hard slash of his frown sent a lick of fear through her. But then his gaze softened and she relaxed. A little.

He turned his attention to Logan. "I see she told you about her memory loss."

Ignoring the comment, Logan closed the distance Megan had created between them when she'd jumped away from him. "You don't remember anything about the murder?"

She lowered her gaze to the floor. "Nothing."

"That must be…" He pulled in a hissing breath. "Terrifying."

Megan's heart kicked hard against her rib cage. Logan understood her predicament. Perhaps better than she did herself.

She wished she could shake the horror of forgetting. She wanted to escape the terrible reality that a portion of her life was gone, perhaps forever.

She fought for her next gasp of air. What if she never remembered? What if Logan had to bring her to trial? What if she was convicted of murder? What if... What if...

What if...

As though sensing her growing panic, he pulled her into his arms again. Muttering soft words of comfort, he kept the embrace light, holding her with the care he might show a wounded animal.

A part of her relished the tender treatment. Another part—the part used to taking care of herself and others—wanted to shrink from the very real desire to rest in Logan's strength, if only for a while.

Even as he whispered soft promises to her, her inner battle continued with the independent side of her nature losing ground quickly. Logan was so strong, so good, so determined to make everything right. She could practically hear his brain working through the problem, his mind sorting and sifting potential solutions in perfect cadence with his heartbeat.

"What does Mattie Silks have to do with this?" he asked.

It was not the first question Megan would have expected from him. The madam had been uncommonly kind to her, wonderful even. But would Logan understand?

When Megan didn't answer the question right away,

Sheriff Scott responded for her. "The murder occurred in Mattie's brothel. In her private suite of rooms."

Logan recoiled. Not enough for the sheriff to notice, but Megan felt his reaction even as he set her gently away from him. She thought she heard him mutter something about the difficult woman and her maddening games, but couldn't be sure. He'd spoken just below a whisper.

Fearing what she might find, she ventured a glance into his eyes. He looked stunned. Indignant. Furious.

Megan had never seen him so angry. She was sure of it. But just as the thought materialized a distant memory triggered a peculiar stinging in her throat. She instinctively backed away from him. One step. Two. The third brought her legs up against the cot.

She sat. Quickly, before she collapsed.

Shivering, she rubbed her hands over her arms. Beneath the thin fabric of her sleeves her skin felt clammy, as though the ugliness of death had attached itself to her and wouldn't let go.

At last, the shadows in Logan's gaze shifted from anger to sorrow to resolve. He turned to glare at Sheriff Scott. "Tell me everything you know."

With slow, precise words the sheriff recounted the events in Mattie's boudoir as he knew them. His smooth, deep baritone lulled Megan into a comfortable daze.

Only half listening, she pulled her feet onto the cot and hugged her knees to her chest. She didn't mind that they were discussing her as though she wasn't in the room. She found it oddly comforting to listen to her story from the viewpoint of an outsider. But as the events unfolded around her, Megan had to swallow back another round of panic.

Why couldn't she remember details from the brothel? She recalled feeling fear. Queasiness. Rage. But nothing more substantial, nothing concrete.

At last, the same tiny thought swam out of the chaos in her mind as it had every other time she'd pushed herself to remember. She'd gone to read to Suzanne, one of Mattie's girls, a woman who'd contracted the same illness that had killed Megan's mother. Megan had gone to the brothel to offer what small comfort she could.

But why had Cole sought her out, specifically? She'd been there on an errand of mercy.

Before confusion overtook her, she made herself focus on the story once again. According to Sheriff Scott, Cole had attacked her, probably assuming she was one of Mattie's girls. All signs revealed that Megan had fought back, at one point pushing the man so hard he'd hit his head against the stone fireplace. But the blow hadn't been what killed him. The sheriff was positive Cole died of a chest wound.

"Someone jammed a knife straight through Kincaid's black heart," he said.

How many times had Megan heard the same series of events, told in the same sequence, always with the same conclusion? A man was dead and his blood was on her dress, as well as on her hands before she'd cleaned them. But no matter how deep she searched her mind, Megan couldn't corroborate any of the sheriff's findings.

Hugging her knees tighter, she fought the familiar fog trying to grip her mind once again. It came anyway, thick and impenetrable.

Logan let out a low hiss when Sheriff Scott began detailing the murder scene. Megan jerked her attention back to the conversation. Catching Logan's hard expression she easily understood why Sheriff Scott had recommended him for the U.S. Marshal position. Not out of loyalty alone, but because Logan could be ruthless when he wanted to get to the truth of a matter. She shivered.

Would he be her ally now? Or her judge?

At last, the sheriff came to the end of the tale.

Logan's conviction was stronger than before. "Nothing you've said changes my mind about Megan's innocence. She couldn't have murdered Kincaid." He tossed her a quick, reassuring look. "Not in the way you just described. You have to let her go. You—"

"Slow down, Logan." The sheriff held up his hand between them. "It's too soon to form any conclusions."

"I said," he clenched his jaw so hard a muscle jumped in his neck, "Let. Her. Go."

"Stop and think," the sheriff suggested. "If someone else murdered Kincaid that means Megan probably saw him."

She shook her head fiercely. "I remember no one."

Neither man acknowledged her.

"Logan." The sheriff's tone turned low and insistent. "He won't know she's lost her memory. She could be in grave danger."

Logan drew in a sharp breath. "Is that why you locked her in here? To keep her out of his reach?"

"It's one of the reasons." The sheriff gave Megan a sad smile, one filled with unmistakable remorse. "But not the only one."

Without warning, Logan lurched forward. He

grabbed the sheriff by the lapels and then slammed him against the wall behind him. "You might have kept her safe from a killer, but you've also broadcasted to the world, including Kincaid's gang, that you think she's the murderer."

Looking cool and composed, Sheriff Scott responded with an even tone. "I'm sorry, Logan, but the truth of the matter is she *could* be the murderer."

Logan shoved his forearm under the sheriff's chin in a brutal choke hold. "You might as well have drawn a target on her back," he growled, ignoring the sheriff's last comment. "Men like Kincaid never travel alone. His gang will want retribution."

As though he knew Logan needed to vent his anger, the sheriff still didn't try to move. Or fight back. "I stand by my decision."

Several heartbeats passed. And then several more.

"Logan, think this through with your brain and not your emotions. Megan is in danger. Whether she committed the crime or witnessed it, she's safer here than anywhere else in town."

After one last shove, Logan threw his hands in the air. Breathing hard, he pressed his palm against the back of his neck and rolled his shoulders. There was such sorrow in his eyes, maybe a twinge of remorse. But mostly Megan noted ruthless determination in his gaze. He'd come to a conclusion.

What was he planning to do?

"No, Logan," Sheriff Scott warned. "I won't let you release her. It's too dangerous."

Logan dismissed the words with a hard flick of his wrist. "We'll discuss that later."

With careful movements, he sat beside Megan on

the cot. The springs gave a series of loud creaks before settling underneath the additional weight.

He touched her wound, then dropped his hand to her shoulder and squeezed. "Have you seen a doctor yet? Did you suffer any other…injuries?"

He spoke so slowly, so carefully. She could tell he was trying not to frighten her but he couldn't contain the fear in his own eyes, fear for her, fear for what might have happened when she was alone with Cole.

In that, at least, she could relieve his mind.

Swallowing back a wave of shyness, she forced herself to hold Logan's gaze. "Dr. Shane cleaned the cut on my neck and then he gave me a tonic to help me sleep. But I…" She shook her head again. This time the gesture sent tiny white dots across her vision. "…can't sleep."

"Logan, don't do this now," the sheriff urged. "She doesn't remember. She's been—"

Logan held up a hand to stave off the interruption. "I want to hear the rest from her."

Nodding in agreement, she pressed her hand to her stomach. She knew how hard this was for him. It was hard for her, too. But they had to speak of this now. And then never again. "He didn't hurt me in any other way." *At least not physically.*

Cole hadn't forced himself on her. There would have been signs. But that didn't mean Megan had escaped free of harm. In truth, she feared the consequences of her night with the outlaw were far worse than cuts and bruises.

Exposed only indirectly to her mother's sinful lifestyle, Megan had thought she understood the gift she'd been given as a resident at Charity House. The gift of escape. The gift of respectability.

Now, as she faced Logan for the first time in five years, she could no longer dodge the one question she'd avoided since Sheriff Scott had locked her in this cell. Because of this single incident, would she end up like her mother, alone and desperate, with no one to love?

Logan followed Trey outside the jailhouse and onto the planked sidewalk lining the street. Night closed in around him like a menacing presence, taunting him. He hardly noticed. Anger still rode him hard, but he forced himself to focus on the facts first. No emotion. No giving in to despair. Just cold, hard logic.

"All right, Trey." He spun around to face the other man. "Tell me the rest, the part you couldn't say in front of Megan."

Trey rubbed a weary hand down his face and then leaned back on one foot. "You've heard most of it."

Not by half. "The blood on her dress. Is it hers or Kincaid's?"

"Mostly Kincaid's."

Logan's breath caught in his chest. Megan had been attacked. By a very bad man. He wasn't sorry the outlaw was dead, but there were too many details that needed explaining. And Megan couldn't remember what had happened to her. That left them with very little to go on.

At least one thing was clear in Logan's mind. "She didn't kill Kincaid."

"We don't know that for sure."

"Yes, we do." A lump rose in his throat. He shoved

it down with a hard swallow. "From what you described—the knife's angled position through bone and flesh, the direction of the blade's entry from above not below—she's obviously innocent. Even if Kincaid had been on his knees, she's not strong enough to have stabbed him in that manner."

Trey looked out in the distance before answering. When he turned his head back to Logan, his gaze was filled with remorse. "Under ordinary circumstances, I would agree with you. But Megan was brutally attacked. The will to survive, the power of the moment, *fear,* any of those factors could have come into play and given her the strength to defend herself."

"With a knife to the man's chest? Through bone? No. That doesn't make sense."

"You know it's possible. Not probable, but possible."

Logan recognized the unbending look in Trey's eyes as he spoke. The other man wasn't going to draw any conclusions about the murder until he had concrete information. That did not bode well for Megan's immediate freedom. *Unacceptable.*

"Release her into my custody."

"No."

"I have the perfect place to take her, a place where she'll be safe."

"She's safe enough here."

"Not as much as she would be with me."

"Look, Logan, I know the situation seems bleak right now, but all is not lost. God has not abandoned Megan. Or you. Have patience, my friend. Pray for guidance. The Lord will direct your way."

Right. He was supposed to stand around and wait

for God to free Megan. The same God who'd allowed the attack to occur in the first place.

Logan didn't have that much faith.

And now he was through taking the passive route. He was through shoving his emotions aside in the name of reason. To what end? To stand around and talk about a silent God who didn't seem to care what was happening here?

"Release Megan into my custody," Logan demanded again.

"I said, no."

Logan went for Trey's throat. But this time the other man was ready. At the last moment, he shifted to his left. Logan stumbled into empty air. Before he caught his balance, Trey spun him around by the shoulder and slammed him back against the wall, securing him in place with the same choke hold Logan had used earlier.

He fought against Trey's grip. "If I wasn't so angry you wouldn't have gotten the chance to subdue me like this."

"But you *are* angry." Trey tightened his hold. "Allowing your emotions to rule your actions is what gets a man shot."

Logan was in no mood for a lecture, especially from Trey Scott. "This? From you?"

"You know I speak from experience." Trey rolled his right shoulder, reminding them both of the time he'd taken a bullet when he'd confronted Ike Hayes over the cold-blooded murder of his first wife. Trey had been bent on revenge and had lost his perspective. Logan had saved the man's life because he'd been the rational thinker.

Now Logan was the one losing perspective. He dropped his chin and let out a long breath. "I can't leave her in jail. Let me take her away from here. I'll keep her safe."

"I know you will." Trey released his hold and stepped back. "But we need answers first."

Absently, Logan rubbed his throat. "We have to find Kincaid's real killer. Before he finds Megan."

"Right now, all we have is supposition. We need more information."

Then Logan would get them more. And he knew exactly where to start. "Promise me you won't let Megan out of your sight, not for any reason."

"That goes without saying."

Logan took two steps in the direction of Market Street but Trey blocked his path. "Where do you think you're going?"

"To Mattie's."

"Waste of time. You know the woman will run you around in circles if she decides to speak to you at all."

"She'll talk."

Trey tried a different tactic. "My deputy has been there for several hours, looking for any clues we may have missed earlier. You'll just be in the way."

"I don't plan to interfere. I plan to get answers." From the most likely source, Mattie Silks herself. "I'll be back as soon as I can."

He shoved past Trey.

This time, the man didn't try to stop him.

With each step he took, Logan calculated how best to go about questioning Mattie. There was no room for emotion now. Only harsh, unyielding intent. Someone in that den of iniquity had seen the real killer. Someone besides Megan.

And Logan wouldn't rest until *someone* started talking.

Chapter Four

By the time Logan rounded the corner onto Market Street, the wind had taken on a nasty bite. He turned up his collar against the cold and instinctively increased his pace. Hollow laughter rang out in the distance, followed by the slam of a door.

He hated this time of day. In the eerie, predawn light, when the world stood poised between night and day, a desolate sheen seemed to cover everything. The oppressive stench of rotting garbage and stale liquor added to his already bleak mood.

A shadow slithered across his feet, then disappeared.

He turned quickly, scanning the area with a narrowed gaze. He found nothing more than a stumbling drunk and a scrawny mutt digging for scraps in the frosted earth.

Frowning, Logan resumed his trek toward Mattie's. Every few steps he stabbed a covert glance over his shoulder. He couldn't shake the notion he was being followed, yet he didn't get a sense of imminent danger.

Puzzling over the contradictory sensations, he arrived at his destination. The most elegant house on the block, the brothel's pale pink stucco, sweeping ivy and heavily sloping roof presented an inviting picture of hearth and home.

It was a lie, of course. The temporary pleasure offered in this house only resulted in despair. For all parties involved.

What Logan couldn't fathom was Megan's decision to come here at all. What had she hoped to accomplish with her charity work? What had been worth putting herself in harm's way?

When and if the time was right, he would ask her.

For now, he lifted the ornate knocker and let it drop with a loud bang. The abrupt sound helped focus his thoughts on the matter at hand.

He would get his answers this morning. Calmly. Methodically.

One question at a time.

The door swung open. Jack, Mattie's notorious bodyguard, stood just inside the gaudy foyer. He stared at Logan with an unreadable expression on his round, scruffy face. With more brawn than brains, Black Jack O'Malley was as much Mattie's lapdog as her protector. Nevertheless, the man had always shown Logan respect.

Logan would return the favor now. "Jack," he said in a courteous tone. "Is Mattie here?"

Jack nodded. "She's been expecting you."

"Of course." Logan didn't bother hiding the frustration in his tone. The woman could have given him vital information when he was here before, but she had chosen to send him away with a head full of confusion and worry.

Games inside games.

When it came to Mattie Silks, some things never changed.

As though sensing his annoyance, Jack stepped aside and motioned Logan forward.

"I'll let Mattie know you've arrived." The big man circled around him. "Wait here."

Logan remained in the foyer a total of five seconds before he'd had enough of cooling his heels. He strode past the entryway and looked around the main parlor.

Nothing had changed in his five-year absence. And yet everything about the decor seemed more…sinful. Alone, each piece of furniture might be able to pass for tasteful, but together the red velvet divans, ornate paintings and gold filigree defined decadence.

Megan did not belong in this house. For any reason. Logan would have to make sure she understood why she could never come here again.

A movement in the back of the room cut off his thoughts. Mattie Silks had arrived in all her overstated grandeur. Arms outstretched, a flirtatious smile pasted on her lips, she glided to a spot in the center of the room then relaxed into a scandalous pose. Typical Mattie Silks behavior. Control the situation simply to prove she could, even if that meant hurting people in the process.

Logan knew his role in this particular drama. He was supposed to take a moment and admire the woman.

He wasn't that much of a hypocrite.

Biting back a wave of impatience, he shifted his weight from one foot to the other and did his best not to glare.

Satisfied she had his attention, Mattie spun in a slow circle then continued toward him. With her blond, corkscrew curls bouncing wildly and her dress two sizes too small, she looked like a caricature of herself.

Adding to the absurd picture, she slowed every fourth or fifth step and struck a more ridiculous pose than the last.

Subtlety was not the woman's strong suit.

Controlling the situation, now that was where she excelled.

She eventually came to a halt directly in front of him. Slipper to boot, she stood close enough for him to get a whiff of her cheap perfume. Normally, he'd step back and reclaim his space.

Not today. *Today* Logan had his own point to make.

"Mattie." He studied her dress with a critical eye. The frothy concoction of lace and blue silk was cut dangerously low in front and even lower in the back. "You're as obvious as ever."

"And you're still the rude boy of years past."

"Be careful," he warned. "I'm also the U.S. Marshal of this territory now."

"Ah, well, I won't hold that against you. You see... *Marshal*." She looked pointedly at the tin star on his chest as she gave him a condescending pat on the arm. "I find myself in an accommodating mood at the moment."

Logan firmed his jaw. Mattie Silks was never in an accommodating mood. Unless it suited her.

He opened his mouth to argue the point, but shut it just as quickly. Patience was his greatest weapon. He would let Mattie play her game, knowing there was too much at stake to lose her cooperation.

That didn't mean he had to give the woman all the control.

Slanting a hard glance in her direction, he pushed past her and strode deeper into the room.

She was forced to follow him or stand staring at empty air.

It was a small victory, to be sure, but one he would use to his full advantage.

Unfortunately, his plans changed when his gaze landed on a chair off to his left—a very occupied chair. One of Mattie's girls had yet to go to bed. Seemingly oblivious to his presence, she tugged absently at a loose thread on her dress.

Even with the glazed look in her eyes, Logan recognized the girl. Her name was Emily, no… Emma. She'd been a child when he'd left, barely thirteen. Her mother had raised her under this very roof. And all that that implied. By the way Emma was dressed, it was clear she was now a second generation "employee" of Mattie's.

But that wasn't the only thing that bothered Logan about the girl. With her slight build and pale blond hair, she looked a lot like Megan. Too much.

Logan experienced a moment of panic at the alarming similarities between the two, but quickly shoved the emotion aside. Unlike this girl, Megan had escaped her mother's profession. She'd been given the chance to pursue a respectable life. With Logan.

He would *not* let her down.

But what if he did? What if he couldn't save her?

Mattie chose that moment to move back into his line of vision. Again, she stood too close. *Again,* he remained unimpressed. He wasn't the green lawman anymore, the one who'd been taken off guard long enough to get another man shot.

"Just so we're clear, Miss Silks." He glared at the hand she'd rested on his sleeve. "I'm here for one reason only. To rescue Megan from her current…predicament."

The madam smirked at him. "Your devotion is admirable."

Her goading tone set him on edge. "Never doubt my loyalty. I will do anything." He peeled away the fingers on his bicep, one claw at a time. "And I mean *anything,* to ensure Megan's safety."

"Well, then." She perched on a nearby chair and folded her arms around her waist. "For once we have the same goal. Who would have thought?"

Who, indeed. As much as it galled Logan to admit it, even to himself, this woman—this brothel owner—could be the key to Megan's freedom. Yet how could he trust such a person as this?

A jolt of helplessness whipped through him. But in the next moment, Trey's words came back to him. *The Lord will direct your way.*

Was God at work even now? Could the Heavenly Father mean for Logan to ally himself with a woman like Mattie Silks? Even for a moment?

Logan was well versed in the Old Testament story of Rahab, the prostitute. God had used the most unlikely of women to help the Israelites defeat Jericho.

The Lord will direct your way…

For Megan's sake Logan would try anything, including an unlikely alliance with a notorious madam. If only temporarily.

Swallowing his misgivings, he focused his thoughts on Megan, then addressed Mattie with a cool tone. "Look, Mattie, I'm not here to argue with you. I'm here to get information that will free Megan. Nothing more. Nothing less."

To Logan's utter surprise, the woman nodded. "You may rest easy, Marshal." Her gaze turned serious. "I'll do everything in my power to help your Megan."

His Megan. Yes. She was his. She'd always been his. And always would be. "Good enough. First, I need to know how—" He broke off at the sound of rustling silk, only just realizing Emma was still in the room with them, openly listening to their conversation.

He grimaced at the girl.

Mattie's gaze followed his. "Go to your room." Her tone brooked no argument, but the girl didn't budge.

A foolish mistake. One Mattie would surely punish her for later.

"I said leave," Mattie ordered. "Or I'll lock you in your room for two days without food."

Logan knew the madam meant every word. Apparently, so did Emma. Shoulders hunched, eyes glued to her feet, she made her way toward the staircase leading to the second floor.

Mattie kept her hawklike gaze trained on the girl until she disappeared from sight.

Finished with the delays, Logan got straight to the point. "How did Megan end up in your private boudoir, when she'd come only to read to a sick woman?"

Mattie swung around, parked one fist on her hip and zeroed in on a spot just above his head. As she stood in that particular pose, ignoring him completely, Logan feared she wouldn't answer his question. But then she flicked her hair off her forehead and focused on him once again.

"I moved her as soon I discovered Cole had arrived

earlier than expected," she said. "I wasn't about to let that vile man get a glimpse of our dear girl."

Logan pulled in a tight breath of air. "Why would you have worried about Kincaid seeing Megan?"

"Cole was one of my regulars. He had a penchant for…" Mattie cleared her throat. "Innocents."

A wave of fury threatened to overwhelm him. For a blessed moment Logan let the anger come, let it flow through him and guide his next words. "If that was true, why didn't you send her back to Charity House? Why move her to a place where he could easily get to her?"

Obviously used to dealing with angry men, Mattie held Logan's stare without flinching. "Time was of the essence. I knew if Cole caught sight of her leaving, he might follow her. And then, well…" She held his gaze. "You understand my meaning."

Yes, he did. It was her meaning that made it nearly impossible for Logan to think rationally. Too many terrible scenarios ran through his mind. "So you thought she was safe in your sitting room," he said, forcing down his fury enough to avoid doing anything rash. Like shake the truth out of Mattie.

"That is correct."

"Still doesn't explain how Kincaid got to her."

Mattie blinked. Then blinked again. "I had to leave her alone for a moment."

Logan drew in another sharp breath. "Why would you do that?"

"Because a business matter required my attention."

"What business matter?"

"I had to break up a fight between two of my girls." She lifted her hand in a dismissive gesture. "I was gone

no more than twenty minutes. When I returned, Cole
was lying flat on his back with a knife stuck through
his chest."

Despite the growing urge to shake the woman,
Logan made himself piece together the details in his
mind. So far, Mattie's story matched Trey's. But there
was a part of the tale where his friend had been unclear,
a minor point that only Mattie could answer.

"Where was Megan when you first entered the
room?"

Looking everywhere but at him, Mattie shifted to a
spot just behind the chair. Only after the barrier stood
between them did she continue. "Dig too deep into this
murder, Marshal, and you may not like what you find."

He scowled at the remark, wondering why she was
warning him off. To protect herself? Megan? Or someone else entirely?

What did this woman know? Or rather, what was
she refusing to tell him?

Only one way to find out. He kept his gaze on hers,
reading every nuance in her body language, and repeated the question a second time. "Where was Megan
when you entered the room?"

Mattie sighed in uncharacteristic resignation.
"Lying on my settee, out cold."

Shock rippled through his body, making him shudder. "She wasn't on the floor?" Like he and Trey had
assumed?

"Uh…no."

Logan gaped at the woman for several heartbeats.
Focus, he told himself. He had to focus on the facts.
No more assumptions. No more mistakes. He had to
think like a lawman. Not a man who's greatest love had

been attacked earlier tonight. "Tell me how Megan was positioned on the divan. Exactly."

"She looked rather…" Mattie screwed her face into a look of deep concentration "…comfortable. Yes, that's the word."

Logan clenched his teeth together. Mattie was hiding something from him. "Comfortable, how?"

"Oh, I don't know." She lifted a shoulder. "Her head was propped on a pillow and she was covered with a blanket. That sort of comfortable."

A thousand questions exploded in his brain. But Logan kept his breathing slow and easy, his mind focused on his questions. "Could she have gotten that way by herself?"

"No." Mattie's fingers drummed along the chair's rim. She continued avoiding direct eye contact. "The blanket was tucked neatly around her."

Clinging hard to his composure, Logan worked the new information around in his head. Instinct told him there was only one explanation. The real killer had moved Megan to the settee. And then—*then*—he'd covered her with a blanket.

But why?

Neither gesture rang true.

Despite the fact that the details didn't add up, Logan was certain of one thing. Megan hadn't killed Kincaid. Now he could take her away from here, to the one place where he knew she'd be safe.

Then why did a sense of foreboding slide down his spine? What was he missing?

"I need you to think hard, Mattie. Did you see anything suspicious last night? Anything out of the ordinary?"

Her fingers tightened on the chair, the gesture turning her knuckles white. "I've been over the events in my head a hundred times. Nothing comes to mind." She took a shuddering breath, but there didn't seem to be any subterfuge in the act. "Nothing, that is, that will change the very real fact that Cole Kincaid is dead."

An odd choice of words.

For once in their volatile eight-year acquaintance, Logan sensed she was telling the truth.

And yet...

There was something still missing from her tale, some valuable piece of information that would fit the other details smoothly together. Unfortunately, Logan had been down similar roads with Mattie Silks. She would never volunteer everything she knew, not unless he asked the right questions. If only he knew the right ones to ask.

The Lord will direct your way...

Logan rubbed a hand down his face. *Please, Lord, what's my next step?*

As soon as he voiced the prayer in his head, he knew what he had to do. "I want to interview everyone who was in this building last night," he said. "Starting with your girls."

After a momentary hesitation, Mattie nodded. She actually nodded in agreement!

As much as Logan wanted to rely on her cooperation, he would be wise to remember this woman had been known to harbor criminals in her own bedroom. She could not be trusted. Not fully.

Dig too deep, Marshal, and you might not like what you find.

What was she hiding from him?

"When would you like to begin questioning my girls?" she asked.

Her cooperation was at odds with the Mattie Silks he knew. "After I look around the crime scene."

Her eyebrows lifted in surprise. "Cole's body is already gone. Sheriff Scott's deputy took him away over an hour ago."

"I want to see the room where he was stabbed." Trey was always thorough, but maybe he'd overlooked an important piece of evidence. Logan clung to that small hope.

Mattie pushed away from the chair and started out. "Follow me." Without a single argument, coy look or detour, she led Logan directly to her private sitting room.

He didn't second-guess her continued cooperation. Yet.

"Here we are," she said, moving aside so he could enter the room ahead of her.

With a quick glance, Logan surveyed the small, confining space. Cataloguing the contents of the room, he counted a fireplace, a small sofa, a winged-back chair and a bookcase actually filled with books.

Surprised by the hominess of the decor, Logan worked his way around the perimeter quickly, with a smooth economy of motion that belied his sense of urgency.

There was something here. He could feel it.

Noting the trace of blood on the mantel, he ran his hand along the wood, searching for the groove where Kincaid had hit his head. After he'd attacked Meg—

Focus. Logan had to focus on the facts alone. No

emotion. No thoughts of Megan. No dwelling on what had happened to her in this room.

"Give me another ten minutes to look around," he said through a tight jaw. "Then send in the first girl."

"Whatever you wish." She turned to go.

"And Mattie?" he called after her retreating back. "I'll need the names of last night's clients, as well. *All* their names."

She stiffened at the request, but didn't turn around. "Are you sure this is the route you wish to take, Marshal?"

The woman was warning him off? A huge mistake on her part, especially if Logan found out she had a personal connection to the killer.

"One way or another I *will* find out who murdered Kincaid," Logan said in the kind of ruthless tone a woman like Mattie understood. "I know that doesn't mean anything to you, but it could mean life or death for Megan."

Mattie lowered her head and sighed. "I'll draw up a complete list of names later today."

"Thank you."

Normally, those two simple words would earn him a snide remark. But when Mattie spun around to face him, her eyes were filled with gratitude. And genuine sincerity.

"It's good you're home, Logan. Megan needs you, now more than ever."

Caught off guard by the woman's heartfelt words, Logan didn't have a ready response. What the woman didn't realize, what he hadn't fully understood himself until last night, was how much *he* needed Megan in return.

And no matter who tried to stand in his way this time, he would never desert Megan again.

Chapter Five

Megan burrowed deeper under the blanket and forced her mind to relax. But no matter what position she attempted, peace eluded her. Too tired to sit up, she squeezed her eyes shut and tried to capture a few moments of sleep.

Every part of her body hurt, resulting in an all-over ache that went far beyond the physical. The pain brought an odd sense of relief, a bold reminder she was alive.

Alive was good. That meant God still had a plan for her life. Megan clung to that hope, even as dark thoughts tried to surface.

Shivering from a sudden burst of cold air, she pulled the blanket tighter around her shoulders and took a slow, steady breath. The smell of blood and death hung in the air. She didn't want to know why that scent was so strong. Why it seemed so real, so tangible.

Best to forget, a voice whispered in her head. Yes. *Yes.* She let her mind go blank, let her sense of time and place garble in her head. The nothingness soothed her.

Distant, hollow voices buzzed around her, like an annoying mosquito.

She took another, slower breath.

At last, sleep began to claim her, promising a temporary respite, if only she could give in to the blessed darkness. She reached out to the void. But then the watery sounds in her head began to form into clear, distinct words.

"You must allow me to wake her." The urgent request came from somewhere close by. "It's not good for her to sleep this long."

A low, menacing growl followed. "I said, leave... her...alone." There was a deadly calm in the carefully spoken words. And an unmistakable threat. "I mean it, Shane."

Dr. Shane was here?

"You have to trust I know what I'm doing, Logan."

Logan, too?

Megan wanted to see him for herself, wanted to know he was real and not a dream like she feared. But opening her eyes required too much effort so she tucked the blanket under her chin and prayed for sleep to return.

"Step back, Logan. Or I'll have the sheriff personally escort you out of here until I'm through examining her."

A brief moment of silence filled the room.

"All right. Wake her." Another pause. "But do it slowly. *Don't* scare her."

A masculine sigh accompanied the sound of footsteps. Very loud footsteps. Like hammers to nails, pounding relentlessly in her head.

She shied away from the noise.

"Megan." A gentle hand touched her shoulder. "Megan, you need to wake up now."

She moaned in protest, even as her mind placed the familiar voice. It did indeed belong to Shane Bartlett, the doctor from the clinic connected to Charity House. She knew the man well. Trusted him implicitly. Not only because he was married to her good friend Bella, but because he was an exceptional doctor. Compassionate and thorough.

"Megan." The hand shook her again, a little more firmly this time.

"Sleep," she mumbled.

"No. No more sleep."

She tried to protest again, but her mind drifted over a dark void of shifting images, images she couldn't quite capture.

Best to forget...

If only her head didn't hurt so badly.

Eyes still firmly shut, she lifted a hand to touch the tender spot above her temple. The movement sent unspeakable pain spearing behind her eyes.

Another moan slipped through her lips.

"Megan. You need to open your eyes." Dr. Shane's voice came at her stronger this time. More insistent. Closer.

Too close.

She snapped awake and sat up with a jerk.

A burst of light flashed before her, momentarily blinding her. She breathed in a quick gasp, blinked past the grit in her eyes, but the room remained hazy. The sickly odor of mold and something else filled her nose. What was that other smell?

She didn't want to know.

"Sleep," she muttered again, then squeezed her eyelids shut and started to lie back down.

"No." The doctor's hands caught her by the shoulders before her head connected with the pillow. "Stay with us." He urged her back to a sitting position.

She managed a squint. The sun spread golden fingers of light across the floor, chasing shadows to the outer edges of the room. She opened her eyes fully and connected her gaze with a long row of iron bars. She'd spent an entire night in jail.

Her eyes filled with tears.

"Megan, darling, don't cry." The words washed over her like a soft plea.

She turned her gaze in the direction of the voice. *"Logan,"* she breathed.

He moved toward her slowly, his steps relaxed, careful, as though he didn't want to scare her with any sudden movement.

The dear, dear man.

"Logan, wait just a moment." Dr. Shane stopped his progress with an outstretched hand.

Ignoring the command, Logan continued toward her. No hesitation. No hitch in his step. Just bold purpose.

Dr. Shane muttered something about "arrogant, single-minded lawmen." Megan didn't listen to the rest of the words. She was too busy watching Logan's approach.

He crouched down in front of her and placed his palms on her knees.

His movements were still slow, but the fierce angles of his face and the severe expression in his eyes said he was anything but calm.

At the sight of all the intensity directed at her, a quick jolt of fear slithered down her spine.

Megan instinctively leaned back. *Away* from Logan.

There was a flicker of hurt in his eyes but then he gave her a wide, nonthreatening smile.

Remorse instantly filled her. This was Logan. *Her* Logan. There was nothing to fear from him. Just being near him was all she'd ever wanted, all she'd ever craved. "You're still here," she whispered.

He swung around then sat beside her on the cot. As before, the ancient springs creaked in protest under the additional weight.

Reaching down, Logan took her hand and laced her fingers through his. "I'll never leave you again."

The magnetic force of his sincerity took her breath away. For one fleeting moment, every dream she'd ever had about this man and their future together seemed possible.

In the next moment, an onslaught of images beckoned for release and a feeling of dread balled in her stomach.

Her vision blurred.

Logan slung his arm across her shoulder to steady her. "Doc. Do something. She's losing color."

Dr. Shane was at her feet in an instant. But he was too close.

She suddenly felt trapped.

"No. Please. Step back." She waved her hand in his direction. "I need…" She let her voice trail off, not sure what she needed. "Just…give me a moment."

Breathing slowly—very slowly—she pressed her thumb and forefinger to the bridge of her nose and ordered her mind to slow down. But her thoughts continued running in countless directions. There were too many images fighting for release.

Sights, sounds, smells all came at her at once, attacking her in rapid succession.

"Breathe, Megan," Logan urged softly in her ear. "Just breathe."

She tried to do as he suggested. In. Out. In. Out.

Her efforts only made matters worse.

Blood roared in her ears.

Logan's grip on her shoulder tightened, reminding her she wasn't alone in this terrible, terrible mess.

Why was there no comfort in the thought?

Was she fooling herself? Was she grasping at a dream she'd built in her head over the last five years?

Confusion and panic tangled together in her mind. Rather than giving in to either, she called on one of her favorite verses. *Come unto me, all ye that labour and are heavey laden, and I will give you rest.*

One heartbeat passed.

And another.

By the third she shrugged away from Logan's support and tried to stand.

"Megan," he began.

"No." She thrust a palm in his direction. "Don't help me. I need to do this on my own."

Brave words. Necessary words. She had to call on her strength, like always, or risk losing more control than ever.

Unfortunately, she couldn't quite get her feet underneath her. Logan grasped her elbow gently. Once she caught her balance, she stepped away from him.

Pain shot through her right foot. And she lowered back down on the cot.

"What is it?" he asked. "What—"

"Just wait a minute, Logan." Dr. Shane cut him off. "Give her a moment to find her bearings."

Logan gave an unhappy grunt in reply, but surprisingly didn't argue this time. Keeping his eyes on her, he moved to the opposite end of the cell in three ground-eating strides, then leaned a shoulder against the brick wall.

The hard look he shot Dr. Shane reminded her of… of…

She pressed a shaky hand to her quivering stomach and felt the knots tighten beneath her touch. What was wrong with her? How could she possibly be afraid?

This was Logan. *Her* Logan.

Confused, she turned her attention back to Dr. Shane. There was certainly nothing threatening about him. His clear blue eyes held compassion while a hint of concern showed on his handsome face. His dark hair shot out in every direction, as though he'd run his hands through it too many times.

He slowly crouched in front of her, placed his fingertips on the inside of her wrist and began counting her heartbeats. After a moment, he nodded in approval. "Do you hurt anywhere other than your head?"

"My back aches a little. But that could be from sleeping on this cot."

He cracked a smile. "I wouldn't rule out the possibility." His smile disappeared. "Where else does it hurt?"

"Sometimes…it hurts to breathe." She drew in a sharp breath and winced. "In my ribs."

Nodding, Dr. Shane probed the area gently. She pulled back and hissed when his fingers landed on an especially tender spot.

At the sound of her gasp, Logan pushed away from the wall and rushed forward. *"Megan."*

Dr. Shane glared him back a step. Then another. Impatience flared out of both men, but Logan finally relented.

Muttering under his breath, the doctor turned back to Megan. "Do you hurt anywhere else?"

"My ankle."

He lifted her foot and Megan stifled a gasp. The swelling told its own story. Sometime during the evening she'd acquired a minor sprain.

Still holding her foot, Dr. Shane reached for his bag. Digging inside with his free hand, he pulled out a roll of linen bandages and began wrapping her ankle with deft fingers.

"Do you remember falling?" he asked, eyes focused on his work.

Megan forced her mind to concentrate. To focus. Surely a fall that had resulted in a sprained ankle would be somewhere in her memory. "I remember…" She searched her mind. And searched. And searched. *"Nothing."*

The doctor must have heard the panic in her voice, because his eyes softened. "Don't worry." He tied off the bandage with a firm knot. "Your memory will return with time."

If only she could believe him. If only she could remember what had happened in Mattie's boudoir. If only she could say that she knew, without a doubt, she hadn't killed Cole and that she knew who did. The man who killed him was…

He was…

She glanced at Logan. Then just as quickly folded

her hands in her lap and looked away. Her gaze caught sight of the blood on her dress and she choked back a sob. "I have to change my clothes." She couldn't hide the desperation in her voice.

"Of course." Dr. Shane touched her clasped hands and squeezed. "Bella is gathering everything you'll need. She'll soon be here to help you."

"Bella?" Logan hissed. "Who's Bella?"

"Pastor Beau's sister and my lovely wife." Dr. Shane rose and turned to face Logan.

"Your wife?" Logan stared at him for a long, tense moment. "You got married?"

"Two years ago."

Blinking hard, Logan ran a hand down his face. "You're married," he repeated, his voice filled with disbelief. "And I never knew."

"Our first child is due any day now."

"A child, too." Something flashed in Logan's eyes, something sad and regretful, but he didn't comment again.

He paced.

Even in the confines of the small jail cell he moved with unmistakable authority. There was no hesitation in him, no pause. Every step he took said Logan Mitchell knew who he was and what he wanted out of life. Handsome, kind, capable, he could have his pick of women.

And he'd chosen Megan.

But five long years have passed. The thought settled over her like a heavy weight. In that time she'd changed. She'd gone from a child who helped around the orphanage to a woman in sole charge of the nursery. She'd grown in her love for the Lord, as well. Best of all, she'd discovered her artistic talent and had used it to turn the bedroom walls of Charity House into joyful expressions of God's unconditional love for His children.

In Logan's absence, she'd learned so much about herself. Surely he'd discovered things about himself, as well.

Was he still the man she remembered?

It was disloyal to think otherwise.

As if sensing her change in mood, Logan stopped pacing and turned to face her. "Megan, everything's going to be all right. I promise."

How could he be so confident? How could either of these men stand here and give her such promises? She'd lost a part of her life last night and everything hinged on her remembering those forgotten hours.

"What if I never remember?" she whispered to no one in particular.

"You will," Logan said. "You just need time to heal."

Time. There was that awful word again. Time had kept her and Logan apart. Time threatened them now.

She swallowed back a sob, chagrined at her inability to contain her emotions.

Logan moved closer and searched her face as though he could pull the missing memories forth by his will alone.

If only he could.

She knew she was letting him down. Yet some other instinct, something buried inside her lost memories, hinted that the blackness in her mind was about protecting Logan.

How could that be?

"Megan," Dr. Shane interrupted her thoughts. "Focus

on getting well. Once your body heals, your mind will follow."

Logan took her hands in his. "And until then I'm going to make sure you're safe."

Those were the same words Sheriff Scott had uttered to her last night. Fighting a sense of defeat, Megan lowered her head and sighed. "You're going to leave me in here until you find the real killer."

It made the most sense, even if she couldn't bear the thought of another night in this cold, drafty, depressing jail cell.

"No." Logan shook his head fiercely. "I'm not going to leave you locked up like a common criminal. I went to Mattie's this morning. I have proof of your innocence."

"You…you do?"

"Yes." But he didn't expand, which made her wonder if he really had proof or if he was still basing his assumption on what he thought he knew about her.

Before she could press him for more information, for *anything* to give her a sense of the truth hidden deep within her mind, he steered the conversation in a different direction. "As soon as I make the arrangements I'm going to take you home."

Home? No. *No.* They couldn't take that risk. "I can't go to Charity House," she said in a panicked voice. "We can't put the children in danger."

"That's not what I meant. I'm taking you to *my* home, where I grew up."

His words took a moment to settle over her. "You want to take me to your family's ranch?" Pure joy spread through her. Logan came from a large, happy family with a mother. And a father. And lots of siblings.

"It's the best solution," he said. "The only one."

Glory.

"Will that be all right with you?" he asked.

She wanted to jump off the cot and fling herself into his arms. She wanted to tell him, yes, yes, yes.

But reality held her back. She was the daughter of a prostitute, raised in an orphanage with children from similar backgrounds as hers.

His family might never accept her.

Then again, surely the people who'd raised this wonderful, kind, godly man would have equally gracious hearts.

"I…" Not sure what to say, she lifted her arms in the air and he immediately tugged her into his embrace.

She rested her cheek against his hard, muscular chest and breathed in his scent.

For the first time since she'd walked into Mattie's brothel yesterday Megan felt at peace. "Yes, Logan, I want to go home with you."

"Good." He blew out a long breath then set her away from him. "We'll leave immediately. We'll—"

"Logan, no." Sheriff Scott slammed into the jail cell, his lips twisting at a furious angle. "You can't take her away."

At the sound of those five angry words, spoken with such conviction, Megan's hope shattered.

Sheriff Scott wasn't going to let her leave with Logan.

That meant she would have to spend another night in jail, alone, with no relief in sight.

How would she ever bear the torment?

Chapter Six

Logan had been shot once. In his leg. The bullet had seared through his flesh with a burning agony he'd never experienced before that moment. Yet compared to the pain sweeping through him now as he stared at the anguish on Megan's face, the bullet wound seemed a mere pinprick.

A fierce, almost primal urge to wipe away her suffering nearly brought Logan to his knees. The sensation was so sharp, so raw, he had to fight for outward control.

He slowly released his hands from around Megan's waist, sucked in a quick breath, then shifted her behind him, literally shielding her from Trey's angry glare.

Logan slid his gaze across both men in the cell. "Who's going to stop us from leaving town? You?" he demanded of Trey. "Or maybe, you?" He stabbed a finger in Shane's direction.

Neither man appeared in a rush to answer him. After a moment, Shane broke eye contact. Trey, however, continued staring at Logan with an all-too-familiar look in his eyes. Trey wasn't going to back down any-time soon.

Neither was Logan.

Flattening his lips in a grim line, he dug in his heels and held his ground.

After another moment of silence, Trey finally looked away. "Logan," he said with unmistakable frustration. "You have to be smart about this. You have to think through every possibility. You—"

"We're done negotiating."

"Are we now? There's still the pesky matter of the law." Trey casually stuffed his hands in his pockets. He looked deceptively nonchalant. "You can't just whisk Megan away. She's a suspect in a murder."

"She's innocent."

Trey shook his head sadly. "We've been through this before. Until her memory returns, or until we can prove her innocence, she stays put."

"I have the evidence we need."

Trey's eyes narrowed. "What evidence?"

While Logan silently considered how much to reveal in Megan's presence, Shane's light footsteps sounded in the cell as he moved away. Excellent decision on the other man's part. The good doctor didn't belong in this conversation.

Neither did Megan.

"Let's finish this outside," Logan said to Trey.

"No." Megan hobbled around him, stopping when she stood by Trey's side. "I deserve to know what Mattie said about me."

Although Megan's voice sounded stronger, Logan noted the pallor on her face. "I'm not sure you should hear this right now."

"Yes, Logan." She lifted her chin at a stubborn angle. "Now."

Logan found himself gaping at her uncharacteristic tenacity. And her inflexibility. The Megan of the past had always been even tempered, tolerant. Gracious even, with the kind of patience that could nurse a child's injured knee in one breath and laugh off a garden snake stuffed in her pocket the next.

"I think Megan should stay," Shane said as he stepped out of the shadows. "Hearing the story might spark something in her memory."

While he spoke, Shane glided to a spot next to Megan. Shoulder to shoulder to shoulder. Trey, Megan, Shane, all three stood in a single row, facing Logan with various levels of resolve in their gazes.

The proverbial three against one.

Logan let out a sharp hiss. There was no way around the inevitable now. He would to have to reveal what he'd discovered at Mattie's, including the unsavory details of the madam's business dealings with Kincaid, since he was one of her regular clients.

Without looking at Megan directly—how could he with some of what he had to say?—Logan ran through Mattie's revelations in a quick, rapid-fire staccato. He finished with the final piece of evidence that cleared Megan of any crime. "Mattie found her lying on a small divan with a pillow under her head and a blanket tucked neatly around her legs."

"Logan," Trey began. "We still don't know—"

Logan lifted his hand to stop Trey from continuing and instead focused on Megan for the first time since he'd started his tale.

She wasn't looking at him, though. Her gaze darted

around the jail cell and she'd gone completely still. A series of complicated emotions ran across her face, while her breathing quickened to quick, short gasps.

Was she on the verge of remembering something important?

Logan wanted to physically pull the hidden memories free for her. If only he knew how. There had to be a way. But then she moved her head from side to side, sighed heavily, and let her shoulders drop at a dejected angle.

At the sight of her obvious despair, Logan wanted to offer her whatever comfort he could. He wanted to tell her matters weren't as hopeless as they seemed. That with prayer, time and God's help everything would turn out well for them.

He opened his mouth to tell her all that, but Trey's voice stopped him. "I'm afraid none of this changes Megan's situation."

Logan's jaw flexed with the heat of renewed fury. "On the contrary. Everything has changed." He spoke slowly, carefully, keeping his tone even. "It's clear someone else entered the room and killed Kincaid. Nothing else explains how Mattie found her."

"*Mattie* being the operative word here," Trey said, regret filling his eyes. "Consider your source."

"I have." Realizing his shooting hand had started shaking—from anger—Logan wiped his palm against his thigh. "I've interrogated Mattie Silks more times than I care to count. I know when she's lying. Perhaps for the first time in her life, the woman is telling the truth."

Well versed in Logan and Mattie's turbulent history, Trey faltered. "I'll want to check Mattie's story myself," Trey said in way of concession.

"Suit yourself, but we both know Megan is innocent." Logan smiled at her as he said the words.

She smiled back. And for that single moment in time, everything seemed to stop and pause. *Everything* felt right between them.

Then Trey ruined the moment. Again. "Logan, you should think about this one thing. You're basing your entire decision about Megan's innocence on information Mattie didn't divulge last night. Why cooperate now?" he asked. "And with you, of all people?"

"Because she's Mattie Silks. We both know she reveals what she wants, when she wants, to whomever she wants. I believe in her own, twisted way, Mattie's been protecting Megan all along." Like a mother would.

The realization didn't sit well with Logan. He didn't like the idea that a woman like Mattie Silks might actually think of Megan as a daughter. It was yet another reason to get her out of town quickly.

"I don't disagree with anything you've said," Trey admitted. "But for Megan's sake, I won't allow you to act in haste."

"Megan is innocent," Logan reiterated. "And the primary witness to a murder. That puts her under my protection now."

"I'm aware witness protection is under your jurisdiction," Trey said through snarled lips. "I'm not going to fight you on that. What do you have to say about this, Shane? Is Megan capable of making a journey like Logan is suggesting?"

Shane nodded. "Yes, as long as he makes frequent

stops." He turned to speak to Logan directly. "You must allow her to rest whenever necessary."

"I have no intention of pushing her beyond reason."

"Of course not," Shane acknowledged. "Didn't mean to imply otherwise."

"She'll also need a chaperone for the trip," Trey pointed out, in a tone more like a father than a lawman.

"I know that, too." In fact, Logan had already begun working up a list of chaperones in his mind.

He knew of several suitable women he trusted implicitly, all of them connected with Charity House. He didn't see a problem with asking any of the ladies to accompany him and Megan to his family's ranch, until his gaze met hers.

There was something in her eyes he couldn't quite define. That look, it was the same one she'd given him earlier, as though she was...afraid?

Was she afraid of him?

Surely not. Something else had to be causing her worry.

"Megan, I'm confident we can find you a suitable chaperone, one we can both agree on."

His words seemed to upset her more, so much so that tears gathered in her eyes.

Tears!

Megan was going to cry.

No, Lord. Please, no.

Logan could stand anything but that. Unlike his brother, Hunter, he'd always been powerless in the face of female tears. Even as a boy, Logan's baby sisters had wrapped him around their little fingers with nothing more than a whimper. It hadn't taken the little darlings long to learn how to use that particular weapon mercilessly against him.

But with Megan, her tears were different. They'd always been...terrifying. Gut-wrenching.

"Please, sweetheart, don't cry." Hoping to avoid the inevitable, he took her hands in his and blurted out the first thing that came to mind. "We'll get married instead. Before we leave."

She gasped at his blunt delivery, her eyes wide with shock.

You're botching this, Logan.

He softened his voice, took a deep breath and tried again. "Megan, I want to marry you." At the sight of her skepticism, he added with more force, "I do."

"You two can't get married right now," Trey and Shane said at the exact same moment, their voices melding into one, cruel sentence.

Paying no heed to either man, Logan gripped Megan's hands a bit tighter and stared into her eyes. His mind traveled back to the time when her guardian had told him to wait until she was older, until he could provide for her properly.

For five years, he'd followed another man's advice. He'd worked hard to prove himself as a lawman, moving up the ranks until he was no longer someone's deputy but a U.S. Marshal in his own right.

What good had come from that route? Megan was in trouble. Her life was at risk. And where there had once been love and affection between them, strain and tension now reigned.

"Megan." He raised one of her hands to his lips. "Will you marry me?"

Her eyes continued filling, the tears wiggling to the very edges of her lashes.

One lone tear escaped. Another soon followed.

He stopped the third with the pad of his thumb. "We've always planned to marry," he reminded her. "It's what we promised one another before I left for San Francisco."

Another tear slipped free.

He swallowed. Hard.

This wasn't how his marriage proposal was supposed to go. He'd had a plan, a good one that included dinner at a fancy restaurant and the ring he had tucked away in his pocket. He'd prepared a heartfelt declaration and even toyed with the idea of picking a bouquet of her favorite flowers to start off the evening on the right note.

But nothing in the last twelve hours had gone as planned. Logan wasn't supposed to find his future bride in jail. He wasn't supposed to feel uncertainty and confusion growing between them. And he certainly wasn't supposed to make her cry.

He trapped another rogue tear with his fingertip.

"It won't be a grand wedding, there's no time for that, but we'll be together, like we planned." *Wasn't that what mattered?* "What do you say, Megan? Will you marry me?

She blinked up at him, sorrow shimmering inside her gaze. But, if he wasn't mistaken, the desire to say yes to his proposal was swimming in her eyes, as well.

Hope swelled in his heart.

Then Shane cleared his throat. "Logan, give her a moment to think," he said softly. "She's been through an ordeal. She deserves a bit of time to consider your proposal."

Logan was in no mood for a lecture, but he knew Shane was right.

What if she says no? He swallowed back a jolt of apprehension. *Lord, release me from this doubt. Whatever happens next, however she responds, help me to trust it is for the best. Not the end, but the beginning.*

"If this is all too sudden for you," he added in a surprisingly steady voice. "We can wait to be married until you're completely ready."

She cocked her head at a slight angle, a sense of wonder evident in her gaze. "You'd still marry me, even if I said no now?"

"Yes." He smiled at her and satisfaction filled him when she returned the gesture.

"I've always wanted to marry you," he said. "From the first moment I laid eyes on you I knew you were the one for me. I love you, Megan." It was the truth, his defining truth these last five years.

It was also the right thing to say.

Her expression cleared and she flung herself back into his arms. Right where she belonged.

"Yes, Logan." She choked back a sob. "Of course, I'll marry you."

Praise God, he thought. Something was finally going their way.

Chapter Seven

Half fearing Logan would vanish if she released her hold on him, Megan clung longer than was proper.

But, oh, Logan loved her. He *loved* her. And he was going to marry her. Today.

She rubbed her cheek against his shoulder and breathed in his warm, masculine scent. How she'd missed him. How she'd longed for his strength. His kindness. His patience.

Although she didn't want to rely on anyone, not even Logan, not completely, she couldn't help but give in to her joy now.

For this one, brief moment in time, it was easy for Megan to believe God's promise in Romans 8:28. *And we know that all things work together for good to them that love God, to them who are the called according to His purpose.*

She tightened her grip on his shoulders, only half aware the other two men were leaving the building, giving her and Logan a moment alone with one another.

Megan sighed. All her dreams were coming true at last. Her plans for the future were no longer vague and shadowy. There would be no more waiting. No more wondering "when" or "if." No more serving other people's purposes, but those of her own family.

The one she would build with Logan.

Megan should be happy.

And yet...

She was tempted to hold a part of herself back, like always, even after Logan's bold declaration of love in front of a highly unlikely audience—her doctor and the town sheriff.

Confusion and sadness tumbled through her. Surely, this bleak feeling in the pit of her stomach was caused by her memory loss and not some ridiculous fear that Logan would leave her like her father had left her mother. Like her mother had in turn abandoned her to the care of others.

No, this doubt had to be caused by recent events. She'd been through a terrible trauma.

Or so everyone kept telling her.

The thought brought no relief. Only more sadness. She dug her fingers into Logan's shoulders, reminding herself this was Logan. *Logan,* the man who'd remained constant these past five years. The man who had returned to her, just as he'd promised.As though sensing her shift in mood, he pulled slightly away and stared into her eyes. She quickly lowered her head, away from all that consideration staring back at her.

He gently lifted her chin with his finger. "Megan?" Concern filled his voice. "What is it? What's wrong?"

Rather than answering his question, she bolted back into his arms, letting the strength of his body erase her sudden melancholy.

"Nothing's wrong," she said in a rushed tone, her

voice catching on the words. "It's just…everything has happened so fast. I'm a bit overwhelmed. That's all."

"Of course." He released a slow exhale of air. "I suspect that's only natural."

Why did he have to be so agreeable, so kind? So understanding?

Frowning at the unexpected jolt of frustration at him—at her—at them both—Megan stepped back again. With a slight shake in her hands, she pressed her fingertips to her temples and tried to rub out the ache behind her eyes.

"Do you want me to stay with you awhile longer?" Logan asked, worry still evident in his voice. "Time is short. But not that short. I can wait to start making plans for our wedding if there's something you want to discuss first?"

He was giving her a chance to change her mind. Instead of feeling grateful for his thoughtfulness, panic clogged in her throat. Did he want her to change her mind?

"No. I…" Her throat grew tighter. She wanted to push him away from her. At the same time, she wanted to pull him close and never let him go. What was wrong with her? "I want you to start making our wedding plans. As soon as possible, please."

He held very still. "You're sure?"

Was she? Of course she was. But her hands started shaking harder and the dark, hazy feeling that hovered just out of reach threatened to consume her all over again.

Her life might be simpler if she relied only on her own strength, but that wasn't God's plan for His children. *Two are better than one; because they have a good reward for their labour. For if they fall, the one will lift up his fellow...*

She wanted that kind of unity with Logan.

Pulling her bottom lip between her teeth, Megan laced her fingers together and set them in front of her. They fell directly across the bloodstains at her waist. She *had* to get out of this dress. At once.

"Please, Logan, I don't want to wait any longer to get married. But I need to prepare a few things on my own, without you here. I need..."

A friend, she thought a little desperately, someone to help her dress for the wedding ceremony. To share a few words of wisdom that would alleviate her worries about this hasty marriage.

As if in answer to her silent wish, the outer door swung open with a flourish. The scent of jasmine floated on the air while the sound of rustling material and soft footsteps echoed off the walls.

Megan turned her head in time to see Bella, Dr. Shane's wife and one of Megan's dearest friends, approaching. With her honey-gold hair, amber eyes and aristocratic features, Bella O'Toole Bartlett was the most beautiful woman Megan had ever met. She was also a ferocious and loyal friend. *Exactly* the person Megan needed right now.

Arms full of what looked like expensive dresses made of shiny silk and lace, Bella half glided, half waddled into the jail cell. Despite being eight months with child, she was all grace and style. No longer touted as the international opera sensation of her generation, the woman still knew how to make an entrance.

"Oh, Megan, my dear," Bella said in her breathy, British accent. "I've been beside myself with worry. It's just not right, you, all alone and trapped in this hideous jail cell." She drew in a dramatic pull of air. "Well, I'm here now. We'll get you changed and feeling like new in no time. I've brought several dresses with me. You can choose the one you like best."

Barely glancing in Logan's direction, she shoved the bundle of silk and lace at him. Ignoring how he fumbled to keep one of the dresses from falling to the floor, Bella tugged Megan into a fierce hug.

"Shane told me what happened last night at Mattie's." She rubbed Megan's back as if she were one of the smaller children at Charity House. "What an ordeal you've suffered."

Megan relaxed under her friend's sympathetic care, then glanced over at Logan. He stared back at her, wide-eyed, blinking rapidly and so adorably handsome in his confusion. Clearly, he had no idea what to make of Shane's wife. Bella had that particular impact on people.

He bobbled the dresses in his arms again, crumpling the bulk of them against his broad chest in an effort to secure his hold. He should look ridiculous, standing there with all that silk and lace tumbling around him.

He stole her breath away. This man, this dear, dear man, would soon be her husband.

Two are better than one; because they have a good reward for their labour. For if they fall, the one will lift up his fellow. Megan sighed in satisfaction.

Bella let out an answering sound deep in her throat, then stepped back. "Let's have a look at you." She gripped Megan's shoulders, scowled at the wound on her throat, then searched her face for...what?

Megan shifted under her friend's scrutiny, putting

far too much weight on her tender ankle. She gasped at the sharp pain shooting up her leg.

Logan was instantly by her side, but the dresses in his arms made it impossible for him to reach out to her.

No matter. The fact that he'd moved that quickly was enough to tell her how deeply he cared. Maybe it wouldn't be so terrible to rely on him. Just a little.

Megan had to fight to keep from bursting into tears, whether from happiness or confusion she couldn't say. Her emotions were so raw, so close to the surface. One moment she was happy, the next she was confused. Would she ever feel like herself again?

She didn't have long to ponder the question before Bella released her and moved to stand directly in front of Logan. "You must be Megan's fiancé, Logan."

He blinked several more times, obviously thrown off by the censure in her tone. "Yes. I'm Logan Mitchell. And you—" he cleared his throat "—must be Shane's wife, Bella. He said you were coming to help Megan change her clothing."

"And here I am," she said, continuing to eye Logan with her face bunched into an uncharacteristic glare.

At the sight of the two squaring off, a moment of desperation spread through Megan. What was her friend about to say to Logan? Bella had never pretended to agree with Megan's decision to wait for his return. She'd gone so far as to encourage Megan to leave Denver altogether and travel abroad so she could study her art.

Megan had resisted.

What was wrong with not wanting to leave Denver? What was wrong with desiring a simple life with Logan, and producing a handful of children together?

"You know, Logan," Bella said, jamming her fists on either side of her waist. "I don't mind saying, we've been anticipating your arrival for some time now. Years, to be precise."

"As have I, Mrs. Bartlett." Logan eyed Bella carefully. "In fact, I've been counting down the days for five years, one month, six days and eighteen hours."

His answer did not impress Bella. "And how many minutes, since we're counting?"

"Twelve."

Bella's lips twitched, but her eyes gave away nothing of what she was thinking. "Well, now that you've finally arrived, I find it necessary to speak plainly."

He tilted his head at her. "Of course."

"You stayed away too long."

Something like pain traveled across his features. "I agree."

"You…" It was Bella's turn to blink in shock. "Agree?"

"Yes." He didn't expand, or explain himself further.

"Well, hmm." Bella tapped a finger against her chin and studied him silently.

He simply held her gaze.

Letting out a feminine sniff, she tossed him a dismissive wave. "You may go now. I wish to speak with Megan. Alone."

"I understand." He set the bundle of dresses on the cot with exaggerated care. But instead of leaving right away, he pulled Megan's hands into his and said, "But I'll go only if that's what you wish of me."

How sweet to ask her. How…wonderful.

He drew one of her hands to his lips. "Do you wish for me to leave?"

No. Yes. Maybe? She wasn't sure what she wanted so she hedged. "I'll be perfectly fine with Bella."

"Then I'll begin making plans for our future." He dropped a chaste kiss on her forehead. "When we meet again, it'll be at our wedding."

"Our wedding." As she repeated his words, the bottom dropped out of Megan's stomach. For the first time since Logan had returned home she felt secure. "Yes, I'll see you at our wedding."

"Once all is made ready, I'll return." Smiling broadly, he turned back to Bella and regarded her with a sense of amused tolerance. "I leave my future bride in your care, Mrs. Bartlett. Watch over her for me."

Before Bella could respond, he was gone.

"Well," Bella said, still watching the door after he'd clicked it firmly shut behind him. "Perhaps I underestimated his attachment to you."

Megan felt her mouth curve up at the corners. "It takes a confident woman to admit when she is wrong."

"I said, *perhaps*." Bella flipped her hair over her shoulder. "Time will tell."

Megan did laugh then, the sound coming out rusty and a little off-key. "You are my most loyal friend, Mrs. Bartlett."

"So I am." Bella let out her own pitch-perfect laugh. "Now, come." She steered Megan toward the cot, moved the dresses aside and forced her to sit with gentle pressure on her shoulders. "Tell me everything you remember about last night."

The request brought a sudden ache flooding hot and fast through Megan, making her head spin. How many times must she answer the same endless round of questions before people quit asking her?

"Didn't your husband explain the situation? I can't tell you what happened," Megan said, her words coming out harsh. "Because I don't *remember*."

"So, it's true." Bella touched Megan's hand. "You've lost your memory of last night's events."

Megan nodded.

"Oh, my dear girl." Bella joined Megan on the cot and immediately turned into the trained nurse she'd become in the past year. She brushed Megan's hair off her forehead, then lifted her wrist and placed two fingers at the tender spot below her hand.

While Bella counted heartbeats, Megan closed her eyes and tried to slow her breathing. She wanted to clear her mind, to relax, but she was getting married in a few hours. Her life was about to change forever.

In her heart she knew it was time for her to leave Charity House at last. Although she loved them dearly, the babies she cared for weren't her own. The murals she'd painted on the bedrooms walls weren't her creations, not really, but rather an expression of all that the orphanage stood for.

Even her charity work at Mattie's brothel had been done by Bella first. Nothing Megan had ever done in her life was a reflection of who she was as a person, or as a woman.

Who was she then, really?

She wanted to know the answer. Craved it. But until her memory returned she feared she would be at a disadvantage. How could one know oneself when parts were missing?

Bella released her hand and then swept her fingertips across Megan's forehead again. "You're a little warm."

Megan snapped her eyes open. Everything in her

hurt, her head, her body, maybe even her soul, an ache borne from her helplessness. "It's…it's stuffy in here."

"Is it?" Bella looked around the tiny jail cell. "I was thinking it was a bit drafty."

For some reason, the offhand remark loosened the tears Megan had barely gotten under control once before. But she couldn't cry. Not now. She swiped at her damp cheeks with the back of her wrist.

Wordlessly, Bella pulled Megan into her arms. "Go ahead, my friend. Cry. It's a perfectly acceptable reaction to all that's happened to you."

"No." Megan shook her head sternly. "No. It's my wedding day. I will *not* cry on my wedding day."

"Megan, don't do this to yourself." Bella shifted to her left and sighed. "You've been through a waking nightmare, with a portion of your memory locked deep inside your mind as a result. There's no shame in a few tears."

"No," Megan said again. "I'm getting married today, to the man I love. I'm supposed to be happy. I… I…" Megan let her words trail off as a memory shoved for release.

She closed her eyes and grasped for it, but the elusive thought was just out of reach. Like always.

There *had* to be a way to unlock her mind. She thought briefly of praying, but no words formed in her head.

Bella patted her arm. "Look at me, Megan."

She slowly opened her eyes again, stricken and uneasy but determined to hide her suffering from her friend.

"Here's what I know for sure." Bella smiled kindly, tugging a handkerchief from her sleeve and handing it over to Megan. "God never gives us more than we can bear, at least not with Him by our side. You're a strong woman, Megan, but sometimes even strong women need to call on the Lord for help. With His assistance, you will get through this."

Megan wasn't so sure.

"I also know that crying, when done properly, is never a sign of weakness but a show of strength."

Megan blinked at the sheer cloth in her hand. "Perhaps that's true, for you," she said, holding on to her emotions by a thread. "You are, after all, a famous opera singer known for her dramatic range."

"Then I'd say that makes me something of an expert, wouldn't you?"

Megan managed a wavering smile. Obviously, she wasn't going to win this battle of words with her friend. But she wasn't going to cry either. No more tears on her wedding day. No. More. Tears.

"Well." Bella rose and stretched out her hand. "If you aren't going to indulge in a good cry, like any self-respecting female would, let's get you dressed for your wedding."

Instinct told Megan to focus on one thing at a time, and not get ahead of herself. Forcing a smile onto her lips, she took Bella's outstretched hand and stood. "All right. What have you brought me?"

"Let's see." Bella sorted through the pile of dresses. "What about—" she picked up one, quickly discarded it, went for another but eventually settled on yet a third "—*this* one."

Smiling in triumph, she raised the light blue silk dress. "It's one of my favorites."

Megan let her gaze linger on the gown. The thin

line of navy lace running along the collar and cuffs looked far too delicate to touch, much less wear. "It's too elegant."

"It's perfect. Here. Let's see how it looks against your skin."

With shaking hands, Megan took the dress and held it up under her chin. "What do you think?"

"I think—" Bella clapped her hands together with glee "—you're going to make a beautiful bride."

Chapter Eight

For the next two hours, Logan finalized his wedding plans with one objective in mind: get Megan out of town as quickly as possible.

After purchasing a marriage license from the county clerk, his next stop was Charity House, where he discreetly informed Marc Dupree of the situation. The owner of the orphanage was understandably worried about Megan's safety, but didn't fight Logan over his decision to take her away from Denver. Even when Logan explained a killer was still on the loose, possibly gunning for Megan, Marc didn't appear overly concerned.

Did the man trust Logan to keep Megan safe? Not likely. Something else must warrant his lack of worry.

At least he'd agreed the wedding needed to be kept a secret. Not even his wife would know about the blessed event until Logan had Megan safely away from Denver.

Satisfied Marc understood the gravity of the situation, Logan turned to leave. But before he could exit Charity House, Marc stopped him with a hand on his shoulder. "Logan, wait. I want to show you something first."

Logan studied the man who had prevented him from marrying Megan once before. Dressed in a brocade vest and matching tie, with his hair immaculately cut and styled, Marc looked more like a banker than the proprietor of an orphanage that catered to prostitutes' mistakes.

There were things Logan wanted to say, but so far he'd held his tongue, determined to show this man his due respect. Marc was, for all intents and purposes, Megan's father.

That didn't mean Logan didn't harbor a large dose of resentment toward him. If Marc had relented five years ago and allowed Logan to take Megan as his wife she wouldn't be in danger now.

"I don't have much time," Logan said through clenched teeth, surprised to hear a trace of resentment coating his voice.

Eyeing him thoughtfully, Marc released a slow breath. "I realize you're in a hurry, but it's important you know what Megan's been up to in your absence. She's been…well, you should see for yourself."

It was the earnest look on Marc's face, rather than his odd choice of words, that had Logan nodding in agreement. "All right. Show me."

"This way."

Marc ushered Logan upstairs, directing him around one corner and then another, stopping at the end of a long hallway with a row of closed doors on either side.

Since the children were at school the orphanage was all but deserted at this hour. Marc threw open one of the doors and Logan stepped inside. His mouth dropped open. Shock stole his ability to speak. It was as if he'd been transported to another world, a world of whimsy and dreams and eternal hope.

For a long moment, he simply gaped at the beautiful, intricate designs on the walls. Each one depicted a different scene from the Bible. The accompanying verses scrolled in a bold, swirling script were a testimony to God's love for His children. Verses such as, *Let the children come to me,* and *I am the Way, the Truth and the Life,* along with several more.

"Who painted this?" he asked.

"Megan."

Of course. No wonder Marc had wanted Logan to see this room. The insight the paintings gave into Megan's character was extraordinary. No, it was mind-boggling. Logan had always known she had a tender heart, but he hadn't realized she had such a vivid, whimsical imagination inside her beautiful head.

The discovery left Logan unsettled. How would he ever make such a woman happy? He was too pragmatic, too single-minded, jaded even. He knew nothing of fancy ideals and castles in the sky.

A moment of despair nearly brought him to his knees, but then an idea formed, one that just might help release the memories trapped inside Megan's mind.

He made a mental note to stop by the nearest mercantile before returning to the jail. He would worry about the rest later.

Marc cleared his throat. "There's more."

Logan swallowed. "More?"

"She's painted every room upstairs," Marc said. "Each one is more special and unique than the last."

"I want to see them."

"Of course." Marc led Logan from one room to the next.

Leaning against the doorjamb of the last one, Marc crossed his arms over his chest. "I hope this helps you understand your future wife a little better."

Logan swallowed again. "I… Yes, it helps immensely." As disconcerting as it was to discover how little he knew about Megan, Marc had just given Logan a gift and a peace offering of sorts.

Marc pushed away from the door, an unreadable expression on his face. "Understand, Logan. I showed you her artwork because Megan is precious to me. I consider her my daughter. I would do anything, *anything* to protect her." His gaze turned hard, ruthless. "As far as I'm concerned, the man who attacked her deserved to die."

Logan didn't argue, not since he secretly agreed.

"But she's no longer mine to watch over. She's yours. I beg you to take care of her as I was unable to do."

They both knew he was speaking of last night's attack.

Choked with emotion, Logan wasn't sure what to say. Megan had been hurt while in Marc's care. It was something he would have to come to grips with on his own.

"I wish you well in your marriage." Marc patted him awkwardly on the back then dropped his hand and quickly looked away. But not before Logan saw the sorrow and grief welling in his eyes.

Marc had just given Logan his blessing. Until that moment, Logan hadn't realized he'd been waiting for it. "You can trust that I'll do whatever it takes to keep Megan safe," he said. "Even lay down my life if necessary."

"I know." Marc ran a hand down his face and sighed. "May God be with you both."

"Thank you."

There was nothing more to say. Logan left the orphanage, his feet heavier than usual as he walked across the backyard in search of Reverend Beauregard O'Toole. After Logan explained the situation all over again, the pastor agreed to perform the marriage ceremony at the jailhouse. Without his wife accompanying him.

Wedding plans complete, Logan made his way back to the heart of Denver. He told himself all this secrecy was necessary for Megan's protection. Nevertheless, regret pushed its way through his resolve.

Megan deserved to be surrounded by her friends and loved ones on her wedding day. She deserved to be married in a church, not a jail cell. Perhaps there was a way...

No. Logan couldn't relent. Megan's safety *had* to come first. All this secrecy was necessary. He would make it up to her later. Somehow, someway.

Charging across the grounds of the Arapahoe County Courthouse he eyed the white, puffy clouds drifting overhead. They created a carefree mood Logan found oddly annoying. He focused his gaze solely on the courthouse.

The building looked the same as it had five years ago. Made from a mixture of solid stone and marble, the three-story structure was a perfect representation of law and order.

Would justice be served in Kincaid's murder? Or had it already been served? With a knife jammed through his black heart?

The thought went against everything Logan believed in as a lawman and a Christian. It was the type of rationale his brother had always used to justify years of walking on the opposite side of the law from Logan.

And yet...

Logan wasn't sure he disagreed with his brother, at least not in this situation. Kincaid had attacked Megan, had tried to steal her innocence. Just like Marc had said, the man had deserved to die.

Logan balled his hand into a tight fist. The gesture did nothing to stop the rage sweeping through him. When he found Kincaid's killer, would he arrest the man? Or congratulate him for a job well done?

A wave of unease spread through him.

Logan turned quickly, scanning the area behind him. He looked from left to right, right to left, taking note of each person, what they wore, the expressions on their faces. No one seemed to care that a lawman was watching them. Yet there had to be a reason for this powerful sense of foreboding, this sense that someone had Logan in his crosshairs.

What was he missing?

Guard what has been entrusted to your care. The Scripture from First Timothy came so fast, so powerful Logan's shoulders bunched with tension.

He searched the sea of faces again.

Kincaid's killer could be among them. He could be watching Logan now, which only added to his sense of urgency.

Logan wouldn't rest easy until he had Megan tucked safely away on his family's ranch.

Darting up the marble steps of the courthouse, he shoved inside and circled his gaze around the wood-paneled lobby. Men and women of all ages milled about. Seeing no threat, he wound through the labyrinth of activity and made his way to the back of the building. Every breath he took smelled of leather and wood varnish. The scent of important business.

Rounding the final corner, Logan entered a tiny office and slammed the door shut with a bang. The room contained a wooden chair, a functional desk and a thick layer of dust. The sparse surroundings spoke of the lack of respect the former U.S. Marshal had afforded his administrative duties.

Logan allowed a smile to play at the edges of his mouth. Like Trey, Logan preferred pursuing outlaws over the paperwork the federal government demanded of his position. Unfortunately, once an outlaw was apprehended a trial had to be scheduled, conducted and the proceedings painstakingly recorded.

Every expenditure had to be documented, checked and rechecked, until the accountants in Washington were satisfied.

Grimacing, Logan reviewed the court schedule for the coming months. He nodded in satisfaction. The next trial under his jurisdiction wasn't scheduled for another three weeks, plenty of time to get Megan settled on the ranch.

Letting out a slow breath, Logan flipped open the top ledger and began sorting through the mess Trey had left him. A half hour later, he gave up.

Ledgers tucked under his arm, he left the courthouse and made his way to the telegraph office. He sent a brief message to Washington explaining that he would be delayed at least one more week before he could start his official duties.

After making a quick stop at the mercantile, he headed back to the jail with a present for his bride.

It was time to begin their life together at last.

Megan watched as Bella and her husband spoke softly to one another just outside her jail cell. They'd left the door slightly ajar, but the iron bars served as a barrier, a reminder that Megan was not a part of their world.

Heads bent, hands lightly touching, the Bartletts made a single unit, one that seemed to shut out everyone else. They slowly pulled apart and then shared a look of quiet understanding, as though they could read each other's mind.

Megan fought a pang of envy. She wanted that kind of relationship with Logan. She wanted the certainty and deep connection that went beyond words. But they didn't have anything like that. Not anymore.

Had they ever?

Of course they had.

There was no doubt she loved Logan, and he loved her. They simply had to get to know one another again. But if her memory never returned would they ever be completely happy together?

Doubt swept through her like a cold blast of mountain air. But in the next moment, the outer door swung open and a burst of light from outside temporarily blinded her. When her vision cleared, Logan wasn't the one standing in the doorway.

It was…it was…

Mattie Silks?

Why would Denver's most notorious madam come

here? The last time Megan had seen the woman she'd been hovering over Cole Kincaid's dead body.

Her mind drifted back to that moment, but the images shifted, blurred. Then disappeared altogether.

Frustrated, Megan focused on Mattie's approach.

Hand on her hip, the other one bent at the elbow and swinging in time with her steps, Mattie sashayed across the floor. Catching sight of the woman, Bella broke away from her husband and stepped directly in Mattie's path.

The two proceeded to carry on a harsh, whispered conversation. Megan thought she heard the word wedding, but couldn't be sure. After several hard shakes of her head, Bella relented and stepped out of Mattie's way.

"Remember, Mattie. Don't overtire her," Bella said as she pulled her husband toward the outer doorway. "Shane and I will be just outside."

Mattie tossed her a careless wave in answer.

Once the Bartletts left the building Mattie stepped closer to Megan, sending the sickeningly sweet scent of musk and jasmine wafting over her.

Her stomach roiled in protest, but she bit her lip and forced her body to relax. "Mattie? What are you doing here?"

"I came to check on you, of course." A ridge of concern dug between the woman's eyes.

The look was so atypical, Megan found herself more confused than before. She pressed a thumb and forefinger to the bridge of her nose and ordered her mind to slow down. But her thoughts continued running in countless directions.

"Megan, darling. You look absolutely…" Mattie smiled. "Stunning."

Megan dropped her hand and smiled back, oddly pleased to discover that the blue silk dress suited her well enough to earn a rare compliment from Mattie Silks.

"But your hair." The older woman clicked her tongue in mortification. "We simply must do something about all those knots."

Not waiting for Megan's response, Mattie entered the cell, set the carpetbag she'd brought with her on the cot and proceeded to rummage through its contents.

"Sit down," she ordered without looking up. "We'll get you presentable yet."

Suddenly too exhausted to argue, Megan did as the other woman requested.

Standing over her, Mattie proceeded to comb out Megan's tangles with a surprisingly gentle hand. "Now, tell me, dear. Have you remembered anything from last night?"

Shying away from the sympathetic tone, Megan shut her eyes. Her lower back still ached. Her head still spun. And she still could not recall a thing prior to Mattie's appearance in her boudoir. "I remember nothing after I first arrived, except waking up and seeing you leaning over Cole's body."

"Well, never mind." Mattie gently released another tangle. "It'll come eventually."

"Dr. Shane said the same thing."

"He would know."

Silence fell over them, interrupted only by the sound of the brush stroking through Megan's hair.

Once she'd combed out all the tangles, Mattie wound

Megan's hair on top of her head. She shifted around her, studied her creation from the front, pulled a few tendrils loose then nodded in satisfaction. "Perfect."

"Really?" Megan asked.

"Of course." Mattie looked insulted. "I don't give false praise."

Unable to deny the truth in that particular statement, Megan lifted her hands in surrender. "No, Mattie. No, you don't."

"I almost forgot." She began digging in her bag once again. "I brought you a present."

"You did?" Megan's voice rose then broke over the last word.

"Now where is it?" Mattie continued digging. "Ah, there you are." She pulled out a package that was small enough to fit in her hand.

"This was your mother's." She thrust the gift at Megan. "I thought you should have it."

"Oh." Megan had nothing left of her mother but sad memories. She took the small bundle with shaking fingers and slowly peeled away the corners of the box.

A beautiful diamond bracelet winked back at her. She'd never seen anything so delicate. The sparkling piece of jewelry reminded Megan of the mother she'd known before the bad times had hit, when there'd been nothing but laughter and smiles and a strong sense of safety. Unable to speak, Megan turned the box around in her hand.

"Your mother sold it to me years ago." Mattie snatched the bracelet free and then clamped it around Megan's wrist.

Even in the dim light of the jail cell the stones glittered. For a second, it was if her mother was as close as the bracelet around her wrist, telling her to be happy, telling her she *deserved* to be happy.

Tears welled, but Megan swallowed them back. Aside from her earlier vow to resist crying on her wedding day, Mattie wouldn't appreciate the sentimental reaction. "I don't know what to say. I've never had anything of my mother's."

In the next moment the door to the jail swung open, cutting off her words.

Five people filed into the tiny building. Bella led the way with Dr. Shane and Sheriff Scott on either side of her. Pastor Beau came next. Logan entered last, carrying a bouquet of flowers and a package with a red bow tied on top.

He smiled at Megan, his handsome face all but dancing with joy, but then he caught sight of her visitor and scowled. "What are *you* doing here?"

Hands on hips, nose in the air, Mattie glared right back at him. "Visiting a dear friend on her wedding day."

As the two proceeded to stare each other down, Megan sighed. For one dreadful moment she wondered if it was too late to change her mind about this wedding.

But despite this discouraging start, despite all the animosity flowing through the room, she wanted to marry Logan. Not for decency's sake, not for expediency, but because she loved him.

With all her heart.

Chapter Nine

Logan settled into his stalemate with Mattie as though he had all the time in world. Which, unfortunately, he did not. But there were some situations that required careful handling. *This* being one of them.

No matter how badly he wanted to toss the unsavory madam out on her ear he wouldn't do so unless Megan asked him. She deserved a wedding free of strife. If that meant he had to play nice with Mattie Silks, so be it. His bride's happiness must come first.

Of course, Mattie was in one of her surly moods. Bad temper flared out of her, while an unpleasant snarl curled her lips. Logan had dealt with the woman often enough to know this standoff could last all day.

Unless he relented first.

Finished with the ridiculous battle of wills, he broke eye contact with the madam and focused his full attention on Megan.

The air immediately left his lungs in a hard, burning whoosh. Megan was…

She was…

Exquisite. Breathtaking. Beyond beautiful.

And, best of all, she would soon be his.

His.

Until death do them part.

He couldn't take his eyes off her. Standing in a splash of sunlight, she looked almost ethereal. Her hair was piled on top of her head in a complicated design, with a few pieces hanging loose along her face, framing her eyes. Eyes so blue, so clear Logan was reminded of the San Francisco Bay under a cloudless sky.

Oh, Lord, help me do right by her. Help me to protect Megan in the coming days.

Pushing down a thread of misgiving, he breathed out slowly but his thoughts refused to untangle. Clearing his throat, he carefully set Megan's wedding present on Trey's desk and went to her, flowers still in hand.

Unsure how he put one foot in front of the other, he entered the jail cell and fumbled for words. "Megan. I…" Disgusted with his clumsiness, he forced a smile and tried again. "You look…remarkable." He touched her cheek. "So. Very. Beautiful."

Blushing, she lowered her eyelashes and sighed. In that moment, she created such a picture of beauty and grace his heart gave two hard knocks against his ribs.

She lifted her gaze at last and smiled up at him. "You look wonderful, too, Logan."

Her voice shook as she spoke and the sound of her nervousness made his gut stir with apprehension. *What if I let her down? What if I can't make her happy?*

"These are for you." He shoved the flowers at her. For a man who'd hunted down the vilest criminals in the country he felt surprisingly stupid and tongue-tied.

Megan did that to him. Even after all these years.

"Thank you." She buried her nose in the bouquet for a moment. "They're lovely."

Their gazes connected again, and a pleasant warmth settled over him. *This* was where he belonged. With this woman. Always. They would work through the rest in time.

Certainty filled him.

At the same moment Megan's eyes brimmed with an emotion he recognized at once. *Love.* She might not have said the words out loud yet, but Logan saw the truth in her gaze.

Despite his five-year absence, despite the long days of silence broken only by sporadic letters Megan's feelings for him hadn't changed.

He would make sure they never did.

Nervous for an entirely different reason now, he dipped his hands in his pockets and rocked back on his heels. As much as he wanted to continue staring at his beautiful bride, time was running out.

They needed to be on the trail before nightfall.

Logan took Megan's hand and held it close to his heart. "What do you say? Want to get married now?"

She curled her fingers into his shirt and let out an engaging little laugh, the one that had first attracted him to her all those years ago. "Oh, yes. Let's."

Logan was suddenly very impatient to make this woman his wife.

Hitting his cue perfectly, Reverend O'Toole stepped forward. "Shall we begin?"

Logan nodded, then turned to face the man directly. With his tawny hair, chiseled features and charismatic presence, Beauregard O'Toole could have easily been a star on the international stage, like the rest of his famous acting family.

But the Lord had called him into ministry. And while most preachers tried to keep the unpleasant types out of their church, Beau opened his doors to everyone, especially the lost and broken. He was a man who lived Christ's example daily and Logan admired him greatly. He couldn't think of a better person to perform his wedding ceremony.

Smiling now, Beau opened his Bible and motioned the others forward. "Everyone, please take your places."

Logan pulled Megan flush against him. She leaned in closer still, the gesture turning them into a single unit.

It was a very good beginning.

There was a moment of jostling as the others moved into the jail cell. Trey and Shane stood on Logan's right, Bella on Megan's left.

Mattie hovered just behind Bella, but Logan chose to ignore the woman. He would have succeeded rather nicely had he not breathed in a large whiff of her cloying scent.

The woman was a menace. But at least she comported herself with a small amount of dignity—by keeping her mouth shut.

Thank God for small blessings.

Megan clutched the flowers in her hand so tightly her knuckles turned white. Her mother's bracelet felt heavy around her wrist and despite her best efforts to focus on the positive aspects of the moment, nerves consumed her.

She should be happy. Ecstatic, even. But she felt rootless and adrift, nothing like herself at all. She shouldn't feel so unmoored on her wedding day.

Then again, who could blame her?

She was getting married in a jail cell, for goodness' sake. To the man she loved, yes, but with only a handful of her friends as witnesses. Worse yet, she was wearing a dress that was not her own.

She let out a weary sigh.

During all the lonely nights she'd lain awake dreaming of this moment, a borrowed dress had never factored into the equation. Nor had a row of iron bars. She certainly hadn't expected the smell of mold and Mattie's nauseating perfume to waft over the proceedings.

Oh, Lord, Megan prayed. *I want to believe the odd circumstances of this wedding are part of Your plan for Logan and me. Please, I beg You, help me to see this from Your perspective, not my own.*

"Dearly beloved," Pastor Beau began and Megan snapped to attention.

"We have come together in the presence of God to witness and bless the joining together of this man and this woman in Holy Matrimony."

The reverend was speaking words Megan had heard countless times before at other wedding ceremonies, yet they sounded distant and cold to her now. Like frost under hazy fog. Yet the air in the room was so unbearably hot and sticky Megan had to fight to take a decent breath.

Feeling more disjointed than before and needing an anchor, she let her gaze drift toward Logan.

He was watching her in return.

His smoky blue eyes skimmed her face with a look

she couldn't quite decipher. Fondness, perhaps? No, conviction. Logan Mitchell knew exactly what he wanted.

And he wanted her.

Her stomach dropped.

Even as Pastor Beau continued blessing their union, Logan held her stare. Then he enfolded her free hand in his and squeezed gently.

A moment of apprehension took hold of her. Logan was so big and she was so small. He was so strong and, at the moment, she was so unsteady. She didn't know what to say, or how to act.

But then a slow, warm smile spread across Logan's face and he touched his lips lightly to her knuckles. The intimate gesture put her immediately at ease.

Tightening her grip around her flowers, Megan spent the next few moments trying desperately to re-focus her attention on the solemn words Pastor Beau spoke.

She missed several lines, but easily honed in on the vows.

"Logan," the reverend addressed him directly. "Will you have this woman to be your wedded wife, to live together in the holy estate of matrimony as God ordained it? Will you nourish and cherish her as Christ loves the Church? Will you love, honor and keep her, in sickness and in health, and forsaking all others remain united to her alone, as long as you both shall live?"

"I will," he said with quiet intensity, commanding Megan's gaze as though she was the only person in the room. He pressed another heartfelt kiss to her knuckles and repeated the words a second time. *"I will."*

Bella sighed. Mattie blew her nose, loudly.

Megan looked down at her feet.

"Megan."

She quickly lifted her gaze. "Yes?"

"Will you have this man to be your wedded husband, to live together in the holy estate of matrimony as God ordained it? Will you love, honor and keep him, in sickness and in health, and forsaking all others remain united to him alone, as long as you both shall live?"

"Oh, yes." She glanced over at Logan, who was looking expectantly at her. "I will." Her voice barely shook.

She was slowly getting a handle on her nerves.

"Is there a ring?"

Megan's heart plummeted. Logan had been gone only a short time this afternoon. Surely with all the other tasks he'd had to complete, there hadn't been time for him to purchase a wedding ring.

But, oh, how she wanted the symbol of their unity wrapped snugly around her finger. She wanted the world to know she was this man's wife.

Looking rather pleased with himself Logan opened his mouth to speak, but Mattie beat him to it. "You may borrow one of mine."

She thrust forward, jockeying for position until they were forced to step apart.

"This will do quite nicely." Mattie tugged at one of the massive, ostentatious jewels on her left hand. When the ring didn't budge, she applied considerable effort to the task, popping it free. The gesture sent her elbow straight into Logan's stomach.

He released a grunt.

"Oh, dear, so sorry, Marshal." Mattie didn't appear sorry at all.

Ever the gracious gentleman, Logan didn't call her out on the lie. Instead, he nudged her back to her place behind Megan.

"No need to trouble yourself, Miss Silks." He gave her a warning glare. "You may keep your ring. I have one of my own."

"You do?" Megan asked, unable to keep the surprise out of her voice as she moved back into place beside him.

"Of course I do." He dug into his pocket and retrieved a tiny, velvet-covered box. "I made the purchase before I left San Francisco."

Tiny sparks of joy danced along Megan's skin. "You…you did?"

He flipped open the lid. "Actually," he said, looking a bit sheepish. "I acquired it two years ago, in anticipation of today."

Megan placed her hand over her heart. "You bought my ring two years ago?"

"Well, I made an offer for it that long ago."

She lowered her gaze and caught her breath at the sheer beauty of the rather large, perfectly round sapphire surrounded by what looked like hundreds of tiny diamonds.

"It took me two full years to pay it off."

"Oh, Logan, it's perfect." She lifted her gaze back to his.

"The color of this particular stone reminds me of your eyes when you're happy. I promise I'll make you happy."

Bella sighed again. Several of the men cleared their throats. Mattie blew her nose, louder than before.

Ignoring them all, Megan stared at her groom. Oh,

she knew she was looking at him with stars in her eyes, but she couldn't help herself. Logan had bought her a beautiful ring. *Two years ago.* "I... I didn't get a ring for you."

"It's all right, my love." He cupped her cheek. "This was all a bit sudden."

"Not to worry. One will do for now." Pastor Beau plucked the ring from the box with deft fingers. "Whenever you get a ring for Logan, I'll bless it then."

Grateful for the promise, Megan nodded. "Thank you."

Smiling his pastor smile, the reverend placed the ring on his Bible and continued the ceremony. "Bless, O Lord, this ring to be a sign of the vows by which this man and this woman have bound themselves to each other: through Jesus Christ our Lord." He handed the sapphire to Logan. "Amen."

Holding her hand gently in his, Logan slid the ring onto Megan's finger and then nodded in satisfaction. "It fits."

Despite her promise to avoid any more crying today, the back of her eyelids stung with unshed tears. She parted her lips to speak, to say something, *anything,* but nothing came out.

"Megan," Logan began, rubbing her finger absently as he repeated the words Pastor Beau said first. "I give you this ring as a symbol of my vow, and with all that I am, and all that I have, I honor you, in the Name of the Father, and of the Son, and of the Holy Spirit."

Still too choked with emotion to speak, Megan busied herself with admiring her new ring. Unfortunately, a rogue tear slipped free. Several more threatened.

Blinking rapidly, Megan kept her gaze averted. She

didn't dare look at Logan just yet, or the rest of her tears would surely break free.

Thankfully, Pastor Beau proceeded with the conclusion of the ceremony. "Now that Logan and Megan have given themselves to each other, I pronounce that they are husband and wife."

Bella clapped her hands excitedly.

"Those whom God has joined together let no one put asunder."

The entire room responded in unison. "Amen."

Chapter Ten

Standing on the planked sidewalk just outside the jail-house, Logan spoke softly with the three men who'd been kind enough to witness his marriage. He held himself at ease, with his heavy wool coat closed against the biting wind.

When the topic turned to child rearing, Logan could only summon up a halfhearted smile. Although he definitely wanted children with Megan, that wasn't the first thing on his mind. Getting his new bride to a safe haven, now that was another matter entirely.

Needing a moment alone, he casually broke away from the group.

Mired in what the Bible had to say about child rearing, Shane and Beau continued conversing with one another, completely forgetting Logan had ever been a part of their discussion. Just as well. He had nothing to add.

Trey slid him a knowing look and what might have been a sly smile, but he didn't try to stop Logan from leaving their friendly huddle.

Grimacing, Logan moved closer to the rail. While Megan changed into something more suitable for their journey, he mentally considered the best, fastest route to his parents' ranch.

But no matter how hard he focused, his mind kept shifting to the fact that Megan was his wife now—*his wife*.

Logan had been waiting for this day for five long years. His future was finally set, no more wondering. No more waiting. Now he and Megan could get on with the business of living their lives together as husband and wife.

Except...

There was still the matter of Kincaid's murder, not to mention Megan's memory loss hanging over them. And no matter how happy Logan was to be married to Megan at last, there was a shadow of darkness cloaking this day.

A killer was on the loose, possibly gunning for his new bride at this very moment. He had to close his eyes to fight back a surge of anger.

Leaning forward, he scanned the bustling activity before him with a trained eye. Horse-drawn carriages, women herding their well-behaved children and men hustling about their daily business created an idyllic scene, one that spoke of a prairie boomtown on the cusp of becoming a bustling, modern-day city.

Although Logan didn't sense any immediate danger, he was impatient to leave Denver. Looking past the mountains in the distance, he tried to see into the future and couldn't. With all the thinking he'd done about his wedding day, he hadn't focused much on his marriage.

Now the future stood before him as a blurry shroud of unanswered questions.

How many children would he and Megan have?

Where would they live? Near his family's ranch? Or in Denver, close to Charity House?

Perhaps somewhere else entirely?

So engrossed with his thoughts, Logan didn't hear Trey's approach. "Congratulations, my friend." Trey slapped him on the back. "Megan is a fine woman. She'll make you a good wife."

But would he make her a decent husband?

The question was something he wasn't sure he wanted to explore. Not now, at any rate. "God has blessed me tenfold."

Beau chose that moment to break away from Shane and join them. He no longer looked like a pastor, but a friend. "Your patience and trust in the Lord has paid off. Or as my lovely wife likes to say, good things come to those who wait."

Yes, the Lord had finally rewarded Logan's patience. With a few surprises added to the mix. "Megan's more beautiful than I remember," he said, his breath growing tight in his chest. "And far more talented than I ever realized."

Trey's mouth curved into a smile. "So you've seen the walls she painted in Charity House."

"I have." Logan felt a line of worry creasing his brow. Megan was an artist, a romantic through and through. Logan was neither.

A soundless whisper of doubt gripped him and his heart constricted with alarm.

He'd always thought he and Megan were well suited. But now...

He wasn't sure.

As though reading his mind, Beau clasped his shoulder with an encouraging grip. "Megan's still the same woman you once knew. The fact that she's discovered a hidden talent doesn't change who she is at the core."

A skeptical glare was Logan's only reply.

Unmoved, Beau chuckled. "You and Megan are well suited. Have a little faith."

Faith. Such a simple word and yet so hard to put into action when he'd just married a woman he didn't know as well as he'd always thought.

At least some good had come from his discovery of Megan's artistic talent. An idea had formed that just might help unlock her memories.

Or so he hoped.

There was one person who might know.

Logan searched for Shane, found him leaning against the jailhouse wall. The man certainly knew how to fade into the background when no one was looking.

Needing him front and center, Logan gestured Shane forward.

The good doctor pushed away from the wall.

"I'd like to know your honest opinion. Will Megan regain her memory? Or is there a chance the loss is permanent?"

"I believe she'll eventually remember everything, given time."

Logan didn't like Shane's answer. He'd have preferred a more concrete promise. "But you can't say when?"

"No. I can't."

"I might have an idea to help speed up the process."

Shane lifted an eyebrow. "Go on."

"I stopped by the mercantile this afternoon and purchased a sketchbook. I figure if Megan starts drawing, maybe she will…that somehow the act of putting pictures on a page might…that it might…" He let his words trail off, not sure how to proceed. Now that he'd spoken his idea aloud Logan couldn't say what he hoped to accomplish. Precisely.

Nevertheless, he began again. "I don't know much about art but I thought maybe something will come back to her as she starts to draw."

Shane remained silent for an endless moment, making Logan wonder if the man had heard a word he'd said. But then he nodded his head and smiled. "I think what you suggest makes perfect sense. In fact—" he looked off in the distance, his eyebrows drawn together in concentration "—it's really quite brilliant."

Relief flowed through Logan. "Then you think it might work?"

"Maybe, yes. Maybe, no. There's no guarantee the act of drawing in and of itself will bring back her memory," Shane warned with an apology in his voice. "But it might be exactly what Megan needs to relax her mind enough to allow her thoughts to flow freely. I'd say it's worth a try."

At this point, Logan was desperate for anything. "Thanks. I'll give her the sketchbook tonight."

Beau moved forward and shook Logan's hand. "In the meantime, I'll pray for you both. May you have a safe journey and may God go with you."

Logan blew out a slow breath. "I appreciate your prayers, Beau."

"We'll all pray for you," Shane added.

Trey pulled Logan into a quick bear hug then stepped back. Way back, as though the friendly gesture left him uncomfortable. "Godspeed, my friend."

Touched by the show of friendship from all three men, Logan struggled for words. He was saved from responding when Megan exited the jail.

Thankful for the interruption, Logan studied his new bride. She wore a simple, light pink dress with a long row of buttons running down the front bodice. Her hair hung in long, loose curls past her shoulders, making her look more like the girl he remembered.

But then she stepped forward, flattened her palm against his heart and gave him a woman's smile.

His mind wiped clean of all thought, smooth as glass.

This new Megan, this thoroughly adult version of the girl he'd loved for years, completely mesmerized him.

He wanted to pull her against him, wanted to hold her close and protect her from everything bad in the world.

Especially the "bad" gunning for her now. "We should be on our way."

She held her smile in place as though sensing the new power she had over him. "I'm ready."

He took her small reticule and other bag, her only two pieces of luggage and more than likely not her own. The contents of both cases were probably borrowed, as well. Wishing there'd been time for her to gather a few of her own things, but knowing they couldn't risk a stop at Charity House now, Logan directed his new bride toward the wagon he'd purchased from the livery stable.

A twinge of panic shot through him when her steps faltered. She righted herself, lifted her chin giving him a clear view of the angry wound at her throat. In that moment, Logan couldn't stop the notion from forming in his head that he wasn't escorting his new wife to safety.

He was taking her straight into the heart of danger.

Megan hunched her shoulders against the brisk wind and moved slowly toward the rickety wagon Logan had just indicated. They certainly weren't traveling in style. But perhaps that was for the best. They'd attract less notice this way.

She took another careful step and grimaced. Having stood on her ankle far too long this afternoon, it now ached with a constant, throbbing pain. Nevertheless, she was determined to walk to the wagon on her own. She'd already received too much pampering in one day, enough to last a lifetime.

"Megan, wait." Bella stopped her midstride with a light touch to her arm. "You're going to need this." She whipped off her cloak with a flourish.

Balancing most of her weight on her uninjured ankle, Megan stared at the bulky garment in Bella's hand, unable to stop a wistful sigh from slipping past her lips. The black cloak was made of very fine wool and had a bejeweled collar that must have cost a fortune.

The beautiful garment would look ridiculous on Megan, and certainly had no place on a cattle ranch.

"Go on." Bella waved the cloak in the air between them. "Take it. You'll need something to cover you once you leave the streets of Denver."

Yes, Megan would definitely need something to keep her warm in the open air. But a blanket would do just fine. And besides, she'd already received too much from her friend. She would never be able to repay the debt. "Thank you for offering, but I can't possibly take your cloak."

"Oh, but you can." Bella's amber eyes filled with a stubborn look Megan knew well. "And you will."

Knowing the battle was already lost, Megan found herself nearly relenting. But not completely. "I'll be fine with a blanket."

As soon as the words left her mouth, the wind slapped her in the face. Logan returned to her side at that exact moment when she started shivering.

He frowned, but didn't comment directly on her reaction to the cold. Instead, he took the cloak from Bella with a quick word of thanks and then wrapped the heavy wool around Megan's shoulders.

There'd been no arguing. No cajoling. He'd simply taken charge. The competent way he commanded every situation had been what had initially attracted her to him.

But now as he pulled the cloak closed at her neck, apprehension slammed through her. Megan wasn't sure she wanted Logan taking over her life so completely. She was used to taking care of her own needs, ruthlessly so. No one could hurt her if she didn't rely on them. At least, that had been her motto before today. There was comfort in knowing she was a giver rather than a taker.

She opened her mouth to tell Logan she could take care of herself, but then he smiled sweetly at her, almost shyly and gathered her close. The next instant, he covered her mouth with his in a brief kiss.

Well, all right, yes. Maybe she did want him to take charge. At least until she was feeling more like herself.

She stepped back and tilted her head to keep her gaze level with his. For a moment, for just this *one* single moment, Megan allowed herself to drown in his gaze.

His face was all rugged planes and sharp angles. There were times when the light caught him just right and she actually found herself slightly afraid of him.

But now, out in the open with several of their friends standing beside them, somehow all that hard, masculine beauty made him more approachable. Appealing even. And very, *very* handsome.

Megan drew in a quick breath. She was suddenly aware of her new husband with a sharp-edged clarity that made her feel completely exposed. And very, *very* female.

A ball of nervousness dropped in her stomach but instead of dwelling on her new condition, Megan spun to face Bella. "Thank you for loaning me your precious cloak. And for…well, everything."

"Oh, Megan." Bella yanked her into a bone-rattling hug. "I'll miss you so much."

To Megan's dismay, tears threatened. Again. Really, this penchant for crying was so unlike her. "I'll miss you more."

Laughing at that, they pulled apart.

"Please, my friend, stay safe," Bella said. "And whatever you do, don't take any unnecessary risks." The last was directed at Logan.

"No, ma'am. I won't."

"Good, good. May God go with you. And… *Oh,* I hate goodbyes." Bella dabbed at her eyes and, sniffling, rushed to stand next to her husband.

Mattie pecked Megan on the cheek then gave a dramatic flick of her wrist. "Now stop your dawdling and get out of here."

Smiling at the very real emotion she heard in Mattie's voice, Megan hugged her mother's friend then said a quick goodbye to the rest of their group.

With a solemn look in his eyes, Logan silently assisted her into the wagon. Settling her skirts around her, Megan placed her feet on the footrest and lowered her gaze to her hands. If she looked at Bella, or even Mattie, she knew she would cry. And maybe never stop once she started.

What was wrong with her? She really needed to get a handle on her emotions.

This was supposed to be a happy day. Her wedding day.

Logan joined her in the front seat, then leaned forward and pulled the hood of her cloak over her head. "Ready?"

"Ready."

Winking at her, he picked up the reins and released the brake lever.

In the next beat, they were off.

A block into their journey Megan's heart started a fast, painful drumming. She chalked it up to the anticipation that had been building inside her for five long years. *This* was the next step in her life.

Her very own new beginning.

No matter what happened in the coming days, she would always be Logan's wife. They'd said their vows in front of witnesses and were pledged to one another in the name of the Lord. Nothing could take him away from her now.

Stopping the wagon to let a mother and her three

children pass, Logan reached out and laid his hand over hers. Megan rotated her wrist until their palms met. Her racing heartbeat slowed to a steady tap, tap, tap.

Oh, yes, she thought. *No matter what may come, I will always be this man's wife.*

Chapter Eleven

Logan didn't mind putting in long hours on the trail—when he was in pursuit of an outlaw. But *this,* this clipping along at a snail's pace while seated in a rickety old wagon was not his idea of a favorable experience for anyone. *Especially* not for his new bride.

Unable to find a comfortable position on the hard wooden seat, he shifted. And then shifted some more. As he had every few minutes since leaving town, he tracked his gaze across the endless, open country up ahead. He looked to his right, to his left, back to his right, everywhere but directly at Megan. He couldn't bear to witness the disappointment in her eyes.

How could she not be disappointed? She would be spending her wedding night in a slow-moving wagon headed to a strange destination. Logan felt a sharp pain of regret.

His wife deserved a real wedding night, with soft words, heartfelt compliments and extraordinary patience from her very attentive bridegroom. Tonight should have been special for them both, one of the best moments of their lives. But it wouldn't be the wedding night either of them had imagined. Megan was in a fragile state and Logan couldn't allow himself to think of what might have been, only what lay ahead.

Frowning, he rubbed the base of his neck where most of his tension had settled. He wanted to look at his wife and smile. He wanted to break the awkward silence that had fallen over them.

He kept his eyes trained on the view up ahead.

They'd left Denver just as the sun had begun its descent over the mountains in the distance. Dusk painted the sky in a kaleidoscope of muted purples, reds and oranges.

Wondering what Megan thought of the view, Logan still kept his gaze locked on the trail.

The sound of the creaking wagon wheels brought memories from long ago rushing back. He'd made this trek from Denver to his home many times, both as a boy and a young deputy marshal.

As the crickets harmonized with one another and a breeze tousled his hair, Logan realized how much he'd missed his childhood home. Too many years had passed since he'd last traveled this route, a trek he could make with his eyes closed.

He shouldn't have stayed away so long. Especially when his reasons had nothing to do with his parents or younger siblings.

Unpleasant memories threatened, pulling him toward thoughts of his brother and what they'd lost in a moment of unbridled anger.

Refusing to allow his mind to go back to that terrible night when accusations had flown as fast as fists, Logan forced himself to look out over the mountains. The approaching night had colored them a rich, midnight blue. A slight chill in the air warned that spring hadn't fully settled over the land yet.

Logan grimaced. He'd forgotten how cold the nights could get in this part of the country, even in late March. He and Megan were in for an uncomfortable journey.

He hoped traveling at night wasn't a mistake, not that he could change his mind now. Logan had wanted the cover of darkness to hide their progress. And he knew this route so well, knew any dangers they might face along the way, that he felt comfortable taking Megan out in the wild at this late hour.

The four-legged predators, he could handle. He was fast with a gun, any gun. He'd made sure to set his rifle close at hand, his six-shooter even closer. Nevertheless, he was still concerned about the two-legged danger chasing Megan. At least no one would expect them to travel at this late hour. The thought gave Logan a sliver of comfort.

But what if Megan was afraid of the dark? He sucked in a hard breath. He hadn't thought to ask.

As if in answer, she sighed happily and gripped his arm in a loose hug. After another moment, she leaned her head against his shoulder and sighed again.

A shock of masculine pleasure went through him, warming his heart. She smelled so good. Too good. For one terrible, wonderful, insanely confusing moment Logan considered stopping the wagon and kissing his bride properly.

He abstained. Barely. The feelings stirring in his gut were unlike anything he'd ever experienced before. They were so strong he was afraid he might unintentionally hurt her.

"Are you cold?" he asked, his voice tight from holding on to his control.

"Not at all." She snuggled closer, then rubbed her cheek against his shoulder. She was practically purring.

He gritted his teeth.

As if to test his resolve, she lifted up and kissed him on the cheek. Shyly. Sweetly. Engulfing Logan in a riot of warmth and chaotic emotions. Thrown off guard by his reaction, he clutched the reins tighter.

She's suffered a trauma, he reminded himself sternly. *You have to be careful with her. Extremely careful. This isn't a normal wedding night.*

Logan closed his eyes and swallowed. Hard.

"How long before we arrive home?" she asked.

Home. The softly spoken word quieted the loud, thumping din in his ears. Yes, they *were* heading home, where Megan would be safe. And Logan could finally breathe easier. "I'm afraid in this old wagon it's going to take us most of the night."

"Oh?" She didn't sound overly disappointed, merely curious.

"The ranch is about twelve miles due north," he explained. "I predict we'll arrive at the Flying M by sunrise."

"The Flying M. Is that the name of your family's ranch?"

"Yes."

"I like it. And do you know? I just realized that I've never been this far out of Denver." She angled her head to stare out over the mountains. "That makes this my first real adventure." She let out a husky laugh. "I'm glad it's with you."

Logan's heart swelled. "Me, too."

Setting the reins in his lap, he took her chin and gently guided her to look at him. "But, Megan—" he dropped his hand "—I never wanted to take you away so quickly, without allowing you time to say goodbye to everyone."

She reached up and cupped his cheek. "I know."

A brief moment of understanding passed between them.

"It can't be helped," she said.

"No. It can't."

He leaned forward, but Megan looked quickly away. "It's so beautiful out here. Look at the mountains over there." She swept her arm in a dramatic arc. "They're almost purple under the fading light. And the uneven slope of the foothills is magnificent. How could anyone look at all this and not believe in God?"

Logan squinted in the direction she indicated. "I have no idea," he said. But as soon as the words left his mouth he thought of his brother and the bitterness that had permeated Hunter's soul even in childhood.

"I don't understand how so many people can reject the Lord." Her voice held a large dose of sadness, as though she was thinking of someone in particular.

Logan was doing the same thing. "I think some people don't want to believe in God because it means they have to answer for their actions." He wondered if that was the case with his big brother. "Or maybe they're simply running from the Lord." Another likely scenario. "Or maybe—"

"They're comfortable in their own misery," Megan finished for him, lifting her arm so she could touch the pretty bracelet dangling from her wrist.

Logan considered her words. "Perhaps that's true. For some."

In the case of his brother, Logan didn't believe comfort had anything to do with the road he'd chosen. Willful from a young age, obedience hadn't been in Hunter's nature. Respect for authority had been a foreign concept, as well.

Though they'd butted heads many times and had never agreed on much, Logan missed his brother. Or rather, he missed the man Hunter could have been.

Had Hunter been predestined for wickedness? Was it in his blood to do wrong?

A dull ache swirled in the pit of his stomach. If that were the case, Logan would have turned in that direction, as well.

Maybe he still could. The possibility was why he held such a tight rein on his temper. Always. As long as he controlled his baser emotions he would be the better man.

"Tell me about the Flying M," Megan said, her innocent request cutting into Logan's unpleasant thoughts.

Happy for the distraction, he thought for a moment, trying to decide how best to describe a slice of paradise.

"If you think the land out here is beautiful, wait until we arrive at the ranch," he said. "The main house and outer buildings are huddled in a large, flat valley at the base of the Rocky Mountains. Just north of the homestead, there's a long tree line filled with a mixture of aspens, Colorado firs and other vegetation. The colors are spectacular in the fall."

"I can only imagine. But you said outer buildings, as in more than one. How many in all?"

Logan's heart filled with satisfaction. He wasn't

bringing his new bride to some run-down homestead off the beaten track. He was taking her to one of the most successful cattle ranches north of Texas. "There's the main house, of course, a bunkhouse that sleeps ten, a smokehouse, a barn, a separate stable for the work horses, a small guest cabin on the north range and a matching one in the south pasture."

"Oh, my." She sounded fascinated, and not at all intimidated.

His pleasure increased tenfold. "Much like Charity House, the Flying M requires a lot of coordination to run properly."

A wistful sigh slipped past her lips. "It sounds wonderful. An artist's dream."

Her words made him smile. "Speaking of which, I never gave you your wedding present."

"Oh, Logan, the ring is more than enough." She lifted her hand and studied the sapphire from several different angles. "I can't imagine a better gift."

At the sound of all that genuine happiness, words backed up in his throat. His new bride was so easy to please. Maybe too easy. He couldn't shake the notion he was going to let her down somehow, that he was going to hurt her in some unimaginable way unless he was vigilant.

He would simply have to be vigilant. *Always.*

It would come easier once he got Megan to the ranch, where she could begin the healing process.

Which reminded him…

He reached under his seat and retrieved her present.

Megan watched, fascinated, as Logan placed a package on her lap. She glided her finger along the silky red ribbon tied around the plain brown paper. Trying to guess what he'd bought her, she lifted the gift closer to her face. The gesture sent her slightly off balance.

"Go ahead," he said, helping her steady herself with a hand to her arm. "Open it."

"All right." She blinked, then lowered her gaze.

Inexplicable emotion gathered inside her, turning into something she recognized but couldn't quite name. Dismay, perhaps? Fear?

For crying out loud, this was a wedding gift from her husband. There was nothing to fear. Not from Logan.

Then why were her hands shaking? And why, *why*, was she hesitating?

For a dreadful moment Megan lost her bearings. She didn't feel in the moment. Not fully. She felt overwhelmed with emotion from the day. Surely that explained why every thought simultaneously slowed down and sped up, becoming a tangled ball of confusion in her mind.

Just open the gift, she told herself.

Fingers still shaking, she untied the ribbon and in one quick flick of her wrist tore off the wrapping paper.

"It's a book." Relieved, she opened the cover and flipped through several pages. Then several more. "With blank pages." She swung her gaze to Logan. "I don't understand."

He lifted a shoulder. "It's a sketchbook."

A sketchbook? She turned another page. Well, of course. Why hadn't she realized that at once?

"I saw your paintings on the Charity House walls when I went to speak with Marc this morning." A sweet, almost vulnerable note entered his voice. "I thought, maybe, that you might…that is, I thought you might like to practice your drawing?"

The uncertainty in his voice made her smile. "It's wonderful."

And it was. But not because she'd have a chance to draw, freely, whatever she liked, whenever she wished. Although, that was quite an exciting prospect. No, what struck her as completely wonderful was that Logan had put so much thought into her gift.

He was giving her a chance to pursue her art on her own terms. No pressure. No hidden expectations.

What a dear man.

"You really like it?" he asked, sounding as shy as he had that day long ago when he'd first asked her to go for a walk with him down the lane. It had been love at first sight for both of them, which had made them unbearably shy around one another.

Much like they were with each other now.

"I love it." She hugged the sketchbook and then kissed him on the cheek. "Thank you."

"You're welcome."

Logan continued looking at her, but night had descended and she could no longer read his expression.

Something about the way his hat sat on his head, something in the off-center angle sent a cold thread of alarm spinning through her.

Confused at her reaction, she fiddled with the corner of her new sketchbook.

Logan patted her trembling hand. "Try to get some rest. We have a long, tedious night of travel ahead of us."

"Of course." But she knew she wouldn't sleep, not with her mind in such turmoil. She must focus on happy thoughts, if only to escape the darkness looming inside her own head.

Picturing the look on Logan's face as he'd stared down at her during their wedding ceremony helped. But not completely. Reminding herself he was her husband now, she buried her face in his sleeve. His heat enveloped her and she relaxed at last.

"I love you, Logan," she whispered, certain he couldn't make out her muffled words through the thick layer of wool.

A full minute of silence passed, cut only by the sound of a hundred crickets fighting to be heard over one another.

But then, Logan covered her hand with his once again. "I love you, too, Megan." He let her go. "More than you know."

Chapter Twelve

By the time Logan guided the wagon onto Mitchell land, a shelf of patchy, orange-colored clouds peppered the early morning sky and the tension in his chest had finally eased.

Despite the dark circumstances behind this journey, Logan had felt God's protection surrounding him and Megan all along. In fact, they'd made the trek out of Denver without a single incident. Not even a coyote had crossed their path.

Allowing himself a moment to enjoy the quiet solitude of dawn, Logan breathed in the familiar scent of pine and wild sage. Off to his left was a small lake that had once been his and Hunter's favorite swimming hole.

They'd made a lot of happy memories here. A few bad ones as well, like the day Hunter had thrown a rock straight at their younger sister's head. Callie, barely five at the time, had been rendered unconscious for several minutes.

At first Hunter had looked stunned, frightened even,

but then he'd hardened his expression and had fixed the blame back on Callie. "I told her to move."

Logan shook his head. It had always been that way with Hunter. A thoughtless act followed by pointing blame everywhere but where it belonged...on himself.

Logan released a slow expulsion of air and glanced down at Megan. She'd fallen asleep on his shoulder. His arm had gone numb, but she looked so peaceful he didn't have the heart to move her just yet.

A rush of tenderness spread through him. Closing his eyes, he dropped a kiss on the top of her head.

Lord, I never knew I could love someone this much.

Without a doubt, he was deeply in love with his wife. When she'd finally declared her feelings he'd been unprepared for his intense reaction to the softly spoken words. Joy had coursed through him at first. But fear had quickly followed. Fear that he would somehow let her down. The conflicting emotions had rendered him speechless for a full minute.

Once he'd found his voice, though, it had been easy to tell her how much he loved her in return.

Shifting on the seat, Megan nuzzled his arm with her cheek. Instead of soothing him, a flash of desperation took hold. What if he'd allowed her to sleep too long? Shane had been explicit with his instructions, warning Logan of the dire consequences if he failed to wake her at measured intervals.

"Megan." Suffocating panic rolled over him. "Time to wake up."

She mumbled something incoherent and hugged his arm tighter. The strength of her grip didn't fit with her petite frame.

Logan almost smiled. Almost. "No, Megan. No more sleep."

"Unnnhuh."

With his concern mounting, Logan stopped the wagon on the edge of a clearing near the lake and set the brake. One by one, he detached Megan's fingers from his arm. "Come on, sweetheart. Wake up."

Blinking slowly, she lifted her head off his shoulder and looked around. "Where are we?"

Relief shot through him. "About twenty minutes from the main house."

"Oh." She hid a delicate yawn behind her hand. "So close?"

He smiled at her husky, sleep-filled tone. "Let's get down so you can stretch your legs."

Without waiting for her reply, he jumped out of the wagon and opened his arms.

Still half-asleep, her eyes a little unfocused, she scooted across the seat and then set her palms on his shoulders.

Holding her gaze, Logan lifted her to the ground but didn't release her right away. Immobile in his loose embrace, she didn't appear in any hurry to let him go either.

For several intense seconds, they stood facing each other in the crisp dawn air.

Logan's breath halted in his chest. In the pink glow of morning, Megan looked beautiful and delicate, a fairytale princess come to life.

An echo of a smile trembled across her lips and sliced through his self-control.

Logan clenched his jaw so hard he felt a muscle

jump in his neck. He was only a man, after all, one who could stand temptation just so long.

What little hold he had on his restraint disappeared. He leaned forward, certain all the intense emotions he'd desperately tried to control since leaving Denver showed on his face.

Confirming his suspicion, Megan's eyes widened. Then, *then,* she pressed against him and lifted up on her toes.

Logan lowered his head to meet hers, but stopped just shy of touching his lips to her mouth. This was to be their first real kiss as husband and wife. He wanted Megan to be sure this was what she wanted. So he waited, his lips a mere whisper from hers, giving her the chance to turn her cheek if she wasn't prepared for anything more intimate.

She released a very female sigh and closed the distance between them herself.

Lost. Logan was completely and utterly lost to this woman. To this moment. Fully aware of how well they fit together, he wrapped her tighter in his embrace and deepened their kiss.

Instead of shying away, Megan dug her fingers into the thick wool of his jacket. She felt soft and pliant in his arms, but also eager. Bold even.

Logan's mood instantly shifted from tenderness to something more primitive. The intensity of the new emotion frightened him.

Matters were getting out of hand.

Logan tried to stop the kiss, but Megan gripped his shoulders harder.

No. *No.* She was still fragile, he reminded himself. The thought gave him enough strength to tear his mouth from hers.

Breathing hard, he stared into her eyes.

A deep shade of pink danced along her cheeks. She looked fresh, innocent, and thoroughly kissed. He lowered his head again, but stopped himself just in time. Focusing on the jagged knife cut on her throat helped.

This wasn't the right moment for this. Their journey wasn't complete. She was still in danger, still vulnerable.

Logan reluctantly took a full step away from his bride and ran a hand through his hair. He forced a light note in his voice. "Good morning, Mrs. Mitchell."

A dazzling smile was her only response.

It took herculean strength to take yet another step away from her. "We'll head out in ten minutes."

She nodded, then caught sight of the lake and gasped with pleasure.

"Go explore," he urged. "I'll join you in a moment."

She headed toward the water while Logan checked on the horse. Out of the corner of his eye, he kept a careful watch on Megan's progress. She took cautious steps, favoring her sprained ankle. At last, she made it to the water's edge.

Then she threw back her head and opened her arms wide, as if she were surrendering herself to her new life.

Logan's heart flipped over in his chest. He wanted to go to his wife. He *needed* to go to her, needed to bask in her joy of the moment and forget all the trouble they'd faced in the last twenty-four hours.

Quickly unhitching the horse, Logan led the mare

to the lake, then moved to Megan's side, slipping his arm across her shoulder.

She leaned into him and sighed.

They stood that way for several minutes, enjoying the view. A companionable silence fell between them.

"It's so beautiful." She stared out over the lake. "Look how the colors of the dawn are reflected in the water."

He heard the happiness in her voice. "I'm glad you like it here."

She looked serene, at peace. Nothing like the frightened woman he'd found locked in a jail cell just yesterday.

Had it only been a day since their reunion?

So much had happened in that short time. Nevertheless, Logan was confident he'd been right to take Megan away from Denver. This moment erased any doubt. She was blossoming right before his eyes.

Soon her memory would return. And when it did, no matter what happened as a result, they would face the consequences together.

"Ready to go home?" he asked.

"Yes. But first, tell me a little about your family." She swiveled her head to look him directly in the eyes. "Will they like me?"

"They're going to love you."

His words did nothing to ease the apprehension in her eyes and Logan realized he'd told her very little about his family through the years. Practically nothing, in fact, while his parents and siblings knew almost everything about her.

Recognizing his mistake, Logan wondered why he'd told Megan so little about his family. The answer came

quickly. Hunter. Any talk of the Mitchells would inevitably lead to a discussion about the oldest son. And
why he was no longer in any of their lives.

"Logan?" Megan asked cautiously. "Is there something I should know about your family before we arrive at the Flying M?"

Forcing a smile on his lips, he dragged a fingertip down her cheek. "There's nothing unusual about
us." True, from a certain perspective. "The Mitchells
are just like any other family." Didn't most have an
estranged member or two somewhere in their midst?

"I'm not sure I know what you mean."

Fair enough. He *had* been vague. "We work hard,
play harder, laugh well and often. We turn to God in
times of need and praise Him for our blessings. Life
can be rough at times, but the Mitchells always work
together and somehow everything seems easier because
of that." A flash of Hunter's angry face filled his mind.
"Or, at least, tolerable."

"Your family sounds lovely."

"They are, Megan." He no longer had to force a
smile. "Oh, they are."

Something had changed, Megan realized. No, not
some *thing*. *She* had changed—all because her husband
had finally kissed her, as a husband kisses his wife.

Smiling, she pressed her fingertips to the exact spot
Logan's mouth had descended upon hers. His kiss had
brought a feeling of rightness to their union that hadn't
been there before.

For the first time since walking into Mattie's brothel,
Megan felt at peace. Really at peace. The sapphire
on her finger caught the morning light. Although she

couldn't see into the future, she trusted that God was directing her path, leading her to this new chapter in her life. With Logan. And his family, a family that sounded altogether wonderful.

"Look, Megan." He pointed to the hill straight ahead. "The Flying M is just over the next rise."

A shiver of anticipation had her leaning forward in the seat. The wagon seemed to chug along at an impossibly slow pace, but finally rolled to the top of the hill.

Megan's breath caught in her throat. The Flying M was everything she'd dreamed a ranch would look like. The sloped roofs, the rows of windows along the first and second floors, the rocking chairs on the wraparound porch, all added up to a warm, welcoming feel. The corral off to her left, with its tidy wooden fence and large, healthy-looking horses reminded her that this was a working ranch. Even the makeshift swing hanging under a large shade tree was a happy surprise.

Blinking rapidly, breathing harder than usual, Megan darted her gaze in countless directions. Every sight, sound and smell was a delight to her senses. And for this one moment in time, she didn't care that she'd lost a portion of her memory. She didn't care that a killer might be after her. She was home. *Home* at last.

"Well?" Logan asked. "What you think?"

"It's…it's…" She couldn't find the right words as her gaze bounced from the buildings to the lush tree line to the craggy mountains in the distance. "It's…"

"Big?" A hint of amusement danced in his eyes.

"Well, yes. It *is* big. It's also…" She paused, taking note of how the wall of snowcapped mountains created a perfect backdrop for the ranch. Her fingers itched to recreate the scene on paper. *"Breathtaking."*

"You like it, then?"

Hearing the relief in his voice, she dragged her gaze away from the ranch and focused on Logan's face. "I think," she said, covering his hand with hers, "I'm going to be very happy living here with you."

"You will. I'll make sure of it." As if to punctuate his statement, a birdsong sweetened the air around them.

Suddenly the horse reared, nearly tossing Megan out of the seat.

She grabbed Logan as he struggled with the reins, trying to calm the horse with sheer brute strength.

Searching for the source of trouble, Megan swiveled her head to the left. She caught sight of a pair of large, black and white dogs barreling down the lane toward them. Both animals were barking madly.

Much as the horse had done, Megan instinctively reared back in her seat. She wasn't usually frightened of dogs. In fact, she enjoyed most of the ones she came across. But the two snarling brutes heading for the wagon were big, bold and possibly rabid.

"Not to worry," Logan said, still struggling to steady the horse. "That's Sally and Jake, two of our best range dogs."

"Range dogs?"

"That's right. They were bred specifically to work the herds. Whoa, now." He clicked his tongue at the horse. "My father bought the two at a field trial about seven years ago."

Megan tried to smile, but Logan's explanation did nothing to settle her nerves. "Oh."

Setting the brake, Logan jumped to the ground and moved quickly to the spooked horse. He whispered soft words of comfort, running his hand along the mare's sleek neck.

Once the horse was calm again, Logan moved into the direct path of the approaching dogs.

"Hello, you big, beautiful curs."

They leaped into the air, nearly knocking him over with their exuberance.

Laughing, he wrestled both of them to the ground. They immediately jumped back to their feet, licked his face and the process started all over again. As he ruffled their thick fur, Logan talked to the pair as if they were his old friends. Once he had them somewhat under control—*somewhat*—he commanded them to "sit."

Their bottoms instantly dropped to the ground. Their tails slapped the dirt with loud thuds as they watched Logan with expectant gazes.

"Stay."

Neither animal budged.

Turning his back on them, Logan joined Megan again. "Come meet Shaky Jake and Sally Mae." He helped her out of the wagon. "Some of the hardest working dogs you'll ever come across."

Eyeing the two closely and taking special note of their very pointy fangs, Megan allowed Logan to lead her to the animals. One of the dogs started shaking wildly, but he stayed obediently rooted to the spot.

"*That* would be Shaky Jake," Logan pointed out.

Megan gave him a wry smile. "I figured as much."

"And this fine looking female is Sally Mae." He scratched the dog's neck. "She's the most loyal of the two."

Sally Mae proved his point by leaning heavily against Logan's leg.

Now that they weren't running in crazed circles

Megan was able to get a better look at the dogs. Both had long, shiny hair, big brown eyes and were mostly black all over with large white patches in between. Jake was considerably larger than Sally Mae, while Sally Mae was the calmer of the two.

"Let them sniff your hand."

Megan reached out slowly. Very, *very* slowly.

Taking turns, the dog's politely touched their noses to her fingertips. Shaky Jake went so far as to shove his head under her palm and proceeded to whine like a baby.

Charmed, Megan rubbed the dog's head.

Sally Mae wasn't to be ignored. Within seconds both dogs were alternately bumping into Megan's legs and pressing their heads into her hands.

A grin split Logan's face. "They like you."

"They're delightful."

"Here I was thinking the same thing about you." He shoved the dogs out of his way and then tugged her into his arms. "Welcome to your new home, Mrs. Mitchell."

A rush of pleasure shot through her. "I'm glad to be here."

He lowered his head, but just as his lips touched hers a loud whoop rent the air.

"Logan." Another bellow was followed by Jake and Sally Mae's frantic barking. "Is it really you?"

Muttering something under his breath, Logan lifted his head and frowned. "Prepare yourself, my dear."

"Prepare myself?" A shiver of fear traveled up Megan's spine. She tried to peer around her husband, but he stood in her way. "For what?"

"You'll see." He touched her cheek softly, gave her

an apologetic grimace and then stepped farther back. Jake and Sally Mae spun in frantic circles by his side.

Arms outstretched, palms facing forward, he looked as if he were…surrendering?

"Logan?" Suddenly afraid for her husband, Megan's voice skipped over her words. "I… I don't understand."

A corner of his mouth kicked up in a sardonic grin. "Let's just say, some of the Mitchell offspring can be a bit unruly."

With that dubious remark, he took two more very large steps back. And was immediately tackled to the ground by a band of blond-haired ruffians.

Chapter Thirteen

As a longtime resident of a large orphanage, Megan had witnessed her share of impromptu wrestling matches. No matter how many sermons Pastor Beau preached on proper Christian behavior, many of the boys couldn't help being, well…boys.

But what she'd always considered "play fighting" couldn't begin to describe the Mitchell brood's enthusiastic take on the subject.

She was seriously concerned for her husband.

Except, Logan was…

Laughing?

Megan drew in a steadying breath and squinted past the flying dust. She counted three others besides her husband. And if she wasn't mistaken, Logan appeared to be enjoying himself. Never mind the fact that he was buried under a pile of tangled legs, swinging arms, and balled fists. Fists, that seemed to make contact with his midsection far too often.

In all her years around rowdy boys, Megan had never been able to understand what drove them to wrestle with such ferocity. Didn't they realize one of them could end up hurt?

More to the point, how could Logan possibly find this fun? Apparently, she didn't know her husband as well as she'd thought.

Shaky Jake, proving he was as much *boy* as the rest of them, joined in the antics. He ran in frantic circles, leaped over the pile of snarled bodies, barked happily and occasionally nipped at flying fists.

The scene was one big unruly mess.

At least there was no blood. Always a welcome sign.

Sally Mae, decidedly the wiser of the two animals, trotted over to Megan and sat down. She looked up at Megan with a rueful expression, as if to say, "What are we going to do with our boys?"

Megan chuckled despite herself. Their "boys" didn't show any signs of tiring. This could go on for a while. "Well, my furry little friend." She scratched the dog's ear and sighed. "I've found it best to let displays such as these play out to the bitter end."

"My sentiments exactly."

Megan gasped and swung around, searching anxiously for the owner of the amused, feminine voice. Her gaze connected with steel-blue eyes the exact color of Logan's. This had to be his mother. Although there were few lines on the pretty, round face, a considerable amount of gray laced the woman's wheat-colored strands.

Megan smoothed a hand over her own hair, desperate to make a good impression. "You must be Logan's mother. I'm—"

"Megan."

She blinked. "You know who I am?"

"Well, of course." The woman's gaze softened. "Logan has talked about you for years."

What could he have possibly said to put that affectionate, welcoming look in his mother's eyes? Surely nothing Megan could live up to. "He's told you about me?"

"You've been the main topic of his letters since he first met you." Not even attempting to stop her tears, Mrs. Mitchell dabbed at her eyes with a corner of her apron. "We've been praying for the day we could finally meet you. And praise God, here it is at last."

The ground seemed to shift beneath Megan's feet at the woman's heartfelt words. If she'd ever doubted Logan's devotion during his five-year absence, if she'd ever feared he had only fulfilled his promise to marry her out of duty, this was her proof otherwise. His family had been waiting to meet her, all because he'd talked about her and mentioned her in his letters.

But if he'd been proud enough to mention her so often, why hadn't he told Megan about his family in return? What was she missing?

"Hey, Ma." Logan called out from the beneath the pile of brothers.

"Yes, Logan." His mother continued smiling at Megan. "What is it, dear?"

"Megan and I..." He jumped up and tried to make his way toward them. His feet were pulled out from under him and he landed flat on his back with a grunt.

"Megan and I," he repeated between gulps of air, all the while dodging fists, "were married yesterday."

His mother shifted her gaze to her son, her mouth hanging open. Her expression cycled from shock to understanding to pure delight.

"Well, my goodness." She turned and lifted Megan's left hand. She eyed the wedding ring with tears in her eyes, then pulled Megan into her arms. "Praise the Lord, you're together at last."

Megan stood stiff in her new mother-in-law's embrace. Despite only knowing her through Logan's comments, the woman was welcoming Megan into the family. No reservations. No questions.

Megan closed her eyes and accepted the embrace. She breathed in the smell of her new mother, a comforting mixture of flour, spices and lemon polish. As the woman stroked her hair, a quiet, indescribable feeling of wholeness settled over Megan.

Oh, she knew she was clinging entirely too long, but there was something about the woman's open affection that brought a comfort she hadn't felt in a long time. Maybe never. Certainly not in the presence of her own mother, a woman who'd demanded Megan call her by her given name to avoid appearing old enough to have a daughter.

Jane Goodwin had done her best, but Megan had never felt truly loved. Not completely.

She'd always known she could count on her Heavenly Father's love, and she believed she was a treasured member of the Charity House family, but Megan had craved a family of her own, a *real* family with siblings and parents and maybe even a few yapping dogs.

Had her prayers finally been answered?

Logan's mother slowly pulled back. She didn't release Megan entirely, but rather kept her hands resting lightly on her shoulders. "Let me take a good look at my new daughter-in-law."

Megan tried to hold still under the inspection, but

with each passing second Mrs. Mitchell's expression become more and more concerned. "You poor dear," she said. "You've been through an ordeal, haven't you?"

Megan flushed. "You can tell that by just looking at me?" This was not the first impression she'd hoped to make.

"I'm a mother." She placed a fingertip near the wound on Megan's throat, not quite touching the tender skin. "Even without such a clear sign I can recognize when a child has been hurt."

At the sympathetic tone, a sob choked in Megan's throat. Something in her threatened to break at the warmth and caring in the woman's voice. What was she supposed to do with all this unexpected outpouring of affection? *She* was the one who offered comfort to people in need, not the other way around.

She hated this newfound weakness, this desire to allow someone else to take care of her, this yearning to be protected. First Logan, and now his mother. Megan felt so unlike herself she couldn't stop the tears from flooding into her eyes.

"Now look what I've done." Mrs. Mitchell dropped her hands to her sides. "I've gone and upset you."

"No." Megan swallowed. "You haven't." Her gaze cut to Logan, half hoping he would rush to her rescue, half dreading that he would. However, he'd gone back wrestling with his brothers. "It's just that, you're right. It's been a difficult two days."

But admitting to an "ordeal" and explaining the details of what had happened to her—especially her memory loss—were two entirely different matters.

As though sensing her discomfort, Logan's mother

linked arms with her. "No need to explain now. Plen⌐
of time for that later."

"I…" Megan quickly looked away. "Thank you."

Still needing a moment to gather herself, she returned her attention to the pile of wrestling boys.

The antics seemed to be winding down. Even Jake's
yapping had become less boisterous. And Logan looked
firmly in control now. Perhaps he'd always been in
control. As if proving her suspicion, he climbed to his
feet. Then peeled away the arms and legs wrapped
around him.

"All right, you bunch of renegades." He pulled Jake
away from the heap and ordered the dog to sit. "That's
enough horsing around."

Logan scowled at each of the boys. He almost pulled
off the menacing look, the one that surely cowed the
hardest outlaws, but then his lips twitched and a
chuckle slipped out. *The fierce U.S. Marshal, indeed.*

"Pull yourselves together," he said, barely holding
back his own smile. "And come meet my wife."

The tallest of the three boys scrambled to his feet.
"You got married?" He sputtered the question through
tight lips. "Without telling us?"

Logan chucked the kid under the chin. "Yeah, well,
I'm telling you now."

Without explaining himself further, he lined up his
brothers in a neat row, largest to smallest. Jake joined
the group, settling in at the end of the line as though
he were one of the boys.

Arm still linked with Megan's, Mrs. Mitchell surveyed the rowdy bunch with an indulgent smile.

Sally Mae yawned and then lowered onto her belly.

:hin on her front paws, she shut her eyes
ed to ignore the lot of them.

over to pat the dog's head, Megan con-
ragtag group. All of the boys looked like
Logan. But the two smallest were identical replicas of
one another, all the way down to the cowlicks on the
right sides of their heads.

Logan moved behind the line. "Megan," he said in
an overly serious tone. "I'd like you to meet part of the
Mitchell brood."

Wide-eyed, she looked from her husband to his
mother. "This is only *part* of your family?"

Mrs. Mitchell shrugged. "Counting Logan, there's
seven children in all."

Megan gaped at her. She knew her husband came
from a large family, but she'd never realized he was
one of *seven* children. How marvelous. How...puz-
zling. "Where are the others?"

"My daughters, Callie and Fanny, are back East attending Miss Sinclair's Prestigious School for Girls."

Megan nodded, thinking it was nice that Logan's
sisters were getting a solid education back East. But
then she did a quick calculation in her head. Counting Logan, the three boys standing in front of her and
the two girls off at school... "That only makes six,"
she said aloud.

"We have one other son." Mrs. Mitchell shot Logan
a look full of complicated emotions and then lowered
her voice. "Our oldest boy, Hunter, hasn't been home
for some time. He's—"

Logan cleared his throat, cutting off his mother in
midsentence. "Let's begin the introductions."

A moment of friction passed between mother and

son. The underlying tension hadn't been there until the mention of Hunter. Megan wanted to ask more about him but Mrs. Mitchell straightened and said, "Yes, Logan, by all means. Proceed."

He erased all emotion from his expression and moved to one end of the line. Ignoring Shaky Jake, he started with the smallest of the three boys. "This scrappy little fellow is Peter. Don't let his size fool you. He has a mean right hook." Logan laughed, even as he absently rubbed his jaw. "And this is Paul." He tapped the middle boy on the head.

"We call them the twins," their mother added out of the corner of her mouth.

"I can see why," Megan said.

Logan moved to the final boy in the line. "And this is our resident tough guy, Garrett." He ruffled the kid's hair hard enough to create a few permanent tangles.

Scowling, Garrett shoved his hand away.

Megan bit back a smile. "I'm pleased to meet you." She made eye contact with each boy, then added, "I'm Megan. Logan's wife."

She didn't have the opportunity to expand before the boys broke formation and rushed straight for her.

Though her heart stuttered, Megan held her ground.

Mrs. Mitchell, however, moved out of the way, abandoning Megan to a series of rapid-fire questions tossed at her from every direction.

All three boys spoke at once, their voices tumbling over one another in a garble. Megan did her best to concentrate, but whenever she focused on one of them another shoved him back and took his place.

Finding their enthusiasm amusing, Megan took a deep breath and answered the boys' questions as best she could, the ones she could decipher anyway. "No, I don't shoot. Yes, I ride like a girl, and, no, I've never tried to rope a cow. Not yet, at any rate. But I'm certainly willing to try."

That last response earned her an approving nod from the tallest of the three.

Although she'd only just met them, she found herself already falling for Logan's brothers. They were bold, pushy and really quite charming.

When one of the brothers asked a rather inappropriate question about kissing, Logan intervened. He pushed through the crowd, looped his arm around Megan's shoulders and quite literally shielded her from his brothers. "Take it easy, boys. Let's not embarrass my poor bride."

Megan opened her mouth to say she didn't mind the attention, but was cut off by the sound of a horse galloping down the lane at full speed.

She turned in the direction of the noise, and found herself looking at an older version of her husband riding a ferocious-looking black horse. He drew the massive creature to a stop and dismounted in a single swoop.

Every head turned toward the deep, gravelly voice that said, "What's the holdup? You boys were supposed to meet me in the stable ten minutes ago."

Without waiting for an answer, Logan's father—surely this was his father—whipped off his hat and slapped it against his thigh. He caught sight of Logan and let out a loud whoop. "Well, look who it is."

Smiling broadly, Logan released Megan and met his father halfway across the expanse of grass dividing them. "Hello, Pa."

"Son." The older man's hands, large as bear paws, landed on Logan's shoulders with a resounding whack. "It's about time you made it back this way."

The two grinned at each other, their genuine affection for one another evident in their eyes. They were similar in so many ways, especially in height, but Logan's father had a good twenty pounds on him. Most of it in his stomach.

Mrs. Mitchell must be a remarkable cook.

"Logan, my boy, you're looking a bit tired." The gruff declaration was tempered with a hearty laugh. "But at least you're alive."

"Alive is always good," Logan said, still smiling but his eyelids had dropped to half-mast.

The two stared at one another, a silent message passing between them that Megan didn't quite understand. When the men began pounding each other's backs, Mrs. Mitchell let out a frustrated huff.

"Oh, honestly." She maneuvered between the two, her gaze filled with equal parts fondness and exasperation. "Cyrus, you're going to beat all the air out of our son. Now let him be and come meet his wife."

"His wife?" Cyrus's voice boomed through the air. "You finally married your little gal in Denver?"

"I did." Still smiling, Logan motioned Megan forward.

She went to him at once, but her steps were slow and careful. Not only had her ankle begun to ache, but her father-in-law was a little intimidating. *A lot* intimidating.

"Megan, darling." Logan kissed her knuckles in a gesture that was becoming pleasantly familiar. "Meet Cyrus Mitchell, owner, operator and resident curmudgeon of the Flying M ranch."

Trying not to smile at the lofty description, Megan looked into the tanned, lined face that was so much like her husband's. Her heart thumped hard against her ribs. She was getting a good look into the future, and she liked what she saw. Even the deep, weathered grooves around Cyrus Mitchell's eyes were appealing. Logan was going to be a very handsome older man.

"I'm so very pleased to meet you, Mr. Mitchell." She reached out her hand to her new father-in-law.

Cyrus glared at her extended fingers as if they were connected to a poisonous snake. "We'll have none of that in this family."

Megan's throat tightened. Had she done something wrong? Never having had a father of her own, she didn't know how to proceed. Nevertheless, she lifted her chin and continued holding out her hand, sensing Cyrus Mitchell would appreciate grit over any other character trait.

Making a grumbling sound in his throat, he pulled her into a bone-crunching hug. Trapped in the strong, fatherly embrace, Megan had never felt so cherished. So *accepted*.

"Welcome to the family, little lady." Cyrus patted her shoulders awkwardly, then stepped back and stared at her with…was that…water in his eyes?

Megan had just made a grown man cry, all because she'd married his son. An odd sense of joy spread through her. Between Mrs. Mitchell's warm reception, the boys' eager enthusiasm and Cyrus's watery eyes, Megan knew—she just knew—she was going to be very happy on the Flying M.

Oh, yes. She was home. Home at last.

Chapter Fourteen

Logan had made a serious error in judgment. He'd failed to prepare Megan for his family.

What must she think? In a matter of minutes she'd been subjected to a pair of barking cow dogs, an infamous Mitchell wrestling match and now one of his father's bone-rattling hugs.

She had to be reeling. After all, Megan was used to life at Charity House, where order and polite decorum reigned supreme. The complete opposite held true on the Flying M. A day didn't go by without some small disaster or another coming to fruition. That was just the Mitchell way.

When his father finally gave Megan room to breathe, Logan pushed between them. Fighting the urge to whisk her away, he ran his gaze down to her bandaged ankle and back up again, stopping at the angry-looking wound on her throat. His gut clenched at the reminder of the attack. "How are you feeling?"

"I'm perfectly well, Logan."

She didn't look well. She looked ready to drop from exhaustion.

He opened his mouth to argue the point. She let out an exasperated sigh. "Truly, I'm fine."

He still didn't believe her. Her eyes had taken on a glassy, unfocused sheen. And her face was leached of color. Shane had warned Logan not to push his bride too hard. He feared he'd done just that.

"All this excitement is too much for you." He kept his voice even. "I'm sorry, Megan. My family can be a bit overwhelming."

"You're family is lovely. *Every* one of them." She smiled at his parents then turned her gaze to his brothers.

Logan tossed all three of them a warning glare. The boys were acting relatively polite. For now. It was only a matter of time before they grew bored and mayhem erupted all over again.

"Still," he said, moving into her line of vision and subsequently cutting off a direct route between her and the boys. "You've had a long journey and not nearly enough sleep in the last two days."

"I dozed most of the night." Her eyebrows scrunched together as though she'd just come to an unpleasant realization. "But you haven't slept at all."

"I'm used to sporadic sleep." It was part of his job description. *"You,* however, are not." He took her elbow and turned her in the direction of the house. "Let's get you inside so you can rest."

He guided her carefully, making sure he took the bulk of her weight so she didn't put unnecessary pressure on her ankle.

"Shouldn't you rest as well?" she asked, leaning heavily on him.

"I will. Later."

"But you haven't—"

"Hey, Garrett," he shot over his shoulder, effectively cutting off whatever additional argument she'd been about to make. "You and the boys unload the wagon while I get Megan settled inside."

She tugged on his arm. "I can walk on my own."

Bold words, spoken in a strong tone. He almost believed her, but then she stepped on a small rock and lost her balance. She would have crumpled to the ground if he hadn't been holding on to her. Evidently, he needed to be her better judgment.

"Megan, darling, you're going to have to defer to me on this."

She lifted her chin at the stubborn angle he was growing to dread. This was a new side of his wife he didn't completely understand. Just how much had she changed in the past five years?

As if in answer, she pulled him to a stop and began to argue with him again. "Can I at least take a moment to—"

"No."

"Not even if I—"

"No."

Giving him an irritated sniff, she drew her elbow free and headed toward the house without his assistance. With her nose in the air and that unbending look in her eyes, she almost looked regal. But then she stumbled, enough to break stride.

He rushed to scoop her in his arms, but caught sight of his mother shaking her head at him.

He knew that look. But why was she warning him off? Megan was brittle, fragile, *injured.* She needed him. She…

Seemed to be making satisfactory progress on her own.

Should he let her continue or not?

Unsure how best to proceed, Logan looked to his father for help. The older man shot him a sympathetic grimace, but didn't offer any advice. Instead, he planted a loud kiss on his wife's lips, jammed his hat on his head and then moved back to his horse.

"Once you boys get that wagon unloaded meet me in the stable. We have a long day ahead of us in the saddle," he said, then clicked his tongue and the dogs obediently fell in line behind his horse.

At this time of year Logan knew his father could use an extra pair of hands. "Hey, Pa," he called after him. "Once I get Megan situated I'll join you on the range."

Cyrus waved a hand over his head. "We'll be in the south pastures today, gotta round up the latest batch of newborns."

Logan knew the difficult task that lay ahead of them. Most new mothers tried to conceal their calves from the rest of herd by moving them to remote spots not easy to get to on horseback. Thankfully, Jake and Sally Mae were experts at rooting out even the most stubborn from their hiding places.

"I'll find you," Logan said.

After he made sure Megan rested. Once she was off her feet he planned to join his father and tell him everything, including the events surrounding her recent memory loss. Later tonight, he'd do the same with his mother. Logan didn't think he'd brought the danger with them, nevertheless he owed it to his parents to warn them of the hazards that might lie ahead.

In a few days Logan would have to leave Megan in his family's care so he could hunt Kincaid's killer. Although he trusted his family implicitly, Logan knew

Megan wouldn't be safe until he found the real killer and put him behind bars. Then—and only then—would they be able to begin their life together as husband and wife.

Megan entered the house with Logan by her side and his mother trailing closely behind. She was tired of all this careful "handling" and longed to get back to her old self, yearned to be strong again, in control, giving to others rather than receiving.

Stepping deeper into the house, the pleasant aroma of cinnamon, apples and baking bread instantly soothed her. So much so that when Logan took her arm, Megan allowed him to direct her into a large sitting room without argument.

She glanced around her surroundings with pleasure. *This* was the kind of large, comfortable space she'd always thought would belong to a family, a real family.

The entire area was happily cluttered. Blankets were tossed haphazardly on the bulky, well-worn furniture. A pile of wooden toys and a bag of marbles sat in the center of the floor, while papers, magazines and books littered every available tabletop. This room looked lived-in, a place to cast aside the cares of the day and simply relax.

"Sit here, sweetheart." Logan indicated a spot on one of the sofas.

Although the large, comfortable-looking piece of furniture beckoned, Megan didn't want to sit. She was too restless, too excited. She wanted to investigate her new home. "I've been riding in a wagon all night," she said. "My legs are stiff."

Logan's handsome face twisted in concern. "Your ankle must be throbbing by now."

It was, but Megan could bear the pain a little while longer. The moment Logan reached out to her, as she knew he would, she dipped out from under his hand before he could get a good grip on her arm.

Trying not to grimace at him, she took a step then winced when her ankle landed at an awkward angle.

Without preamble, Logan scooped her into his arms and headed toward the sofa. "I don't understand why you're fighting me on this. I only want to take care of you."

She opened her mouth to argue, but his mother spoke first. "Logan, you're suffocating your wife."

He drew in an offended breath. "Shane, her *doctor,* told me to keep her off her feet as much as possible. He said—"

Megan touched his lips, effectively cutting off the rest of his words. "My ankle is fine. I moved too quickly, that's all."

Cradling her against him a moment longer, he set her on the sofa and then sat down beside her. "It's just that I can't bear to have anything else happen to you." His eyes held that familiar look of worry, but there was something else in them, as well. An intensity that sent a shiver through her.

Sighing, Megan lowered her gaze to her hands, hands that were shaking. Again. She was growing quite tired of this odd, almost fearful reaction to her husband. She knew—*knew*—he would never hurt her, not even in the most intimate moments of their marriage. But every once in a while when the light caught his face at just the right angle, something in her pulled back from him.

"I would never harm you," he said quietly, as if he could read her thoughts.

She didn't *want* to be afraid of her husband. But sometimes he was just too big, too close, too intense. And yet, her reaction to him made no sense. This was Logan. *Logan.*

Swallowing down her ridiculous fear, she lifted her hand to his face. He caught it and placed a light kiss on her palm.

This time, fear had nothing to do with the shiver sliding down her spine.

Enthralled by the pleasant sensation, Megan leaned a bit closer to her husband. His blue eyes were so compelling, so beautiful. She ran her fingertip along his jaw. His day-old stubble was rough under her touch.

He leaned forward, his lips nearly touching hers.

Megan shut her eyes and sighed.

He brushed a strand of hair off her forehead and she trembled under his tender touch.

"Are you cold?" he asked.

Megan shook her head, but she couldn't stop the heat rising in her cheeks. "I'll be fine with your mother." She smiled up at him, hoping to alleviate his worry even if she'd rather he stay. "Just fine."

After another round of arguing, cajoling and promises of dire consequences if Megan was not kept off her feet, Logan exited the room.

Once he was gone, Mrs. Mitchell let out an amused breath of air. "I didn't think that boy would ever leave."

"He's worried about me," Megan said.

"Well, that certainly needed clearing up," she said with a quick burst of laughter.

Megan couldn't help enjoying her mother-in-law's reaction.

After a moment of smiling at one another, a comfortable silence descended. Megan studied her new mother-in-law beneath lowered lashes. This was a woman comfortable in her own skin.

Would she ever have that sort of confidence, that internal acceptance of who she was deep at the core? Megan sensed she could learn a lot from this woman.

At that happy thought, a wave of guilt crested. "I'm sorry you weren't able to attend the wedding," Megan said. "Under the circumstances there wasn't time to plan anything formal."

Smoothing a wrinkle from her apron, Mrs. Mitchell lowered herself onto the sofa next to Megan. "Am I to assume my son got a little, shall we say…ahead of himself?"

Megan frowned at the oddly worded question. Her instinct was to change the subject immediately, but curiosity got the best of her. "Ahead of himself, how?"

She took Megan's hands and squeezed gently. "Are you with child, Megan?"

"No." She visibly shrank from the blunt question. "I'm not my mother's daughter."

"Oh, dear, I didn't mean it that way." She smiled kindly, so kindly that it took an effort of will for Megan to hold her gaze. "It's simply obvious how much my son loves you."

"But we haven't… Logan would never…that is, he and I haven't…" She lowered her gaze in complete and utter embarrassment. "Of course I'm not with child.

We had to get married quickly because we—" She cut off her own words. How did she explain the circumstances of their hurried wedding?

Mrs. Mitchell simply stared at her, waiting for the rest.

"There was nothing scandalous about our sudden nuptials." Words tumbled out of her mouth in a garbled rush. "Well, yes, maybe there was, but not in the way you would think. When Logan came home he found me in, that is, I was in... Oh, bother, it's complicated."

"With Logan, it usually is."

"Oh?" When it came to her husband, Megan had always thought matters were blessedly straightforward.

"Oh, my, yes." Rather than expanding, Mrs. Mitchell rose. "Now, come. Let's get you settled in a room upstairs, then you can tell me the story behind your hasty marriage to my son."

Megan hobbled up the stairs behind her mother-in-law. There was only time for impressions along the way. The sturdy railing made from knotted pine, the long hallway that came to a T and then split into two identical corridors.

Turning down the left hallway, Mrs. Mitchell stopped at the first room on the right. Megan entered ahead of her and was immediately struck by the scent of pine and woodsy spice she'd always associated with her husband.

"This was Logan's room as a boy."

Smiling, Megan poked around the room. The decor had a decidedly masculine, albeit comfortable, feel. There were two large chairs with matching ottomans, a sturdy chest of drawers and an oversized, cozy-looking bed.

Wanting to surrender to her exhaustion, Megan stared at the fluffy mattress with longing. Much to her horror, tears welled in her eyes.

The last two days had been filled with too much emotion to sort through all at once. Although she was excited to begin her new life with Logan, although she already adored his family, everything was all…so… new. And overwhelming.

A sob slipped past her lips and the tears she'd held on to for days escaped at last.

Without commenting on her sudden breakdown, Mrs. Mitchell handed Megan a handkerchief she dug out of her apron.

"I'm sorry." Megan dabbed at her eyes. "I don't usually cry like this. I don't usually cry at all."

The older woman guided her to the edge of the bed and urged her to sit. "Then it's high time you did."

Megan sank onto the mattress. The blessed softness called to her and she had to fight to stay upright.

"We all need a good cry every now and again," her mother-in-law announced.

Cocooned in the woman's soft smile, Megan sniffled. "That's what my friend Bella said."

"Your friend sounds like a very wise woman."

"Oh, she is." Thinking of Bella brought on another batch of tears. Embarrassed at her loss of control, Megan buried her face in her hands. "I don't know what's wrong with me."

Joining her on the edge of the bed, Mrs. Mitchell tugged her into a motherly hug. "You're exhausted. You've left everything and everyone you know. You're in a strange, new world."

"I'm supposed to be happy," Megan said. "I just

married the best man I know, a man I love with all my heart. And I'm truly glad to be here with his family."

"We're happy to have you here."

Megan pulled back and wiped at her cheeks. "How much do you know about me?"

"I know Logan loves you. That's enough for me."

Logan must have skimmed over the details of Megan's past. "Do you know the circumstances of my birth? That I have no idea who my father is?"

"Logan told us all about your childhood, including why and how you ended up at an orphanage like Charity House." There was compassion in the woman's tone and no matter how hard Megan looked into her mother-in-law's eyes she couldn't find a hint of condemnation staring back at her.

She had to make sure Mrs. Mitchell truly knew *everything* about her. She wouldn't start her marriage with secrets. "Did Logan tell you that once my mother's stage career ended she went to work in a brothel?"

"Your mother loved you enough to send you to a Christian orphanage where you were able to break free of her sinful lifestyle." She touched Megan's arm. "Given the circumstances of your childhood, I predict you understand God's grace better than most."

Too choked to speak, Megan slowly nodded. Thanks to the godly people at Charity House, she'd learned that the Lord loved even the unlovable, including women like Jane Goodwin. The very arms that defeated death on the cross were open to all, including sinners, including a woman of questionable virtue, including her daughter.

"I won't deny that your mother made many bad choices," Mrs. Mitchell said. "But her decision to send you to Charity House ultimately led you to Logan. That's what I call providence. God's providence."

Fresh tears filled Megan's eyes. Jane Goodwin had given her life and had done the best she could with her limited resources. But in a matter of minutes, Mrs. Mitchell had become something more to Megan, more than Jane had ever been. She'd become a mother.

Chapter Fifteen

Logan hooked the heel of his boot on the corral's bottom rail, leaned his elbows on the top and then looked out over the mountains. He rolled his shoulders, hoping to ease the multitude of knots. He'd forgotten what it felt like to put in a long day of hard labor on the ranch. Although every muscle in his body ached, he hadn't felt this satisfied in years. Now all he wanted was a decent meal and time alone with his wife.

His sweet, beautiful Megan.

He hadn't wanted to leave her this morning. Just thinking about what Kincaid had done to her, what he'd *tried* to do to her still made Logan's gut churn with rage. Surely that explained why he'd been on edge all day. Why his instincts were on high alert even at this late hour.

The bulk of his uneasiness should be gone by now. Yet a sense of foreboding rode him hard, as if danger lurked just out of reach—waiting for the right moment to strike.

Unhappy with the direction of his thoughts, Logan waited until his brothers trooped inside the house before turning his attention to the north range. His gut told him something was out there. Or rather, *someone*.

Before he could decide whether he should investigate his suspicions or shrug them off as a result of exhaustion, his father joined him at the railing. "It's a real blessing to have you home, son."

Logan sensed a grim seriousness beneath the words, but he couldn't pinpoint the source. "We had a good day," he said carefully.

"We did." His father dipped his bandanna in the water trough next to him and began scrubbing the trail dust off his face and neck. "More challenging than most."

Logan conceded the point with a short nod. Several of the newborn calves had been hidden in thick, gnarled underbrush. The cow dogs had been undaunted, rooting out the most stubborn with ruthless, well-honed precision. "Sally Mae and Jake are worth their weight in gold."

Smiling, his father continued rubbing the dirt off his neck. "That they are."

As silence fell between them, Logan took in the view with another sweeping glance. The ranch was bathed in the soft, golden glow of late afternoon. He loved the Flying M, and the simple, uncomplicated life that came from working the land.

It was during quiet moments like these that Logan regretted ever leaving home. His fight with Hunter had been the catalyst. Logan had needed to prove he wasn't like his gunslinger brother, that he was an agent for good rather than evil. In the end, the life of a lawman had fit him well. Or so he'd thought.

But now, after the events of the last two days, Logan

wondered if he was only fooling himself. Maybe he wasn't as in control as he'd always believed. Maybe he wasn't the good devoted Christian taking the righteous path to which he'd been called. He knew—knew beyond a shadow of a doubt—that if he'd come across Kincaid hurting Megan, he would have done whatever necessary to save her.

Including killing the blackguard.

What sort of man did that make him? Good? Evil? Something in between?

A sudden urge to see his wife overtook all other desires. He needed to hold her and make sure she was safe.

He turned toward the house.

"Logan, wait." His father set a hand on his shoulder.

Impatience speared through him. He wanted to shrug off the viselike grip but held steady. "I have to check on Megan."

"I know you're worried about your wife. We all are." His father dropped his hand and held Logan in place with nothing more than a firm look, a look that said he had something important to say. Something Logan wasn't going to like. "I've been thinking about what you said, about what happened to Megan in that brothel two nights ago."

Logan's chest tightened at the change in his father's tone. "Are you worried I've brought the danger with us? That I've put the family at risk?"

"No." His father flicked his hand in dismissal. "No. That's not what's bothering me."

"But what if I did?" His gaze automatically shot toward the north range. Apprehension gnawed at him with the tenacity of little rat teeth.

"There's no use worrying over what might or might not happen in the future," he said in his matter-of-fact tone Logan knew well. "If someone comes to hurt your wife, or tries to threaten our family, then we'll deal with it in the same way we always do, as a united front."

Logan nodded, wondering why he didn't feel more reassured. Maybe because he couldn't stop thinking about Megan and the terror she must have experienced when Kincaid pulled his knife.

Lord, give me the strength to protect her and keep her safe.

"Like I was saying—" Cyrus rubbed his chin between his thumb and forefinger "—something doesn't add up about what you said happened that night."

A lot of things didn't add up. "Where are you headed with this, Pa?"

"I don't believe the woman I met this morning, the one who was determined to walk on her own steam despite her injury would have lost her memory just because she witnessed a murder."

"Murder is *never* easy to see," he said. "Especially for someone like Megan. She's been sheltered most of her life."

"You underestimate her. She's stronger than you think."

Under normal circumstances Logan would agree. Megan *was* a strong woman, and more capable than most. But she'd been brutally attacked by a bad man with evil intent in his heart. No woman, no matter how strong, could walk away unscathed from such an experience. "She was traumatized," he said through a tight jaw.

"I'm not denying that what happened to her was a travesty. But what if something else caused her to forget the events of that night, something far worse than witnessing the murder of her attacker?"

Logan lowered his gaze, praying his father was wrong. But he couldn't ignore the thumping of his heart, or the dread sweeping through him. Had Kincaid done something horrible to Megan, something so terrible that her mind refused to accept the truth?

His stomach roiled at the terrible possibilities that came to mind, things too awful to speak aloud. Shane had confirmed that Megan was still innocent. Could he have been wrong?

Logan banished the thought.

"What if your wife knew the identity of the man who killed her attacker? What if that's why she can't remember the events of that night?"

The question took Logan aback. "You think Megan lost her memory because she knew the man who killed Kincaid?"

His father nodded.

"But why?"

"Why else?" Cyrus pushed away from the rail. "To protect him."

Still reeling from his father's theory behind Megan's memory loss, Logan went in search of his wife. He found her in his old room, asleep in one of the chairs. Her legs were stretched out on the ottoman while she hugged her sketchbook tightly against her. The ring he'd put on her finger the day before looked as though it belonged there, as though it had been there for years—a symbol as solid as his love for her.

She looked peaceful in sleep, tranquil even, and yet Logan couldn't shake his uneasiness. He'd thought bringing her to the Flying M would alleviate his worries. Now his father's suggestion had added additional confusion to an already uncertain situation.

Letting out a slow breath of air, Logan moved closer to the chair, careful not to wake his bride. The setting sun spread fingers of pink-tinted light across her face, making her features appear soft and radiant. She was so lovely, so *beautiful*. It took an ironclad will to keep from touching her.

For years, Logan had prayed for the day he could make Megan his wife. Marriage was where the two of them would become one, where their own family would begin. But she was still fragile from her ordeal. He *must* be careful with her.

He brushed a lock of hair off her face. His hand shook from the control it took to keep his touch light. He ached for Megan, had always ached for her, from the first moment he'd laid eyes on her.

But he found it hard to enjoy watching her now. His father's words played through his head, taunting him. He had to consider the possibility that she knew the man who'd killed her attacker.

If Megan knew the man, that meant Logan probably did, as well.

Mattie Silks had warned him he wouldn't like what he found if he persisted with his investigation. What had the madam been hiding from him?

As soon as the question formed in his mind, Marc Dupree's words came back to him. *I consider her my daughter. I would do anything,* anything *to protect her.*

Had those words been a confession? Had Marc killed Kincaid to protect Megan?

It was possible. More than possible. But only a theory at this juncture. None of the evidence pointed to Marc. In fact, none of the evidence pointed to *anyone*. It was as if the killer had vanished into thin air.

Megan sighed in her sleep, the sound cutting through Logan's troubling thoughts. He curled his fingers into a fist and forced himself to remain where he was, to keep his hands to himself.

She sighed again, then wiggled into a more comfortable position.

He gave in to temptation and moved a step closer. He ordered himself to behave like a gentleman. In hopes of distracting himself, he slowly pried the sketchbook out of her grip and flipped through the first few pages.

She'd attempted a handful of drafts of the snow-peaked mountains. None were complete, each drawing nothing more than a series of disconnected lines that hinted at a picture.

Studying the sketches a moment longer, Logan noted a shadowy figure in the lower right corner of all the drawings.

Kincaid's killer?

Hard to tell. The general build and masculine set of the shoulders could belong to a number of men. Even Logan himself.

Patience, he told himself. *All will be revealed in time.*

Shutting the book, he placed it on the ground at his feet. He would ask Megan about the man in the drawings when the time was right. Not now.

Now he just wanted to hold her and assure himself

she was as well as she appeared to be in sleep. Forcing his heartbeat to settle, he sat on the edge of the otto-man, slipped his hands around her shoulders and gently pulled her into his arms.

She murmured his name, her breath warm against his neck. Then she curled into him, hugging him tightly.

Offering up a silent prayer for control, he buried his face in her hair. "I missed you, sweetheart."

"Logan." She rubbed her nose along his neck, her voice husky from sleep. "You smell good."

He loosened his hold and tried to pull back.

She wrapped her arms around his neck and tugged him tighter against her. "I love your scent. I've missed it all these years."

She punctuated her words with a kiss to his bare throat.

Had the woman no mercy? She was quite literally killing him. Unable to stop himself, he pressed his lips to her shoulder.

An answering shiver passed through her.

Logan forced himself to relax. Nothing special going on here, nothing out of the ordinary.

Who was he kidding? Love for his wife burned in his gut.

He closed his eyes and *again* prayed for strength.

It was a hopeless request. His control was all but gone. He had to put distance between them. At once. Rising quickly, he nearly stepped on the sketchbook in his haste to get away.

Breathing hard, he stared down at his wife. The dark smudges beneath her eyes were less noticeable and her face had taken on a bit more color than earlier in the day. "You look rested."

"I feel rested." She stretched her arms over her head and arched her back. The gesture pulled the bodice of her dress tight against her womanly curves.

Logan shifted his gaze. He noticed the sketchbook and retrieved it. "Here, you were clutching this in your sleep."

"I was?" She paused, then took the book and set it on her lap.

Logan stepped closer, not sure what he saw in her eyes. She appeared to be debating with herself, perhaps deciding whether to tell him about her half-finished drawings.

"I attempted to sketch the view from the window over there." She ran her fingertip along the top of the book in a slow, circular motion. "But every time I made it to a certain point in the drawing my head started spinning, aching really, and I'd have to stop to rest my eyes. I must have fallen asleep."

The anguish in her voice tore at him. Logan wanted nothing more than to drag her into his arms and offer her comfort. But he wasn't sure he could stop at just holding her. "Megan, I'm sorry. I—"

"Oh, Logan." Her gaze whipped to his. "What if I'm never able to draw again?"

"Megan, darling, don't despair." He returned to the ottoman and wrapped her hand securely in his. "Shane warned you to expect a certain level of exhaustion in these first few days. Don't try to rush your healing."

"I hope you're right."

"I am."

She stared at their joined hands for a long moment.

Then she shook her head and pulled her fingers free of his.

"Logan, I should tell you. Your mother thought that we...that you and I had already..." Her cheeks turned a becoming pink. "She thought that we had already been...intimate."

The embarrassment in her voice was impossible to miss. His first instinct was to protect her. Not as much from his mother and her inappropriate assumptions, as from himself. Because in the privacy of this room, with the idea of intimacy now hanging in the air between them, Logan found it hard to ignore his natural instincts to make this woman his wife.

He must be strong. He *must*.

"Don't worry, sweetheart." He forced himself to speak slowly. Clearly. For himself as well as for her. "I won't touch you until you're completely healed."

Chapter Sixteen

I won't touch you until you're completely healed. Megan stared up at her husband, unsure how to respond to his bold declaration.

She could feel the heat rising in her cheeks, but had the presence of mind to break eye contact.

From a certain perspective, his vow to wait was terribly sweet. Yet so...very...wrong.

It was as if he thought she would crumble under his touch. She wasn't nearly so weak. Couldn't he see that despite her injury she was perfectly capable of certain...activities? She was a newly married woman, after all. One who dearly loved her husband.

If Logan loved her as much as he claimed, wasn't he supposed to want her as a *man* wants a *woman*?

Maybe love made things different for a man. Megan admitted that her knowledge of such matters might be a bit slanted, colored as it were by her mother's disgraceful example. Even before Jane Goodwin had resorted to selling her affections for money, men had been a staple in her life. The ones that stuck around for any length of time did so for a myriad of reasons, none of them wholesome.

At least Logan's feelings for Megan were pure. She tried not to worry that his lukewarm reaction meant anything but complete devotion.

"I see I've taken you by surprise." He reached to her. But instead of pulling her into his arms as she'd hoped, he tucked a strand of her hair behind her ear. "I realize this is a difficult conversation, but we must speak of this now."

She nodded in agreement.

"You are the most important thing in my life," he said, twirling another strand of hair around his finger. "I'd never do anything to hurt you."

"Oh, Logan." She leaned into his touch. "I know that."

"Then we're in agreement." His words had a final ring to them. "We'll wait to consummate our marriage until you're feeling stronger."

I'm strong enough now, she almost said, but caught herself. "If that's what you want." Disappointment made her voice skip over the words.

He didn't seem to notice her shift in mood. "Now that that's settled, come along." He helped her stand. "Supper is on the table."

"Is it that time already?" Megan launched herself toward the door, but she moved too fast and swayed.

Logan steadied her with a hand to her arm. "Easy now."

"I should have helped prepare the meal." She looked frantically around her, her gaze landing on nothing in particular which only made her dizzier. "What must your mother think of me?"

"She *thinks* you need your rest." With his hand still on her arm, he guided her toward the door.

"No, wait." Megan jerked to a halt then looked down at her dress. "Am I presentable?"

Rather than answering right away, Logan ran his gaze down to her toes and back up again. By the time his eyes met hers again there was nothing careful or tender in them. *Glory.* He was looking at her the way a man looks at his woman.

A thread of pleasure flipped in her stomach.

Perhaps Logan did want her. Perhaps he was merely trying to act the part of a gentleman, which was really sweet.

And completely unnecessary.

Maybe she should test them both. Before she lost her nerve.

Flattening her palms against his chest, she lifted up on her toes. Just before her lips made contact with his, he pulled his head back. "Megan, no."

"Why not?" She angled her head and stared up at him. What was it she saw in his gaze? Alarm? Apprehension? "We're married," she reminded him. "Kissing is allowed."

He lifted his hands in a defensive gesture, a silent plea for her to keep her distance.

Ignoring the request, she moved closer. Close enough to feel his breath tickle her cheek.

She lowered her eyelashes and bit back a smile. He might be standing in that loose, casual way of his, but there was nothing relaxed about him. He was as tense as she'd ever seen him.

She moved closer still.

He groaned.

"Logan, I—"

Gripping her shoulders, he crushed his lips to hers.

Wanting their kiss to last forever, she clung to him in return. One heartbeat passed. Two. By the third he flung himself away from her.

With a strained look in his eyes, he pulled in several tight breaths. Then several more. "The family is waiting." His words came out strangled.

Feeling gracious, Megan decided to let him win this round. She hid her newfound joy inside a demure smile. "By all means—" she offered him her hand "—lead the way."

He blinked at her another moment longer. His eyes grew dark again, filling with bold intent, then he looked quickly away. Still breathing hard, he took her hand and led her from the room.

The ensuing silence as they made their way down the stairs didn't bother Megan. She knew the truth. And no matter what Logan said to the contrary, no matter how many lofty promises he made, he wanted her the way a husband *wanted* his wife as God intended.

Megan touched her lips and sighed. Her marriage had just taken on a whole new dimension and she couldn't be more pleased.

Supper at the Mitchell house turned out to be a chaotic, undisciplined affair, everyone grabbing for whatever they wished. With her hands neatly folded in her lap, Megan stared at the pandemonium in stunned silence.

The only moment of calm had come a few minutes earlier, when Logan's father had blessed the food. Since then, disorder had reigned supreme. Sentences tumbled over one another, making it impossible to decipher a single word.

Blinking rapidly, Megan darted her gaze around the table. She had no idea how to proceed. Meals at Charity House were orderly affairs. Table manners were enforced. Food was passed counterclockwise, one dish at a time. Please and thank you were the most commonly uttered words. Polite conversation prevailed.

A biscuit flew in the air, nearly clipping her on the nose. She leaned back as a second one soon followed the first. Both were caught in midair in rapid succession, one by Paul and the other by Peter. Neither had looked up from their plate.

Glory.

As Mrs. Mitchell smiled indulgently at her brood Megan remembered Logan's description of his family. *We work hard, play harder, laugh well and often.* Well, she couldn't deny the accuracy of those words.

"Megan, darling." Logan leaned close to her ear. "Aren't you hungry?"

"I...well, yes. Yes, I am." The food smelled delicious. The large roast looked especially appealing.

Logan pointed to her empty plate. "You can't eat air."

"I—"

"Here, let me help you." With a slight of hand that displayed his quick reflexes, he reached across her, picked up a bowl and then plopped a mound of potatoes on her plate. He soon had gravy poured and a biscuit situated on the rim. A pile of meat followed. "Dig in."

She stared at him wildly; convinced her eyes were as round as an owl's.

He kissed her lightly on the lips then lowered one

of his eyelids in a lazy wink. "You can't be shy at this table."

"I...of course not. I think I understand."

She picked up her fork, then looked over at Logan's father and nearly dropped the utensil in her lap. Cyrus Mitchell was spreading a thick layer of butter on his biscuit. Then he put another on top of the first. And still another.

He caught her eyeing him and grinned. "Makes 'em slide down easier." He lifted the biscuit in her direction.

Megan smiled back at her new father-in-law. *We work hard, play hard, laugh well and often.*

She closed her eyes and lifted up a silent prayer. *Oh, Lord, I want to work hard and play harder, too. I want to be free to laugh well, just like my new family.*

So what was stopping her? Why was she holding herself back, even as she desperately wanted to join the Mitchell mayhem?

Because life with her mother had always been out of control. Uncertainty had been her only staple as a child. One moment her mother would be her best friend, while the next she'd become an enraged stranger best avoided. Megan never knew which mother to expect at any given moment.

As a result of all the chaos and insecurity, she'd learned to control her own world. With order. And distance. By giving to others and never, *never,* expecting anything in return. Life was easier that way.

But here, with this loving, spontaneous family Megan felt safe. Safe to be herself. Safe to laugh well and often.

Determined to live in the moment, Megan picked

up her fork and did exactly what Logan suggested. She *dug* in to her meal.

And ate twice as much as she'd planned.

After dinner, the boys ran off to wrestle with the dogs. Logan helped his father shut down the stable for the night, while Megan cleared the table.

Her mother-in-law had grown surprisingly quiet once they were alone and maintained her silence during the washing.

Handing Megan the next plate to dry, she spoke at last. "Would you and Logan like to stay in one of our guest cabins for a while?"

Megan's hand stilled on the plate and she gave up any pretense of drying. "I'm sorry. I don't understand what you're asking."

"I was remembering my first days as a new bride." She placed another plate in the soapy water, her eyes a bit dreamy. "I realized there isn't much privacy in this house."

Megan felt her cheeks warm as random thoughts collided in her mind. She squared her shoulders and addressed the most obvious concern. "Are you afraid one of the boys might walk in on us?"

"That has occurred to me." She looked amused, rather than shocked. "But that's not what I meant."

"You don't have to worry about any impropriety. Logan has promised to keep his hands to himself until I'm healed." The frustration in her voice surprised her.

Her mother-in-law's response surprised her even more. "Well, now, that's unfortunate."

Megan gaped at the woman.

"I see I've shocked you."

"No. Well, yes, I suppose you have." Megan picked

up the discarded plate. "Logan and I should set an example for the younger children. A *godly* example."

"Megan, darling, you and Logan are married."

Megan's head spun with confusion. "Nevertheless." She had to work on getting her voice steady. "Our behavior should be above reproach under your roof."

"I see I'm going to have to be blunt."

And here Megan thought that's what she'd been doing.

Ignoring the rest of the dirty dishes, her mother-in-law faced her. "I want grandchildren. The sooner the better."

Megan felt an ice-edged chill claw through her. If she wasn't mistaken, Logan's mother was telling her to consummate their marriage. She could barely draw a breath past her embarrassment. "I…don't know what to say."

After wiping her hands on her apron, Mrs. Mitchell took Megan's hands and steered her to an empty chair against the opposite wall. "What did your mother tell you about relations between a man and a woman?"

Megan picked up a portion of her skirt, smoothed it at the pleat then let it fall again. "She told me men are ruled by their urges." She squeezed her eyes shut before some of the uglier memories of her childhood could interfere. "She said men care only about their own fulfillment."

"That's just about the most foolish thing I've ever heard."

Megan's eyes flew open.

Mrs. Mitchell was staring down at her with pursed lips. "Not to speak ill of the dead, but your mother's chosen profession obviously gave her a biased perspective."

Hope speared through Megan. She knew what she

felt toward her husband, knew what she wanted to happen between them, knew her feelings were based in love.

Surely Logan felt the same way. Surely he would be gentle with her, far more so than the men at the brothel had been toward her mother.

But what if she was wrong? What if her mother had been right? "I should think my mother knew more than most about the subject of relations between a man and a woman."

"Perhaps on one level," Mrs. Mitchell conceded. "But not within the sanctity of marriage."

There was a drumming in Megan's heart, an anticipation that Logan's mother was about to tell her something life-changing. Unable to contain all the emotions running through her, Megan started to rise.

"Sit down, dear." Mrs. Mitchell pressed Megan back into the chair. Her eyes took on a thoughtful look, as if she was gathering her words with great care. "Love between a husband and his wife is never ugly or dirty or one-sided, but rather beautiful and natural for both partners."

Megan stiffened her spine, slowed her breathing, and eyed her mother-in-law warily. The other woman's revelation brought with it a large dose of hope as well as a strong sense of bewilderment. "Are you saying the physical part of marriage can be special and... enjoyable?"

"Of course."

Megan felt everything in her relax. Until she remembered the determined look on Logan's face. "Like I said before, my husband has vowed to remain a gentleman until I'm healed."

"Oh, dear." Mrs. Mitchell sighed heavily. "My son

is an honorable man, perhaps too honorable. He is incapable of going back on his word."

"That's why I love him."

"Ah, but do you want him to remain a gentleman?"

Megan thought about how she felt in Logan's arms. Their love might have transcended the physical for many years, but something had changed since his return.

And now, when Megan thought about how she felt when he kissed her, how her stomach flipped inside itself when his lips touched hers, well, she couldn't help but feel ready for more.

"No," Megan said. "I want Logan to make me his wife." *In the way God intended.*

"Wonderful." Mrs. Mitchell looked ecstatic at the news, as if she were already deciding the best ways to spoil her future grandchildren.

Megan felt the need to remind her of the most important fact. "I don't see how any of this will make a difference. As you so aptly put it, Logan is a man of his word. He won't change his mind on this."

"Then you're going to have to change it for him."

Chapter Seventeen

Logan left the stable ahead of his father. He needed a moment alone to sort the thoughts running through his head.

Tension weighed like a stone in his gut, slowing his steps as he made his way back toward the main house. He wanted to start a life with Megan, but as long as she failed to remember the events in Mattie's boudoir Kincaid's killer would remain a threat. Unless, of course, the man was someone Megan knew, someone who may have killed to protect her.

Logan picked up a small rock and rolled it around in his palm. If Megan didn't get her memory back soon, he'd have to return to Denver and restart the investigation. This time, he would consider *all* the possibilities, including the scenario that Megan knew the killer personally.

Tossing the pebble back on the ground, Logan looked to the heavens. A million stars dotted the cloudless sky, shiny diamonds against black velvet. He shifted his gaze to the mountains. Even at night he could make out the bold peaks standing like sentinels in the distance.

During his five-year absence Logan had forgotten a lot about life on the Flying M. He'd forgotten the messy, boisterous chaos of the Mitchell brood, the sweet smell of pine on the wind, the sound of the horses moving around in the corral, and the satisfying ache in his muscles after a long day of rounding up cattle.

He'd left to make his own way in the world, believing the Lord was directing him along a righteous path. Through the years, he'd caught countless outlaws and brought them to justice. Yet in all that time he'd never come directly in contact with his brother. He'd caught wind of Hunter's trail twice, only to come up a short both times. The man knew how to disappear. Especially when Logan was hard on his trail.

Feeling out of sorts and restless as he always did when his thoughts turned to his brother, Logan squinted into the night, past the corral and the outer buildings. The slam of the stable door alerted him to his father's approach.

"You chose well," Cyrus said, drawing alongside Logan at the bottom of the porch stairs. "Your wife suits you."

Mulling over his father's words, Logan sat on the steps and rested his elbows on his knees.

"Megan is the best thing that ever happened to me." She not only "suited" him, she made him whole. He didn't know what he'd do if he lost her. Which made it all the more imperative to keep her out of harm's way.

"I can see you're worried about her." Slapping his back, Cyrus settled on the steps next to him. "But she's going to be fine."

Too much had gone wrong already for Logan to let go of his concern that easily. Events had taken place that should have never occurred, *would* have never occurred had he come home sooner.

"I stayed away too long." He forced the confession through a tight jaw. "When I finally arrived I gave Megan no choice but to marry me. Then I yanked her away from all she knows."

"The woman I met doesn't appear to have regrets."

Logan wasn't so sure. There'd been a moment tonight—in the privacy of their bedroom—when Megan had looked at him with fear in her eyes. "She's afraid of me."

That earned him a dry chuckle. "Most new brides feel anxious around their husbands."

Logan shook his head. "It's more than that. I think the attack may have left her wary of all men, including me." *Especially me.* "She needs time to be left alone to heal."

He repeated the words he'd just said over and over in his head, hoping that was all there was to Megan's disturbing reaction to him.

"No, son, your wife doesn't need to be left alone. She needs you." Cyrus looked Logan directly in the eyes. "Do you understand what I'm saying?"

Logan shrugged.

"You have to convince Megan she can trust you, in all areas of your marriage. But it's going to take time. You have to be patient."

Logan's heart sank at his father's advice. When he was alone with Megan, when he was *kissing* her patience was not the first thing on his mind.

What if he couldn't find it in him to be gentle with

her? He'd always prided himself on being able to control his emotions.

But lately he hardly recognized himself. There were times when anger consumed him, others when passion for his wife nearly brought him to his knees.

If he let go in one area of his life would he be able to control all the others? "What if I'm more like Hunter than any of us realized?" he said. "What if I lose the power to control my urges, like Hunter did?"

"Your brother's tumble into lawlessness didn't happen overnight and it certainly involved more than a lack of self-control." Cyrus blew out a hard, frustrated puff of air. "Hunter made choices that led him down a bad road. When things got too hard to handle, his anger took hold until it became a part of him."

Precisely Logan's point. "If it happened to Hunter it can happen to me."

"That's not true." His father placed a hand on his shoulder. "Even as a boy, your brother never knew how to rein in his temper. You, on the other hand, always did. It's what makes you a lawman and Hunter a gunslinger."

Logan looked away from his father's admiring gaze. "I'm no different from Hunter. Not anymore. When I think about what happened to Megan—" he clenched his jaw so hard he thought his teeth would crack "—I seethe with rage. You have no idea how badly I want to give in to the violence running through me."

Cyrus dropped his hand and sighed heavily. "I admit, anger is a strong, seductive emotion. It can feel good to give in to it. But you're not that kind of man. You will conquer this."

Logan drummed his fingers on his thigh in a furious tap, tap, tap. "What if this time is different?"

"Then you turn this over to God. Go to the Lord in prayer, Logan. Ask for His help. He'll guide your way."

Trey Scott had given him similar advice. But how could Logan surrender to God now? He had too much rage in him, too much feeling, too much need.

The only solution was to maintain control. At all costs.

Anger, passion. Rage, desire. Two sides of the same coins. If he gave in to one, he sensed it would be easy to give in to the other. And then someone would end up hurt. Most likely Megan.

He couldn't take the chance. He couldn't hurt her any more than she'd already been hurt. He had to put a barrier between them. And if he couldn't do that, then he would leave for Denver. Sooner rather than later.

Megan would understand. Eventually. She'd probably thank him later.

If she was still talking to him.

Much to her chagrin, Megan woke up alone in her bed the next morning. Staring up at the ceiling, she tried not to allow disappointment to take hold of her. She'd failed miserably.

Pressing her fingertips to her forehead, she sighed. Logan hadn't come to bed until well after midnight. In fact, he hadn't come to bed at all. He'd slept on the floor. She'd been too shy to join him. And now regret filled her.

Burying her face in the crook of her arm, Megan sighed again. Something had to change. Logan had to stop treating her like she was going to break. The return of her memory was the surest way to change his behavior toward her. But Dr. Shane had said that could take days, weeks, maybe even months.

Megan couldn't wait that long. She needed to convince Logan that she was ready for the next step in their marriage.

But how?

She needed a plan, one that would put Logan's concerns to rest. First order of business, get out of the bed and dress for the day. That concrete act alone made her feel better, stronger, and now she was ready to face the day. And her husband.

An hour later, Megan sat on the front porch in yet another borrowed dress, *alone* with her thoughts and her new sketchbook. Despite her best efforts she still had no plan to make Logan see her as a woman of strength, not a victim of a terrible attack. She decided to relax and see if an idea would form on its own.

With that strategy in mind, she flipped to a blank page in her sketchbook. The paper was completely free of marks, waiting for her to fill it with charcoal slashes.

She loved this moment of discovery, loved making something out of nothing. At times like these, right before she began a new drawing, she felt most connected to her Creator. The God of the universe was bigger than her problems. *Lord, I give this up to you.*

Smiling at last, she made the first sweep of black on white and tried not to feel guilty for doing nothing more than sitting passively on the porch and drawing. At Charity House she only pursued her art after her daily chores were complete and the babies in the nursery were fast asleep.

Not that Megan hadn't tried to assist her mother-in-law this morning. She'd picked up a rag and had begun wiping away dust particles from the furniture in the living room. When Mrs. Mitchell caught her she'd shooed Megan out of the house with strict orders to rest her ankle.

Megan was sick of resting her ankle. She was sick of resting period.

She wasn't sure what Logan had told his mother about her final hours in Denver, but it was clear she would not be allowed to help with any chores until she was completely healed.

So here she sat, alone, attempting yet another drawing of the mountains. The pages of her sketchbook were filling quickly. With a bunch of half-finished artwork.

Lord, why can't I complete a picture? What's wrong with me?

"I will prevail."

Gritting her teeth, she kept her eyes on the mountains as her fingers flew across the page. Perhaps if she focused on the scenery instead of her art she would be successful at last.

Halfway through the sketch her fingers froze and her heart began throbbing painfully in her chest. Undaunted, Megan stiffened her spine and slowed her breathing. The headache came anyway.

For a frightening moment, Megan's vision blurred completely. The spot behind her eyes pounded like hammers to iron. Misty images beckoned for release. She squeezed her eyes shut, struggling to capture the memories that rode on the thin beams of pain but they were locked too deep in her mind.

A fresh spurt of anger tickled her throat. She was

sick of not remembering, of not knowing what had happened to her.

"I will prevail," she said with greater force than before.

Hunched over her sketch pad, she squeezed her eyes tighter shut. For the first time in her life Megan was afraid to view her own work. She must be strong. She *must* push past this pain and debilitating fear, or risk never healing.

She forced her eyes open and looked at the drawing below her fingertips.

Her vision refused to clear. She blinked. And blinked again. At last, the drawing came into focus. She'd captured the mountains well enough. Their magnitude and strength were evident on the paper. But at the lower right-hand corner of the page, there was the man again. He was always in the same spot. And just like every other time, the shadowy figure looked familiar.

With his broad shoulders, muscular chest and pair of six-shooters strapped to his lean hips he could be any number of men she knew. Sheriff Scott. Marc Dupree.

Logan?

Her mouth went dry. No. *No,* the man was not Logan. He was someone else. Someone—

A sharp pain sliced through her head, cutting off her last thought before it took hold. A sob escaped her lips.

She quickly flipped the page, happy to see pristine, untouched paper staring back at her once again.

Locking her concerns deep inside her mind, Megan began another drawing. Two strokes later a movement in the distance caught her attention. She recognized Logan at once. He was riding straight toward the house, straight toward her.

She drank in the sight of him. He sat tall in the saddle, confident. He'd pulled his hat over his eyes, perhaps shielding his features from the bright sun. A riot of conflicting emotions surfaced at the masculine picture he made. Joy, excitement, pleasure...*fear.*

Why did fear always twine through her other emotions when she couldn't see Logan's eyes? Or when he looked at her too intently. Her reaction made no sense.

Sighing, Megan looked down and discovered her fingers were drifting across the page. She was drawing Logan.

Still not looking at Megan, he dismounted and led his horse to the water trough. He took off his hat, slapped it against his thigh and then caught sight of her at last. He turned in her direction and smiled.

Their gazes connected.

She kept drawing.

"Hello, beautiful." He surged up the steps and dropped a light kiss on the top of her head. "How are you feeling this morning?"

While her fingers worked she studied his face, focusing on his eyes. His beautiful, mesmerizing eyes. "Better. No more swelling." She pointed to her ankle with the piece of charcoal.

He reached out, laid a hand on her booted foot in a show of comfort that was so innate to him. "Looks almost healed."

"It is." Her hand stilled on the paper. She lowered her gaze and sighed at yet another failed attempt. The eyes were all wrong.

"Can I see what you're working on?" His voice didn't sound quite right. There was curiosity there, yes, but some other emotion, as well. Something… calculating, perhaps?

"No." She slammed the book shut.

He lifted an eyebrow. "No?"

"I mean, not yet. It's not complete." Embarrassed at her inability to reproduce a likeness of her own husband, the man she loved with all her heart, she placed a palm flat on the book. "When I'm finished, I'll show you."

Ever the gentleman, he didn't press the issue.

It was only when he looked back over at his horse that she realized he was alone. At such an odd hour of the day. "Where are the others?"

"In the south pasture. Several calves were born last night."

His answer confused her even more. "Why aren't you helping with the roundup?"

"Pa ordered me back home." He gave her a sheepish grin. "He said a newly married man should be spending every free moment he had with his bride. Not with a bunch of cows."

Megan couldn't help but smile at the choice of words. It sounded so much like Cyrus Mitchell. "I think your father is a brilliant man."

"He would heartily agree." Grinning at her, Logan reached out, then quickly pulled his hand back and crossed his arms over his chest. "I have to check on the fencing in the north range. Want to come with me? We can bring a picnic lunch with us."

Yes, she wanted to shout. But before answering, she angled her head and tried to decipher her husband's strange expression. There was something in his gaze, something not at all gentlemanly and yet altogether thrilling. He blinked and the moment was gone.

Glory.

"I think a picnic is a grand idea," she said. No longer worried that she hadn't come up with a plan to convince her husband she was well enough to receive his attentions, she smiled broadly.

She had Logan all to herself. For the rest of the afternoon. With no possibility of interruption. As far as she was concerned, she owed her father-in-law a debt of gratitude.

Megan reached out to Logan. This time there was no hesitation in him. He took her hand and placed a light kiss on her knuckles.

That one, sweet, oh-so-familiar gesture coupled with the soft look in his eyes was all Megan needed to bolster her confidence even more. One way or another, she would not return to this house as Logan's wife in name only.

Chapter Eighteen

Logan helped Megan into the wagon they'd brought with them from Denver. Every decent thought he'd had on the way back to the ranch house, every noble intention he'd tried to cling to since arriving home disappeared the moment he touched Megan's hand.

Keeping his distance was going to prove impossible. Sleeping on the floor last night had worked well enough, but Logan wasn't sure how he was going to remain a gentleman when he and Megan were all alone, miles away from prying eyes. She was his wife. He wanted to love her, to—

An image of her in the jail cell insinuated itself into his thoughts. The memory of how fragile she'd looked, how wounded, cooled any desirous thoughts he might have had.

He couldn't be the source of any more pain in her life. He had to keep his hands to himself.

His father's suggestion to take his bride on a picnic had seemed innocent enough at the time. It was broad daylight, after all.

As if that mattered.

Cyrus Mitchell had known exactly what he was doing. The old man had some serious answering to do.

Trying not to frown, Logan joined his wife on the wagon's seat. Her beauty stole his breath away. Before he picked up the reins he gave in to temptation and closed his hand over hers. His thumb absently stroked the smooth skin of her palm.

Her eyes fluttered shut and she sighed. Something intense, almost dark ran though him at the happy sound.

He brought her knuckles toward his lips but stopped midway when he caught sight of her blackened fingertips smudged with charcoal. Was his plan working? Was she getting closer to discovering the identity of Kincaid's killer through her drawing?

"You've been busy this morning."

She grimaced. "I've attempted a few drawings."

Everything in him froze at the dejected angle of her shoulders. "Attempted? Does that mean you haven't completed a drawing yet?"

"Not one." Her tone told him how frustrated she was.

"Do you have your sketch pad with you now?"

She nodded.

"Maybe something will capture your imagination out on the range."

She made a noncommittal sound in her throat. He could tell the subject upset her so he let it drop and steered the wagon toward the north range.

Megan, for her part, studied the passing scenery in silence. A band of thunderclouds rumbled in the distance, but they would probably stall over the mountain peaks as they usually did this time of year.

Just in case, Logan redirected the wagon, turning the horse in the direction of the small guest cabin built for shelter during storms or other mishaps. He watched to see if Megan noticed the thunderheads in the sky.

As if sensing his eyes on her, she turned in his direction. She looked at him as though she had something important on her mind but wasn't sure how to say it. "Will you tell me about your brother?" she asked.

Everything in him froze and his skin turned ice-cold. "Which one?"

"The one nobody ever mentions."

He went numb at the question, but his shock was tempered with a strong desire to share his burden with the one person he trusted the most in the world. How could he expect her to trust him if he didn't trust her?

Drawing in a slow breath, he fixed a blank expression on his face. "How much do you know about him already?"

"Not much. I know he's not dead, but something bad happened, something that upsets your parents greatly."

Logan nodded. "He's an outlaw, Megan. A gunslinger."

"How can that be, when your family follows the Lord so faithfully?" Her brows pulled together. "There's certainly no lack of love in your household. Your younger brothers are a bit unruly. But they're full of mischief, not evil."

Logan wasn't surprised Megan was confused. Hunter had confused all of them through the years. "Maybe something inherent in Hunter made him go bad." Logan allowed his mind to drift back in time, to the days when he and Hunter were boys. "There were signs of his lack of conscience even back then."

"Signs?"

"He bored easily. When Hunter grew bored he took mischief to a whole new level. Often at the expense of others, never considering the consequences." Logan swallowed. His voice became a strangled whisper as he told her about the time Hunter had thrown a rock at Callie's head. "She was only five at the time."

"Oh, dear."

"When he was told to apologize, he claimed it was an accident and thus there was no need for an apology. Maybe that sort of lack of conscience was in his blood all along. Maybe bad blood runs in all of us, but only Hunter tapped into it."

"I don't believe bad blood runs in families." Megan's soft hand closed over his arm. "If that were true, I would have followed in my mother's footsteps long ago."

He turned to look at her. He *needed* to look at her. Their gazes locked, held. A thousand words passed between them without a sound. "Your situation is different," he said at last.

"How?"

He broke eye contact and focused on steering the wagon over a rocky ridge. "It just is."

"Logan, my mother chose her lifestyle because that's the one she wanted." Megan adopted a breezy tone, as if to deflect the seriousness of the situation. "She surrounded herself with others who chose similar lifestyles. I suppose it was easier for her that way. She needed to be among people living the same way she did."

"Bad company corrupts good character, is that what you're saying?"

"I suppose so. But it can go both ways. All of us want to be around people who think and act like we do. Outlaws surround themselves with outlaws. Christians surround themselves with Christians. It's hard to step away from that." She looked out over the scenery once more, deep in thought. "I know I'm that way. There were times when I had to force myself to walk into Mattie's and read to the women who choose to live so differently from me."

Logan wasn't sure what he heard in her voice? Sorrow? Guilt? "Do you ever regret going into Mattie's?"

She didn't answer right away, but continued looking out over the land. "I don't know. I'd like to say no, I don't regret offering what comfort I can to someone in need. I'd like to say serving fulfills me, and despite what happened to me that night I'd still go back. But I just don't know."

Logan wanted to tell her he didn't want her to walk into Mattie's ever again, but he wasn't sure that was right thinking. Maybe serving the Lord wasn't supposed to be easy or comfortable or safe. Maybe serving the Lord was messy and dangerous because *life* was messy and dangerous.

When Logan shared his thoughts aloud, Megan didn't argue but turned quiet, thoughtful. "I think you might be right. I can't allow one incident to scare me off."

"No, you can't." He reached over and patted her hand. "That would go against the Megan I know."

She pulled her hand away and shook her head fiercely, as if trying to rid her mind of the disturbing thoughts their conversation had stirred up.

"When did your brother leave home?" she asked. "Was it right after he hit your sister with the rock?"

The quick change of subject took Logan off guard, but only for a moment. "No, but not long after that. It's been ten years since he left. He and I had a fight." Logan instinctively battled against the memory but it came anyway. "I don't remember what we argued about, probably something insignificant. But Hunter's anger had a different feel to it that night. Fists flew. Hard words were exchanged. The next morning he was gone." Logan pulled the wagon to a halt fifty yards shy of the cabin. He hadn't realized they'd covered so much ground. "He never returned."

"Was that the last time you ever saw him?"

"No." Logan stared straight ahead, remembering the last time he'd seen Hunter had been right before he'd become a deputy marshal. "Our paths crossed about a year later. Not that Hunter would remember. He was passed out drunk in a brothel."

"Glory." It wasn't shock Logan heard in Megan's voice, but compassion. "Did you try to sober him up? See what had gone so wrong to send him into such a state?"

Shamed by her questions, Logan lowered his head and fiddled with the reins still in his hands. "I left him there to rot in his own sin."

The words came out harsh and surprisingly regretful.

Looking back, Logan realized how selfish and self-righteous his response had been. He should have tried harder to reach out to Hunter. At the time Logan had been too angry, too humiliated that his own brother had sunk so low. A part of him had also been afraid he'd end up like his brother if he got too close.

"I failed him." He knew that now, accepted it.

"Oh, Logan." Megan's voice held nothing but understanding. "You were so young."

Yes, he'd been young, not yet twenty, but did that absolve him? Hunter was his brother. He'd abandoned the man without a single thought. As he'd just told Megan, life was messy. People were messy. And family was often the messiest of them all.

"I left home soon after that night," he said. "I needed to leave, needed to work out my own convictions in my own way."

A clap of thunder shook the air. Logan looked to the sky, glad for the distraction sweeping in overhead. He'd miscalculated the clouds. They were upon them. "Rain's coming in fast."

With a tender smile, she reached up and smoothed her fingers across his forehead. "Then we better find shelter fast."

Her touch raised a powerful reaction in him. Hunter was no longer foremost in Logan's mind. A wistful longing for his wife pulsed through him. "Follow me." He helped her out of the wagon. "The cabin's just over there."

The first raindrop plopped at Megan's feet. A crack of thunder soon followed. Three more drops landed in succession on her nose and then the clouds let loose. The scent of rain carried a strong hint of grass and earth.

"Hurry, Megan." Logan hugged her to him, taking the weight off her ankle.

Two more steps and he scooped her into his arms. They were soaked to the bone after three more steps.

Megan could feel the tension in Logan. Speaking of his brother had left him sad.

Hustling inside the cabin, Logan shut the door behind them with the heel of his boot.

He set her feet on the ground then stepped back.

Megan wrapped her arms around her middle and blinked into the dark. The smell of ash from a recently extinguished fire hit her first, before her eyes had a chance to adjust.

"Wait here." Logan swerved past her. He made quick work of lighting a lantern then turned his attention to the fireplace. Checking the pile of wood next to the hearth, he nodded in satisfaction.

"I'll get a fire started right away. But first…" He pulled a blanket off the sofa and wrapped it around her shoulders.

She tried not to shiver from his touch.

Looking distracted, he dropped an impersonal kiss on her cheek then crossed to the fireplace again.

While Logan built a fire, Megan moved deeper into the cabin. The room was a nice size, not too small, not too large. The furniture was large and bulky with lots of blankets thrown over the edges. The rugs looked well-worn, the colors a nice blend of browns and deep blues.

"What is this cabin used for?"

"We originally built it in case we ever got stuck out on the range during the spring roundup," he said over his shoulder. "There's another one in the south pastures. We only use the cabins if the weather isn't suited for sleeping outside."

"Has someone stayed here lately?"

"Possibly." He rose, stared into the small fire cracking to life then turned and grabbed another blanket. "Why do you ask?"

"I don't know." She looked around, took note of the way the furniture had been moved to face the fireplace and how the stove looked recently clean yet the smell of food lingered in the air. "It feels…" She searched for the right words. "This cabin feels lived-in."

Logan circled his gaze around the room. "Could have been one of the ranch hands out mending fences." His eyes narrowed. "Or a squatter."

A squatter?

As though sensing her alarm, Logan wrapped the additional blanket around her shoulders. "Don't worry, sweetheart."

She shivered anyway.

"No one will harm you here," he said. "You're safe with me. We're completely alone."

Oh, yes, they *were* alone, with nothing but the rain to keep them company. No longer concerned with squatters, a plan formed in her mind, one that involved a little action on her part.

Could she be so bold?

Megan trembled at the possibilities.

Misunderstanding her reaction, Logan stepped away from her. "You're cold. We need to get you out of those wet clothes."

Ah, the perfect opening. "Or maybe—" she closed the distance between them again "—we should both get out of our wet clothes."

Before Logan could respond she laced her fingers behind his head and urged his lips toward her. He remained perfectly still, praying for strength, but then Megan pressed her mouth harder against his.

Something in him broke.

He gripped her shoulders, deepened the kiss, then tore his mouth away and set her out of his reach.

"Logan," she whispered.

"It's hot in here." He looked desperately around him, pulled on his collar, ran his hand through his hair. "Really, really hot."

"Logan? Have I done something wrong?"

"No. I'll be back."

"Where are you going?"

"Out...uh, outside."

"But it's raining."

Yes, it was. Logan looked everywhere but at his wife. If he looked at her, if he stayed in this cabin one more minute, he was going to do something both of them would regret. Megan more than him.

He headed for the door. "I'll be back," he repeated.

"Logan, please." Her voice shook. "Don't leave like this."

"I have to." He couldn't hold on to his control much longer. He needed air. He needed distance.

He needed to keep his back to her as long as possible. No eye contact.

"Is it me? Do you not find me pretty?"

He heard the hurt in her voice and it nearly broke his heart. "I think you're beautiful."

"Then, tell me what I did wrong."

He spun back around and sucked in his breath at her hurt expression. The one he'd caused. He pulled her against him. "No. No, Megan, you didn't do anything wrong. You have no idea how badly I want you." The admission slid past his lips before he could stop it. "I ache for you."

She rubbed her cheek against his shoulder. "Then make me your wife."

"I...*can't*."

She angled her head to look at him. Her blue eyes brimmed with hurt and confusion. "I don't understand why you're refusing to be with me."

He cupped her cheek and his whole body shook from the effort to maintain his self-control. "I don't want to hurt you any more than you've already been hurt."

"You couldn't possibly. I trust you, Logan."

The exact words he needed to hear, but he could not relent. He touched the wound at her neck. Purple bruising surrounded the angry red slash of skin. "I can't risk making matters worse for you."

She shoved out of his embrace. "I won't break. Stop treating me like I will. I'm strong."

His father had said the same thing, but Logan couldn't take that risk. Even if Megan looked angrier than he'd ever seen her, a fact that evaporated the breath in his lungs, he was not going to relent.

"Sometimes, I think..." She stomped away from him then swung back around. "Do you love me, Logan?"

"Yes, of course, I love you." A surge of distress made his declaration sound like an accusation. "I would do anything to protect you, even lay down my life."

She lowered her head and sighed. "Wanting to protect me isn't the same as loving me."

"It *is* the same." He practically growled the words at her. How could she not understand? "One cannot exist without the other."

She didn't look convinced.

"I don't want to hurt you." Even to his own ears, his argument sounded less convincing than before.

His control was slipping.

"How do you know you'll hurt me?"

Of their own volition, his hands reached to her.

When he gripped her waist, he lowered his forehead to hers. "I can't risk making you my wife, Megan. Not when it could have devastating consequences."

His words held no conviction now. She was in his arms, practically reclining against him and all he could think was how good it felt having her close, how right.

She fit perfectly in his arms. The light in the cabin took on a golden glow.

"Oh, Logan. What if…" She boldly pulled his head toward hers, but didn't press her lips against his. He could feel the whisper of her breath on his face. Something more than desire spread through him. Warmth, homecoming, wholeness.

She combed her fingers through his hair. "What if it…our being together…helps?"

Before he lost all control, Logan gazed into Megan's beautiful blue eyes. This was the woman he'd adored since he was more boy than man. He loved her desperately and wanted to be with her for a lifetime. They would build a family together, starting today.

The soft look in her eyes told him she wanted him in the same way.

He gently kissed her lips and the rightness of his decision washed over him. He would do the right thing here, the godly thing. He would *finally* make Megan his wife.

Chapter Nineteen

The afternoon passed in a pleasant blur. If Logan had only himself to consider, he and Megan would have stayed in the cabin long after the rain had stopped. But his wife needed a hot bath and dry clothing far more than she needed another round of—

He cut off his train of thoughts and focused on the fatigue he saw in her eyes. The fatigue she'd just tried to deny when he'd ushered her out of the cabin and helped her into the wagon.

At least she waited to reopen the argument until after he'd settled in beside her on the seat.

"I'm really quite fine, Logan." Her voice carried a pleasant, husky tone, making her sound sleepy and satisfied and altogether lovely. "It won't be dark for hours. Couldn't we stay a little while longer?"

The selfish part of him wanted to do exactly what she suggested. But he couldn't. *They* couldn't. "Please, Megan." He gripped the reins until the leather bit into the flesh of his palms. "Humor me this one time."

Before she could argue again, he leaned over and kissed her full on the lips.

She relaxed into him and made a soft sound deep in her throat, which brought on a whole new collection of ideas. Ideas that had nothing to do with returning to the main house and *everything* to do with walking back into that cabin with her in his arms.

By the grace of God, Logan broke the kiss.

Megan leaned her head on his shoulder and sighed. He loved that sound, had heard it often in the last few hours and would love to hear it some more.

No.

He flicked the reins and set the wagon in motion.

They made the trek back to the main house in a happy glow of companionable silence. But the mood shifted the moment he pulled the wagon to a stop and his mother rushed off the front porch to meet them halfway.

"Look at you two," she said. "You're soaked to the bone."

"We got caught in the rain," Logan said unnecessarily as he hopped out of the wagon and strode around to Megan's side. Smiling up at her, he wrapped his hands around her waist and lifted her to the ground.

She kept her hands on his shoulders a bit longer than required.

A moment of solidarity passed between them, a silent message of understanding that went far beyond words. Then Megan shivered.

"Ma, can you help Megan get out of her wet clothes and into a hot bath while I take care of the horse and wagon?"

"Well, of course. Oh." She clicked her tongue in a motherly show of concern when she got a good look at Megan's face. "You look ready to drop, my dear."

"I'm really quite fine, Mrs. Mitchell." She stifled a yawn behind her hand. "But a hot bath does sound lovely."

"Then come with me."

Before his mother spun her away from him, Logan kissed his wife on the lips one last time. "I'll be up after I take care of things here."

She blushed prettily. "I like that idea."

"I'll hurry."

As he watched his mother lead Megan up the porch steps, his heart tumbled in his chest. She was his wife now, in every sense of the word. They'd had a perfect afternoon together. Sweet, romantic, exactly as he'd always envisioned. Smiling—he couldn't stop smiling—Logan unhitched the horse from the wagon and led the old girl into her stall.

He picked up a brush and began grooming the wet fur. His hands worked from habit, while his mind drifted back to the afternoon with his wife. He and Megan were bonded in body, soul and mind now. Best of all, he hadn't hurt her during their time together.

But had he helped?

Only time would tell.

For now he would focus on his next step. Finding Kincaid's killer, so he and Megan could move on with their life together. Even if it meant discovering someone he admired had murdered the outlaw, Logan wouldn't rest until he found his answers.

Scowling now, he hung the brush back on its hook and went about the chore of filling the mare's bin with oats. Again, his hands worked from memory while his mind filled with other thoughts.

Tonight would be his last opportunity to be with his

wife before he left. They'd only had three days together. He wanted more time with her, especially now, after the closeness they'd shared this afternoon.

The sound of his mother's purposeful footsteps cut through his musings. This time, Logan smiled for a very different reason. Annie Mitchell walked like a person who knew her own mind.

"Your wife is exhausted," she said in a neutral tone from behind him. "But blissfully happy."

Glad he had his back to her, Logan tried not to let out a whoop of joy. "That makes two of us."

"Indeed."

Not liking what he heard in his mother's tone, Logan turned around to face her.

Her left eyebrow lifted the barest fraction, but enough to tell him she knew what had occurred in the cabin.

In a purely defensive gesture Logan threw his hands in the air, then dropped them just as quickly and did what any man would do in the same awkward situation. He changed the subject. "I'm heading back to Denver in the morning."

Digesting his words in silence, his mother followed him out of the stable and helped him secure the latch. "Will you be taking Megan with you?"

"No." He pressed his fingertip to his temple and rubbed. "She's safest here with the family."

Nodding, his mother set a comforting hand on his arm. "Your father and I will take good care of her while you're gone."

Although the promise should make him feel better, Logan's discomfort increased. "I hate leaving her so soon."

"That's perfectly understandable."

He drummed his fingers on his thigh. Was this what the rest of his life would be like? Would he be destined to love Megan one day, only to leave her the next?

Without realizing what he was doing, he increased his pace. "I don't know how long I'll be gone."

Used to fast-walking men, his mother matched him step for step. "Isn't that part of a marshal's job? Leaving for extended periods of time?"

"It is." He sounded as gloomy as he felt. "I've condemned Megan to a life of wondering whether I'll return alive or with an outlaw's bullet buried in my chest."

"She knew what she was getting into when she married you."

But had *he* known? Had he been prepared for the pain he would inevitably inflict on the woman he loved?

Logan stopped at the top of the porch steps and turned to look out over the land. The valley, riddled with wildflowers, led to a line of aspens that swayed gently. The breeze whispered through their leaves in an almost musical swish. Logan's heart filled. This was his home. This was where he belonged.

He'd been homesick for years, and hadn't realized it. Now that he was married to Megan, the thought of leaving her for weeks at a time, of being away from the Flying M, his home, depressed him more than it should.

"Maybe it's me who doesn't want to leave Megan," he admitted.

"Logan." His mother directed him to sit on one of the chairs while she did the same. "Tell me why you became a lawman."

The question took him by surprise, especially coming from his own mother. "You *know* why."

She rocked back and forth. The annoying sound of the creaking chair set him on edge. "Maybe I want to hear it in your own words," she said.

"I became a lawman because I wanted to help people, to see justice served, to…prove I wasn't like Hunter."

Continuing to rock, she lowered her gaze to her hands. But not before Logan saw the sadness in her eyes. "You didn't have to become a U.S. Marshal to do that last part. You've always been a good man, Logan." She looked back up. "It's inherent in you to do the right thing. It's perhaps your greatest strength and your one true character flaw."

As harsh as her words were, they held no sting in them. Nevertheless, he winced. "How can following a righteous path be a character flaw?"

"When you rely only on yourself and your own abilities, you refuse to admit you're human, with human frailties." She fiddled with the edges of her apron. "You aren't in control, Logan. God is."

"I know that."

"Yet you've spent your entire life trying to be your own Savior."

"That's not true." Was it? He thought back over his life, over the choices he'd made, to the control he'd demanded of himself and others. How many times had he turned to God for help in the last ten years? How many times had he admitted he couldn't do something—anything—on his own?

Never.

He'd never asked his sovereign Lord for help.

In that moment, he was painfully aware that he'd always believed in God but had never *relied* on Him. Why should he have done so when he'd been successful relying on himself? Successful, he reminded himself, until the events of the last three days.

Logan jumped to his feet and started to pace. Trey had told him to surrender to God. His father had told him the same thing. Now his mother was chiming in with a similar message.

He needed to think this through. But not here, not with his mother watching him with those wise eyes of hers. Not when he knew he had to walk inside this house and tell Megan he was leaving her again.

Flattening his lips, Logan paced toward the edge of the porch. A walk around the corral wouldn't be a bad idea.

Unfortunately, his mother wasn't finished with him. "Here's something else to consider while you go off by yourself and brood over what I said."

Logan braced himself.

"Your father and I want to give you and Megan a wedding present."

"You…" He spun around so fast he had to take an extra step to catch his balance. "You what?"

"We want to give you a gift."

Logan gaped at his mother with disbelief. In the span of a heartbeat, she'd gone from giving him a spiritual lecture to offering him a wedding gift. Where was the logic in that switch? He stared at her for several more seconds then shook his head. "Opening your home to us is more than enough."

"That's just family being family." She flicked her wrist in a dismissive gesture. "What your father and

I want to do is deed a thousand acres of land on the north range to you and Megan."

Logan's breath stuck in a spot between his heart and his throat. "That's some of your best land. It's too generous."

Smiling at him tenderly, she rose and cupped his cheek with her hand. "It's a gift, Logan. You don't get to decide if it's too much or not. Just say thank you."

"Thank you," he repeated.

"Your father will be home soon to discuss the particulars."

Logan blinked down at his mother. He couldn't deny he wanted the land. He wanted it badly enough to say yes right there on the spot.

But how could he take Megan away from Charity House, from her friends, from all she knew? He'd just accepted a promotion so he could provide for her in Denver. "There's a lot to consider," he said. "I don't know if I can acc—"

"Don't answer yet." She dropped her hand and stuffed it in the pocket of her apron. "Talk it over with your wife before you say anything."

"I… I…" He was too dumbfounded to do much more than stutter. "Yes… I will."

"The land is yours no matter what you decide to do with it." She kissed him on the chin, then walked into the house ahead of him.

Logan rocked back on his heels. He felt amazed. Bewildered.

But most of all, *blessed*.

Megan wondered what was keeping Logan. Her bath had grown cold a long time ago. So cold, in fact, that she'd been forced to dress or suffer a worse chill than before. Apparently her husband had decided to give her privacy, perhaps allowing her to ease slowly into the new aspects of their marriage.

She didn't need time to get used to the change. Megan loved what had happened between them. She'd never dreamed marriage could be so lovely or that she could be so happy. She was at long last Logan's wife, completely, irrevocably. No turning back.

Hugging her arms around her middle, she stared out the bedroom window and smiled. *Thank You, Lord. Thank You for guiding Logan and me into a closer relationship.*

A dozen images of Logan ran through her mind. Megan picked up her sketchbook and turned to a blank page. She needed to capture the tender way he'd looked at her this afternoon, when it had only been the two of them alone, sharing nothing more than the glow of the fire and each other's company.

Logan's eyes had held countless emotions in them, and an undeniable affection that spoke of his deep love for her. Her heart pounded like the wild wind just thinking about what they'd done in that cabin together.

They'd crossed an invisible line, not just a physical barrier but something…more. It was the two of them against the world now, and no matter what life threw their way they were a single unit. A team.

Afraid she would lose the image of Logan's love for her, she worked quickly. When she focused her attention on his eyes, her movements slowed. But there was no headache snaking through her brain this time. Only urgency. And an all-consuming need to get the image of her husband correct this time.

She was nearly finished, the eyes almost there, when the door opened with a soft creak. She looked up from her work just as Logan sauntered into the room, his gait smooth and relaxed, reminding her of the man she'd known all those years ago.

He looked happy and her heart swelled with joy. *She'd* put that smile on his face. Their stares connected with a force that nearly flattened her.

Suddenly shy, she set aside her sketchbook and rose to greet him. "Hello, husband."

"Hello, sweet wife." His eyes shone with love, but his tone sounded a bit…odd.

Megan moved closer, her steps tentative as she took a slow breath. Before she drew in a second, he was kissing her with an intensity that surprised her. When he pulled away his eyes were guarded. What could have put that change in him?

"Logan?" Her chin trembled. "What's wrong? What's happened?"

He moved to his left. Shadows fell across his face, curtaining his expression. "I want us to start our life together without anything standing between us."

"That's my hope as well," she said carefully.

"Then you understand why I have to leave for Denver in the morning." He sounded as sorrowful and unhappy as she felt at the news.

Nevertheless, her heart sank. After this afternoon, Megan had hoped he would find it difficult to walk away from her. "So soon?"

His shoulders tensed as he strode to the window and rested his hand flat against the glass. "I have to find Kincaid's killer. I want this over," he ground out. "For us both."

She stood frozen in place, staring at his back, trying to pinpoint what she heard in his voice. "I want that, too."

"Then you understand why I have to go back now."

Not really. There was something he wasn't telling her. "Maybe you could explain it to me."

He pushed away from the window and started pacing through the room. Back and forth. Back and forth. Every few steps he shot her an odd look, one filled with ambivalence, as if he was trying to sort through several conflicting thoughts.

"My father has a theory about your memory loss." He changed direction and headed straight toward her. "The more I consider his suggestion the more I agree he's probably right."

Her knees suddenly felt wobbly and she lowered to the edge of the bed. "What is this theory?"

Logan sat next to her. There was genuine agony in his eyes. "He thinks you might know Kincaid's killer and that's why you can't remember what happened in Mattie's boudoir."

His words staggered her. "That can't be." She blinked up at him, her hand clutched around her throat. "Do you truly subscribe to that…theory?"

"You must admit, from a certain perspective, the idea holds considerable merit."

She folded her hands tightly together in her lap in the hopes they would stop trembling. "It makes no sense at all, not from any angle."

She could not believe, *would* not believe that anyone she knew could kill.

"We know Kincaid tried to attack you." Logan touched the wound at her throat, swallowed several times, then lowered his hand. "Perhaps whoever else entered that room did so to rescue you from the outlaw. Does that sound..." He looked intently in her eyes. "Possible?"

Megan shook head.

"Think, Megan." Without warning, he pulled her against him and stroked her hair in a slow, mesmerizing rhythm. "Think back to that night and try to remember what you saw."

Lulled by his touch, she closed her eyes and tried to recall the events of that evening. Only misty images floated through her mind, images too muddled to make out clearly.

"I don't remember a thing. Oh, Logan." She gripped his shirt in her fist. "My mind is too fuzzy. The memories simply aren't there. And now my head hurts."

"I'm sorry, Megan." Logan kissed her hair. "We won't talk about this anymore. Why don't you close your eyes and rest a while. We can talk later."

"No." She scrambled off the bed. She wasn't going to cower from whatever was hidden in her mind. Not anymore. *Not. Anymore.* "I want to remember what happened to me."

He stared at her for a long moment without speaking. "But your headache."

"Please, Logan. Let me try again."

He nodded slowly. "All right."

"You said you think I might know the killer. Do you have someone in mind?"

He nodded again, but didn't respond right away.

When several seconds ticked by and he still didn't

answer, Megan lost her patience. "Well? Who do you think it is?"

"Your guardian, Marc. Marc Dupree."

Chapter Twenty

"No." Megan staggered away from Logan. "Not Marc." Horror filled her eyes. "He could never kill a man. *Never.*"

Logan thought about Marc's odd behavior the day he'd shown off Megan's paintings. The man had been unusually nervous. Logan had chalked it up to guilt, guilt over failing to protect Megan. But what if it had been more, what if Marc *had* killed Kincaid? "It's possible."

"No. *No.* Marc is a godly man. He taught me that all the ways of the Lord are loving and faithful and that we're supposed to love our enemies. He wouldn't murder an innocent man."

"Kincaid wasn't innocent." Logan knew he had to be careful with his words, but Megan wasn't hearing him. No, she was *refusing* to hear him. "I've seen men do far worse when it comes to protecting their family. And for all intents and purposes, Megan, you are Marc's family."

She shook her head vehemently. "Even if Marc had come upon us, even if he had killed Cole in an attempt to protect me, he would have never left me alone in Mattie's boudoir. He would have taken me with him."

Logan had thought of that, had found hope in the possibility, but there was enough suspicion to implicate Marc. And Logan couldn't ignore any possible scenario just because he wanted a man that he admired to be innocent of murder.

"And besides." Her eyebrows slammed together. "Marc wouldn't have allowed me to go to jail for something he did."

"You make a valid point, Megan, but I still have to question Marc directly."

She pulled her bottom lip between her teeth. "What if he did kill Cole? Then what?"

Logan looked away from the hurt in her eyes, the accusations. "Then I have to arrest him."

She gasped. "Even if he did it to protect me?"

"Yes."

"Even if killing Cole saved my life?"

Logan swallowed. Seconds ticked by before he could answer her question. If Marc had saved Megan's life, no matter what that entailed, Logan would want to give the man a medal. But matters were never that simple. Murder was *always* complicated.

"I'm a lawman, Megan. Sworn to uphold and protect. I have to do what the law dictates, even if it goes against what I want to do or what I *feel* is right."

"You would arrest the man who raised me, the man who was a father to me most of my life?"

"I would ensure he was given a fair trial."

She regarded him with an appalled stare, giving him the impression she considered him unreasonable.

Logan couldn't blame her for that. This was a hard

conversation for them both. But he was not one to shirk his duty. If Marc was guilty, Logan would arrest him.

Heavyhearted, he rose and strode to the door but stopped with his hand on the knob. "I'll let you rest your head for now. I'll—" he swallowed hard "—see you in the morning. I'll have my mother bring up a tray of food for you."

He waited for her response, half hoping she would call him back to her and they would talk this through, maybe come to some understanding that would relieve the tension between them.

"Yes, Logan." She let out a choked sob. "I think that's best."

He shut the door behind him with a final click.

The next morning Megan awoke to a muddy, gray dawn and a pounding headache. She hadn't slept well. Nor had Logan returned in the night, though she'd prayed he would come back to apologize, to tell her he'd been dreadfully wrong to accuse Marc of murder.

They'd both gone to bed angry. As a result, she couldn't escape a vague sense of rejection.

Let not the sun go down upon your wrath.

Megan had done the opposite. But so had Logan.

Maybe it wasn't too late to fix this mess between them. Surely her husband hadn't left for Denver yet, not without telling her goodbye. She climbed out of bed and quickly dressed.

She found Logan in the kitchen, alone, staring into a mug of strong-smelling coffee.

"Good morning," she said softly, her voice skipping over the words.

He looked up and held her gaze. Exhaustion was

etched in his features while his red-rimmed eyes told of his own sleepless night.

She wanted to erase the sorrow she saw in his eyes. Their argument suddenly seemed smaller in the gray light of dawn. She loved this man. They just needed to talk matters through, come to an understanding that would satisfy them both. Give and take, wasn't that the basis of a strong, godly marriage?

"Oh, Logan," she reached to him, "I'm sorry I let you leave our room angry."

He was out of his chair and pulling her into his arms halfway through her short speech. "No, Megan, I'm the one who's sorry."

They held each other fiercely.

"I don't want to fight with you," she said, clinging to him harder still. "I don't ever want to go to bed angry with you."

"Never again." He kissed her then, with the turbulent emotion of someone who'd nearly drowned but had just been rescued at the very last moment.

"Let's go upstairs," he whispered in her ear. "And I can show you how sorry I am."

She felt her eyes narrow in feminine triumph. "I like that idea."

He chuckled then set her away from him. "Afterward, we can talk about the situation with Marc while I pack."

"You're still determined to go to Denver this morning? Can't you wait—" She broke off, realigned her thoughts. "Until my memory returns?"

"No, Megan. I can't." He gave her one long, frustrated stare. And they were right back where they'd started. "I've been hired as the U.S. Marshal of this territory. I have to fulfill my duty."

"You mean arrest Marc."

"Maybe. Maybe not. I won't know until I review all the facts once again."

Megan swallowed three times. Each time a hot ball of dread expanded in her throat. Maybe if she was with Logan when he confronted her guardian she could prevent an unspeakable tragedy. "Take me with you."

"You'll be safer here."

She turned cold with foreboding. Something deep within her told her that if she let Logan out of her sight, if she let him leave now, nothing would ever be the same between them. "Please, Logan. I should be with you when you question Marc. It might help me remember what happened."

"It might hurt. I can't take that risk." His eyes darkened. "You're my wife, Megan. It's my job to protect you."

She gasped. "How can you say that? When you're heading back to arrest Marc for protecting me?"

"I didn't say I was going back to arrest Marc. I'm going back to get answers."

So cold, Megan thought. Who was this cold man? "Do you really think your notion of protection is any different than Marc's?"

"You're intentionally misunderstanding me."

"Am I?" She rose onto her tiptoes so she could look him eye to eye. "If you had been the one to come across Kincaid when he was attacking me..." She ignored his flinch and continued. "What would you have done?"

"That's not a fair question."

"It's a valid one. Logan, I'm not as fragile as you

think. I can handle whatever happened that night, even if it means discovering that I know the killer personally."

"If that were so then you wouldn't have lost your memory in the first place."

She reared back as though he'd slapped her. "You think that little of me? That I'm so weak-minded I can't face the truth?"

He rubbed a hand down his face and let out a weary burst of air. "Megan, I don't think you're weak-minded, however—"

"However?"

"However—" he gritted his teeth "—you were attacked by a very bad man." He glared at the wound on her throat. "That sort of trauma would make even a strong-minded person buckle."

His words told her what he really thought of her. She was only a woman to be protected, not loved. "Why did you marry me, Logan?"

Her question obviously took him off guard. "What?"

"Tell me why."

"Because I love you. I've always loved you. From the first moment I saw you." He started to lift his hand to her, but dropped it when he caught her expression. "I waited five years to claim you as my bride."

Five. Long. Years. By the end of that time, Megan had feared he would never come back. That he would find someone else. Or maybe quit loving her altogether. The reality was so much worse. "Why didn't you come home sooner? Why did you wait so long?"

"I needed to make my own way in the world. I needed to be able to provide for you and our family."

She lowered her head and blinked back the tears

welling in her eyes. "Your mother told me about their wedding gift."

"What does that have to do with this?"

"Everything." She lifted her chin until her gaze met his again. "You could have brought me here years ago."

"Your life is in Denver."

"My *life* is with you. It's always been with you, even when you were a thousand miles away." She stopped, drew in a careful breath and began again. "You don't love me, Logan, not really. You only love the image of me you've created in your mind."

"How can you say that after yesterday, after what we shared in the cabin together?"

"I forced your hand."

"No, Megan." He knuckled a lock of her hair off her cheek. "You didn't force me to do anything I haven't wanted to do for years."

She desperately wanted to believe him. "Then stay here just a few more days, and help me regain my missing memory."

"I have been helping you. That's why I bought the sketchbook for you."

"What?" It was her turn to be thrown off guard.

"I figured that if you started to draw at your leisure you might eventually come across an image from that night, one that would unlock the rest of your lost memories."

A hysterical laugh bubbled in her throat, but she shoved it down with a ruthless swallow. She'd thought the sketchbook had been a simple gesture of love, a confirmation of his admiration for her talent.

How could she have been so foolish?

Her tears begged for release. She let them come, let them fall unchecked down her cheeks.

"Megan, please." Logan's voice filled with genuine horror. "Don't cry."

Unashamed of her tears, she stared at him through her watery vision.

"Don't look at me like that."

"How am I looking at you?" She swiped at her cheek with the back of her hand.

"Like I've just broken your heart."

"You have."

He lifted his hand.

She shifted to her left.

He frowned, but didn't reach for her again. "I was only trying to help you," he said. "I had nothing but good intentions."

"You'll have to excuse me if I don't believe you." She didn't bother hiding the hurt in her tone.

"Don't be cynical," he said. "That's not you."

"How would you know what is or isn't me?"

"I *know*."

He was wrong, so very wrong. He only knew her as he wanted to see her. A woman who needed his protection, a weaker individual than himself. She might as well have been made of china and placed on a shelf. "You'd best start packing if you want to make it to Denver by noon."

He opened his mouth to speak but was cut off by the sound of his mother's voice coming from the other side of the door. "I'm telling you, Cyrus, I heard something."

"You're mistaken, Annie," came the gruff reply. "It's too early for anyone to be up."

"I know what I heard."

Before either Logan or Megan could school their features into blank expressions the older two Mitchells swept into the kitchen.

"Oh." Logan's mother came to a swift halt. "I knew I heard voices, I..." She let her words trail off and angled her head. In the next moment, her brows pulled together in a frown. "Well, then, we'll just leave you two alone to finish your conversation. Take all the time you need."

Her manner was light and breezy, but she gave her son a warning glare before turning Cyrus around and marching him out of the kitchen.

Megan rushed forward to stop her in-laws' retreat. "No. Stay, please." She focused on a speck just over their heads. "Logan and I are through."

Letting out a sharp hiss, Logan moved forward. "No, we're not." His boot heels clicked on the parquet floor right before his hand rested on her shoulder. "Megan and I still have a few matters to discuss before I leave for Denver this morning."

Before I leave.

Megan struggled to control her temper as she turned to face her husband. A battle seemed to wage behind his eyes, as though he didn't know what to say next. His confusion almost melted her anger. Almost.

"Will you take me with you?" She held her breath. It wasn't fair to put Logan on the spot in front of his parents, but she might not have another chance.

"It's too dangerous." His eyes took on the hard, determined look she'd seen too often since he'd found her in jail. In the past four days that look had been enough to send a shiver of fear running through her.

This time, a surge of anger reared. Anger so strong her entire body shook.

Nevertheless, she found the inner strength to speak calmly. "Can we discuss this further?"

"I've made my decision. You will stay here, under my family's care."

Megan sighed at his imperious tone. He hadn't heard a word she'd said this morning.

Bella used to tell her a woman could stand anything if she prayed hard enough, hoped long enough and loved well enough. But looking at Logan's unrelenting expression now, Megan feared he would forever see her as nothing more than an object to protect. Not his wife. Not his partner in life, just a weak woman in need of a strong man to take care of her.

"Well, then, I suppose I'll see you when you return."

She walked out of the kitchen without another word.

Chapter Twenty-One

Later that morning Logan guided his horse through the streets of Denver. He barely took note of the bustling activity around him. His mind was back on the ranch. With Megan. Before he'd mounted up, he'd tried to reason with her. But no matter in what direction he maneuvered the conversation she'd refused to speak about anything other than the weather.

Prior to their argument, he'd thought nothing could be as heart-wrenching as Megan's tears. He'd been wrong. Her anger—anger at *him*—was far worse.

Why couldn't she see he loved her, as a man was supposed to love his wife?

Hadn't Jesus himself said, "Greater love hath no man than this, that a man lay down his life for his friends"?

There was no way Logan could love his wife and not want to protect her. Trust, faith, laying down one's life, weren't they all rooted in the nature of love?

Frustrated with his own thoughts, he took a ragged breath and turned his horse down Larimer Street. No good would come from brooding so he cleared his mind and focused on what had brought him back to Denver—finding Cole Kincaid's killer.

Taking the final corner, Logan entered one of the most exclusive neighborhoods in Denver. Modern gas lamps sat atop ornate poles on every street corner. Each house he passed was more elegant than the one before. He reined in his horse outside Charity House and dismounted in a single swoop.

For a moment he studied the orphanage from his vantagepoint on the street. Despite the grubby clouds that swallowed the pristine sky above, the structure was awe-inspiring with its clinging vines, stylish brick and soft angles. A safe haven in a fallen world.

Had one of the people living in this house killed to protect Megan?

There was one way to find out.

Logan bounded up the steps, taking them two at a time. He knocked, but no one answered. He pushed open the door. "Anyone home?"

"Back here," a familiar voice answered in return, "in my study."

Logan wound his way through the labyrinth of corridors on the main floor. He had to fight the urge to rush his steps. Even the homey scent of baking bread couldn't pacify his impatience. He didn't want Marc to be guilty of murder. Then again, if he *had* killed Kincaid, Logan would no longer have to worry about Megan's safety.

Lord, Logan prayed, *let truth be revealed here today. Give me the wisdom and clarity to know what questions to ask.*

Taking a deep breath, he pushed open the door to the study. Marc sat behind a sturdy mahogany desk, reviewing what looked like a ledger. The man looked like a respectable businessman, not a killer.

Marc set down his pen and leaned back in his chair. "Logan. This is a surprise. I wasn't expecting you today. Is Megan with you?"

Logan's heart pinched tight in his chest. He wasn't in the mood for pleasantries, but a certain amount of finesse was required before he jumped right in and accused his wife's guardian of murder. "She's back on the ranch and growing stronger every day."

"Praise God," Marc said. He steepled his fingers under his chin and studied Logan with the kind of penetrating stare that belonged to a man used to controlling tense situations.

Marc Dupree was no pushover.

But was he a killer?

"What brings you back to town so soon after your wedding?" Marc asked.

"I'm here on official business," Logan said. "I have a new theory about Megan's memory loss."

Marc lifted a single eyebrow. "Indeed."

Considering Marc was as much a father to Megan as any man, Logan decided not to mince words. "I believe she knew the man who killed her attacker and that's why her mind has shut off the memory. To protect him."

"Ah." Placing his hands flat on his desk, Marc leaned forward. "I take it you have a theory as to who that person might be?"

Logan gave him one swift nod. "Did you kill Cole Kincaid to protect Megan?"

"No, I did not." Marc's mouth flattened. "But given

the opportunity, I wouldn't have hesitated slamming a knife through that blackguard's chest."

"Where were you the night Kincaid was murdered?"

"He was with me all evening," a soft feminine voice said from the doorway. "Here, at the orphanage."

Logan shifted in his chair and faced Laney Dupree, Marc's wife of ten years. She was dressed more casually than her husband, wearing a simple green dress with a white lace collar. Her dark, mahogany hair was pulled into a fashionable bun. As she walked deeper into the room she moved with an inherent grace that reminded Logan of his own wife.

"Did anyone see you two together that night?"

"About forty children of different ages," she said, her eyes filled with a mixture of chagrin and amusement. "Logan, please, you can't possibly think my husband killed a man."

"I believe he would stop at nothing to protect the children in this house."

Laney whisked around the desk and placed her hand on her husband's shoulder. "I can't disagree with you on that. Nevertheless, Marc was with me the night of the murder." She held Logan's gaze without flinching. "Would you like to interview some of the children to check out our story?"

"That won't be necessary." Logan rose.

Marc did the same.

The realization that the man was undoubtedly innocent should have pleased Logan. He should feel relieved that Marc Dupree, a man he admired, hadn't committed murder. But deep down, in the dark place where Logan feared most for Megan's safety, he'd hoped Marc had done the deed. At least then she would be out of danger.

Panic tried to gnaw at his control. He replaced the useless emotion with ruthless grit and forced his mind to consider the facts rationally, logically.

There was something he was missing, some vital piece to the puzzle that was just out of reach.

"If you think of anything that might help me uncover the killer's identity," he said, "send word."

"We will." Marc walked out from behind his desk and placed a comforting hand on Logan's back. "Where can we find you?"

The only logical place. "Mattie's brothel."

Mattie made Logan wait over an hour in the main salon before deigning to see him in her private boudoir. By the time he followed her bodyguard through the kitchen, Logan's patience had vanished.

He reviewed the last conversation he'd had with Mattie. One sentence kept coming back to him. *Dig too deep into this murder, Marshal, and you may not like what you find.*

At the time, Logan had assumed Mattie was simply being her usual difficult self. But now he wasn't so sure.

Whatever her reasons, Mattie hadn't wanted Logan to discover the identity of the murderer. Which could mean a number of things, none of them good.

Jack stopped outside the door to Mattie's private suite of rooms. "Go right in. She's expecting you."

Right. The ornery woman had been *expecting* him for almost an hour.

Logan took a deep breath and reminded himself why

he'd come here today—to find Kincaid's killer. One way or another, he was not leaving this house until he knew everything Mattie had hidden in that devious brain of hers.

Arranging his features into a blank stare, he strode into the boudoir. The outrageously clad madam reclined on her brocade divan. Regardless of what she thought, pink was not a good color for her.

"Ah, Marshal. What a pleasant surprise to see you again. And so soon after our last meeting. To what do I owe this honor?" She stretched out her hand to him, which he patently ignored.

"You know why I'm here."

"Of course." She sat up and patted the spot next to her. "Do tell me how my Megan is fairing."

He had to give the woman credit. She'd asked about Megan right off the mark. "My wife is doing quite well, thank you."

"How is she taking to ranch life?"

Before answering, Logan thought back over the past few days. "She's...thriving." It was the simple truth, a truth he hadn't taken the time to explore until now.

"Ah, yes." Mattie gave him a satisfied nod. "I suspected she would find happiness there."

"You did?" He asked the question before he realized the words were out of his mouth.

"You obviously don't know your wife very well if you find that surprising. Megan is a good girl with simple tastes. She was never meant to live in a city like Denver."

Logan resented the implication that she, a notorious madam, knew Megan better than he did. "I won't speak of my wife with you any further. I'm here to discuss Kincaid's murder."

"I was wondering how long it would take you to bring up that unfortunate business."

Unfortunate business? "Mattie, a man was murdered right where I'm standing. *After* he attacked an innocent woman."

"Ah, yes, a very regrettable series of events, wouldn't you say?"

Her patronizing tone set Logan's teeth on edge. "I think the reason my wife lost her memory is that she knew Kincaid's killer."

Mattie twirled a lock of her hair around a finger. "I didn't see the murder, if that's what you're asking."

"But you know who did it." He made sure to phrase his words as a statement.

Laughing again, she unfolded her legs, stood slowly then went to her desk and unlocked the top drawer.

"I came for answers, Mattie," he said to her back. "I won't leave until I have them."

She pretended not to hear him. "It might interest you to know I've gathered the list of clients that were here that night, just like you requested." She handed him a sheet of paper. "One name in particular might surprise you."

Eyeing her with suspicion, Logan took the list. He held her gaze a moment longer before lowering his head. Four names down, he stopped.

"Judge Kavanaugh?" The man who was single-handedly attempting to rid Denver of prostitution?

She chuckled. "A woman likes to keep her enemies close."

"So it would seem."

"The judge might be a hypocrite but he's no killer. Keep reading, Marshal."

Halfway down the list Logan's gut rolled inside itself. His mouth went dry. *Lord, no, it can't be. Not him, dear God, not him.*

The paper slipped from his fingers.

Mattie picked up the list off the ground and began fanning herself with it. "I took the liberty of listing our mutual friend's real name. We'll call it a wedding gift."

Fury, shock, a multitude of other emotions rushed through Logan. The identity of Kincaid's killer had been right in front of him all along. Megan's memory loss, her inexplicable fear of him, her shrinking from his touch when he'd first arrived.

She'd never been fragile or brittle or disturbed by the trauma of witnessing a murder. Deep down, locked in her memory, was the fear that Logan had killed Kincaid. Megan's mind had been protecting him.

But Logan wasn't the killer. It was someone who looked like him, someone with his same features, his same eyes. His brother, Hunter.

Logan knew what he had to do now. For the sake of justice, for Megan's safety as well, he had to hunt down and arrest his own brother.

Chapter Twenty-Two

Heavyhearted and full of regret, Megan sat on the front porch with her sketchbook in her lap. Sally Mae lay at her feet, enjoying the commotion in the front yard from a respectable distance. The twins were playing a raucous game of tag. Shaky Jake, as usual, thought it was a game that included him. Cyrus and Garrett threw well-aimed rocks at various targets from measured distances.

Mrs. Mitchell rocked in the adjacent chair, watching over her brood in much the same way Sally Mae did. With patient indulgence. Although Megan was happy to be a part of this family, her heart wasn't in the moment. Her heart was in Denver, with Logan.

She shouldn't have allowed him to leave without trying to settle matters between them.

She sighed heavily over all she would have done differently, given the chance.

Her mother-in-law looked over at her. "Want to talk about it?"

"Logan and I fought. And now I feel as if there's a big gaping hole inside of me."

She nodded. "The first fight is the worst."

"I don't want to argue with Logan." She thought about the violence he faced as a lawman. She could lose him on any given day. She must remember that, and never, *never ever,* allow him to leave angry, or sad.

"A certain amount of discord is inevitable in any marriage," Mrs. Mitchell added. "Especially in the first year."

Megan swallowed. "Do you know what we argued about?"

Her mother-in-law shook her head.

"I told Logan I wanted him love me for *me*, not some unrealistic image he has of me in his mind."

"That sounds reasonable."

"His idea of protection is…well, it's just smothering."

Instead of being offended, Mrs. Mitchell patted her hand. "Logan is protective by nature. He needs time to get used to the woman you've become. After all, you two have been separated for five years. There's going to be a settling-in period, a time where you'll both have to get to know the older versions of yourselves. Once you do, I predict your love will be stronger."

If only Megan could believe that. "How can you be so sure?"

"By the way you look at one another. Have faith, Megan." Mrs. Mitchell smiled at her, as a mother would smile at her daughter. "The Lord will direct your way, if you let Him. You just have to believe. In God. In love. In each other."

Wise advice. Hard to do.

Nevertheless, she closed her eyes and silently prayed one of her favorite Bible verses. *Lord, I believe. Help me with my unbelief.*

Feeling marginally better, she opened her eyes, only just realizing her fingers had been working of their own accord. She'd finished another picture of Logan. Except...

The eyes were all wrong. They were too hard, too unforgiving and entirely too ruthless. Logan never looked at her with that much anger. Not even at his fiercest.

As she traced the lines around the man's eyes her thoughts grew thick and uneasy.

The sketchbook slid to the ground.

Shimmering images flooded her thoughts. A knife coming at her, pressing against her throat. The smell of stale whiskey. A threat. Anger, her own, so strong she thought it might consume her. A hard shove. A loud crack. A door swinging open.

"Megan? *Megan.* What's wrong?"

Her mother-in-law's words seemed to come from very far away.

"I..." She flattened her hand against her temple. "My head hurts."

"Did you remember something?"

"My sketchbook." She looked frantically around her. "Where is it?"

Mrs. Mitchell lifted the book off the floor and glanced down at the drawing. Her brow furrowed. "When did you meet Hunter?"

"Who?"

"Hunter. My eldest."

"I've never met him."

"This picture," Mrs. Mitchell pointed to the opened page of the sketchbook. "You've captured Hunter perfectly."

Megan blinked down at the drawing. No wonder she hadn't been able to draw Logan's eyes correctly. The man in the picture wasn't her husband.

With an odd sense of distraction, she studied the image again. Where had she seen the man in the drawing? When?

Like a bolt of lightning coming out of the sky everything fell into place in her mind. Logan's brother had been the one who'd entered Mattie's boudoir. He'd argued with Cole. There'd been a tussle.

Shuddering, Megan looked up at Logan's mother. There was pain in the woman's eyes, the kind of pain that said she suspected where Megan had seen her son and what he'd done.

Megan opened her mouth to explain, or maybe to apologize, but she couldn't make the words form in her mind in the proper order. She had to sort through her thoughts, had to force her mind to remember every detail of that night in Mattie's brothel.

She leaped to her feet. "I need to…" She turned toward the house. "I'll be in my room."

"Megan, wait," Mrs. Mitchell said. "Sit back down. Please. We'll talk about this calmly."

"Not yet." Her eyes begged for her mother-in-law to understand. "I just need a little bit of time. Alone."

Without waiting for a response, Megan rushed inside the house. But the air was too stifling in there, too confining. She swerved toward the kitchen and left quickly out the back door.

Once outside she picked up her pace. She didn't know where she was going, but found her feet heading toward the cabin where Logan had taken her yesterday.

Had it been only a day since they'd shared their mutual love for one another?

Practically running now, she stayed parallel to the tree line, using the mountains as a natural compass to help her maintain her bearings.

She swerved around a fallen branch and then collided into a hard wall of unforgiving muscle. "Oh."

She looked up. And up farther still. Until her gaze connected with...

Hunter.

Glory. The man who had killed Cole Kincaid was standing right in front of her. He'd come for her after all, just like Logan had warned.

She opened her mouth to scream, but his hand covered the sound.

"Can't have you alerting the folks I'm here," he said in a harsh whisper.

Megan's head swirled with images of the night she'd last seen this man. Hunter hadn't killed Cole in cold blood, she remembered that now. He'd made the outlaw stand, had even given him a knife to defend himself. It still hadn't been a fair fight. Not with Cole drunk from alcohol and wobbly on his feet from a head injury.

"We can do this the hard way or the easy way," Hunter said, breaking through the images running through her mind. "Promise not to scream."

Megan nodded.

He removed his hand from her mouth.

She broke eye contact and tried to decide her best route of escape. She might have said she wouldn't scream, but she'd never said she wouldn't run.

In the next heartbeat, she took off in the direction of the main house. Before she'd gotten far Hunter scooped her off the ground and then tossed her over his shoulder. "The hard way it is."

She squirmed, trying to break free but he tightened his hold on her, gripping her so hard the breath whooshed out of her lungs.

"Don't worry, *Mrs.* Mitchell. My brother is a smart man. I predict he'll be coming to rescue you very shortly."

Everything in her froze. "You aren't going to hurt Logan, are you?"

"That, my dear girl, will be entirely up to him."

"What do you mean Megan is gone?" Logan growled out the words through clenched teeth.

His parents shared a look before his mother stepped forward and touched him on the sleeve. "She was upset. She asked for a moment alone. I'm sorry, Logan. She must have slipped out the back without us knowing."

Maybe she'd just gone for a walk. Maybe Hunter hadn't come for her. The despair curling in Logan's throat and clogging the air in his lungs told a different story.

"Before you go searching for her, you should know what upset her." His mother handed him Megan's sketchbook.

"Turn to the last page," his father urged.

Fearing what he'd find, Logan flipped quickly through the book, barely taking note of the various drawings. Until he noticed a pattern. There was a shadowy figure in all the scenes, a man that looked a lot like Logan, but not completely.

His hand stopped turning pages as his gaze connected to a picture of him just outside the cabin. His eyes were full of love and adoration. It was as though Megan had looked straight into his heart and captured his feelings for her.

His mother leaned over him and sighed wistfully. "Everything's going to be all right between you two."

Logan nodded. Yes, everything would work out between them. He would see to it, even if it meant begging her forgiveness every day for the rest of their lives.

"There's one last drawing." She flipped the page for him. "*This* is what upset Megan."

Just as it had when he'd seen Hunter's name on Mattie's list, Logan's heart picked up speed and his mouth went dry. The look of anger and hatred in his brother's eyes was unmistakable. Megan had seen Hunter clearly. Too clearly.

This cabin feels lived in, she'd said yesterday.

Logan had foolishly told her not to worry. He'd believed they were completely alone. They had been at the time. But the cabin had definitely been lived in.

Hunter had been the squatter.

How could Logan have missed something so simple, so basic? By bringing her to the Flying M, he thought he'd brought his wife to a safe place. Instead, he'd put her straight into the heart of danger.

Fighting against his own panic, he took off at a dead run, jumped back on his horse and headed north.

"Logan, wait," his father called after him.

"I'm going to get my wife back."

He just prayed Hunter hadn't gotten to her first.

Twenty minutes later Logan caught sight of the smoke coming from the cabin's chimney, calling to him like a beacon. He pushed his horse harder.

For the first time in his life, Logan feared he

couldn't protect Megan. *Lord, help me. Help me protect Megan from Hunter.*

Mere feet from the front door, he jumped off his horse and burst inside the cabin. The room was cast in shadows, with only a small portion illuminated by a fire in the hearth. Despite his inability to see well, Logan was aware of everything in the room with sharp-edged clarity—the snap of the fire, the smell of pine, the sound of heavy breathing. His own?

"Megan." He shot his gaze in every direction. "*Megan,* where are you?"

"Over here." The sound of her voice nearly flattened him, but he managed to turn in her direction.

All his fears vanished the moment he saw her face. Although shadows fell over most of her body, Logan could still make out her expression. There was no fear in her eyes.

"Megan." He started toward her, but stopped cold at the sound of a shotgun's hammer clicking into place.

"Stay right where you are, little brother."

Logan swung in the direction of the voice. Alert, watchful, *angry,* he focused on the barrel pointed at his heart. He'd been so concerned about Megan's safety he'd made an amateur lawman's mistake. He hadn't checked to make sure the cabin was clear.

Desperation had made him stupid. And now Megan was in danger.

"We aren't brothers." He all but spat the words, then lowered his gaze over Hunter. He noted the look of strain in the lines around his eyes and mouth. "No brother of mine would hurt the woman I love."

Hunter's eyes went dark and turbulent. "I haven't

hurt your wife. Go on. See for yourself. But first, re-move your weapons."

Logan calculated his next move. If he jumped Hunter he'd have the element of surprise on his side. But even if Logan managed to avoid catching a bullet in his chest, Megan could be hurt. Logan unstrapped his gun belt and lowered it to the ground.

"Kick it over to me."

Growling, Logan did as requested.

Hunter grinned at him. "*Now* you may check on your wife."

Still holding Hunter's gaze, Logan inched toward Megan. At the last minute, he broke eye contact and dropped in front of her. He rested his hands on her knees and took a good look at her. She was tied to the chair in a manner that secured her arms against her waist.

"You tied her up," he said, struggling to control his temper.

"Couldn't have her running back to the folks." He chuckled. "Your wife certainly has...spirit."

Before Logan could tell Hunter to leave his wife out of this, Megan's voice cut through his thoughts. "Lis-ten to what your brother has to say," she urged. "His story will surprise you."

Logan's hands clenched into fists at his side as he rose to confront his brother. "Did you kill Kincaid?"

"The man had it coming." Hunter's gaze turned hard and unrelenting, his gun still pointed straight at Lo-gan's heart. But when he stared into his brother's eyes, Logan did not see an outlaw. Rather, he saw a man stricken with grief.

"Did you kill him to protect Megan?"

"She had the blackguard subdued before I arrived." He looked over at her with a hint of admiration.

"Then why'd you do it?" Logan took a miniscule step forward.

"Don't come any closer," Hunter warned.

Logan complied midstep. "Why did you kill Kincaid?" he repeated.

"He murdered my wife." Hunter's gaze turned haunted.

"You got married?"

"Five years ago."

"Cole attacked your brother's wife, in the same way he attacked me," Megan said when neither man spoke again. "But she wasn't able to fight back because she'd just had a child who'd died in her arms. She was too weak to defend herself."

Logan's heart tumbled in his chest. "Is that true?"

Hunter nodded. His eyes were so wounded Logan knew there was no doubting the story. "I've spent the last two years hunting the bast—" he looked over at Megan "—er, outlaw."

Sadly, Hunter's tale was not a new one. Logan had spent much of his career tracking men like Kincaid. He'd brought most to justice. "You should have let the law handle it."

"Would you have?"

"I *am* the law."

"We both know you wouldn't have waited for a trial to determine the outlaw's fate."

Logan didn't argue the point. But he wasn't the one who had to face up to his actions. He wasn't the one who'd killed a man.

Despite understanding why his brother had murdered Kincaid, vigilante justice was never the answer. "There are laws in this land for a reason."

"Justice was served."

"Now who's kidding himself? What you did to Kincaid wasn't about justice. It was about vengeance."

"And what, Logan? Vengeance is God's alone?" Hunter sneered at the sentiment. "Always taking the righteous path, huh little brother?"

Logan ignored the goading tone. He knew his duty. There was no joy in the knowledge, only a deep sense of regret.

"I have to arrest you, Hunter." He shook his head sadly, wanting to rage in frustration at the unfairness of the situation. "But I'll do whatever it takes to make sure you get a fair trial."

"You know I can't take that chance."

Before Logan could make a move, Hunter rushed him. The last thing Logan heard before his world went black was Megan's scream.

Chapter Twenty-Three

Logan wasn't moving.

Please, God. Please, Megan prayed. *Don't let him be dead.*

Swallowing back her panic, she focused all of her efforts on the rope securing her to the chair. Hunter had positioned the knot at an awkward angle, which required extra concentration on her part.

Her arms protested in the twisted position in which she held them. Megan ordered herself to relax, to focus only on freeing herself and not on the pain in her cramping muscles, or on the fact that Logan was... still. Not. Moving.

The knot slowly released, enough for Megan to wiggle out from under the rope. Free at last, she dashed to her husband.

"Logan." She knelt beside him, ran her fingers across his cold forehead. Fear unfolded in her chest, crowding out the breath in her lungs. He looked terribly pale. Too pale.

Had his brother killed him?

Oh, Lord. Please, let Logan be alive. It was the most desperate prayer of her life.

"Come back to me," she whispered, tears running down her cheeks. The force of her love was so fierce it nearly blinded her. "Logan, do you hear me? Wake up."

She placed her hand on his chest, felt the slow rise and fall of his breath and blew out a sigh of relief. "Still alive."

He murmured something incoherent, moved his head around, moaned heavily and then—*finally*—he opened his eyes.

"Oh, Logan. Praise God." She dropped a kiss to his lips. "Welcome back."

Wincing, he reached up and touched her wet cheek. "Don't cry, sweetheart."

She blinked back her tears. "Can you sit up?"

"Won't know till I try." He lifted slowly to a sitting position but then cupped the back of his neck. "My head is pounding." She could see him struggling through the pain.

Gripping his shoulders, Megan supported his weight while he caught his breath. Eventually, he pulled himself to a standing position, took two unsteady steps then collapsed on the sofa with a hiss.

Megan sat beside him and lightly touched his arm. "Where do you hurt?"

"My head." He rubbed his palm over his temple. "What happened?"

"Your brother hit you with the butt of his gun."

"Right." He took a ragged breath of air then looked furiously around the cabin. "Where's Hunter?"

"Gone. And if I'm not mistaken—" she gave him an apologetic grimace "—he took your horse with him."

"Smart. It's what I would have done." There was no respect in his tone, only a sad note of acceptance.

Megan moved her hand to Logan's chest. His heartbeat was stronger, steadier. Wanting a more personal connection, she leaned forward, hoping to place her cheek next to her hand, but he stopped her progress midway.

"Hunter tied you up. How'd you get free? Did he let you go before he left?"

"I freed myself." She motioned to the pile of discarded rope now lying on the floor.

"You freed…" His eyebrows pulled together in confusion. "Yourself?"

"You weren't moving, Logan. I didn't know if you were alive or dead. I *had* to get to you, make sure you were all right." She gave him a frustrated glare. Really, did he not know her at all? "I'm perfectly capable of heroic feats when the situation warrants."

He continued staring at the rope. Wonder eventually took over the confusion in his gaze. "Of course you're capable. I never should have doubted you or your ability to take care of yourself. Or me, when the *situation warrants.*"

She cupped his cheek and smiled into his eyes. "Is that an apology?"

"No, this is." He tugged her onto his lap and pressed his forehead against hers. "I'm sorry for misjudging you. You are a strong, beautiful, capable woman in your own right. You are amazing, spectacular, worthy of poetry. Songs should be written in your honor. You are the sunshine of my life."

Who knew her husband could be such a romantic? "Well, I—"

He kissed her on the lips, cutting off her words. "I'm sorry for not taking the time to get to know the real you." He pulled away and rubbed the back of his head. After a moment, some of the pain left his eyes. "I was wrong to hold on to the image of you I'd created in my head while we were apart. That wasn't fair to either of us."

"Well, now, that's an even better—"

He kissed her again, this one lasting longer than the first. When he pulled away a second time, they were both gasping for air.

"Most important of all, I'm sorry I waited five years to make you my wife."

"Oh, Logan, apology accepted." She lowered her gaze as her own remorse reared. "But you aren't the only one to blame for our misunderstanding. I was too proud to let you take care of me. I've spent so many years fending for myself I had no idea how to surrender to someone else's strength, even when I needed to."

"Apparently, submission comes hard for us both."

"Well, I for one made a promise to live with you in the holy state of matrimony as God ordained it," she repeated the words from their marriage ceremony with fervor. "That means there has to be a certain amount of give and take on each of our parts. I'm good at giving, but I still have to work on the receiving portion of the Lord's command of me as your wife."

He touched the wedding ring he'd put on her finger less than a week ago. "I promise not to overdo the protection portion of His command for me as your husband."

He seemed truly remorseful. It took a very strong

man to admit he was wrong. Was there any wonder why she loved this man?

"I like you worrying about me," she admitted. "I like knowing you will protect me in times of trouble. It's just that, for the last few days, you've—"

"Smothered you with my notion of protection?"

"Maybe you did overdo it a bit." She kissed his lips then scooted off his lap so she could look at him directly. "I don't want you to stop caring for me. I just want you to remember I won't break under a little adversity now and then."

"I won't forget. And if I do, simply say the word *rope* and I'll remember how you untied yourself while I was lying on the ground completely subdued and unconscious." The tender, honest way he looked at her confirmed the truth far more than his words. Her husband finally saw her as she was today.

Megan wanted to pull him to her, but now that he was fully alert she steered the conversation in a more difficult direction. "What about Hunter?" Her lips quivered with the compassion and pity she felt for her brother-in-law. "Are you going after him?"

Logan sat motionless for a long while, his gaze locked on the cabin's door. "No," he said at last. "Hunter will eventually be caught and brought to trial, but not by me."

"Surely you understand why he killed Cole."

He rubbed a hand down his face and released a long burst of air. "No matter how much I sympathize with his reasons, Hunter killed a man. I'll have to write up a report. Wanted posters will have to be hung across the territory. But I'm going to let another marshal track him down."

"I'm sorry, Logan." The sorrow in his eyes was so real, so mournful, Megan's heart broke for her husband. "I can see how hard this is for you."

"Hunter is my brother. My family. I allowed myself to forget that over the years. Maybe if I'd have reached out to him that night in the brothel he wouldn't have become what he is today."

"You mean a man grieving the senseless death of his wife?"

"No." He shook his head sadly. "I don't begrudge him that. What I can't ignore is that he resorted to vigilante justice. He broke the law. The law I'm sworn to uphold."

"Logan—"

"Don't worry, Megan. I won't turn my back on him again. When he's caught, and he will be caught, I'll ask for leniency and do everything in my power to ensure he receives a fair trial." He fell silent.

Megan could practically hear his mind working through the rest of his thoughts. She didn't press him further. Instead, she switched the conversation yet again. To a much happier subject. "You realize where we are. And what we did the last time we were here."

His gaze darkened with an altogether different range of emotions. "I remember."

"Do you also remember which one of us took matters into their own hands when the other one was being overprotective and...smothering?"

"Yes, Megan. I remember." Grinning now, Logan pulled her back into his lap and buried his face in her neck. "I love you, sweetheart."

"I love you, too." She wrapped him tighter against her. "So very much."

For a moment, they simply held each other. But Logan knew the time had come to discuss one last matter. "There's something else we need to talk about," he said.

"Oh?" She gave him a saucy swish of her shoulders. "Sure it can't wait?"

He looked over at the crackling fire and swallowed. If his head wasn't pounding he'd forget everything except showing his wife just how much he loved her. Then again, his head didn't hurt *that* much. Their discussion could wait.

He reached to her, then quickly dropped his hand. No. They needed to clear the air between them first. "My parents' wedding gift," he blurted out. "We have to decide what we're going to do with the land."

She sat up straighter. "You're asking for my opinion?"

"You're my wife, Megan." He took her hand. "My partner in life. Every decision we make from this day forward we make together."

"Oh, Logan." She wrapped her arms around his neck and kissed him soundly on the lips. "If I wasn't already married to you, that speech would have sealed the deal."

There was such satisfaction in her eyes, such joy, he forgot what they were talking about and merely basked in the moment. His head was feeling better by the minute.

"What do *you* want to do about the land?" she asked, her tone serious as she scooted back to her side of the sofa. "Tell me the truth."

Had she asked him that question a week ago, Logan

wouldn't have known what to say. Today, however, he knew exactly what was in his mind. And his heart.

"I want to work the land," he admitted. "I want to build our family here, together, on this ranch, in our own house. I want to stand by your side every day and spend every night in your sweet arms. I want to watch our children grow and mature into godly adults because we were good examples as individuals *and* as a couple."

When he finished speaking, she stared at him for several long seconds. Logan saw the hope in her eyes, and the hesitation, as well. "But you've spent years making a name for yourself as a lawman," she said. "You would walk away from all that to be with me here?"

"Yes."

"Why? When you're so obviously good at what you do?"

"Being good at something doesn't make it a life calling." He held her gaze, trying to communicate the truth that was in his heart. "I believe God has a different plan for me. *For us.* And it's here, on this land. Unless that's not what you want."

"As long as we're together, I'll be happy."

"I need to hear you say the words, Megan. Tell me what you want."

"I want to work hard with you and play harder," she began with a dreamy look in her eyes. "I want to laugh well and often. I want to turn to God in times of need and praise Him for our blessings. And no matter how rough or messy life becomes everything will seem easier because we're together."

Logan's heart swelled with satisfaction. But he had

to be sure she knew what she was leaving behind. "What about your friends in Denver?"

"Denver isn't so very far away," she reminded him.

"A short distance on horseback," he said.

"Precisely."

"So what do you say, Mrs. Mitchell?" He went on bended knee and took her hand, the one with his ring already on it. "With God as our guide, will you be the love of my life? Will you bear my children and let me stand by your side always?"

"Yes, Logan. Oh, yes."

"Will you let me protect you, and our children for the rest of our lives?"

She frowned. "I—"

"Within reason, of course."

"Well, since you put it that way. Yes, my handsome husband. *Yes.*"

He stood, then pulled her up to join him. "Will you love me until death do us part? As I will love you?"

Lifting on her toes, she kissed him on the chin, the cheek and then firmly on the lips. "I wouldn't want it any other way."

Epilogue

One year later

Megan reached out her arms to her mother-in-law. "I can take her if you need a break. She tends to get fussy at this time of day."

Making a sound of dismissal, Mrs. Mitchell swung around until her back faced Megan. "Go away," she shot over her shoulder. "I'm having a private conversation with my granddaughter. Isn't that right, little Janie?"

Knowing her sweet, two-month-old baby couldn't possibly engage in a "conversation," Megan nevertheless indulged her mother-in-law. "Pardon me." Her lips twitched, but she kept a serious tone. "Do carry on."

She watched as the older woman headed toward the blanket they'd spread out earlier for their family picnic. Her mother-in-law whispered secret promises Megan knew she would do everything in her power to keep. Because that's what family did for one another.

Full of unspeakable joy, Megan spun in a circle, silently thanking God for the many blessings he'd bestowed on her in the past year.

Thank You, Lord. Oh, thank You.

Arms outstretched, she breathed in the fresh scent of pine on the light breeze blowing across her face. The sound of hammers pounding nails made her smile all the more.

She turned toward the noise and looked up in time to see her husband, his three younger brothers and their father set their hammers on the ground. They stepped back as a unit to survey their work. It looked as though they'd completed the last section of the frame for Megan and Logan's new house. When finished, their home would be a smaller version of the one where Logan had grown up.

"I'd say we've earned ourselves a break," Cyrus said with a slap of satisfaction on Logan's back.

Before Logan could agree with his father, a loud whoop rose up from the three younger boys. Giving Cyrus no chance to change his mind, they rushed off to the open field and proceeded to engage in a rousing game of tag. Really, Megan thought, it was a wonder no one ever got hurt.

Logan turned and caught Megan's eye. Smiling, he sauntered toward her with a lazy, relaxed gait. "Hello, beautiful." He kissed her firmly on the lips.

"You've done some excellent work already," she said, hitching her chin in the direction of the house.

"It's going to be a fine place to raise our children."

"Speaking of which." Megan tried for a stern expression, but failed miserably. "Your mother is already spoiling our daughter."

"Is she now?" He didn't seem overly concerned.

"I'm pretty sure I heard her make a few outrageous promises, including one that would involve a trip to Paris when Jane comes of age, just like the one she'd given Jane's aunts before they'd gone off to finishing school."

That made Logan scowl in a way that warned Megan his mood had shifted. "No Paris. That city is full of Frenchmen."

She tried not to laugh at his overprotective tone. "*Men* being the operative word?" she teased.

"Precisely." His scowl deepened as he watched his mother playing with their daughter on the blanket.

In hopes of distracting him, Megan cupped his face and kissed him on the lips, making sure their mouths stayed connected long enough to ensure he forgot everything on his mind, especially Frenchmen.

He came up sputtering. "What were we talking about again?"

"Our new home." She steered him toward the unfinished structure. "It's going to be beautiful, Logan."

"And large enough for us to have lots and *lots* of children."

"I like the sound of that."

He wrapped his arm around her shoulders and smiled up at the structure with her.

Settling against him, Megan sighed happily. "When do you want to get started on those other children?" she whispered low enough for only his ears to hear.

His grip tightened. "How about later tonight?"

"Perfect."

"But no more girls," he said in a stern voice. "Our little Jane is killing me."

"She's only two months old."

"And I'm already dealing with Frenchmen."

Megan laughed at him. She couldn't help herself. He looked so handsome when he was flustered.

"Stop laughing. Boys are easier. *Boys* I understand."

Garrett chose that moment to rush up behind him and swat him on the shoulder. "Tag, you're it."

With lightning speed, Logan reached out and tapped Garrett on the back before he could make his getaway. "You're it again," Logan said with the superior tone only a big brother could pull off.

Garrett spun around and gaped at him. The look in his eyes was so forlorn, so full of grief, Megan was reminded of the last time she'd seen the oldest Mitchell. Hunter's gaze had held a similar expression.

When Garrett shuffled off, muttering something to his other brothers about Logan cheating again, Megan decided it was time to ask her husband about his trip to Denver the previous afternoon. "What did you find out about Hunter?"

"His trail has dried up again." Logan shook his head. "The marshal was a day behind him, just one day, when all signs of Hunter evaporated. It's like he vanished into thin air."

"You're relieved." She heard the truth of it in his voice.

"I guess I am."

"We'll keep praying for him."

He nodded. "That's all we can do at this point."

"I'm sorry, Logan."

"Me, too." When he turned and put both his arms around her waist she felt the sadness in him, hated that she'd been the one to put it there by asking about his brother.

"Come with me." She tugged on his hand. "Let's go rescue our daughter from her doting grandmother. Before the woman makes any more promises to the poor girl."

"Not yet." He pulled her back against him. "Thanks, Megan."

Confused, she looked up into his eyes. "For what?"

"For knowing exactly what to say to make my sadness go away, for being a good mother and a wonderful wife. For loving me, even though I waited five years to claim you as my bride."

"No, Logan. No regrets. The years apart made our union all the sweeter."

"I promise I'll always love you, Megan. And I'll never leave you again. Not for more than a day at a time." He lowered his mouth to hers and proceeded to prove his point.

And that, Megan decided, was the best promise of all.

* * * * *

Catherine Palmer is a bestselling author and winner of the Christy Award for her outstanding Christian romance. She also received the Career Achievement Award for Inspirational Fiction from *RT Book Reviews*. Raised in Kenya, she lives in Atlanta with her husband. They have two grown sons. A graduate of Southwest Baptist University, she also holds a master's degree from Baylor University.

Books by Catherine Palmer

Love Inspired Historical

The Briton
The Maverick's Bride
The Outlaw's Bride
The Gunman's Bride

Steeple Hill Single Title

That Christmas Feeling
Love's Haven
Leaves of Hope
A Merry Little Christmas
The Heart's Treasure
Thread of Deceit
Fatal Harvest
Stranger in the Night

Visit the Author Profile page
at Harlequin.com for more titles.

THE GUNMAN'S BRIDE

Catherine Palmer

Don't worry about anything; instead,
pray about everything. Tell God what you need,
and thank him for all he has done. Then you will
experience God's peace, which exceeds anything we
can understand. His peace will guard your hearts
and minds as you live in Christ Jesus.
—*Philippians* 4:6–7

To my faithful readers, who bring me such joy.
I thank you for all your years of loyalty.

Chapter One

~~❧~~

April 1883
Raton, New Mexico Territory

Keeping his six-shooter aimed at the sheriff, Bart Kingsley crouched at the corner of a white picket fence. He was bleeding bad. The bullet that caught him in the side hurt something awful. But Bart knew he couldn't let pain overcome him. He was on a mission to find the woman he loved.

Laura Rose Vermillion's window stood out as a black patch on the dull gray wall of the dormitory just over the fence. Bart knew it was Rosie's window because he had caught sight of her shaking out a pink rug that morning. His Rosie…his beautiful Rosie.

"Kingsley!" a voice echoed through the darkness. "Kingsley, I know I winged you, boy. Come on out like a man and maybe the doc can save your sorry hide."

Bart gritted his teeth. He was too close. Too near Rosie now to let a bullet stop him. Hiding in some shrubs near the depot, he had waited all day until the sun went down and the last train left town. But when he made his move, Sheriff Mason T. Bowman had appeared out of nowhere.

"I've got help, Kingsley," the lawman called out now. "The Pinkerton National Detective Agency out of New York City sent their best man after you. You ain't never going to get away. Not with a Pinkerton detective on your trail. You know that, boy. So, put your hands up nice and slow, and we'll hold our fire."

Bart grimaced. A Pinkerton man? Now that was serious business. Those fellows could track outlaws better than a pack of hound dogs. The damp blood on his buckskin jacket told Bart he was leaving a trail nobody could miss.

But he couldn't be captured now. Not this close to his Rosie. Bart tugged the kerchief loose from his neck and pressed it against the bullet wound. He set his gun on the ground and worked his jacket's buttons into place to hold the kerchief tight.

Taking up his pistol, he began to creep along the boards of the fence. The dormitory housed young women who worked as waitresses for Fred Harvey's famous railway restaurant. Bart surmised that a fence built to keep eager young bucks away from the pretty females inside it would have a gap or two.

"Kingsley, we've got every street blocked!" Bowman barked. "You'll never leave Raton alive unless you surrender now. Come on out, boy!"

Bart pushed against the pickets as he inched toward Rosie's window. *Aha.* A loose board swung outward, leaving just enough room for a man to slip through the fence. Bart edged himself between the securely nailed pickets, then reached back and eased the loose board back into place.

"Look at this!" a deep voice called out. "You plugged him all right, sheriff. There's blood right here by this fence. Good shot. He won't get far."

The Pinkerton detective, Bart guessed. He touched his jacket and prayed the kerchief would hold. Slinking across the grass, Bart tried to think about Rosie. Beautiful Rosie with long brown hair and pretty little ankles. Six years had passed since he'd seen her, but Bart knew he would always love her.

"The blood trail stops at the corner," the Pinkerton man announced. "He's close."

Bowman shouted into the night. "Men, search under every woodpile and behind every fence. Shoot him if he runs."

Bart pushed himself up against the rough stone wall of the dormitory until he was standing. Dark mists swirled before his eyes. Don't faint. Not now.

He reached up and caught the edge of a protruding stone. Then he lifted one leg and found a foothold. *Rosie,* he reminded himself. Overhead was Rosie's window.

"'Spose he could have gotten over the Harvey girls' fence?" someone asked.

Bart pulled himself upward until he found another stone ledge to grab.

"Nah, the sheriff pegged him good," came the response. "If he ain't dead already, it won't be long."

Now Bart ran his fingertips along Rosie's wood windowsill. He set his foot on a protruding metal pipe. As he placed his weight on it, the pipe cracked.

"You hear that?"

"Sounded like it came from the dormitory!"

"Who's got a light? Sheriff, over here! Bring a lantern!"

Bart had slipped down a good two feet, scraping the skin on his palms. Now he found another foothold, this one of stone, and he heaved himself up again.

Coming up in line with the sill, he lifted a prayer. *God, let this window open.*

He gripped the lower edge of the casement and pushed. The window slid up. The scent of lavender and roses drifted out into the night. With a grunt, Bart dragged his body over the sill and tumbled to the floor of Rosie's room. A wave of dizziness came over him as he fought to stay conscious.

"Hey, here's a place where a picket is loose on the fence! Bring that lantern over here!"

"You see any blood?"

Without waiting to hear the response, Bart reached up and pulled the window shut. For a moment, he sat on the floor, head bent as he sucked in air. At the sound of girlish voices outside the room, he stretched out flat. Then, with the last of his strength, he scooted his big body under the bed.

Lying in the darkness, Bart anticipated the moment Rosie would enter the room. Or would it be the Pinkerton man who had finally cornered him? Or the sheriff, gun drawn, ready to blast the fugitive?

Bart closed his eyes. He was close now. So close. He had spent the past two months tracking a runaway woman who didn't want to be found. Trailing her halfway across the frontier. Spotting her at last in this two-bit mountain town.

"Oh, my," a light voice sang out as the door opened and a shaft of light sliced the darkness. "I don't know about you, Etta, but I am just whipped. Good night."

Rosie!

Another girl spoke. "I'm so tired I could fall asleep right where I'm standing. Morning's going to come early. Sleep well."

Rosie shut the door to her dormitory room and sat down on the bed. Beneath the hem of her black skirt, Bart caught sight of those pretty little ankles he remembered so well—worth every drop of blood he had shed.

Until Sheriff Bowman shot him, no one had ever spilled a drop of Bart's mixed Apache and White Eye blood. Not his stepfather, who'd sure tried enough times. Not Laura Rose's pappy, who would have liked to, whether he had the guts to pull the trigger. Not any of the string of lawmen and bounty hunters who had tried to gun down Bart and had found themselves eating cold lead for supper.

But here he lay, his blood soaking into the edge of Rosie's pink hooked rug. All this because of a woman he'd tried to forget for six long years.

Laura Rose. From underneath the bed, Bart studied those ankles as she unlaced her leather shoes and worked her stocking feet around in tiny circles. God didn't make many ankles that slim, that fragile, that downright luscious. Rosie had ankles worth fighting for.

Not that Bart had ever fought for them.

No, sir, there was no way he could deny that when push had come to shove, he had skedaddled out of Kansas City as if a scorpion was crawling down his neck. He'd been only seventeen at the time, but strong as an ox and twice as stubborn.

He could have stayed in Missouri and challenged Rosie's pappy for her. He could have pulled out the marriage license he still carried with him everywhere.

He could have argued his case in court as her pappy had threatened to make him do. But Rosie's father wasn't a highfalutin doctor for nothing. After the shouting, warnings and threats had failed to make Bart give in, Dr. Vermillion had resorted to the only weapon left in his arsenal—the truth.

Under the bed, Bart grimaced as he probed the seeping wound in his side. The physical pain seemed almost easier to bear than the memory of Dr. Vermillion's accusations. He shut his eyes for a moment, fighting the self-contempt that had made him silent and withdrawn as a boy, the shame that inflamed his angry loneliness as a man.

Breathing steadily, he willed a wall of iron around the hurt inside and watched Rosie's feet moving around the room—small feet for a woman so tall. A ragged hole in the heel of one dark cotton stocking revealed tender pink skin.

"Etta, come in here, would you?" She had opened the door to her room and was calling down the hallway. Bart wished he could shrink farther into the space beneath her bed, but it was mighty hard to fit a six-foot-three-inch, two-hundred-pound man under a brass bedstead.

"Do you smell anything odd in here?" Rosie was asking her slipper-footed neighbor. "The minute I came in from the restaurant, I noticed the scent of leather and dust—as if the outside air had gotten into my room."

Beneath the bed, Bart bent his head and took a whiff of his buckskin jacket. He couldn't remember the last time he'd had a good wash. Come to think of it, his hair probably needed combing in the worst way—maybe a cut, too—and his boots hadn't been polished since he took them off that horse thief in Little Rock.

"Phew!" Etta exclaimed. "I hate to say it, but the smell's probably coming from your own shoes, Laurie. These laced boots Mr. Harvey makes us wear cause all kinds of problems for a girl in a busy restaurant. I've gone through two pairs of stockings a month since I started here."

Bart saw Rosie lift one foot and heard her little gasp. "Would you just look at this, Etta? An awful blister right on my heel!"

"What did I tell you? You'll have calluses in a month and corns before you know it. Someone should write a letter to Mr. Harvey and tell him how we suffer. You soak your foot in a basin of water, and I'll fetch some vanilla from my room."

"Vanilla?"

"Put a drop in each shoe and set them in the hall all night. By morning that scent will be gone, you'll see." Etta paused a moment. "Although I must admit your shoes really do have the oddest odor I've ever smelled."

As her friend shut the door, Rosie hurried to the window. Bart heard the sash drawn up and felt a blast of chilly air. The sound of male voices drifted into the room from the street below, and Bart stiffened.

Etta breezed back into the room. "What on earth are you doing, Laura Kingsley? You'll catch your death!"

Turning his head with some difficulty in the tight space, Bart watched as Rosie stood on tiptoe to lean out the open window of the second-floor room. Laura *Kingsley,* Etta had called her. The name Rosie had chosen for herself sent a warm thrill down Bart's spine.

"What's going on outside, Etta?" she asked. "Look at all those men and horses right under my window."

"Ma'am?" someone shouted from below. "Excuse me, ma'am, but have you seen a wounded man about these parts?"

"Shut the window!" Etta hissed. "Quick! Shut the—"

"I'll have you know men aren't allowed near our dormitory," Rosie called out. "It's against Mr. Harvey's regulations. You'd better take your horses out of this yard before the sheriff arrests you."

"I'm the sheriff of Colfax County, miss. Sheriff Mason T. Bowman. This fellow with me is a detective from the Pinkerton National Detective Agency out of New York City."

"Oh, my!"

"I told you to shut the window," Etta whispered.

"Don't mean to frighten you ladies, but we're in search of a desperate outlaw. He was wounded about an hour ago in a gun battle just outside of town—shot two or three times. He's lost a lot of blood, and we've tracked him as far as this backyard."

Shot *once,* Bart corrected silently under the bed. He might have needed an excuse to get close to Rosie, but he wasn't fool enough to let two bullets plug him.

"This man is armed and dangerous. He's a hardened criminal with a price on his head in Missouri. You ladies had better keep your windows shut tight and your doors locked."

"Yes, Sheriff Bowman." Rosie's voice quavered. "I'll tell the other women."

"What has this man done?" Etta called down.

"You name it. Robbed banks, trains, stagecoaches.

He's a horse thief and a cattle rustler. And he's wanted for murder."

Under the bed, Bart frowned. He was *not* a horse thief and cattle rustler.

"What's his name?" Etta asked.

"Goes by two or three aliases—Injun Jack, Savage Jack, Jack King. His legal name is Bart Kingsley. He ran with Frank and Jesse James before Jesse got killed last year. The detective is after him for three train robberies in Missouri. Been trailing Kingsley all the way from Kansas City."

Kansas City? Bart frowned. The Pinkerton detective had been tracing him since Kansas City? Rosie had left a trail a mile wide, but Bart didn't think he had given any clues to his own whereabouts. Maybe he was a chuckleheaded fool after all. No wonder the sheriff had plugged him.

"If we see anything suspicious, we'll send for you right away," Etta assured the sheriff as she shut the window. "A murderer! Can you imagine, Laurie? Right outside the dormitory, too. The other girls will be scared out of their wits at the thought. I'm going to tell Annie and Mae right away. Won't they just swoon? Laurie? Are you all right? You're trembling!"

"Oh, Etta."

"Don't be scared of that outlaw. The sheriff will have him rounded up by morning."

"Etta, I want you to open my wardrobe door right this minute and look inside. Wait—take this!"

Rosie knelt by the bed, and Bart prayed she wouldn't see him in the shadow as she fished a pistol out from under the mattress. He let out a stifled sigh when she stood and gave the weapon to her friend.

"Laurie! You're not supposed to have a gun," Etta squealed. "It's against regulations!"

"If he's in there, shoot him! Just shoot him right through the heart."

Bart scowled. Well, that was a fine attitude.

"Take your gun, Laurie. The wardrobe's empty."

"Don't leave me here alone. Please, I beg you!"

"That man's not going to get in here. I locked your window, and you can bolt the door after I'm gone. I never expected you to be so—"

"Etta…" Her breath was shallow. "Etta… I know that man. The outlaw. The killer. I know him. Or I used to know someone by that name."

"Injun Jack?"

For a moment the room was silent. Then Rosie let out a ragged breath. "Bart Kingsley," she whispered. "I was married to him."

A knock on the door by one of the girls who had come to investigate the shouting had taken Etta out of the room for a moment. As soon as she informed everyone about the sheriff's warnings, she hurried back into Rosie's room and sat down on the bed beside her friend.

"I swear my heart is about to pound right out of my chest! I could barely hold my tongue after what you told me, Laurie. You think you were married to the outlaw?"

"Etta, please," Rosie pleaded, trying to still her own heartbeat. "I don't want to talk about it. It's all in the past."

"Oh, Laurie, how can you just up and say you were married to a murderous outlaw and then not tell the story to me—your very best friend in all the world?"

"I wasn't married to an outlaw, Etta. The Bart Kingsley I knew in Kansas City was no killer. He was a boy. Seventeen. And I was only fifteen. It happened a long time ago."

"You got married when you were fifteen years old?" Etta's blue eyes sparkled as bright pink spots lit up her cheeks. Her hair had escaped its roll to form a wildly frizzy blond spray across her forehead.

"I don't want to talk about it," Rosie repeated. She felt hot, miserable and suddenly close to tears as a flood of memories washed through her. All she had ever wanted was to teach children. How she loved little ones with their wide eyes and fertile minds! She longed to open those minds and pour in knowledge that would create successful, happy adults who could change the world into a better place.

But schoolteachers were working women, Pappy always said, and far beneath her social rank. She would never be allowed to stand in a classroom, he informed her, with chalky fingers and eyes tired from reading late by candlelight. No, she was to marry—marry someone well situated—and forget her schoolmarm notions.

Then Bart Kingsley came along.

"Laurie, please tell me," Etta begged.

"It's not romantic like you think. It was all a mistake."

"Was he cruel? Did you know he was going to become a killer?"

"Of course not. In fact... I couldn't have known the Bart Kingsley they're hunting. At least... I don't think it could be the same man."

"But it *might* be," Etta stressed. "Remember how

scared you were when you first heard his name—same as yours."

With a sigh Rosie smoothed down her black cotton skirt. Right now she wanted nothing more than to untie her soiled white apron, slip off her stockings and soak her sore feet in a basin of water. She didn't want to think about the past. She didn't want to remember Bart Kingsley.

"He was handsome," she murmured, unable to look at Etta. "My Bart Kingsley had green eyes...strange green eyes with threads of gold. And straight hair, black as midnight. He was skinny—rail thin—but strong. Oh, my Bart was *so* strong. He was kind, too. Always soft-spoken and polite to everyone. He loved animals. Stray dogs and cats followed him around the farm. When he sat down to rest, there'd be one cat on his shoulder and another on his lap."

"He worked on your father's farm?"

"In the stables. He was wonderful with horses. He broke and trained them with such gentleness. It was like magic the way they obeyed him. And you should have seen my Bart ride."

"What do you suppose turned him into a cattle rustler and a murderer?"

"It couldn't be the same man," Laura Rose retorted. "The Bart Kingsley I married never hurt anybody. He wouldn't even say a harsh word if someone was cruel to him."

"If he was so kind, why would anyone be cruel to him?"

"The other farmhands taunted him because...well, because he was part Indian. His father was an Apache."

"Apache!" Etta cried. "The sheriff just told us that

outlaw they're hunting for goes by the name of Injun Jack. I'll bet it's him, Laurie. How many men could fit that description?"

"A lot," she shot back with more defiance than she felt.

"So you married him when you were fifteen. Did you actually keep house together?"

"No, of course not. We weren't even…we didn't sleep together like married people. We were just children really—children with such beautiful hopes and dreams."

"I don't see how you could bring yourself to marry a savage even if he was nice to you," Etta rattled on. "Did you get a…a *divorce?* Harvey Girls aren't supposed to be married—it's against regulations. You could be fired."

"We were married two weeks before my father found out," Rosie explained. "He was furious. The two of them had a long talk, and Bart left the farm that afternoon."

"He *left* you? Just like that?"

"There was a note." Her voice grew thin and wistful as she thought of the special place in the woods where they had first kissed each other. The place where she had found the note. "Bart wrote that he realized the marriage had been a mistake. He said we were too young to know what we were doing, and he'd begun to realize it right away after we got married. He said… he said he didn't really love me after all, and I should forget about him. I was to consider that nothing had ever happened between us."

"Nothing?"

Rosie focused on her friend. "*Nothing.* So there… I

wasn't really married to him at all. Not in the Bible way. Our marriage didn't count. And that's the end of the story, so if you'd please just leave me alone now, Etta, I want to go to bed. I have the early shift tomorrow."

"You've got that blister, too," Etta added, her voice sympathetic as she gave her friend a quick hug.

Pulling out of the embrace, Rosie stood and smoothed the rumples in the pink quilt on her bed. There were probably lots of Bart Kingsleys in the world. Besides, she was about as far as she could be from Kansas City and the life she had shared with him. No one was going to find her in Raton, New Mexico. Not her pappy. Not the man who had been her fiancé for the past two years. And certainly not Bart Kingsley.

"Lock up now, Laurie," Etta said from the doorway. "I've put your shoes out in the hall. You'll see how much better everything will be in the morning."

Under the bed, Bart watched as Rosie bolted her door and set a chair under the knob. He knew she was afraid. But afraid of Bart, the murdering outlaw? Or afraid of *him,* the Bart who had married her and then had run off and left her high and dry?

It wasn't going to matter much either way if he up and died right under her bed. He needed to slide out from under this bed, wash his wound with some clean water and try to take a look at the damage. He needed ointment and bandages. He needed water. His mouth felt like the inside of an old shoe.

But he couldn't risk scaring Rosie by edging out into the open. She'd holler, her friends would come running and that would be that. The sheriff would cart him off to jail, the Pinkerton agent would haul him back to

Missouri and the law would hang him high. A half-breed Indian who had robbed trains and banks with Jesse James wouldn't stand a chance in court.

Bart swallowed against the bitter gall of memory as he recalled the years he'd squandered. And now, after all this time, he'd found his Rosie again. She had been the one bright spot in his life, and once again she was his only hope.

He studied her feet as she peeled away her stockings. There had been a time when she would let him hold those feet, rub away their tiredness, kiss each tender pink toe. Her black dress puddled to the floor and a soft white ruffle-hemmed gown took its place, skimming over her pretty ankles.

She began to hum, and Bart worked his shoulders across the hard floor in hope of a better look. The thought of dying this close to his Rosie without ever really seeing her face again sent an ache through him. He tilted his head so the pink quilt covered just one eye and left the other exposed.

Her back turned to him, she sat on a chair, let down her hair and began to pull a brush from the dark chocolate roots to the sun-lightened cascade that fell past her waist and over her hips. "Forty-eight, forty-nine, fifty," she counted in a soft voice.

She swung the mass of hair across her shoulders and began to brush the other side. "Fifty-one, fifty-two, fifty-three…"

She had put her feet into a basin of water while she worked on her hair, and Bart could see those bare ankles again. He shut his eyes, swallowing the lump that rose in his throat at the memory of the first time he'd caught a glimpse of Rosie's feet.

They had been down at the swimming hole where he and his stepbrothers liked to fool around. But this was a chilly autumn afternoon, and Bart's stepbrothers were nowhere in sight. Rosie had agreed to meet him at the swimming hole, and he'd been waiting for her like a horse champing at the bit.

When she finally came, she was full of silliness and laughter, her head tilted back and her brown eyes shining at him with all the love in the world. She had dropped down onto the grassy bank, unlaced her boots and taken off her stockings. Then, while he held his breath, she had lifted the hem of her skirt and waded right into the icy pool.

Hoo-ee, how he had stared at those pale curvy legs and those thin little ankles. She hadn't known, of course, what havoc her childlike impulse wreaked in his heart. His prim, sweet Rosie was the essence of innocence.

Under the bed, Bart suppressed the urge to chuckle at the memory of her sauntering back onto the bank, pulling up her stockings and lacing her boots—annoyed that he had not joined her in the water, and unaware of the reasons why he couldn't trust himself.

They had sat together in silence for such a long time that Bart had begun to fear she really was mad at him. So he did the only thing he could think of—he grabbed her, kissed her right on the mouth, and then ran off lickety-split like the devil was after him.

"Ninety-eight, ninety-nine, one hundred," Rosie said now from the chair. She lifted her feet out of the water and dried them with a cotton towel. She checked the bolt on her door and tested the window latch before crossing to the wardrobe. Breathing heavily, she jerked open the door. After a moment she shut it again and let out yet another sigh.

"Dear God," she said, dropping to her knees beside the bed, "please watch over me tonight. I'm so scared. Don't let Bart be out there, dear Lord. Please don't let that horrible killer be *my* Bart."

She was silent for a long time, and under the bed Bart held his breath. Eyes squeezed shut, he found himself praying along with her, as if he could will away the truth: *Don't let me be that Bart, dear Lord. Please don't let me be that killer they're after.*

"Dear God, please help me to like Etta as much as she likes me," Rosie prayed on. "Give me patience, and please don't let her blabber the things I told her tonight. Bless Pappy, but don't let him find me—not until I've started teaching school and gotten myself established here in town with a house and enough money so I can keep him from hauling me back to Kansas City. Bless...bless Dr. Lowell and help him to understand why I never could be a good wife to him."

Bart's eyes flew open. Dr. Lowell's *wife?* But she was married to Bart Kingsley! Could she have married another man, too? Or been engaged to him? She was Rosie—*his* Rosie!

"Forgive me, Father, for my sins. My many sins," she murmured in a voice so low that Bart could hardly hear it. She sniffled as she spoke, her voice tight with suppressed tears. "And please take care of Bart. Amen."

The bed creaked as she climbed into it. Lying underneath, Bart heard her sniffling. She hadn't yet blown out the lamp on her dressing table, and Bart studied her shadow on the opposite wall as she twisted the coverlet in her hands.

He felt sick. Dizzy with loss of blood. And knotted up inside like a tangled vine. Had Rosie promised to marry someone else? Had she actually gone through with it? How long had it been? Why hadn't his half brother told him?

Some other man had touched his Rosie! How could she have gone and gotten engaged or married to another man when she knew good and well she was already married to him? He had the license to prove it! He wanted to shake it in front of her face and shout, *Why? Why, Rosie?*

But she could simply throw his question back. Why, Bart? Why did you run off and leave me? Why is the sheriff hunting for you? Why did you kill and rob and throw in with a gang of outlaws? Why, Bart?

He heard her breathing grow steady, her tossing ease and the bed cease to groan. He touched his side and found that blood had finally begun to clot over the ragged, burned hole in his skin. He had to get out from under the bed, and soon. He couldn't go much longer without water.

Should he slip out the window and hope the posse had given up hunting for the night? Should he leave Rosie sleeping, never to know the cause of the bloodstain on her pink hooked rug?

He ran a dry tongue over his lower lip. Quietly, he began to shrug his shoulders across the wood floor and out from under the bed. The pain in his side flared, movement relighting a fire inside his gut. Clenching his teeth, he scooted his hips clear of the iron bed, then dragged his legs out into the open.

The world swung like a bucking bronco as he rose onto his elbows. Dizzy, he shook his head, but the fog refused to roll back. Fighting to keep silent, he rolled up onto his knees. His breath came in hoarse gasps.

There she was! His beautiful Rosie, sleeping like an innocent babe in her bed of pink. She was prettier than ever. Rounded cheekbones, delicate nose, full lips barely parted.

Grabbing his side, he tried to haul himself to his feet. The floor swayed out from under him, the lamp-light tilting crazily. He groaned, caught the bed rail, felt the iron frame jolt at his weight. Rosie's eyes drifted open, focused and jerked wide. She sucked in a breath just as he clamped his hand over her mouth.

"Don't scream, Rosie," he croaked as the bed seemed to turn on its side and his feet began to drift on cotton clouds. "Don't scream, Rosie, Please. It's me. Bart."

Her skin and lips melted under his palm as black curtains fell across his vision.

"Bart!" he heard her gasp. Then the curtains wrapped over his head, and his feet floated out from under him. He tumbled like a falling oak tree across his Rosie's soft body.

Chapter Two

Faster than a cat with its tail afire, Rosie pulled herself out from under the deadweight of the unconscious man. She grabbed the oil lamp from the dressing table across the room and nearly doused its flame as she swung back to the bed to take a closer look.

Clamping a trembling hand over her open mouth to keep from crying out, she studied the intruder. He wore leather boots caked with dried mud. Two six-shooters and an arsenal of cartridges hung on belts at his waist. He lay face down, his nose pressed into a rumple of pink quilt. Every breath he took sounded like a distant train engine as the air struggled in and out of his lungs.

Eyes focused on him, Rosie reached for the pistol Etta had held earlier that evening. The heavy metal felt reassuring, and she hugged it close. Bart, the man had called himself. And he had known her name—her real name!

But this shaggy bear draped over her bed couldn't possibly be the Bart she once knew. She lifted the lamp until its yellow glow spread down his entire length. No, she thought with relief, this certainly wasn't her Bart.

Her Bart had been much shorter. This man more than filled up the bed. Her Bart had been as lanky as a colt, but the stranger's weight made the metal bed frame bend toward the middle.

Certainly her Bart would never have let his shiny black hair get into such a state as this. The tangled mop that covered his broad shoulders couldn't have been washed in months. His bloodstained buckskin jacket and faded trousers looked as though the man never took them off. No wonder her room had smelled so odd. Who knew how long this great malodorous hulk of an outlaw had been hiding under her bed?

Shivering, Rosie wondered what on earth she was going to do with him. If he regained consciousness, she wouldn't stand a chance against such a brute.

"Okay, mister," she said, jamming the pistol barrel against his skull. "I've got you now, you hear?"

He didn't budge.

What if he were dead? A dead man, right on her very own bed! Swallowing, she bent toward him to listen for the ragged breathing that had sounded so loud only moments before.

"Rosie..." The moan came from deep inside his chest.

"Don't move!" she cried out. "I have a gun, and I'll use it."

A muffled groan welled out of him. "Rosie? Rosie... help me."

Her hand shook as she brushed a hank of hair from his face. "Oh, dear God, please don't let this be happening," she mouthed in a desperate prayer.

But there was no mistaking the angle of the man's high cheekbone or the smooth plane of golden skin that sheered down from it. Rosie knew those lips, that jutted chin. No doubt about it. The man on her bed was Bart Kingsley. And yet he *couldn't* be. This was a huge shaggy outlaw with a bullet in his side. This man was wanted for murder.

Then he opened his eyes. Green eyes, shot with golden threads, just as she remembered.

"Bart?"

"Where are you, girl?" Grimacing, he lifted his head. "Rosie, I think I'm gonna die."

Rosie carried a glass of water from the washstand and knelt at Bart's side. His mouth felt like a dry creek bed, parched and sandy. Somehow she had known.

"I gotta turn over," he whispered. "Help me, Rosie."

She let out a breath. "Raise your shoulders if you can."

"Tarnation," he muttered through clenched teeth as she helped him up onto one elbow. He grabbed at his side. "Hurts like the devil."

"Hush your cussing and drink this." She sat on the bed beside him.

Pain ripping through his gut, Bart took a sip and then fell back. "Blast that Pinkerton son of a—"

Rosie clamped a hand over his mouth. "You stop swearing this minute, Bart Kingsley!" she snapped. "You're turning the air in my room blue. You never used to talk like this."

No, he hadn't always cussed. There had been a time when he hardly said a word, bottling his frustration, anger and rage deep inside. But if he hadn't allowed himself to swear, neither had he permitted the good words inside to come out. Now all he could think about was how much he wanted to tell Rosie what it meant to see her again. How beautiful she looked. How black the years without her had been. How soft her long hair was as it brushed against his hand.

"Bad enough you had to sneak in here and bleed all over everything, and stink like a pair of old leather shoes and scare me half out of my wits…"

Her admonitions trailed off as he slid his hand down her arm. Oh, but she smelled good, he thought as he pressed his lips lightly into her palm.

With a squeak of dismay, she snatched her hand away. "What are you doing here, Bart? Nobody passes through Raton, New Mexico, but miners and homesteaders. And how did you come to climb in my window and hide under my bed?"

Eyes shut, he forced down deep breaths. "I came looking for you, Rosie. I tracked you here."

"But I changed my name!"

"Kingsley?"

"It was all I could think of when I applied for the Harvey job. I was scared about running away. I had planned everything down to the last detail, but when the recruiter asked my name, I went blank and just blurted it out."

"It *is* your name. Laura Rose Kingsley."

"Stop that!" She pushed him away and stood with her arms crossed. "I have a good mind to call for the sheriff this minute."

"No, Rosie! They'll haul me back to Missouri and hang me."

"The law *should* hang you if you've done all the wicked things Sheriff Bowman told Etta and me tonight. You rode with Jesse James. You robbed banks and trains, stole cattle and horses, killed people."

"I'm no stock rustler."

"Oh, *that's* a relief!" She glared down at him. "You don't look a thing like you used to."

"It's been six years. I grew up."

"You grew up into a gunman. An outlaw."

He closed his eyes. Rosie was right, of course. He'd grown into a man, and he'd done everything he was accused of—except rustling livestock.

The James brothers had a policy against that. Their grievance wasn't with small-time Southern farmers and ranchers. No, Jesse, Frank, and the others set their sights on northern banks and trains. Trained by Charley Quantrill and Bloody Bill Anderson, they had served as guerrilla raiders until the end of the war.

But when the rest of the Confederate guerrillas returned to their homes and farms, the James brothers and their pals, the Youngers, elected to continue raiding. Others joined along the way, men who came and went as part of the gang during its sixteen-year reign.

Bart swallowed against the knot of regret in his throat. He had known every one of the fringe members of the James-Younger gang—most of them killed by lawmen or captured and lynched. Others were serving time in prison or, like him, hoping to escape the law.

The men had accepted a half-breed homeless boy when no one else would. They fed him, boarded down with him at night, saw to it that he had clothes and boots…and guns. They taught him to shoot and let him join them playing checkers, swimming in the river, hunting deer and squirrels. Oh, they had a fine time, Bart and the boys.

Until the day that was burned into his memory like none other: October 7, 1879. Glendale, Missouri. The Chicago & Alton train.

Bart opened his eyes, knowing that light always erased the haunting blackness of his past. And there was his Rosie, gazing down on him with her velvet eyes.

"Rosie," he whispered, hardly able to believe he had found her at last. Porcelain skin, delicate cheekbones, lips the color of roses. Rosie, his prim-and-proper, educated, high-society lady. Rosie, his tree-climbing, pond-wading, horse-riding love. His Rosie.

"You're going to have to leave," she said abruptly. "I'll help you to the window."

But she didn't move, and he couldn't stop staring at her.

"If I leave, the detective will find me," he murmured.

"I suppose he will."

"He'll take me back to Missouri. I won't get a fair trial. Not a half breed like me."

Her brown eyes deepened. "If you did, would you be cleared? You robbed trains."

"I was following orders. Jesse's plan, his guns, his horses."

"You killed people."

"People who were trying to kill me first."

"Bart, how could you? You used to be so kind."

"Rosie." He reached for her arm, grasped her hand. "Let me stay here tonight. I'll leave tomorrow."

"You can't stay in my room." She jerked away. "Etta fetches me in the morning, and she'll know at once.

Mrs. Jensen will faint if she hears even a rumor of you. I'll lose my job."

"Please, Rosie. Don't turn me out."

Opening the heavy lid of her trunk, Rosie took out the bag of pills, lotions and cures she had brought from her home in Kansas City. Pappy always kept an ample supply of medicines on hand in case he had to leave the house to tend someone in the middle of the night. She had decided the medicines might be of use in Raton— though she hadn't needed them until this night.

Don't turn me out. If Bart had said anything else, she would have forced him to the window at gunpoint and made him climb right out into the cold. But how could she turn him out? The Bart Kingsley she knew had been turned out far too often in his life.

Taunted by the farmhands. Beaten, whipped and burned by his stepfather. Neglected by his own mother. He wore ragged clothes and boots that pinched his toes and rubbed blisters on his heels. In the winter he had no coat. In the summer he had no hat. The schoolmarm refused to allow him into her classroom. The preacher made him sit outside on the church steps to hear the sermon.

No, Rosie knew she couldn't turn him out. Not tonight. Once the decision had been made, there was nothing left but to treat the awful wound in his side.

"You'd better take one of these liver pills," Rosie said, carrying her stash of Dr. Vermillion's medicines to the bedside. "Only the good Lord knows where that bullet is."

Though Dr. Lowell had been her fiancé for three long years, Rosie recalled, she had never gotten past calling the man by his formal title. He kept daytime office hours and never saw patients at home. It was the new way of practicing medicine, he had told her.

She helped Bart lift his head to swallow the tiny brown pill, followed by a teaspoon of Dr. Hathaway's Blood Builder.

"Where did you get this nasty stuff, Rosie?" he asked with a grimace as she poured a spoonful of something black. He swallowed and nearly gagged. "I'll be horsewhipped if that doesn't taste like a—"

"Don't you swear, Bart. I mean it." She drew back the edge of his jacket and caught her breath. "You need a doctor!"

"No, I can't do that."

"It's a mess, and I don't know the first thing about nursing. I've got to get this jacket off. I'll fetch my scissors."

"Don't cut it!" He grabbed a handful of nightgown to stop her. "This is all I've got, Rosie. I'll work it off, just give me a minute." Releasing her gown, he began to shrug his shoulders and arms out of the buckskin jacket.

His face was beaded with perspiration from the effort, and she bent over him to help pull away the garment. The scent of woodsmoke and leather clung to his skin. She wished it were unpleasant, but the smell stirred something deep inside her. A memory. A trace of pleasure. Although she tried to keep from touching him, the effort was hopeless, and she ended up wrestling his big shoulders and long arms out of the sleeves.

"There!" she said, letting out a breath as he collapsed. "You don't even have on a shirt! Oh, good heavens, when was the last time you took this off?"

With two fingers she carried the bloody jacket across the room and dropped it into a basket in the corner. It would likely fall apart after a good scrubbing with lye soap. At least the hole ought to be mended. There wouldn't be time for any of that, of course, not with Bart leaving first thing in the morning.

She glanced over her shoulder to find him breathing deeply, his eyes shut and his huge chest filling her narrow bed from one side to the other. When did he get to be so big?

She poured water into her basin and carried it to the bed. When she sat down beside him, his green eyes opened—reminding her that even though he didn't look like her Bart or act like her Bart, he *was* her Bart.

"Now bite your tongue," she told him. "And don't you dare start cussing at me."

She dipped a towel in the water and blotted his skin. *Dear Lord,* she breathed up in prayer as she studied the damage, *don't let him die on me. Much as I've wanted to kill this man, please keep him alive.*

"How's it look?" he grunted.

"Terrible."

"Can you feel the bullet?"

"Feel it? I'm not sticking my finger in there!"

"Rosie, it's not coming out unless someone takes it out. And if you don't patch up the hole, I'm liable to bleed to death. I reckon if you'd do that for me, I wouldn't ever ask another thing of you."

"Why should I trust a murdering outlaw?" she asked.

"Especially one who ran off two weeks after he married her," Bart finished.

"We never were married," she said softly as she rummaged through the bag. "You said so yourself."

"You found the note?"

"Of course I did." Wishing he hadn't brought up their impetuous wedding, she set the lamp on a table near the bed. If only he hadn't tracked her down. If only he hadn't crawled into her bedroom all shot up. Now she was stuck with him. But only until morning.

Before she could begin, he caught her hand and held it to his chest. "Rosie," he whispered, his eyes depthless. "Thank you, Rosie-girl."

"You won't be thanking me in a minute." She focused on the tweezers in her bag. How could it be that his gaze drew her back through time with an ache that wouldn't go away—in spite of everything she knew about him?

She had to concentrate. Bart had lost so much blood. As she dipped the tweezers into the wound, she felt his hand slide into her hair. Eyes squeezed shut, he arched back in pain. His hand closed over a hank of her hair and she could feel him working it between his fingers.

Running a dry tongue over her lips, Rosie centered her attention on the wound again. She moved the tweezers deeper, then wiped the blood with a towel. Nothing. Where could the bullet be? She worked the tool farther in. Suddenly his hand clamped over hers, squeezing hard.

"Bart!" she gasped, jerking out the tweezers.

"Rosie, we *were* married," he murmured. "We were."

"I can't find the bullet."

"You were my Rosie," he whispered, relaxing his hand. His fingers moved through the hair at her temple. "Once you were my Rosie-girl."

She closed her eyes, fighting tears. His fingertips stroked across the down on her cheek, feathering her skin. A finger traced the arch of her eyebrow. Another found her eyelid and rested lightly there a moment before fanning down to her lashes and cheek.

"Remember how you shinnied down the oak tree by your bedroom window that night?" he was saying, his voice almost inaudible. "We ran through the fields to Reverend Russell's place? You wore a white dress and lilacs in your hair. The reverend was drunk as usual, but we hardly noticed because we were so scared and excited to get married and—"

"No!" She pushed his hand away. "It was only a game, Bart. We were children. You said so yourself."

Leaving him, she hurried to the wash stand, rinsed the tweezers and fumbled the medicines into the bag. Six years ago she had convinced herself that she had never married Bart Kingsley. No one knew except her pappy—and neither of them had ever mentioned his name again.

The disaster had been put away like one of Pappy's old textbooks. Hidden on a back shelf. Forgotten. Denied so completely that Pappy had arranged for Rosie to marry Dr. William Lowell. Denied so totally that she had silently submitted, as she always did, to Pappy. Denied so thoroughly, that every night when she lay in Dr. Lowell's bed in his big fancy house, she didn't give Bart Kingsley a thought.

She didn't remember the way he had held her hand, gently weaving his fingers through hers. She didn't remember how he had touched her face, his green eyes memorizing every feature as though it were precious beyond belief. She didn't remember his mouth moving against hers, his lips tender and his breath ragged.

"Rosie," he said from the bed.

She stiffened, unable to look at him.

"I don't play games, Rosie. You know I never have."

"You'd better get some sleep, Bart. You'll need it to climb out that window in the morning."

She rinsed her hands in clean water, then she stepped to the wardrobe for a cotton petticoat she had brought from Kansas City. The strips of clean white fabric would make a good bandage. As she ripped the cloth, she resolved that Bart was part of her past and he must stay that way. Come sunup, he would be back in the past where he belonged.

She laid the bandages across his stomach. "I didn't find the bullet, and you're still bleeding. I'm going to put this around you until you can get to a doctor."

"I reckon you've done me such a good turn I won't need to see a doctor, Rosie."

"You can't go around with a bullet inside you for the rest of your life."

"Most of the men I know have been shot so full of holes you'd think they'd leak every time they took a drink. They carry a few lead souvenirs just to make their stories ring true."

"That's a fine bunch of friends you have, Bart." As she smoothed the cloth bandage over his skin she could feel his eyes on her. Watching her. "Men walking around with bullets inside. Great ghosts, who ever heard of such a thing?"

"Cole Younger's been wounded upwards of twenty times. He reckons he's got a good fifteen bullets buried in him."

"Cole Younger!" she snapped, straightening suddenly. "So you really are in leagues with those outlaws, just like the sheriff said. Oh, Bart, how *could* you?"

"Rosie, it's not like you think." He reached for her, but she had already swung away.

A blanket bundled in her arms, she knelt to pull her pink hooked rug into the center of the room. One glimpse of the blood-soaked wool and she let out a gasp of horror.

"Bart Kingsley, you have ruined my rug! I brought it all the way from Kansas City on the train because it was the only thing I ever liked out of that ugly house my fiancé bought for us last—"

Catching herself, she clamped a hand over her mouth. Her eyes met Bart's.

"You and I *weren't* married," she whispered. "We never were married. Not really, were we?"

When he didn't answer, she spread her blanket on the bare wood floor. Then she curled up and pulled the edges of it over herself. Bart lay nearby, his breathing easier now. In the darkness she wondered if he could hear her crying.

Chapter Three

Rosie woke to find Bart sprawled half on and half off her bed, a sheen of feverish perspiration covering his body. He writhed in the agony of a dream, and she feared his moans would bring someone to investigate.

"Bart, wake up!" she pleaded, placing her hand on his damp shoulder. "Bart!"

At once he sat straight up and grabbed her arms in a powerful grip. His green eyes were bright with fever. "Rosie, don't let them get me! Don't let...don't..."

He winced in pain, then sagged back onto the bed. "Ah, blast that good-for-nothing sheriff—"

"Hush, now!" Rosie ordered. She glanced at the door and wondered if the voice of a fevered man would carry down the hall. Brushing her hair back from her face, she studied the massive figure on the bed.

What on earth was she going to do with him? In the light of day, she felt foolish not to have sent for Sheriff Bowman immediately. It wouldn't be long before someone would hear—or maybe smell—the intruder. She ought to head down the hall to Mrs. Jensen's suite and confess the whole thing.

The truth of the matter was, Rosie didn't owe Bart Kingsley one shred of kindness. He had wooed her, misled her, tricked her, abandoned her. And now he had endangered the one sure thing in life—her job as a Harvey Girl. If anyone discovered an outlaw in her room, her dream of teaching in one of the local schools would end. She would never have a home of her own, a classroom filled with eager children, freedom from her past.

"Rosie?" he murmured as his head tossed from side to side, his black hair a tangle on the white pillow. "Rosie, where are you, girl?"

Fingers knotted together, she fretted over her dilemma. She couldn't let Bart stay in her room, but he was too ill to climb out the window and escape. If she called the sheriff, everyone would wonder why she had let the fugitive renegade sleep in her bed all night. Her bloody sheets would bear witness to the fact that he hadn't been hiding under her bed forever.

"Oh, dear Lord, please show me what to do!" she whispered in prayer as she checked the gold pocket watch she had inherited from her mother.

Six-thirty! The uniform inspection bell would ring in half an hour. Then she would have to rush downstairs, eat a roll, sip some coffee and prepare the dining room for the eight o'clock train. Dare she go off and leave a feverish, groaning man in her bed?

As she turned away in search of her apron, Rosie decided Bart could stay through the first shift. She would return to her room before the lunch train came through and check on him. If he was the slightest bit better, she would insist that he leave.

"Rosie." His voice startled her as he struggled to

sit up. "I promised I'd go this morning. I'll need my jacket."

Her shoulders sagged. "Oh, Bart, you're in no shape to go anywhere."

"No, Rosie-girl. I made you a promise." For a moment he sat hunched over, breathing heavily. Then he hauled himself to his feet.

Rosie watched him sway like a great tree about to topple. He means to do it, she thought. He actually means to keep his promise to me. One of his long legs started to crumple, but he grabbed the iron footboard to steady himself.

His guns and cartridge belts weighed him down as he shuffled across the room toward the corner where she had tossed his jacket. His bandage was stained with a dark red blotch. He propped one big brown hand on the windowsill and bent to pick up the torn buckskin.

"I'm sorry," he said. "Sorry I messed up your sheets and rug. Sorry about when we were young and how much I hurt you. I'm sorry I made you cry last night, too, and—"

"For mercy's sake, Bart!" She snatched the jacket out of his hands. "You're delirious, plain and simple. Now get back to bed this instant. I'll check on you after the breakfast shift."

"No, Rosie, I—"

"Let go of that windowsill and grab on to me before you fall down with a crash and bring Mrs. Jensen running."

Rosie clenched her teeth and heaved Bart against her. This man could drive me to drink, she thought. All those ridiculous apologies. If he weren't so sick, she'd give him what for. She didn't need anyone's apologies for the way her life had turned out. She had made her own choices and now she would live with them.

"Get in this bed," she ordered, shoving him down. "And don't get up until I say. You're going to make me late for inspection, and then where will I be?"

Working quickly, she tugged off his boots and set them on the floor. My, but they needed a good polishing. She pulled the sheets and blankets over his chest and tucked the edges under the mattress.

Opening the window to freshen the room, she didn't take her usual time to pray and gaze out over the little town of Raton and its encircling range of snow-capped mesas. Instead, she quickly washed and then stepped behind the changing screen to put on her uniform. Black stockings. Chemise. Corset—oh, she had to hurry! Black skirt. Black shirt buttoned up to the neck.

Rushing to the hook by the door, she grabbed a fresh white apron, tied it around her waist and buttoned the bib. In two short months she had worked her way almost up to head waitress, but one moan from Bart Kingsley could undo everything.

Nerves jangling, she laced her boots and pinned her hair up in a thick, glossy knot. There had been a time when a lady's maid had helped her dress in silk and velvet gowns, pretty slippers and kid gloves. Necklaces and bracelets that sparkled with gems had adorned her as she called on ladies of her social circle.

Now she wouldn't trade her black-and-white Harvey Girl uniform for all the lace, ruffles and taffeta in Kansas City.

"Uniform inspection!" Mrs. Jensen called in the hallway.

Heart thumping, Rosie flew to the bed where Bart lay. "Now don't do anything foolish," she whispered, smoothing the sheet over his chest as though he were a sick child and not a gunslinger. "I'll come back after the last breakfast train, so just—"

"My beautiful Rosie-girl," he murmured as he caught her hand and brought it to his lips. With a gasp, she pulled away and hurried out into the hall.

Filling silver-plated urns with Fred Harvey's famous coffee, Rosie tried not to think about the possibility that any moment Mrs. Jensen would storm into the restaurant screaming about the outlaw in Laura Kingsley's room.

"Did you sleep all right?" Etta called from her station near a wall of windows. "I reckon that outlaw will be long gone by now."

"If he's smart, he will." Rosie fretted as she folded napkins for her four assigned tables. "Of course, if he was smart, he never would have gotten himself shot in the first place. We'll find out from Mr. Adams."

Charles Adams, editor of *The Raton Comet,* boasted that his eight-page weekly never missed a good story. How shocked he would be to know that the scoop of the year lay just overhead in room seven.

"Twenty-two omelets are coming in on the eight-o'clock!" Tom Gable, the Harvey House manager, called out the food order that had been wired ahead. "Fourteen hotcakes, six biscuits and gravy, thirty-three coffees and nine milks. The train'll be here in seven minutes!"

With a collective gasp, the five Harvey Girls rushed to finish their preparations. Rosie loved her work. Respected, protected, well paid, she couldn't have found a better place to make a new life for herself. Once she had saved enough money, she would apply for a teaching position and buy a little house. It was a hope she had cherished for years. But she knew that at any moment, her past might catch up to her and snuff it out.

A deafening *whooo,* and the dining-room floor began to shake. Glasses rattled. Cups wobbled. Spoons tinkled against knives. Steam billowed across the platform as the enormous black-and-silver engine of the Atchison, Topeka and Santa Fe train rolled into the depot. As the brakeman set the brakes, the train squealed in protest. Chunks of red-hot coal spilled from the firebox. Railway men rushed to stomp them out. The smell of oil and smoke enveloped the Harvey House.

Like wraiths, the passengers descended through the steam onto the platform. Their hats askew and coats not quite settled, they stretched, waved and stared at the blue sky after the long ride. Children scampered to the rails to inspect the big engine. Tails wagging, a pair of dogs known to the whole town as Tom and Griff trotted through the crowd.

Then one of the busboys stepped into the crowd and raised his large brass gong.

"Breakfast is served," he called, giving the gong a hard whack with a stick. "Breakfast is served!" Rosie stood silently, hands behind her back, as the passengers walked into the dining room and took their seats.

The moment one table had been settled, she started around it.

"What do you care to drink this morning?" she asked. "We have coffee, milk or orange juice."

As each patron stated a selection, Rosie quickly arranged the cups according to the code she had been taught. She hurried off to fetch the food while another girl poured beverages. Rosie could almost hear the customers marveling that the drink girl knew exactly what they had requested. It was all part of the Fred Harvey mystique, an air of magic that delighted patrons and filled the staff with pride.

While the diners were munching on apple wedges, oranges and grapes, Rosie went around her station taking orders for omelets, hotcakes or biscuits and gravy. The dining room filled with the spicy-sweet aroma that seemed to rouse the passengers even more effectively than the famous Harvey coffee did.

Standing motionless, hands behind her back and the required smile on her face, Rosie kept her eyes constantly roving her station for the slightest possible indication that she was needed by a diner. On most mornings she was so absorbed in her work that she never gave anything outside it a second thought. But knowing Bart lay upstairs in her bed, Rosie found her concentration wandering. What if he took it into his head to try to climb out the window? What if he lost his balance and fell out? She glanced uneasily through the long side windows, suddenly fully aware of the impossible situation she was in.

Outside the front of the red board-and-batten Harvey House lay a long porch, a row of widely spaced trees and the depot and train tracks. Behind the building was the small, fenced private yard for the House's female employees, and beyond that stretched the town of Raton. Now that Rosie thought about it, how on earth could Bart ever hope to escape in broad daylight? He'd be spotted immediately.

But how could he stay in her room for the rest of the day? Someone would find out for sure. And what if his fever grew worse? She lifted her head, listening for thumps, bumps and moans.

The silence was almost worse than the anticipation of noise. What if Bart had died? She wrung her clasped hands behind her skirt. If Bart died, she would never have the chance to chew him out the way she'd always intended. On the other hand, she'd never learn exactly why he had followed her all the way from Kansas City, or how he had fallen in with Jesse James and his gang.

More important, she wouldn't be able to tell him how miserable her life had been after he went away… how awful the prospect of marriage to Dr. Lowell had made her feel…

"All aboard!" The cry startled Rosie. Her passengers were hurrying off, leaving the table littered with coins and dirty dishes.

The moment the train pulled away, Mr. Gable bounded into the dining room. "Sixteen omelets coming in on the eight forty-five!"

Rosie scrambled to clear her tables. There was no time for worry. And no time for longing.

Along about ten o'clock, Bart felt his fever break. Bathed in sweat, his body suddenly began to cool. The hammering in his head eased. The room stopped spinning.

He could hear the sounds of clinking glasses and chatter from a dining room somewhere. The tantalizing aromas of cinnamon, bacon and freshly brewed coffee drifted up through the floorboards and swirled around his head.

Rosie was downstairs, he remembered suddenly, and this was her room. Her hairbrush lay on the table. Her clean, starched aprons hung by the door. He had found her!

But as the truth set in, Bart closed his eyes. Rosie didn't want him. She had made him promise to leave. And all he had done was bloody up her rug and sheets, smell up her room with his old leather jacket and dusty boots and put her in a position to lose her job. Rosie would be hoping he was gone by the time she returned to her room.

No surprise there. Who would want a no-good half-breed gunman like him around anyhow?

With a grunt he pushed himself to his feet and lifted the lace curtain at her window. The town was twice as big as it had looked the night before. From Rosie's bedroom he could see a shoe shop, a bakery, an undertaking parlor and enough saloons to keep the whole town drunk as hillbillies at a rooster fight. There was the Five-Cent Beer Saloon, the 1883 Saloon, the Mountain Monarch, the Bank Exchange, the Progressive Saloon, the Cowboy's Exchange Saloon, the El Dorado, the Green Light, the Lone Star, the Dobe Saloon and O'Reilly's. And those were just the ones Bart could make out.

A church or two had elbowed out some holy ground amid the saloons. A meeting hall, a hotel, a bank and a water tower near the bank showed that the town of Raton, New Mexico, meant business. The whole place swarmed with people—folks heading in and out of the hardware stores and mercentiles, a milkman stopping off at every house in town, men loading wagons with lumber from Hughes Brothers Carpenter and Building Supply and women carrying bundles out of D. W. Stevens, Dealers in General Merchandise. Wagons, carriages and horses filled the packed-dirt streets.

Bart brushed a hand across his forehead. He would never be able to climb out a second-story window unnoticed. He let the curtain drop and sagged against the sill. He would have to wait until dark to try an escape.

Before he did, he would make up for the trouble he had caused Rosie. Some of it anyhow.

"See you at one o'clock!" Rosie called to Etta, who was chatting with the new cook.

Heart thundering, Rosie swung into the kitchen and filled a plate with food. What if Bart had already gone? she wondered as she climbed the stairs. Worse—what if he was still there?

She pushed open the door. The bare-chested man leaning against her window frame looked nothing like the pale invalid she had tucked away at dawn. In the sunlight, his bronze skin gleamed. A towel hung around his neck. His hair, still damp, had been washed and combed away from his face.

For the first time Rosie fully saw what time had done to the gawky boy she once loved. From the raven eyebrows that slashed across his forehead to his burning emerald eyes, from the squared turn of his chin to the solid breadth of his chest, Bart Kingsley was all man.

Disconcerted, she focused on a makeshift clothesline that stretched across the room. Denim trousers, a torn cotton shirt and a couple of white sheets hung dripping.

"You washed," she blurted out.

"Everything but the rug." He straightened, and she realized that he had tucked her blanket around his waist. "Cold water. All I had."

"Cold water's the best thing there is for bloodstains." Steadying her breath, she held out the plate. "I brought you something to eat."

"Thanks. I'm hungry. The fever broke a while back. I'd be much obliged if you'd allow me to stay until dark, Rosie."

At that moment she would have allowed him to do almost anything he wanted. If she hadn't known his veins ran with both white and Indian blood, Rosie might have mistaken Bart for a pure Apache. With his copper skin and long, black hair, he could pass for a mighty warrior straight out of a dime novel. But he was too tall, and his eyes were too green to deny the heritage of his English mother.

"You'd better stay put," she said, busying herself by straightening her dressing table. "Unless you want Sheriff Bowman nabbing you first thing."

"You reckon I should hang for my crimes, Rosie?"

"You'd have to answer that one."

"I can tell you this. It'll be a cold day in—" He caught himself. "I'm sorry, Rosie. Cussing's a hard habit to break."

"Sounds like you've got a lot of new habits these days."

"I did some things I'm not proud of, but I can't just turn myself in. The law would just as soon shoot a man dead as let him try to make a new life for himself."

Rosie set her brush on the table and turned to face him. "Do you want a new life, Bart?"

"I didn't come all the way here to rob trains—you can bet your bottom dollar on that."

"Why did you come?"

Bart let out a breath. "About the time Bob Ford shot Jesse James in the back of the head, I was doing some thinking. I looked back over the years of my life and all I saw was a long tunnel. A black, cold tunnel. There was only one bright sliver. One spot of light."

"Is that right?" she asked. He was staring at her with a look she couldn't read, a look that sent her pulse skimming.

"That light was you, Rosie," Bart said. "It was you. And that's why I came to Raton, New Mexico. I came to find that light again, to see if I could touch it, to see if it could shine away some of that darkness in the stinking black pit I've made of my life."

Oh, Bart, she wanted to say, *I forgive you. I forgive you!* But the one-o'clock lunch train pulled into the depot with a whistle and a rush of steam that obliterated every sound in the tiny room. Rosie felt the floor shake and heard the window rattle. And she was thankful—so thankful—she hadn't said anything to Bart.

As she left her room and hurried down the stairs to the lunchroom, Rosie saw the faces of her disappointed father and her angry fiancé. She saw the wreath of rosebuds and lilacs she'd worn in her hair the night she married Bart Kingsley, the glade where she had cried her eyes out over him, the parlor where William Lowell had knelt to ask for her hand and her heart—the heart she had promised to another man.

Rosie realized that with all these things, a blackness

had crept into her own life. A blackness so intense she had fled it on a midnight train to a frontier town where no one could ever find her again. A blackness so dark she was not at all sure that even a flicker of light remained—the light that had been Laura Rose Vermillion. The light Bart had come seeking.

Chapter Four

Minutes after the last lunch train pulled out of Raton, Sheriff Bowman and the local pastor strolled into the lunchroom looking for a bite to eat.

"I'll have a ham sandwich, Miss Laura," Reverend Cullen said as he seated himself at her table. "And a dish of that wonderful Harvey ice cream."

"I'll take the same," the sheriff said. "Been out all night and most of the morning chasing that outlaw. I'm hungry enough to eat my own horse."

Rosie tried to smile as she hurried to the kitchen. When she returned and began setting out the meals, the two men were deep in conversation.

"Bart Kingsley is a skunk," the sheriff said. "Nothing but a no-good half breed."

"Now, only the Lord knows a man's heart," Reverend Cullen reminded him. "This Kingsley fellow may not be bad through and through."

"You didn't hear what the Pinkerton man told me before he left for Kansas City this morning," the sheriff insisted. "The gunslinger's got a file as thick as this sandwich. The things he's done would make your hair curl."

"Did the detective think Kingsley got away last night?" the preacher asked.

"Not sure. We lost track of him right here at the depot. I figured he hopped a train, but the Pinkerton man wanted to search the girls' rooms. I set him straight on that real quick. Tom Gable would have a fit if I let any man set foot upstairs. Ain't that right, Miss Laura?"

Rosie swallowed. "I believe it's Mrs. Jensen who would have the fit."

"Ain't that the truth! Anyhow, I figured the minute a stinkin' outlaw set foot in one of the girls' rooms, there'd come a hollerin' and bawlin' like you never heard."

The elderly preacher smiled at Rosie, his blue eyes warm. "But I'm sure our fugitive is long gone."

"The gals will do well to be cautious. Bart Kingsley ain't got proper parentage. The mother's said to be a…" The sheriff glanced at Rosie. "A woman of the evening."

At that the preacher thumped his hand on the counter the way Rosie had seen him do in church. "I've heard enough. A man can't be held responsible for his lineage."

"Kingsley ain't responsible for his family tree, but he's sure accountable for them three trains he robbed over in Missouri. Two men was killed during one holdup. No half-breed gunman is gonna get away with nothing while I'm sheriff. There's a price on his head. Fifty dollars. If I have to, I'll shoot him on sight."

"Fifty dollars would go a long way toward the new

house you're building," Reverend Cullen said. "But you don't even know what the man looks like."

"I saw him well enough to shoot him, didn't I? Besides, he's half Apache. He'll have black hair and a chest like a barn door. He'll be packin' guns and wearin' some kind of buckskin getup like the one he had on last night. If he's anywhere around here, it won't be long before I put a window in his skull."

The sheriff stood and palmed a nickel onto the counter. "Afternoon, preacher," he said, settling his hat on his head. He nodded at Rosie and strode out of the lunchroom.

Hands trembling, Rosie began gathering up plates and glasses as fast as she could.

"Now, don't give the sheriff much heed," Reverend Cullen told her as he stood. "He's fit to be boiled because he lost the outlaw's trail last night. Will I see you in church as usual this Sunday, Miss Laura?"

"I imagine so, sir." Rosie was fairly scrubbing the varnish off the counter as he made his farewell and stepped outside.

Oh, but she felt ill! Bart was an outlaw and a killer. He had admitted as much himself. Now she realized that he was the cause of every trouble in her life.

If Bart hadn't asked her to get married, she never would have disobeyed her father. She might have learned to like Dr. Lowell and been a good wife to him. And if she had cared for her husband, he might not have been as cruel as rumors insisted. After all, her pappy had liked the man and admired his medical skill. Maybe if Rosie had been a quiet and gentle wife, Dr. Lowell might never have felt the need to hurt or shame her, as her friends so often predicted he would.

If she had been more sure of Dr. Lowell's temperament, she might not have run away from him a mere two weeks before their wedding. And she wouldn't be fighting for her future with such slender hopes. Bart was the reason she was shaking like a leaf. Now he had followed her to Raton, he was up in her room and the sheriff intended to kill him!

Rosie wrung out her washrag and scrubbed the same patch of counter for the third time. Bart had told her she was the only light in his life. But she felt more like a snuffed-out oil lamp—black, empty and cold. Bart himself had turned down the bright wick of her dreams, doused her flame and blown away the final sparks.

She picked up her tray of empty plates and started for the kitchen, determination growing with every step. She hadn't come all this way and worked this hard to let some gunslinging outlaw ruin her hopes—no matter how his green eyes beckoned.

In a mere three years, Raton had grown from four ragged tents to a row of inhabited boxcars to a full-fledged bustling town. As Rosie marched down First Street, she felt a surge of hope. Her black-and-white uniform set her in crisp contrast to the ragged coal miners and rough-hewn cowboys on the street, and she held her head high. Maybe she did have an outlaw in her bedroom, Rosie thought. And maybe she had taken some unhappy paths in life. But none of that doomed her to failure.

Ever since she could remember, Rosie had loved children and had wanted to teach them. Pappy, of course, wouldn't hear of such an absurd notion. Schoolteachers were *working women* and therefore far beneath her in social status. She could almost see his face, his dark eyes snapping as he lectured her from behind his huge desk.

"Working women are socially suspicious," he had informed his stubborn daughter more than once. "They're just one step away from the very cellar of society—prostitution. My dream for you, Laura Rose, is marriage to a prominent man, a bevy of healthy children and success as a full-time homemaker."

Rosie had to smile as she crossed Rio Grande Avenue onto Second Street. Pappy would be downright apoplectic if he knew she had taken a job as a waitress. Women who worked in eating houses were at the bottom rung of the job ladder. Considered coarse, hard and "easy," they were usually believed to be doubling as women of ill repute.

One look at Fred Harvey's establishments, however, had convinced Rosie otherwise. Here in Raton she was held in as high esteem as any other reputable female. Men tipped their hats, women greeted her with genuine smiles. Rosie and the other Harvey Girls were invited to every community picnic, baseball game, dance and opera show in town. The fact of the matter was, in the two short months she had lived here, she had had more wholesome, refreshing fun than she could ever remember in her twenty-one years of life.

Never mind about Bart Kingsley, Rosie thought as she climbed the wooden steps to a small one-room structure at the corner of Clark Avenue and North Second Street. Rosie had come to Raton to build a new identity. Fred Harvey had laid her foundation, and Mr. Thomas A. Kilgore would build the platform on which she would at last find freedom.

She knocked on the door of the local schoolhouse. A middle-aged man with a walrus mustache and round spectacles greeted her. "May I help you?"

"Mr. Kilgore?" Rosie asked. At his nod, she continued. "I'm Laura Kingsley, sir. Recently of Kansas City. I work at the Harvey House, but I've come to speak to you about a teaching position."

His eyebrows lifted. "We're in class, Miss Kingsley. But come inside."

She entered a dimly lit room filled with children, each one standing at attention beside a chair.

"Students, I'm pleased to introduce Miss Kingsley," Kilgore said.

"Good afternoon, Miss Kingsley," the children chimed.

"I'm pleased to meet you. All of you." Rosie caught her breath at the realization that she was standing in the place she had dreamed of for so many years. A schoolroom, desks and flags, slates and readers, inkwells and chalk dust. How she had longed to teach—guiding small hands to form letters, listening to recitation, drying eyes and bandaging knees. The children looked exactly as she had pictured them—some clean and neat, others ragged and dirty; some bright with intelligence, others more dimly visaged; some giggly and mischievous, others solemn.

What would it be like to stand before them and open doors in their young lives? Rosie could hardly wait to find out.

"Students, you may be seated," Mr. Kilgore stated as he gave the children a quick scan through his spectacles. "Grade three, continue your history recitation without me for the moment. Lucy, you may lead the group. The rest of you carry on as you were."

As young heads bent to work, he led Rosie to his desk at the front of the room. "Now, Miss Kingsley, may I ask your teaching qualifications?"

"My father is a physician in Kansas City. I attended Park College, in Platte County, to study Latin, art, music and science. My marks were excellent, and I'm confident I can pass the examination of any school board."

"Miss Kingsley, I founded this school with the intent of forming a much larger institution. My wife and I have high hopes of establishing an independent school district in Raton according to territorial law. As you can see, we suffer from overcrowding here, and I fear my students are lagging behind other pupils of like age who have enjoyed better school privileges. At my request the school commission recently voted to extend our school term in order to give the students better preparation as they continue in their education. A good many of these boys and girls will one day attend high school, and some will even want to go on to college. We intend for them to be able to compete with their peers."

"Wonderful," Rosie said, impressed with the man's dedication.

"The voters of Precinct Six have petitioned an election for this purpose, and it will take place the last Saturday of the month. If it passes, the school term will continue through July."

"July! That should allow plenty of time for the students to make up what they've missed."

"Should the election turn out favorably, however,

I'm afraid I will be without a teacher. My regular instructor has…" Here he paused to survey the room, then he leaned closer toward Rosie. "The primary school teacher has elected to return to Chicago as the bride of a young lawyer of her acquaintance."

Rosie's heart swelled with hope. "I would be honored to fill the teaching position your difficult situation has made available."

He pulled at his mustache for a moment before responding. "Return tomorrow morning, Miss Kingsley, after I've had time to ponder this."

"Yes, Mr. Kilgore. Thank you for considering me."

Light-headed with optimism, she shook his hand firmly before making her way to the door.

As she raced back to the restaurant, Rosie laid out a plan. If she were to get Bart Kingsley safely out of her room and on his way, he would need something decent to wear. Her Harvey Girl salary of seventeen dollars and fifty cents a month plus tips, room, board, laundry and travel expenses left plenty of spending money. She had saved nearly all her income toward her goal to buy a small house. But she was more than willing to spend a dollar or two on a new shirt if it meant she could send Bart away. Far, far away.

After the evening trains had pulled away and the dining room had been set in order, the Harvey Girls climbed the long stairway to their dormitory hall. Even though it was well after ten, Rosie was wide-awake as she clutched the shirt she had purchased and opened her bedroom door.

"Bart?" she called softly.

"Over here, Rosie." His deep voice came from the

corner by the window. "I waited for you. I wanted to say goodbye."

She lifted the glass globe of her lamp and lit the wick. Bart was dressed in his buckskin jacket and denim trousers. But the warrior with shining black hair and bright green eyes was not the wounded wreck who had crawled out from under her bed.

She looked away. "The sooner you leave, the more of a head start you'll have on the sheriff. He's still after you. He was in the restaurant talking about how wicked you are."

"I reckon I am, Rosie."

She shrugged. "As the Bible says, sow the wind and reap the whirlwind. If Sheriff Bowman gets his hands on you, he's going to shoot you dead. He wants the fifty-dollar reward."

"Then I reckon I'd better not let him find me." With a gentle smile on his face, he walked toward her.

Rosie winced at the thud of his boots on the hollow wood floor, but it was the nearness of the man that made her face go hot. "W-what are you going to do?" she stammered.

"Right now I'm planning to say goodbye to the only woman I've ever loved."

"I… I mean after you leave. Where are you going?"

"I'm glad you care about me, Rosie."

"I don't care. Not a bit. But I think I should know where you'll be, just in case."

He stopped a mere two feet in front of her. "In case what?"

"In case…" She moistened her lips. "In case I should ever need to know what became of you. Last time you went off without leaving a clue. Now I know you were running with an outlaw gang. Is that what you're planning to do again?"

His eyes searched her face. "I reckon a man who truly loves a woman ought to think of something better to do than robbing banks."

He lifted his hand to touch her cheek, but she caught her breath and pushed it away.

"You made that same sound the first time I kissed you," he said in a low voice. "Remember, Rosie-girl? We were at our special place by the stream. I grabbed your hand and kissed it. You gasped…but you didn't pull away from me."

Her eyes trained on the lamp, she shook her head. "I'm a different woman now, Bart, and you'd better leave my room right this minute."

"You're no different, Rosie. Not really. You're the same girl I married six years ago."

"No, I'm not." She whirled on him. "I've been engaged to Dr. William Lowell for three years and—"

"And you've never forgotten me. We loved each other back then, Rosie."

"We were children! We didn't even know what love was."

"And you're telling me that you do now? If you love your rich fiancé so much, how come you ran off and left him? Why are you hiding out in New Mexico?"

"Stop it, Bart! You don't know one thing!" Her eyes stung with unshed tears.

"I know one thing. I know I aim to make a new life for myself. And finding you is the beginning of it."

She crossed her arms and stared at the ceiling in hope that he could read nothing on her face. Oh, why couldn't this confusing man just leave her as he had before—with no farewells, no speeches, no tenderness?

Why was he standing so close, smelling so good and looking like the man in her dreams? Why did her heart have to hammer and her throat swell up in a lump? And why, oh, why did she long to feel his arms around her just one more time?

"We're both trying to start over, Bart," she said when she trusted herself to speak. "If finding me is the beginning of your new life, it could be the end of mine. I don't want any reminders of the past. I want to be a new person. I want to be alone, Bart. Alone!"

"Rosie," he murmured, unlocking her arms and letting his big hands slide down to take hers. "Rosie, don't push me away. Give me a chance."

"I've always done what people told me to—my pappy, Dr. Lowell, you. I don't have to live that way anymore."

"But I'm not telling you to do anything, Rosie-girl. I'm asking. Please…give me a chance."

She studied the design on her pressed-tin ceiling. "A chance to what?"

"To touch your face, Rosie." He ran the tip of one finger down her cheek. "Remember how I used to pull the ribbons from your braids? I'd untwist your hair until it hung loose around your shoulders. You used to laugh and scold me because I could never put your braids back the right way, and you worried that your pappy would find out we'd been together. But I knew you didn't really care, because you always leaned against my shoulder and let me slide my fingers through your hair."

As he spoke, he slipped his fingers through the bun she had so carefully knotted that morning. Oh, how she tingled at his touch! The desert in her heart came to life for the first time in six years, and Rosie closed her eyes as a powerful yearning washed through her.

When he drew her closer, she sighed and moved against him. But she remembered too well the pain a broken heart could bring. At the sudden realization of her peril, her eyes flew open.

"Bart, you'd better leave," she breathed out. "Just go!"

"Rosie?" Confusion darkened his eyes.

"I—I have to work the early shift tomorrow."

"I've scared you, haven't I?"

"I'll be tired if I don't get a good night's sleep. You ought to head out while the moon's up."

She looked into his face. She longed for this man and she loathed him. She feared the feelings he evoked in her, and she craved them. She hungered for his touch, yet the thought of it terrified her.

"Goodbye, Bart." She forced the words out. "It was good to see you again, and I sure hope your wound heals up."

Before he could see the quiver in her lower lip, she turned away from him and hurried to the hook where her aprons hung.

Chapter Five

B̲art studied Rosie in the lamp's glow. With shaking fingers, she fumbled to release the buttons on her bib. Unable to watch her in such distress, he stepped behind her and set his hands on her shoulders.

"Rosie," he murmured against her ear. "Rosie, I don't mean to upset you. I just want you to know that a day hasn't gone by without my thoughts going over and over those times we spent together. I want you to understand how I felt while we were apart. Rosie?"

His hands circled her waist and he turned her to face him. Her fingers kept working at the bib buttons as she trained her focus on her uniform.

"You're all atremble," Bart whispered as he covered her hands with his own and began sliding each tiny button out of its hole. "Did I ever tell you how crazy I am about your ankles, Rosie?" he asked.

As he let the bib fall, she shook her head. "My ankles?"

"When you were fifteen, you used to take off your stockings and wade in the swimming hole. You were so prim, but seeing you that way just about killed me."

His focus lifted to her face. "Once you slipped on a mossy rock and fell in the water, remember?"

She shook her head and shrugged. "Anyhow, I bought you a shirt today. I decided against a collar. They cost twenty cents each."

"I remember everything about us. You've changed a lot in six years. You're more beautiful than ever. I've been half loco missing you, girl."

He wouldn't hurt or frighten his Rosie for anything in the world. But he couldn't abide the thought of leaving without saying the things he'd needed to say for six long years.

Even though she had told him to go away, she was having trouble meeting his eyes. In spite of what she said, maybe she had missed him just a little, and maybe she'd thought about him now and then. But she was still trembling and her hands were locked behind her back as though they'd been handcuffed. Was he scaring her?

"Rosie," he whispered. Her eyes, dark brown and liquid, focused on him at last. "Rosie-girl, will you put your arms around me the way you used to? Will you hold me just once before I go?"

"Oh, Bart, I can't."

"Because your pappy made you promise to marry another man? Or do you love your rich Dr. Lowell? Is that what holds you back?"

"Bart, it's not like you think. I don't love him and I don't want to be attached to a man again. Not ever."

"How come?"

She squared her shoulders. "You might as well know I can't have children, Bart. After you left me, I was sick a long time. Months and months. I couldn't eat, I didn't sleep much at all. My normal functions…well, everything stopped working right. My father took me to several doctors, friends he trusted, and they said I was barren. All of them agreed I'll be childless. Since having children is the only reason I can think of for… for going through all that rigmarole, I've decided to be a spinster for the rest of my life."

He couldn't hide a grin. "Rigmarole?"

"You know very well what I mean." Pulling out of his arms, she walked across her room, sat on the edge of her bed and began unlacing her boots. "As far as I'm concerned, God made beds for sleeping in, and I don't intend to put my arms around you or anyone else."

Bart hunkered down on one knee beside her. Taking her blistered foot, he set it on his thigh and began rubbing her reddened heel and each sore toe. It bothered him that Rosie had spent time with another man. But it bothered him a lot more to realize that maybe he himself had killed the spark he had once loved so much.

Maybe not quite killed it. Squelched it.

"Rosie, you reckon I could get a job here in Raton?"

"Not a chance. The sheriff would recognize you. He said he saw you before he shot you."

"How well could he see me in the dark?"

"Well enough to shoot you again."

"What if I wore that new shirt you gave me? Would you cut my hair, Rosie?"

She shivered. "It wouldn't do you a bit of good. Your skin is as brown as a berry, Bart. The sheriff said he'd be on the lookout for a man with a face like yours."

"Would you cut my hair anyway, Rosie? I want to give the straight life a chance."

"But here in Raton? Why, Bart?"

Raising his head, he covered her fingers with his

big hands. "Once upon a time, all it took was a few harsh words to send me scampering. But I've changed in six years. I learned to do things. If I set out to break a horse, I'll have him gentle as a kitten in no time flat. If I aim to rob a train, I'll rob it plumb dry."

"Bart!"

"That's the facts. I came to Raton to find you and make a new life. So if you'll give me a haircut, darlin', I'll get on with it."

As she combed and snipped away at Bart's coal-black mane, Rosie berated herself over and over again. Crazy. She was just crazy, that's all! She should have sent him off long ago. Instead, she'd let him hold her hand, whisper in her ear, rub her foot. And now she was actually cutting the man's hair so he could stay in Raton and make her miserable!

"Reckon there's any chance I could pass for a gentleman dandy just off the train from Chicago?" He studied himself in her silver hand mirror.

"Bart, you look just like what you are—an outlaw. A big, brawny gunslinger."

"I'd better leave my six-shooter and holster with you."

"Don't you dare! Bad enough I have to hide a bloody rug and a pile of chopped-off black hair."

He chuckled. "You've done me a good turn, Rosie. Much as my side still hurts, I wouldn't have made it this far without your kindness."

Softening, she ran her brush through his hair. Now that it stopped just above his collar, she could see the tremendous breadth of his shoulders. "In spite of the haircut, you still look like an Apache to me."

"Does my blood make a difference to you now, Rosie?"

"I always told you to be proud of who you are, Bart. It's what's inside a man—what he chooses to do with himself—that makes him who he is."

"And I chose to be an outlaw. I'm a no-good half-breed outlaw."

Rosie stepped around his chair. As she gazed into his green eyes, she saw that he had become the little boy again, wounded by the cruelty of others. "When I knew you on the farm, you never hurt anything. What happened to you? What changed you?"

He stood suddenly. "Aw, why does it matter anyhow? I can't turn back time. I've dug myself a grave and I'm just one foot out of it. All my life I've been searching for something, but I don't know what. The only thing I'm sure of, Rosie, is that when I'm near you, I'm close to the answer."

"Oh, Bart, I can't mean so much to you! I have to get on with my own life and find what I'm searching for."

"What are you looking for, Rosie?"

"Freedom," she whispered. "I want freedom."

"Don't tell me that, girl," he groaned, his face twisting with pain. In one step, he took her hand, lifted her from the floor and drew her into his arms.

"Oh, Bart, why did you run off and leave me?" she murmured. "And why did you ever come back?"

"Hush, girl. Stop your frettin' now and let me hold you the way I used to."

Rosie slipped her arms around Bart and laid her cheek against his chest. A wash of memory soothed her heart. *Let me hold you the way I used to,* he had said. Between these two who had loved so young, there had been only kisses and avowals of devotion, passion tempered by moral restraint.

But who was *this* Bart, this gunman? She drew back and searched his face. As his fingertips trailed down her neck, she realized that they were no longer children.

"I remember so well how we used to hold each other close—and how much I liked it," she said. "But you never touched me. Not the way married people do. And, Bart, I don't want that now either."

"It's all right, Rosie. This is enough for me. More than enough."

The touch of a hand on her shoulder woke Rosie. "Laurie, wake up! You're going to miss uniform inspection."

Sitting bolt upright, Rosie stared at her friend's wide blue eyes. "Etta?"

"Well, who did you expect?" Etta shook her head. "Come on, lazybones. You've got ten minutes before Mrs. Jensen gives you what for."

Unable to speak, Rosie glanced at the empty chair Bart had slept in the night before. She surveyed her room. His buckskin jacket was gone. His holsters and six-shooters had vanished from the shelf. There were no boots on the floor and no trousers hanging on a line overhead. Rosie's white curtains danced in the breeze at her open window.

"Look at you," Etta exclaimed. "You slept in your uniform!"

Rosie slid out of bed and brushed past her friend. Bart must have climbed out the window during the night.

"Hurry," Etta cried. "Mr. Gable will have a hissy fit if he sees you looking like that!"

"Etta, give me a minute alone." Rosie ushered her friend into the hall. She shut the door and leaned against it as the inspection bell began to ring. "Dear Lord, Bart's gone," she murmured in heartbroken prayer. "He left me again. How can I go through this another time?"

But she had little time to mourn, Rosie realized as she pinned her bun in place and tossed a clean apron over her wrinkled black dress. She buttoned the bib while wiggling her bare feet into her shoes. Bolting through the door, she snapped to attention just as Mrs. Jensen approached.

"Miss Laura, you're late." The elderly woman scanned her up and down. "Mr. Gable will not be pleased."

"I'm sorry, ma'am," she mouthed.

Mrs. Jensen gave a cluck. "That dress is dirty. Change it at once. You haven't even laced your boots. You'll scrub the hallway after the breakfast trains."

"After breakfast?" She was to meet with Mr. Kilgore at that time. "But I can't! I have to—"

"Have you found another occupation more interesting than Fred Harvey's restaurant, Miss Laura? If so, I'll inform Mr. Gable that he may hire your replacement from the long line of young women waiting in Kansas City and Chicago for just such an opportunity."

Rosie lowered her head. "No, ma'am. It won't happen again."

Soapy water dampening her cuffs, Rosie sniffled back tears as she scrubbed the dormitory walls. Bart was gone. When she had returned to her room to change into an ironed dress, she searched every nook and cranny of the little place. Bart was gone, along with his boots, guns, jacket, britches and even the shirt she had bought him.

Her heart fluttered a little every time she thought that he might actually have gone into town to look for work. But the spark of hope was quickly quelled by the reminder that for six long years Bart had not been a working man. He'd been an outlaw. And for all his talk about haircuts and new shirts, he still looked like an Indian. She had no doubt he had either left town or been shot.

The sheriff didn't come in for breakfast, and neither did Mr. Adams of the *Comet*. It was all Rosie could do to keep from approaching her minister. But Reverend Cullen was visiting with another preacher, and none of the other locals said a word about town news.

The time passed when Rosie should have been at Mr. Kilgore's school, and her heart sank even further. Such a responsible man would never hire a teacher who couldn't bother to show up when she had promised. What kind of an example was that? The lunch trains started through the depot just as Mrs. Jensen approved Rosie's newly scrubbed walls, and she rushed down the stairs to her station. Swallowing the knot in her throat, she served up sandwiches and soups and plates of fresh fruit by the score. She scooped tips into her pockets, scrubbed countertops, and pasted the Harvey smile on her face.

But as she stood with her hands locked behind her back and her eyes scanning her station, she felt sick with unhappiness. Bart had kissed her last night and made her feel things she'd never even imagined. The memory of his touch was so strong that it rocked her off balance every time she allowed it to creep through her thoughts.

Then he had gone away. Sometime in the night, he must have strapped on his guns and climbed out her window to start his new life without her.

Buttery afternoon sunlight gilded Rosie's hand as she knocked on the schoolroom door. From inside the small frame building she could hear high-pitched voices lifted in song. When the accompanying guitar hit a discordant twang, the choir dissolved into giggles.

"Good afternoon, Miss Kingsley," Mr. Kilgore said, none too warmly. "You are late for our meeting."

"I'm sorry, sir," Rosie replied. "My services were unexpectedly required at Harvey House."

He pondered for a moment. "I'm afraid a meeting is no longer necessary. After discussing your request with my wife, I concluded that your services will not be required here."

"But why not? I'm qualified, and you need a teacher."

Mr. Kilgore stepped outside and spoke in a low voice. "Miss Kingsley, you have neither a teaching license nor any professional recommendations. You have no training and no experience at all."

"But I shall obtain the license as soon as possible. As for experience, how am I to acquire it unless someone like you is willing to employ me? I have the education, the dedication and above all the sincere desire to become a teacher."

His face softening, Mr. Kilgore tipped his head. "I appreciate your enthusiasm, Miss Kingsley, but you lack one other attribute I have decided to insist on for any teacher in the town of Raton, New Mexico. A husband."

"A husband?"

"A local man with steady employment. In the short time since I opened this school, I've lost both my teachers to the lure of matrimony. With all the railway men, homesteaders and cowboys in town—each one eager to find a wife—I wager every Harvey Girl will be wed within the year. Wed and gone."

"I have no intention of marrying, sir," Rosie responded hotly. "I can assure you of that."

"A woman as fetching as you? With those big brown eyes, I daresay you'll have your choice of husbands. I'm sorry, Miss Kingsley, but you're too great a risk. Good afternoon."

He bowed, backed into his classroom and shut the door on Rosie's dreams.

For a long time she stood on the porch and listened to the children reciting multiplication tables. She could never admit she already had a husband. And a fiancé, for that matter. Of course Dr. Lowell would be loath to marry her now. Her desertion would have placed him in a perilous social position. It may even have endangered his professional standing. But she had never loved him or any other man…except Bart.

Plenty of men in Raton had made passes at Rosie, asked her to dance and escorted her to picnics. Wanting to seem like the other girls, she had gone along with these attentions to some degree. But she had always pushed away any serious advances with the excuse that eventually she wanted to become a teacher—and good teachers were always *single!*

Perhaps if she truly wanted a husband, she could bat

her eyelashes and secure one in no time flat. But what a price to pay for a teaching position. Not for anything in the world would Rosie trade away her freedom.

As she headed for the Harvey House, she studied the townsmen delivering goods to the mercentiles, swabbing saloon floors, marching in and out of banks and driving cattle to the stock corrals by the depot. None of them had the broad-shouldered, rugged physique of the one man Rosie actually might have considered allowing on the fringes of her life.

Bart Kingsley was gone. She had no doubt of it. The town felt empty to her, devoid of the presence she felt sure she would sense were he there.

With a sigh she climbed onto the porch of the Harvey House and fixed her eyes on the distant blue mesas. She didn't want Dr. Lowell for a husband. She didn't want a cowboy or a railwayman either. Even if she wanted Bart, she couldn't have him, and she might as well accept that she never would. Now she had lost her chance at the teaching job.

As the first dinner train whistled through the distant pass, Rosie molded her lips into the Harvey smile and hurried to her station in the dining room.

Chapter Six

Any small hope Rosie might have held that Bart was in town faded as the days turned into weeks, and the month of April headed for May. Raton came to life with sweet wild grasses that greened the patchy yards around newly white-washed clapboard houses. Lilacs, roses and violets brought from the east blossomed among budding native piñon, aspen, juniper and cottonwood trees.

True to Mr. Kilgore's prediction, spring fever took its toll. One of the girls up and married a cowboy from the J. R. Jones ranch, and she moved out of the Harvey House to take up her new job raising hogs. Another fell in love with a brakeman from Chicago who wanted to marry her and take her back to the big city. But she was also crazy about a welder from C. A. Fox's hardware and tin shop, who aimed to make her his wife and settle her in a quaint little house in town. Etta and Stefan Braun failed to keep their romance a secret, and Mrs. Jensen was in favor of firing them both. It was only Tom Gable—who knew he couldn't find a better chef than the young German—who kept them employed at the house.

Rosie dragged herself to town picnics, horse races and egg hunts with the rest of the Harvey Girls, but it was all she could do to keep her chin up. One afternoon, the sheriff dropped by with some news for the coffee drinkers in the Harvey House lunchroom. The Pinkerton agency had sent word that Bart Kingsley had been rounded up in Albuquerque and carted back to Missouri to face the judge. He'd be hanged, Sheriff Bowman assured anyone who asked him. A man with a record as black as that outlaw's would be left gargling on a rope for sure.

So that was the end of that. Rosie had to accept it. Bart Kingsley really was no good after all. He had come into her life twice, toyed with her twice and left her twice. Not only that, but she had also been fool enough to believe everything he had told her—twice. All his sweet words and gentle ways had been a sham. His tender touch had served his own selfish aims. How she had managed to fall for such a man twice, Rosie would never understand. She certainly wouldn't let herself act so harebrained ever again.

In fact, as April wound to a close, Rosie decided she would pursue her goal of teaching just as she had planned. She had heard rumors that Mr. Kilgore had not yet filled his vacant position. If the resolution to extend the school year passed during the coming election, he would be in need of a teacher.

And if not Mr. Kilgore, one of the other school owners in town might be looking for a determined young spinster, though her inquiries at the other schools had come to nothing.

Still hopeful, Rosie scheduled an appointment with the district school board in Springer, hours away by rail. One Friday, she used her free vacation train pass to travel south to Springer where she sat for examination.

"You have passed with distinction, Miss Kingsley," the commissioner announced as he handed her a crisp certificate that afternoon after she had sat through five hours of grueling questions. "Any school in the district would be proud to employ you."

All the way back to Raton on the train, those words curled through Rosie's thoughts. As the engine struggled up the mountains, her determination grew. She would not think about Bart any longer—no matter that he was locked away in a Missouri jail. No, she would set her sights on that teaching job. Mr. Kilgore's school had the finest reputation in the area, and with her exemplary performance on the exam, she would secure a position there.

The moment the train whistled into town, Rosie smoothed and dusted her city skirts, descended onto the depot platform and marched straight to First Street. By the time she turned onto Second Street, her heart was pumping harder than it had the whole time she'd been facing the school board. She climbed the schoolhouse steps, tucked stray wisps of hair into her knot and knocked on the front door.

"Ah, Miss Kingsley," Mr. Kilgore said at the door. "Again."

"Yes, sir." Rosie handed him the document. "I passed the examination."

"My goodness, these are high marks," he commented as he studied the certificate. "Mathematics, Latin, history, geography, grammar. Even French. Well done."

"Mr. Kilgore, will you please reconsider my application for a teaching position?"

He chuckled lightly. "Persistence is indeed a virtue. But, Miss Kingsley, I am assailed by doubts. I simply won't hire another unmarried woman. Why don't you take your certificate back to Kansas City and teach there?"

"I've made my home here," she protested. "I belong to a church, I have friends, I'm part of a community I love. I've put my savings in Raton's bank and I've proven myself a reliable worker here. Why do you ask me to start all over when you need a teacher?"

"I don't know that the school election will pass, Miss Kingsley. I'm sorry, my dear. Truly, I am."

Once again, he shut the door on Rosie. She stood outside, fingers gripping her skirt and jaw clenched against threatening tears.

"I will have that job, Mr. Kilgore," she whispered over the lump in her throat. "I *will* have it."

Discouraged but undaunted, Rosie hurried back to the Harvey House and climbed the stairs to her room. Having taken the day off for her trip to Springer, she still had several hours to herself while the other girls waited on the dinner-train passengers. Even though she had thought the free time would be a blessing, she discovered that her mind insisted on traveling down a wayward track.

As she sat on her chair by the window, Rosie couldn't keep back the memories of those hours she had spent with Bart. How badly she had been fooled! He had told her he'd come to Raton to find her, that she had been the one bright spot in his life. And so she had doctored his wound, fed him, boarded him and clothed him.

Then he had taken his new haircut and his new shirt and gone away again.

They had spent such a short time together, but Rosie knew she would never be the same. In those brief hours with Bart, she had fallen under his old spell. She had trusted every word from his lying lips. She had trembled at the sight of his now-so-masculine physique.

Worst of all, she had allowed him to kiss her in a way no man ever had. Certainly Dr. Lowell had never kissed her in such a way. In fact, she could count only two times he had attempted such a liberty, and both had been utterly repulsive.

Dabbing a silk handkerchief to the corner of her eye, Rosie stood from the window seat and went to her dressing table. She spread her rolled teaching certificate and slid it into the edge of the oak frame around her mirror so that she could see it from any part of her small room. She might be a fool when it came to Bart Kingsley, but she was brilliant in every other area of her life.

As she changed out of her city clothes into her white nightgown, Rosie decided that she had taken enough of what other people dished out. She had come to Raton to get a teaching position, and against all odds, she would have one.

"Dear God," she whispered as she folded her hands. "I've made some whopping mistakes, as You very well know. There was all that with Bart…and then I let Pappy talk me into accepting Dr. Lowell's proposal… and then Bart again. You can't be any too pleased with me. But, Lord, I had good intentions in coming out here to Raton to be a schoolteacher, only now Mr. Kilgore says he doesn't want me. Father, please work out this problem. Give me a sign so I'll know what You want me to do. Amen."

As she slipped between the cool sheets and shut her eyes, Rosie felt the first peace she'd known since Bart Kingsley crawled out from under her bed.

At one o'clock in the morning the screaming whistle of the switch engine woke Rosie with a start. Gunfire shattered the night's silence. Shouts and cries echoed through the streets.

"Fire! Fire!" someone hollered below the Harvey House dormitory. "O'Reilly's Saloon is afire!"

Rosie threw open her window to an ebony sky lit with an orange glow. Red sparks shot upward to mingle with the stars and then vanish. Smoke billowed over shingled rooftops. The members of the hose company dashed down the street.

"Laurie!" Etta barged into Rosie's room. "Laurie, everyone's going out to see the fire!"

Wide awake now, Rosie pulled on her robe as they ran into the hall. "O'Reilly's Saloon is a frame building, Etta! It'll go up like a matchstick!"

"The whole town might burn down! Oh, isn't this thrilling?" Etta, frizzy blond hair bouncing, hopped up and down in the hall as the other girls assembled. Even Mrs. Jensen, ruffled nightcap in place, had started for the stairs.

Clad in billowing white gowns, the Harvey Girls followed their matron across the street. Gray smoke hung thick in the night air.

Rosie noted with relief that no wind had sprung up to blow the fire from building to building. Even so, the whole town had come out to view the blaze. Children clung to their mothers' nightgowns. Fathers lugged buckets of sloshing water toward the saloon. Against the bright orange fire, silhouetted men wrestled heavy hoses to shoot streams of water onto the flames.

"There's Sheriff Bowman!" Etta cried. "I heard he was the first to spot the fire!"

Through the smoke, Rosie could barely make out the man kicking down O'Reilly's door. She recognized a good many townsfolk, including some of the sheriff's deputies and Reverend Cullen.

"There's Stefan!" Etta gasped. "Oh, Laurie, I hope he doesn't get hurt! That's Cheyenne Bill with him."

Rosie could see the young German's blond hair backlit by the blaze as he unrolled hoses from the hose cart. A stocky, long-haired man on the cart was shouting orders.

"Is Cheyenne Bill a real Indian?" Rosie asked. She had heard rumors the man was popular at glove contests. Some townsmen were said to wager large sums on him.

"Sure he's a real Indian," Etta said. "Who's that other Indian with him? I've never seen him before."

Rosie focused on the broad-shouldered silhouette of a man who had leaped onto the hose cart beside Cheyenne Bill. The stranger's short black hair glistened in the firelight, and his arms gleamed like bronze as he pulled at the tangled hoses. When he straightened to toss a length of hose to a waiting volunteer, ice washed through Rosie's veins.

"He's an Indian, all right," Etta said. "Oh, look, Laurie. The saloon roof is caving in!"

But Rosie could not tear her attention from the tall man on the hose cart.

"She's done for," someone shouted. "Let 'er go, boys!"

As the structure collapsed, the stranger vanished in the throng of men running for safety. But Rosie didn't need to see him again to know who he was.

Bart Kingsley was back in town.

"I'd open for you, fellers," one of the local saloon owners was saying, "but me and my cook are too tuckered out to fix up a meal this time of night."

"Who cares about a meal?" someone shouted in reply. "Open 'er up for the whiskey! Couple snorts of snake poison ought to be good for what ails us."

As the men laughed, Tom Gable elbowed his way into the street and waved his hat. "There are too many women and children here for you to turn this into a moonshine party. Come on over to the restaurant, and my gals will fix you up with some hot coffee and cinnamon rolls!"

"How-dee!" someone hooted as a stampede for the Harvey House got under way. Children in nightshirts, women in robes and soot-blackened men abandoned the charred saloon.

"Lord have mercy!" Mrs. Jensen shrieked as the full impact of Tom Gable's invitation hit. "Skedaddle, girls!"

Hand in hand, Rosie and Etta raced down a side street. The other girls were close on their heels. As they scampered up the back steps into the kitchen, they found Stefan and the other cooks already slamming oven doors.

There was no time to think. Rosie and her companions rushed into the empty dining room to take up their positions. In moments, the front door burst open as more than a hundred laughing, chattering Ratonians poured into Harvey House. Formality went by the wayside as the waitresses hurried to brew and pour hot coffee.

In no time the aroma of cinnamon, sugar, raisins and hot yeasty bread blended with the tang of smoke. As Rosie raced out of the kitchen, she ran smack-dab into Etta and nearly dropped a whole plate of rolls. In spite of her jitters, she laughed, lifted her tray a little higher and wove her way among the crowded tables.

How silly and free she felt to be dressed in her nightgown and robe. The counter was crowded with children who had managed to escape their parents. Rosie patted sleepy boys on the head and tucked napkins under the collars of wiggly girls.

"Hello, Miss Kingsley," a lad called out. "We saw you at our school." Amid a cacophony of giggles, Rosie waved at the young redhead she recognized from Mr. Kilgore's classroom.

"Are you going to teach us, Miss Kingsley?" a blue-eyed girl asked.

"Lord willing, I am." She glanced at Mr. Kilgore, who was surrounded by children at a small table.

"Miss Laura!" The shout came from Mr. Gable. "We've got fifteen cinnamon rolls coming through the door. Can you help?"

"Sure thing!" Rosie gave the children a wink as she skipped away.

"Right here, Miss Laura." Mr. Gable was seating a group of Raton's prominent townsmen at a large table. "They're asking for coffee, too."

For a moment Rosie thought she wouldn't be able to make her legs move. She was staring into a pair of green eyes that sparkled like rainwashed leaves. The buckskin jacket was gone. So were the holsters and six-shooters. But she knew that collarless white shirt, thick black hair and confident grin.

"Miss Laura!" Tom Gable shouted.

Jumping to attention, Rosie hurried into the kitchen and grabbed a tray of steaming rolls. *Bart!* But Bart had left Raton weeks ago! Bart had been captured in Albuquerque and sent to Missouri to be hanged.

Balancing the tray, she returned to the table and began setting a roll at each place. As she circled the table, she glanced across to find Bart watching her.

"Miss Laura, you got any refills on this coffee?" Sheriff Bowman held out an empty white cup.

Sheriff Bowman at the same table with Bart!

"I worked up a powerful thirst fighting that fire." Now she recognized Cheyenne Bill at Bart's elbow. With a broad grin, he eyed the other men. "I reckon I organized the whole affair from start to finish."

"Chances are you lit that fire in the first place," the sheriff said with a laugh as Rosie filled his coffee cup.

"Would I do a thing like that, now, Sheriff Bowman?" He feigned a hurt expression. "You just ask my cousin Buck. We was over at the Mountain Monarch playing billiards right up until we heard the switch engine whistle."

Buck? Rosie's eyes darted to Bart, who had just set his coffee cup in its saucer.

"Worst of it is, I was winning," Bart...or Buck said.

"Naw!" Cheyenne Bill clapped him on the back. "You boys think I should call a glove contest to settle this matter between me and my cuz?"

"You wouldn't want to spar with the Terror of the

Wicked West, Buck," the sheriff said. "Ol' Cheyenne Bill would drive you into the ground like a stake."

As if a signal had been given, all the men at the table chorused, "Cheyenne Bill is a hard, hard man."

Amid the ensuing hoots of laughter, Rosie fled to the kitchen. Bart was back! But why? Oh, why now? She leaned against a cupboard and clutched at her churning stomach.

How long had he been in Raton? How had he managed to become the *cousin* of Cheyenne Bill? And how on earth had he eluded Sheriff Bowman?

She pushed her heavy, loose hair behind her back. *Bart.* He was a liar, a trickster, an outlaw. And he was the handsomest man in the entire world! Oh, those green eyes. With his short hair and white shirt, he might have passed for a white man except that his high cheekbones and copper skin gave him away. But he certainly was not a full-blooded Cheyenne. He certainly wasn't named Buck.

And he most certainly *was* back in town.

"Miss Laura!" Mr. Gable bellowed. "Three more cinnamon rolls just walked in the door!"

Rosie squared her shoulders and hurried back into the dining room. But the big table had emptied, and Bart Kingsley had disappeared just as certainly as he had returned.

Chapter Seven

If any day in Raton could be given over to a little extra sleep, a fishing trip or a train ride to Springer for supplies, it was Saturday. With all the excitement over the Friday-night fire at O'Reilly's Saloon, Rosie wasn't sure how many men would haul themselves out of bed to cast a school election vote. Only a scant number of townsmen had appeared at Harvey House for breakfast, and she feared the inactivity didn't bode well for extending Mr. Kilgore's free public school for an extra three-month term.

Tired and on edge after the busy night, she scrubbed her dining-room station after the last morning train had chugged away from the depot. The exhilaration of the previous evening had faded during the long sleepless hours in which she had turned the reappearance of Bart Kingsley over in her mind.

When she asked permission to visit the voting boxes, Rosie acknowledged inwardly that she was driven out into the brisk morning by more than a desire to watch men cast ballots.

As she walked, she scanned the front of every building, peeking into windows and glancing through open front doors. She scrutinized every carriage that rattled past her down the street. She carefully inspected every rider, tradesman and merchant.

Several men were surveying the blackened ruins across the street from the Bank Exchange Saloon. Wisps of gray smoke curled into the blue sky to be wafted toward the distant snowy mesas. The local doctor's dog, an enormous brindle mastiff named Griff, was sniffing around the broken kegs and bottles. Griff had a well-known fondness for hard spirits and had been known to knock a man flat to get at his whiskey. Griff was accompanied by Tom, a mutt that was a favorite of the schoolchildren.

Among the charred beams, a group of boys played hide-and-seek. Rosie recognized one of them as the young redhead who had hailed her the night before.

"G'morning, Miss Kingsley," he called as he leaped over a charred piano. "Them sure was good cinnamon rolls!"

"Why, thank you, sir," Rosie answered, lifting a hand to wave. "And how are you today?"

Before the lad could answer, another began to jeer, "Manford Wade is sweet on Miss Kingsley! Mannie has a sweetheart!"

At that moment Griff took it into his massive head to chase the taunter and his pal down the street. Rosie watched the boys' scrawny legs churn as they ran around a corner, followed paces behind by Tom and Griff.

Mannie had ducked behind a blackened porch post, and now the redhead grinned at Rosie. "Where ya goin', Miss Kingsley?"

"I thought I'd take a look at the voting booths." She paused. "I'm hoping Raton will decide to keep you in school another three months, Manford."

"Three months is a long time. It'll be hot in the classroom, and most of us boys will be workin' on the farms or in the mines."

"Mr. Kilgore believes that if you want to keep up your studies, you'll need those extra months of school."

Mannie stuck his hands in his pockets. "I'm a good reader, Miss Kingsley. I wouldn't mind keeping a book handy this summer. But I don't cotton to figures. When it comes to numbers, I'm as chuckleheaded as an old prairie dog."

"If the proposal passes and your father lets you stay in school, you'll have time to concentrate on mathematics."

"I don't have a pappy, and my mother don't care a lick about arithmetic. She needs me to bring in a good wage come summer." He kicked his heel against a charred window frame. "So you're gonna have a look at the voting. One of these days, I'll get to vote. Mind if I come along?"

"I was hoping you'd join me." Rosie suppressed a grin as the youngster swaggered along beside her. Clearly Manford Wade regarded himself as a gentleman—not easily swayed by the teasing of his mates. Unlike the ragged boys he had been playing with, Mannie wore his shirtsleeves buttoned at the wrists and his tails tucked into his pants.

"You made them cinnamon rolls, Miss Kingsley?" he asked as they neared the line of men standing outside the assembly hall. The large building served as a gathering place for dances, socials, school plays, meetings, even church services.

"Our baker is in charge of the breads," Rosie answered before making an announcement that would have curdled her father's blood. "I'm a waitress."

Rosie stepped onto the wooden walkway and scanned the faces of the men in the line. Bart was not among them.

Had she dreamed he had been sitting at the table with Cheyenne Bill and Sheriff Bowman? If not, where was he now?

"You reckon women ought to get the chance to vote, Miss Kingsley?" Manford asked.

"The right to vote is a highly debated issue," she told the boy. "My father believes women aren't meant to take an interest in public affairs. His views led me to consider suffragettes as nothing but a hen party bent on making trouble. But, you know, Mannie, if women could vote, this school resolution would have a good chance of passing."

"Not if my mama could vote. She'd hold out against it. She wants me in the fields come summer."

Rosie was formulating a response when someone brushed past her elbow.

"Morning, Miss Kingsley."

She swung around to find Bart Kingsley already halfway past her. He and Cheyenne Bill were headed for the end of the voting line. He greeted several of the men, hooked his thumbs in the pockets of his britches and took up his position to vote in the school election of Raton.

Bart—a wanted outlaw! Rosie clamped her mouth shut and tried to make herself listen to Manford, who was lamenting the possible results of women attaining the right to vote.

"We might even have a lady sheriff," he was saying. "A lady sheriff? Now that would be bad."

While Cheyenne Bill bragged about how he had organized the hose company to fight the fire, Rosie studied Bart. As he had the night before, Bart wore the white shirt she had bought him, a pair of new denim trousers and the old boots she had once pulled off his feet.

"What about a lady governor?" Manford piped up. "Ain't no way a woman could manage all them governor jobs and be cookin', warshin', ironin' and such as that. My mama says if women got to vote, they'd turn into men and start smokin' cigars, drinkin' whiskey, wearin' britches, cussin'."

"Not every woman hankers to cook and clean, young fellow," Bart put in, his deep voice sending Rosie's nerves skittering.

Manford stared at the tall, green-eyed stranger. "You're Cheyenne Bill's cousin. What's your name?"

"They call me Buck. I work at the livery stable over by the depot." Though the words were spoken to the boy, Rosie knew the message was meant for her. "I claimed a homestead near the mesa, and I've started building my dugout."

For the first time since he'd joined the line of voters, Bart looked directly at Rosie. He tipped his battered black felt hat. "Howdy do, ma'am."

Before she could answer, Bart addressed Manford again. "I've got one hundred sixty acres of prime land, and I'm aiming to grow sugar beets for cash, run a few cattle and build myself a snug soddy to live in. I could use a man with a shovel on afternoons and weekends. What do you say to that, young man?"

"I say yahoo! I'd better run tell my mama!" Manford hightailed it across the street before sliding to a stop. "I'll be right back, Injun Buck. Don't leave town without me, hear?"

Before Rosie could fall under the spell of those green eyes, she stepped away from the line of men and hurried down the wooden sidewalk.

The dinner crowd brought news that the proposal to extend the school term by three months had passed, and Mr. Kilgore's free school would hold classes through the end of June.

"And he's looking for a teacher," Sheriff Bowman said around a bite of hot apple pie. "Tom declares he's going to bring our children up to par with every child back east. He says he'll go to Kansas City to fetch a new teacher if need be, but he'd rather hire a lady right here in Raton."

"What about Miss Hutchinson?" someone asked.

Rosie was serving at a station near the sheriff's table. As she poured cups of dark brown Harvey coffee, she leaned toward him to hear.

"Tom wants a married lady," the sheriff said. "He needs a teacher who's got roots, a gal who ain't goin' nowhere."

"I reckon Mrs. Poole might do a dandy job. Mrs. Poole or Mrs. Bell. Both of them's got education."

Rosie had knotted her fingers together behind her back and she wasn't even trying to wear the Harvey smile. The men were right. Any number of married women in town could take that teaching position.

I'm the best teacher for the job, she wanted to shout. Oh, how could Bart Kingsley just swagger into town and wangle himself a good job? Nobody expected him to be married before hiring him. Well, Rosie was married! Legally married for six years, as a matter of fact.

And her husband was right here in Raton. If Bart could lie his way into town, convince everyone he was someone he wasn't, get a job and claim land, why couldn't she get what she wanted the same way? And if Bart—conniver that he was—could toy with her, why couldn't she use him, too?

Her father had brought her up to be a moral Christian lady, but did that mean she couldn't have what she deserved? Why shouldn't she use a man who owed her for all the trouble he'd caused, a man who couldn't risk anyone tattling to the sheriff about who he really was…a man who belonged to her in the first place?

"Buck!" the stable boss hollered. "A pretty lady wants to see you. Better step to it before she gets away."

Surprised at the sight of Rosie standing in the doorway, Bart started across the hay-littered barn. He liked his work at the livery. The air was fragrant with well-oiled leather, sweet straw, fresh oats and dusty horses. Sunlight filtered through holes in the roof. It was a good place to be when so much was at stake.

"Howdy, ma'am," he said in greeting. He regretted his appearance—the sleeves of his blue chambray shirt were rolled up to his elbows, and he knew his collar was damp. Wondering if he smelled like a horse, Bart brushed bits of straw from his hair.

"Buck, is it?" she asked.

He nodded as his boss headed toward the back storage area. "What can I do for you, ma'am?"

She fixed her big brown eyes on him and took a deep breath. "You can do exactly what you promised six years ago before you ran off like a yellow-bellied coward. You can convince Thomas Kilgore that I'm your wife. I want to take a teaching position, and you're going to help me. After that, I don't care what you do with yourself."

Bart rubbed the back of his neck, concerned that Rosie might have gone a little off kilter. "You say you want to be my wife? You want people to know I'm your husband?"

Her eyelashes fluttered a moment. "Just until I've earned enough money to buy a house. Meanwhile, you'll take me out to that homestead you somehow got hold of and set me up comfortably. You'll earn a lawful, decent living for once in your life. You will do as I ask, or I'll march right over to Sheriff Bowman and tell him that you're not Cheyenne Bill's cousin and your name is not Buck. It's Bart Kingsley."

"Now hold on a minute—"

"I'll tell the sheriff you're the outlaw he shot that night when the Pinkerton detective was searching Raton. I'll tell him you used to ride with Jesse James and you robbed three trains. All he has to do to get his fifty-dollar reward is stroll over here to the livery stable and put you under arrest. So you'd better do as I say and take me for your wife without a word of argument."

Bart worked to hold back a bemused grin. "All right," he said finally. "Since you put it that way, I reckon I could do what you ask."

Her eyes widened as if she had expected a protest.

Bart leaned one shoulder against the side of a stall and chewed on the end of a piece of hay. How could his little Rosie know that she'd just made his dream come true? He had risked his life by hiding out in the New Mexico wilds while his bullet wound healed. Then he put his neck on the line by confiding in Cheyenne Bill, returning to Raton, taking a job in as public a place as the depot livery stable and staking a homestead claim in Springer.

He'd done it all in the hope that he could someday take Rosie back into his arms forever. He had supposed it would take months, maybe years, to earn her trust. Yet here she was, commanding him to marry her.

But at what cost?

"You might get the fifty-dollar reward yourself," he said. "Ever thought of that, Rosie?"

"I don't want fifty dollars. I want that teaching job." Her brown eyes sparked with determination. "I don't have much time, so here's what you're to do. Come to the House tonight and ask Mrs. Jensen if you can take me to church."

"Church?" Bart hadn't been to church in years. As a boy, he'd spent many a Sunday sitting on the church porch listening to the preacher. His pals didn't cotton to religion—never had seen much good in it. But Bart liked to hear the Bible read out loud. He liked what the preacher said, too.

Although he'd never had the chance to walk the aisle and proclaim himself a Christian, he figured he was one—in his heart anyhow. Of course, riding with the James gang prevented any churchgoing. The way he was living didn't make Bart any too eager to listen to sermons.

"Reverend Cullen is a good man," Rosie was saying, "and you need to try to prove you're moral. You'll court me every night next week. On Saturday we'll take the train to Springer. When we come back, we'll say we're married."

"We *are* married, Rosie."

She shot him a look of fury. Before she could argue, he continued. "So, when you get that teacher job, you'll up and walk out on your new husband? What will Mr. Kilgore and the school board say to that?"

"They'll think I'm such a fine teacher that they won't care a lick. Anyhow, I'm sure it won't take you long to go back to your wicked ways, Bart. All you know how to do is rob trains and banks. You'll get tired of sweating for your pay. A tiny dugout soddy, a field of sugar beets and a job shoveling horse manure won't hold your interest. Everyone will understand why I left you."

"What you really want to know is how long it'll be before I get tired of you, isn't it, Rosie?"

"You've left me twice, and I survived just fine." She turned away. "I'm sure I can do it again, Bart Kingsley."

Etta hammered on Rosie's bedroom door at exactly seven that evening. "Laurie! There's a man come to call on you. He's talking to Mrs. Jensen, and you should see him!"

Rosie's heart slammed into her ribs as she pulled a fringed shawl around her shoulders and opened the door. "I've been expecting him," she said with forced calm. "We spoke today in town, and he asked to accompany me to church tonight."

"He's the best-looking fellow I ever saw!"

"Better looking than Stefan?" Rosie hurried down the hall.

"Stefan's as cute as butter, but this man is so handsome it's plumb dangerous!"

Rosie took the last step down into the lobby, caught one look at the man who stood waiting for her and realized he was no longer the wild man who had crawled out from under her bed. Bart Kingsley had begged, borrowed or stolen a starched white wing collar that framed his bronzed face. A fine black cutaway jacket and a new pair of trousers completed the transformation.

"Evening, ma'am." Bart came toward her and held out an arm. "Mrs. Jensen has given me permission to escort you to church."

Rosie glanced at Mrs. Jensen and noted the high color in the woman's cheeks. Obviously the starchy matron wasn't completely immune to the charms of a dashing man.

"You'll stay with the others on the way to church," she told them. "And you'll have Miss Laura back at the dormitory at nine o'clock sharp."

"Yes, ma'am." Bart tipped his hat as Rosie slipped her arm through his.

Joining a crowd of young men and women, Rosie and Bart left Harvey House and headed for church. She could feel the hard lump of his biceps beneath his jacket sleeve, and his bay rum scent wafted around her head.

"Nice night," Bart commented. "It's a grand moon. Brisk wind down the mountainside sure sets up a chill, doesn't it?"

Rosie saw he was grinning at his own silly conversation. She rolled her eyes and gave him a sharp jab to the ribs. "It's windy around here, all right."

He chuckled as he led her up the steps. But as they entered the sanctuary, he leaned close and whispered in her ear. "You look beautiful tonight, Rosie-girl."

Without responding, she made her way to the pew where she usually sat. But when she had seated herself, Rosie looked around to find that Bart had vanished. Not again! She whisked out of the pew and marched back up the aisle. Bart wasn't going to pull this! Not tonight. Sheriff Bowman sat two pews in front of Rosie, and she would just tell him exactly who had escorted her to church.

But the moment Rosie set foot on the narrow porch, her heart melted. Bart was sitting on the stoop, his hat in his hands, just as he had when he was a little boy. With his head bowed, he was studying a small wrinkled Bible he had pulled from his pocket.

"Bart?" Rosie whispered. "What on earth are you doing?"

He lifted his head and smiled. "I figured I'd be more comfortable out here. Hope you don't mind."

"I do mind. You're no outcast that you have to hide like this." She crouched beside him, her blue dress billowing into a pouf. "Please come in and sit with me, Bart."

"I'm Buck, and I'm a half breed. I won't be welcome in there, no more than I was in the church back home."

Rosie laid a hand on his shoulder. "Please," she whispered. "You look fine tonight. Just fine."

"Fine clothes don't change the color of my skin, Rosie-girl. Much as I try to act decent, I don't know about manners in church and other high-society places. My mama used to say poor people have poor ways. She was right. Now get on back in there where you belong, and I'll meet you out here after the service."

Rosie shook her head. She wouldn't be the obedient little girl any longer. "I'm not going in without you, Bart Kingsley," she told him. "Now get up and escort me like a gentleman should."

It was a moment before he clambered to his feet and offered Rosie his arm. As they took their seats, it occurred to her that this was probably the first time in a long while that Bart had obeyed an order he didn't cotton to. She knew it was the first time ever that he had set foot inside the lily-white walls of a church. But before she had time to ponder all this, he took her hand, wove his fingers through hers and bowed his head in prayer.

Chapter Eight

When the church service ended, Bart wished he could ease right out a side door and escape for a few minutes alone with Rosie. The last thing he wanted was to be hauled to the church door where Reverend Cullen stood shaking hands with everyone.

For one thing, Bart was feeling convicted. From the time he was a boy, he had known preachers could really lay a sinner out—and Reverend Cullen was no exception. After nearly two hours of the minister's preaching that evening, Bart was squirming in his pew. He envisioned his transgressions stretched out across the heavens like a headline in *The Raton Comet*. Worse, he pictured God and the angels looking down on him and shaking their heads in disappointment.

Another reason Bart was hoping to bypass the preacher had to do with his uncertainties about trespassing in such a sacred place. If a half-breed Apache hadn't been wanted in the Kansas City church, what would make Reverend Cullen welcome him now? In spite of his bath, shave and the fancy duds he had bor-

rowed from the owner of the livery stable, Bart knew
he looked just as much like an Indian as ever.

The third reason for slipping out of church was to
talk to Rosie in private and get to the bottom of her
feelings for him. He had never known her to be so
downright cold. Miss Prim and Proper was in her element. If the angels were shaking their heads over Bart,
they were smiling with pleasure at the uppity Laura
Rose.

No doubt Rosie never felt a moment's conviction all
through that sermon. She didn't have a single thing in
her upright life to feel guilty about. As he made his way
up the aisle, Bart steeled himself for the disapproval
he would read in the preacher's eyes. Sure, the elderly
man had a handshake and kind word for everybody
else. But Bart didn't hold out much hope that he'd get
the same treatment. He had seen too many grins dis-
solve into thin air when he walked into a room.

"Reverend Cullen," Rosie said as she shook the
preacher's hand. "What a thought-provoking sermon.
I was truly moved."

"All credit goes to the Lord, Miss Laura."

Rosie turned to Bart, who wished he could disappear. "Reverend Cullen, I'd like you to meet..."

"Buck Springfield," Bart said.

The preacher stuck out his hand and grabbed Bart's,
giving it a firm shake. "Welcome to Raton, Mr. Springfield. I understand you're Cheyenne Bill's cousin."

Bart glanced at the ceiling, wondering if he could
be struck dead for telling two bald-faced lies right inside a church. "That's right," he managed. "We're like
family."

"Splendid! I've done my best to lure that gentleman into church. Now that you're in Raton, perhaps you'll be able to convince him of the need for spiritual renewal."

"I can try, sir." Bart discovered he was still shaking hands with the minister. "But you know Cheyenne Bill is a hard, hard man."

Reverend Cullen threw back his head and gave a hearty guffaw. "That he is! And you're escorting Miss Laura tonight. A fine young woman. You couldn't have chosen a better lady to court in this entire town."

"I agree, sir. Well, that was a real nice sermon. Good evening to you." Bart detached his hand and took Rosie's. Feeling hot around the collar, he lunged out into the night.

Rosie was fairly running alongside him. "Bart!" she cried. "Slow down. What's gotten into you?"

He shortened his stride and took a deep breath. "Did you hear what I said? I told him I enjoyed his sermon! He was preaching about sin and eternal damnation."

Rosie grinned. "I always tell him I like his sermons, even when he's been pounding the pulpit and shouting about Satan, iniquity and the fires of hell."

Pondering this, Bart eased to a stroll and tucked Rosie's arm inside his own. "I never met a preacher who'd welcome a man like me inside his church."

"There's nothing wrong with your bloodlines, Bart. And you certainly aren't responsible for them."

"But I am for all the other things I've done. If Reverend Cullen ever found out about my riding with the James gang and robbing those trains and being wanted in Missouri—"

"He'd treat you the same. He often quotes the Scripture where Jesus told a group of men who wanted to stone an adulterous woman, 'Let him who is without sin cast the first stone.' Everybody's done wrong, Bart. Anyhow, it's a good idea to go to church. People will think you're honest and upright. If Mr. Kilgore believes I've married a decent man, it'll help me get my job."

"You're doing all this hoo-ha with me just so you can teach school, Rosie?"

"Of course. After all I've been through, there's not a man alive who could persuade me to marry him for keeps."

"Just because you don't cotton to that doctor your pappy wants you to marry doesn't mean another man wouldn't treat you right."

She glanced at him. "I hope you're not referring to yourself, Bart Kingsley. You haven't done one right thing by me since I've known you. Now you've come to live in my town, and you'll probably mess things up for me here, too."

He stopped and pulled her around to face him. "What makes you so sure I'm going to mess up?"

"You haven't let me down so far."

He studied the tops of the cottonwood trees lining the street. Although the air was clean and fresh, his gut was twisted into a knot that grew tighter with every word from Rosie's mouth. Sure, those big brown eyes called to him. Those sweet, full lips beckoned. Yet Bart knew that when it came to him, Rosie had a chilly streak a mile wide.

"You don't believe I can lead a straight life?" he asked.

"Frankly, no. The last time you walked the straight and narrow you were seventeen years old. All your adult life you've been living on the wrong side of the law. Don't tell me you can up and change just like that."

"I reckon I could if I had a reason to."

She pushed his hands from her shoulders and crossed her arms. "Don't make me your reason to change, Bart. I remember the sweet words you said about me being the light of your life. Well, listen here. I'm not interested in being your light. If you want to change, go right ahead. I want my freedom and I moved to Raton to claim it."

"What are you so all-fired hot about, Rosie?"

"You've tangled me up as usual. I don't know why I let you talk me into that wedding nonsense when we were kids. I don't know why you ran off and left me like you did, or why you tracked me down after six years. I don't understand any of it!"

"Why don't you just ask me?"

"Because I don't trust a word out of your mouth." Her voice quavered for a moment, as if she were struggling not to cry. "You can go on blaming your mama, your Apache pappy, the boys who teased you, the preacher who wouldn't let you into church and everyone else for the way you turned out. But you're an outlaw because you chose to be one!"

"Hush now," he pulled her close, pressing her head against his shoulder. "You're going to scare up the sheriff with all this carryin' on."

Bart knew he was bad. Gritting his teeth, he stared up at the moon and acknowledged the truth. He was a sinner in league with the devil. And he felt just as mean and nasty as she had made him out to be. A hot flame of bitterness curled through him as he thought about Rosie's taunts and accusations.

Every instinct that had been honed over six law-less years told him to force her to do what he wanted. He could hold her down and kiss her the way he'd imagined during all the long nights alone. With bru-tal strength, he could bend her to his will, make her pay for hurting him.

She didn't believe he could ever change. So why should he struggle to suppress the animal inside him? Maybe he should show her just how bad Bart Kings-ley could be.

"Haven't you done your share of sinning?" he asked. "Haven't you lied to your pappy and pretended to be someone you're not? Weren't you married to one man and engaged to another at the same time? Come on, Rosie, answer me."

Her brown eyes met his. "Yes, I'm a sinner, Bart. Everyone is. I know I hurt my pappy and Dr. Lowell, too. Believe me, I've lived these past months torn be-tween wanting to make amends and needing to take care of my future."

"So you rank your desire for a happy life above the agony in your own father's heart?"

She caught her breath in a gasp. "Oh, Bart, it's true what you say. I've thought only of myself. But I'm sure that when I'm settled—with a teaching job and a home of my own—then I'll telegram my pappy."

"And in the meantime, you'll let him suffer?"

With a cry, she covered her face with her hands. Her hair had come loose from its knot. Long glossy ten-drils, silvered by the moon, spilled over her shoulders.

"Aw, Rosie," Bart cried in a muffled voice, "this ar-guing and fussing is killing me." Catching her tightly to him, he kissed her soft lips. "I'm sorry darlin'. You're right to call me a bad man. I'm used to punching anyone who makes me mad, stealing money when I need it, taking what I want without asking. But, Rosie, I want to change. I swear it."

Once he finally let her go, she backed away and stood shivering, her shawl clutched tightly at her throat. "You've made me see my own sins, Bart," she said in a hoarse whisper. "I will find a way to repair the damage I've caused. But I've never seen anybody change as much as you're going to have to. I expect it'll take a miracle."

"Reverend Cullen said miracles can happen."

"God's in that business, not you."

"So, maybe God will help me." He took a step toward her. "Rosie, can't you give me a chance?"

She shook her head. "I've given you too many chances. I've trusted you too much. If you want me to believe you're a different kind of person, you'll have to prove it to me."

"I will show you. If I can convince Sheriff Bowman I'm decent, I can convince you, too."

"Sheriff Bowman doesn't know who you really are." She turned and walked quickly toward the house. "Come for me tomorrow at four. We'll go skating at the rink."

For a moment Bart felt elated at her invitation. Then he remembered that Rosie didn't want to be with him because she enjoyed his company. She was out to get what she had set her sights on: that teaching job. And her freedom.

All the next day while Bart curried, fed and saddled horses, he thought about how he had told Rosie he wanted to change. The man she wanted wouldn't get drunk on a bottle of rotgut or shoot up a town. Changing meant he would have to put a lid on his urges. If she made him angry, he would find a way to let her know gently. He would listen better, be kinder, take life more peacefully.

He would go to church and read his Bible, too. But instead of just believing all those great things about Jesus, he would start showing his faith by doing right. He wouldn't just understand goodness. He would *be* good.

As he washed and dressed in his dandy clothes that afternoon during a break between trains, Bart made up his mind to win back Rosie's heart. She had loved him once. The memory of her at fifteen—those brown eyes gazing into his face and her sweet soft kisses—told him how much she had cared.

With his hair combed and his old boots shined, Bart presented himself to Mrs. Jensen at the Harvey House. But as Rosie walked into the room, he felt just as awkward and rough as ever.

Hat in hand, he stood to meet her. My, she was a beauty! She had brushed her hair up in a knot high on the back of her head and tied it with a ribbon. Her pink dress had a draped front that fell over her knees like a curtain swag and a pretty ruffle over the bustle.

"Good afternoon, ma'am," he said, managing a bow.

"Mr. Springfield, how kind of you to call." Rosie tucked her hand around his elbow as they took leave of Mrs. Jensen and headed down the boardwalk. The square skating rink was a crude structure constructed of rough-hewn planks. Its owner charged Rosie and

Bart twenty-five cents each for roller skates and an hour of skating.

The rink was almost deserted as Rosie laced her skates. Bart couldn't resist sneaking glances at her pretty little ankles. Anything but acknowledging the truth: He had never skated in his life. He'd have preferred to walk in the park. Maybe then he could steal a kiss or two.

But now Rosie was swirling out across the bumpy rink, her dress fluttering around her ankles like a blossoming rose. She wore a grin as big as Lincoln County as she spun around in a circle that lifted her hem clear up to her knees.

"Glory be," Bart muttered. If Rosie was going to expose herself in public like that, he'd better stay by her side. He lunged up from the bench, rolled out onto the rink and fell flat on his backside.

"Oh, Bart!" Rosie giggled behind her hands. "Don't you know how to skate?"

"The name's Buck, and does it look like I know how to skate?" She grabbed his hand and helped him to his feet. In moments he began to wobble. Then his legs spread-eagled and he crashed onto the boards with a thump and a whoosh of dust.

"Bart!" Rosie was beside herself by this time.

So was everyone else at the rink. Bart glanced at the other skaters and felt his hackles rise. "What's so funny?" he growled.

"It's just that you're so big and brawny," Rosie said as she reached for his hand again. "You look as if you could wrestle a bull to the ground with your bare hands."

"I *can* wrestle a bull to the ground with my bare hands."

"But you can't roller-skate? Bart, we have to teach you how to skate."

"Not me." He eased up into a crouch, then straightened his knees. "I haven't taken a fall like that since I was learning how to break a wild bronco."

"Take my hand, and we'll go around together. It's easy."

Rosie began skating slowly around the rink. Bart felt vulnerable hanging on to her like a frightened child, his jaw clenched and his eyes locked on his feet. He didn't like it.

"You're doing fine," she said when they had completed their second circle around the rink. "You want to try it alone?"

"To tell you the truth, Rosie-girl, I'm enjoying your company."

Though she blushed, she didn't move away from him, and Bart felt a thrill of victory as they swung in circles around the rink. Rosie's slender arm curved around his waist, and her laughter lightened his heart. It seemed they had barely started when a train whistled in the distant tunnel.

"I've got to go!" Rosie exclaimed. "I'll be late."

"So what? In a few days you're going to marry me and quit that job anyway. Why don't you stay with me, Rosie? I'll take you over to the Mountain Monarch for a bowl of ice cream."

"You're forgetting our deal, Bart Kingsley. We're here to show everyone that you're courting me. Besides, I can't quit work. I need every penny so I can buy myself a house in town."

She sat on a bench and began unlacing her skates. Her message was clear. There could never be anything between her and Bart. She just didn't trust him. Not one bit.

* * *

For a week Rosie kept tabs on Mr. Kilgore's unfruitful search for a new teacher. She and Bart made a public display as a courting couple everywhere in town. They went out to eat, attended Wednesday-night prayer meeting at church, strolled the streets of town and accompanied a group of Harvey House employees to a band concert at Bayne and Frank's Hall.

Etta was beside herself. She couldn't get over how much her friend had changed since the dashing Buck Springfield came to town. Whereas once Laura had chosen the most severe dresses in her wardrobe, Etta explained to the other Harvey Girls, she was now wearing those luscious things she had brought with her from Kansas City—bright blues, greens and pinks; drapes, waterfall frills, lace cuffs and fringes, checks, stripes, plaids and florals; taffetas, silks and velvets. From her traveling trunk, Rosie produced hats Etta had never even seen—straw hats with wide brims, small hats with upturned brims and lace edgings, tall felt hats and flowerpot hats.

More significant, Rosie was always giggling. Etta insisted her friend was falling in love.

It was all a ruse, Rosie told herself. She wanted everyone to think she cared for Bart to fulfill her plan. Although it was easy enough to spend an hour or two a day with him, Rosie knew she couldn't put much stock in those moments of laughter and fun. Every night when she went to bed, she knelt to pray that Bart wouldn't run off before she had gotten that teaching job.

As the days passed, it became clearer to Rosie that Bart would never last in Raton. He tried to keep his rough ways hidden, but it was hopeless. Not only couldn't he roller-skate, but he didn't know any popular songs. And he'd learned his manners in a pigsty.

When he and Rosie went out to eat at the Mountain Monarch with a group of Harvey employees, Bart leaned his chair back on two legs, picked his teeth with the end of a matchstick and told a wild story about a bear hunt. Then he slipped up and started to call her Rosie instead of Laurie in front of everyone. It took all his doing to explain that Rosie was just his pet name for his girl.

One of these days someone was going to fit the pieces of Bart Kingsley's puzzle together. One of these days someone would remember a half-breed outlaw who had come to town and been shot by Sheriff Bowman. And one of these days someone would link that man to Buck Springfield. There wasn't a doubt in Rosie's mind, and she had better set her plans in motion as soon as possible.

"We're leaving on the six-thirty train for Springer," she told Etta one evening. "We're going to get married."

Etta's blue eyes widened. "Married! Oh, Laurie, how wonderful!"

"Don't tell, Etta. Not even Stefan," Rosie warned her friend, knowing the news would be out before she got back to Raton.

"If you get married, you'll be fired the minute Mr. Gable finds out! Mrs. Jensen will have a hissy fit."

"I don't care. Buck has filed for a homestead and he has built a soddy on his land. He's planting sugar beets."

"You're going to trade being a Harvey Girl for a soddy and sugar beets?"

Rosie was silent for a moment. "I love him, Etta."

Etta caught her friend in a warm hug. "Marriage!

Your very own cookstove, ironing board, washtub, jam jars, and…and babies! You'll have scads of children. Just think, you'll be a man's wife for the very first… time…"

She drew back and faced Rosie. "You've been married before, haven't you? You said you had a husband once."

"But I told you we never were…together. Not in the way husbands and wives are. I kept on living at home, and he ran off two weeks after the wedding. It wasn't really a marriage."

"He was a half breed, too, wasn't he? And you told me that boy you married had black hair and green eyes."

Rosie's breath shook as she drew it in. "I guess I'm just a sucker for a man with green eyes. Lucky thing Buck is nothing like the kid I married when I was fifteen. That boy was so skinny and short…and ugly," she added for good measure.

"You've got a good man in Buck Springfield. He would never run off and leave you. Your first husband couldn't have been half the man you're marrying tomorrow."

"Really?" Rosie whispered without thinking.

"Sure. Buck may not know better than to wear the same suit for five days in a row, but he's as good a person as a girl could ever find. He's going to give you a snug home and plant crops to feed your family. He works hard at the livery stable. I've never seen him squander money—not once. Buck Springfield doesn't have a mean bone in his body. If I weren't so stuck on Stefan, I'd be after Buck. So there!"

"Oh, Etta!" Rosie laughed.

"Go get ready for your wedding trip," Etta said, giving Rosie a little push. "Wear that blue dress, the one that looks like ice."

"All right, Etta." Rosie stepped to the door and glanced back at her friend. Etta was staring out the window.

"Etta?" Rosie murmured.

When her friend didn't look up, Rosie shut the door and walked down the hall to her room.

Chapter Nine

Bart didn't have any intention of showing his face to the justice of the peace at the courthouse in Springer, New Mexico. Such a mistake would have ensured him a one-way ticket to the gallows in Missouri. Rosie knew this, and she understood that their Saturday morning train trip was intended to convince people in Raton that they'd gotten married. It was Rosie, in fact, who had set the date, and it was she who had purchased the tickets.

So when Bart arrived at the waiting train, caught her elbow and whispered in her ear, "Happy weddin' day, Rosie-girl," she was more than a little surprised.

He wore a brand-new outfit, and she couldn't help but think how much it must have cost and how rarely he would ever wear it again. All the same, she couldn't deny that in his black suit, white shirt and red four-in-hand tie, the man looked positively dapper. He had combed his hair and donned a gray, felt top hat. In one leather-gloved hand, he carried a wicker basket, and in the other he held a gentleman's walking cane.

"A cane!" Rosie cried, louder than necessary. She

hadn't seen a man with a cane since she'd left Kansas City.

"I do believe my trigger finger looks better hooked around a cane than it does around a six-shooter," Bart declared. "Besides, I knew you'd like it."

Rosie didn't want him to see how close he had come to the truth. "You must have spent all your pay and then some, Bart Kingsley," she said in her best schoolteacher voice.

"As a matter of fact, I didn't spend a penny for this getup."

Rosie gasped. "Bart! You *stole* those clothes?"

At that, he gave a loud laugh. "Get on the train, girl, and stop your frettin'. I broke a horse for Mr. Loeb, who owns the Star Clothing House, and I'm going to fix his best saddle for him next week. He traded my work for these fine gent's clothes. All except the cane. I bought that."

Rosie hardly knew what to say as Bart helped her up the iron steps and into the passenger car. As Rosie seated herself, she recalled Etta's assertion that Bart was no lying, dishonest gunslinger. Etta called him faithful, reliable, a good provider. Mr. Loeb trusted him. Cheyenne Bill had deceived the whole town on his behalf. Even Sheriff Bowman had accepted Bart. Did they see something Rosie had been blind to?

"Sure do like your dress," he offered. "Did you buy it for today?"

Rosie studied her ice-blue gown, covered in ruffles, rosettes and ribbons. Actually, her father had given her the money to have a seamstress fashion it for a charity tea last spring.

"I'm afraid I didn't have anything to trade Mr. Loeb

for," she said softly. As the train whistle blew, steam hissed from the undercarriage and the passenger car jolted forward. Bart took one of Rosie's hands and slipped his fingers between hers.

"This sure is different from the first time we got married," he said as the train gathered speed. "I'll never forget you climbing down that sugar maple outside your bedroom window."

"I climbed down that tree every afternoon to escape my lessons and run to find you at our...our place..." She faltered and couldn't continue.

"I was supposed to be working horses," he reminisced. "I'd get my chores done early so I could hightail it to the stream. You brought books to read me, remember?"

Rosie smiled, closed her eyes and leaned her head against the seat. Lulled by the swaying train and memories of those golden summer days, she felt relaxed. Maybe it was just that she was taking a day off work. Maybe the fact that they were leaving Raton calmed her. Or maybe it was Bart's hand in hers, strong and warm.

"*Pilgrim's Progress*—now, that was one I liked," Bart said. "Sometimes when I thought about finding you again, Rosie-girl, I'd remember how Christian stood up, and the heavy bundle of burdens he'd been carrying snapped and fell off his back."

"Christian was standing at the foot of the cross when that happened," Rosie reminded him. "I'm not your salvation, Bart."

"I didn't sit on the church porch for years without knowing where salvation comes from. But I will say that ever since I climbed in your bedroom window, my burdens have felt lighter."

"Mine have felt heavier."

He shook his head. "Aren't you ever going to let up on me, Rosie?"

"Am I supposed to pretend that everything about the past was as wonderful as those afternoons by the stream?" she retorted. "Do you think I can just take up with you where I left off? Do you honestly believe I'm happier since you came to Raton?"

"I know some things in the past hurt you a lot. They hurt me, too. But I wish you could just let it be and start over."

"*You* were hurt?" she said. "What was so painful about high stepping out of Kansas City and joining Jesse James's gang?"

"Shh." He glanced at the only other passengers, an elderly couple at the far end. The woman appeared to be asleep, but the man was staring out the window. "If you don't learn to talk quieter, you're going to get me caught one of these days."

"You're going to get yourself caught!"

"Maybe so. Maybe I'll pay for my sins by having my neck stretched. But don't ever think I was having a rip-roaring good time those six years without you."

"If it wasn't fun, why did you do it?... No, wait!" She held up a hand. "I don't want to hear anything about those evil men and their sinful ways."

"Listen here, Miss Priss, I am one of those evil men, and you might as well accept it. But you ought to know that none of those fellows is bad through and through. And neither am I."

"Are you trying to tell me Jesse James wasn't wicked?"

"Jesse was bad, but he had a good side, too. His brother, Frank, ran with us and he's the best man I ever met. Frank set me on the right track after Bob Ford killed Jesse. Make a life for yourself like other folk, he told me. Get a home, a wife, children. Find a place to live where you don't have to worry about getting a ball in the back when you go out for firewood. That's the life he's been building ever since the jury let him off last August."

Rosie had read in the newspaper about the long, sensational trial. The courthouse had been jammed with people, all shocked to learn that Jesse James's brother had been found not guilty of the train robbery murder of Frank McMillan.

"You think the James gang is evil and the law is perfect," Bart was saying. "Did you know the Pinkerton detective agency set a bomb in the house of Jesse and Frank's mother? That poor lady had to have her arm amputated."

This was news Rosie hadn't heard, but she wasn't going to drop the argument. "I suppose you can find something good to say about Robert Ford."

"Bob Ford doesn't have a moral bone in his body," Bart said. "But one time in Arkansas, I was trapped at a train depot fifteen yards away from my horse. The law was everywhere. Jesse called the boys to head out and leave me to my fate. But Ford pulled his six-shooter and held off the posse while I ran to my horse. Nary a bullet touched my hide. Bob Ford saved my life, Rosie. I reckon the good Lord is the only one who can know a person's heart."

She could hardly argue with that. Yet how could she trust a man who had done so much wrong?

"So, Rosie-girl," Bart said. "What do you say to putting the past behind us? Might be something good up ahead."

With Bart Kingsley in the picture, it might be something bad, she thought.

"Just for today," she said finally. "Just for today we'll let bygones be bygones."

Chapter Ten

Bart spent the morning walking the streets of Springer with Rosie. She had brought four crisp one-dollar bills to buy fabric to make curtains for Mr. Kilgore's school.

With his cane and wicker basket in tow, Bart accompanied Rosie as she went from one dry goods store to another. It wasn't enough to buy just any old cloth. Rosie wanted something special, something that would cheer up the small room and bring life into the summer months. It had to be a fabric that would block some of winter's chill but also let in spring's sunshine.

Bart had started the morning feeling like a citified dude, but by the time he had stared at hundreds of bolts of gingham, silk, taffeta, cotton, muslin and velvet in every color of the rainbow, he was about ready to take off like a wild bronco. His stiff white collar seemed to get tighter and tighter around his neck. The fancy coat he had traded for began to have the weight of a saddle on his shoulders. Even the bullet wound in his side began to hurt.

He was debating the urge to gallop outside for a breath of fresh air when Rosie suddenly announced,

"This is just what I've been looking for! Don't you agree, Bart?"

"It's mighty nice." Despite his glazed eyes and itchy feet, it occurred to Bart that he was actually enjoying the straight life. Especially with Rosie at his side.

"Just look at this pattern!" she exclaimed. "Have you ever seen such lush florals?"

Bart wasn't sure what florals were, but he nodded. "Those are the lushest florals I've ever seen."

"Huge pink cabbage roses," she exclaimed. "Violets. Lilacs. Oh, it'll be just like bringing the outdoors inside!"

While Bart watched Rosie turn the fabric this way and that, it came to him that being with her like this had made his heart feel downright warm. Maybe he didn't know much about cloth and curtains. Maybe he'd never met a man who actually gave a woman's ideas much weight. Maybe shopping and chitchat were foreign to him. But one thing was clear: Bart Kingsley was enjoying the straight life.

"Would you please hold this up to the window for me, Bart?" Rosie was asking. "I'd like to see how the light comes through it."

"Happy to oblige," he said, and he carried the bolt of flowery cloth to the front of the store. He made a sort of curtain rod out of his arm, and draped the fabric over it so that a sunbeam shot straight through the weave.

"Oh, it looks so much thinner now." Disappointment tinged her voice. "I probably should line every curtain, but I don't have enough money to buy twice the fabric."

Bart would have given Rosie every dime he owned to buy lining for her curtains. The only trouble was, he had churned most of his money into his homestead, having bought a team of horses, a wagon, a plow and a collection of tools that already seemed too few and inadequate for the job that lay ahead.

"Didn't you say you were going to ruffle up the cloth?" he asked, searching for something that might bring the smile back to her lips. With his arm still outstretched, he began to a gather the rose-strewn fabric along it. "How's this, darlin'? See, the sun won't come through near so well now."

Rosie studied the fabric for a moment before giving a big sigh. "Oh, Bart."

"Don't fret so, Rosie-girl. Now, you just go ahead and buy this cloth you've set your sights on. The minute I get my paycheck next Friday, I'll give you enough money to buy all the linings you need. Tell Mr. Puckett how many yards you want, and I'll put it right in this basket I brought. Then we'll go get us some lunch. How does that sound?"

Rosie's face broke into a brilliant smile. "Thank you, Bart," she said softly. "That sounds just fine."

Leaving the mercantile with Rosie and an armful of fabric, Bart stopped at the depot livery stable to rent a wagon pulled by an old mare. At the nearest restaurant, he bought a canteen of fresh lemonade, a block of ice and some vanilla ice cream.

"Mrs. Jensen would have kittens if she knew we didn't have a chaperone," Rosie remarked as they headed toward the mountains.

"We're married folk," Bart pointed out as he took her hand. "Don't be scared, Rosie-girl. I'm not going to take advantage of you. A gentleman would never do such a thing."

"Even with his own wife?" she asked.

"A gentleman wouldn't treat any woman roughly," he said. "Especially his wife."

Before he could get the words out of his mouth, she was clearing her throat. "Oh, did I mention that yellow clapboard house on Second Street?" she asked quickly. "It's small. Just the right size for a single lady."

Bart kept his focus on the blue-gray mountains and the sapphire sky behind them. Resting his elbows on his knees, he let the mare set her own pace along the rutted track.

"The fence needs a coat of whitewash," Rosie was saying. "I'll plant flowers along it. In the back, I want to dig a vegetable garden. With school lessons to prepare, I won't have much time to tend a garden, but I can manage carrots and peas. The dining room has a small cut-glass chandelier. I know it sounds like a costly place, but I checked the price with the brokers. Osfield and Adams are offering it, and with what Mr. Osfield told me, I do believe I can afford to buy it once I've settled into my job."

Rosie paused again. "Don't you think it sounds like a good house, Bart?"

He gave a small shrug. "Sounds dandy. For a town house."

"The parlor is lovely. You should see the wallpaper."

"Floral, I'd guess." Bart settled his hat down low on his brow.

He didn't much like the trend of Rosie's talk, but he wasn't sure what to say. He'd been pondering the state of the small soddy he had built on his homestead—and how very far that damp hole in the ground was from a yellow clapboard house with a white picket fence. The wood plank walls were layered against bare dirt.

There would be no wallpaper, no parlor, no roses and tulips. This was a half-buried one-room shelter, and no woman who had her heart set on a town home could ever be happy in it.

"I'd love lace curtains in the bedroom windows," she sighed as Bart steered the wagon toward a clearing beside a stream.

In a soddy, he thought, lace curtains wouldn't last a week. His heart weighed like a millstone when he set the wagon's brake and jumped down into the ankle-high green grass. His palms nearly spanned Rosie's waist as he lifted her up and set her feet in the grass.

"The sky is so blue," she murmured. "Like a big bowl over the mountains. I love the territory, don't you? Oh, look, Bart! A jackrabbit!"

Lifting her skirts, Rosie scampered toward the stream where a large jackrabbit had frozen in surprise, its long ears upright. As the froth of blue silks swished toward it, the jackrabbit took flight, hopping along the streambed, then vanishing around a bend.

"How silly!" She laughed, grabbing her bonnet and gasping for breath. "Did you just see those ears?"

To tell the truth, Bart hadn't been watching the jackrabbit or its ears. My, what a bustle could do for a woman! He could imagine his arms around that narrow waist...the scent of her neck...the brush of her hair against his cheek...

"He went over there by that cottonwood," Rosie was saying as she approached the wagon. "I don't see how anyone can take jackrabbits seriously. If they were eating your crops...well, then, I suppose... Bart... Bart?"

He started. "What?" He rubbed a palm across the

back of his neck. "We ought to eat that ice cream before it melts."

"Hand me the tablecloth and I'll put it under the cottonwood. Maybe we'll get another look at our jackrabbit."

"Tablecloth?" He vainly searched the back of the wagon, knowing full well there wasn't one.

"We'll use this old saddle blanket." She spread it over the grass and began setting out Bart's picnic— sandwiches made with fresh bread and roast beef, boiled eggs and a sack of Huffman's candies.

"*Cream* candies," he clarified proudly.

"Oh, I love cream candies."

"I know." He hunkered down beside her on the blanket and hooked off his boots. "A man doesn't forget things like that about his girl. Do you still like pecan pie?"

"You didn't!" she gasped, turning to him with sparkling eyes.

"I sure did. Finest pecan pie you ever sank a tooth in."

He took out a covered plate and lifted the lid to reveal a golden crusted pie filled with molasses custard and layers of nuts.

Rosie sighed. "It's beautiful."

"Sweets to the sweet." He couldn't remember where that phrase came from, but he knew it was in one of the books Rosie had read to him by their stream. This gurgling New Mexico brook with its gray rocks and grassy slopes was nothing like their secluded glade in Missouri. But Bart was hoping that Rosie might begin to feel a little softer toward him in such a place.

"You're the sweet one, Bart Kingsley," she said. "This is just how you used to be—full of surprises for me, thinking of kind words to say, doing such gentle things."

"You always brought out my good side."

"Sometimes I think you invented all that about being an outlaw. Here you are with your fancy duds and your cane and the pecan pie, yet I'm supposed to believe you're a train robber?"

He toyed with his sandwich for a moment. "Maybe you could just forget about that, Rosie-girl. Pretend I did make it up. It wouldn't bother me if you put my past aside."

"But I can't put aside the part of the past I *do* remember."

He shifted on the blanket before replying, "Did you ever think there might have been a good reason why I went off and left you with your pappy there in Kansas City?"

She set her sandwich on the plate. "I can't think of a single good reason for a man to run off from his bride of two weeks. Besides, you left a note that spelled out your reasons. You said we'd been playing a child's game and you hadn't ever loved me—"

"Stop!" He caught her hands. "I did write that note, but not a word of it was true. Not a word, you hear?"

"Why did you write it, then? A person doesn't just write a letter full of lies."

"He does if he has to."

"You didn't have to do such a cruel thing! People were never able to cow you, Bart, no matter how they taunted. Don't sit there and tell me someone forced you to write those awful words!"

"No one forced me," he said more gently. "But I had to write the letter all the same. I had to do it for you."

"Why? You nearly killed me with that letter."

"I had to set you free to live a better life than the one I could give. Don't you see that? I didn't have a barrel of shucks. You deserved a better life and a better man than I thought I could ever be to you."

"A man like Dr. Lowell? You ran off and left me to marry someone like him?" Tears filled her brown eyes. "You were always kind to me. You believed in me and you treated me right. So you abandoned me to a father who didn't give a hoot about who I was and what I wanted in life? You left me to my pappy, who forced me to accept the hand of a man I didn't love, a man who expected me to act like somebody I could never be? Was that better than a barrel of shucks, Bart?"

With a groan of dismay, he drew Rosie close and wrapped his arms around her. "I didn't know, darlin'. I didn't know it would turn out that way. If I could live my life over again, I'd make everything better for you. Please believe me."

"I'll try."

He kissed away the tears on her cheeks. "Aw, Rosie, after I left your little room in Raton, I missed you so much I could hardly stand it."

"You really thought about me?" As she relaxed against him, he loosened the pins in her hair and released the mass of chestnut waves. Toying with her hair, running his fingers through the strands, he shuddered with the ache of yearning.

"Darlin', you don't know the hold you have over me," he murmured, bending to kiss her lips. And again. "I could kiss you all day."

"Me, too," she admitted as she traced his jaw line with her fingertips.

"When we were kids," he told her in a low voice, "I rushed through my work just to be with you. So I rode over the mountains searching for you, expecting to find my Rosie-girl with her sweet brown braids and her pretty ankles. I sure didn't expect to find a woman with her own dreams and her own mind, a woman with twice the power over me that the little girl had."

"I don't have any power over you," Rosie protested. "The very idea! I've never had an ounce of power to my name."

"Right at this moment, honey, you could knock me over with a breath of air."

"Oh, really?" Laughing lightly, she blew against his cheek.

"I'm a goner," he cried, falling onto his back. As she giggled, he looked up—straight into the double barrel of a shotgun.

"Don't move," the intruder barked.

Eyes veiled, Bart assessed the man even as his own empty hand formed the shape of his missing six-shooter. Wearing a faded brown felt hat darkened around the crown with sweat, the fellow had a mouth full of teeth stained by chewing tobacco.

"Sorry to spoil y'all's little picnic," he said, prodding Bart to his feet. "I rode my horse after your wagon all the way from Springer to get a look at your pocketbook. I reckoned anybody dressed like a city dandy oughta have a wad, huh?"

Bart glanced over his shoulder to find Rosie watching in horror as the man edged him toward an aspen tree by the stream.

"Then I come upon this pretty little picture here," the stranger continued, "and I decide I'll get me two prizes fer the price of one. Ain't nothing' can stir a man's blood like the sight of a pretty woman."

At his words, Rosie clapped her hand over her mouth.

"Get yer back up against that tree, lover boy," the man ordered. "I'm gonna tie you up so you can watch the action."

"Bart!" Rosie cried out.

At her shriek, the stranger turned his head for a split second. Bart slammed his fist into the man's jaw. The intruder staggered backward, his shotgun firing into the air.

Rosie screamed again. Bart hammered the man with another blow to the chin. Scrambling to her feet, Rosie dashed across the clearing to the wagon. As she climbed into the back, Bart picked the man up by his coat and slammed his head against the tree. The stranger dropped the gun, and Bart kicked it away.

"You want action?" Bart growled, throwing a thunderous punch into the man's midsection. "I'll teach you to talk about a woman like that." He rammed his fist into the man's mouth. "Talk now, you good-for-nothing thief!"

Spitting out teeth, the stranger held up an arm to ward off the blows. "Let me go. I didn't mean nothin'!"

"I've shot men for less, you yellow-bellied little skunk."

"Don't shoot me! I'll leave! I swear it."

Bart lifted the man off his feet and threw him across the saddle of his horse. As the air whooshed out of his lungs, Bart grabbed the shotgun and slammed the stock into the back of his skull. Instantly limp, the man hung over his horse, blood dripping from his mouth.

Using the rope with which the man had planned to tie him to the tree, Bart bound his assailant.

"Get out of here now. *Shee-hah!*" he shouted, giving the nag a slap on the flank. As the horse skittered out of the clearing, Bart stood watching with his hands balanced lightly on his hips. Even though his chest rose and fell with the effort he had expended, he felt no pain in the hands that had battered the thief. He felt nothing but the raw male power that had been a daily part of his life for so many years.

Anger ate at him. How dare anyone think he could get away with trying to rob Bart Kingsley? And the things he'd said about Rosie were—

He turned suddenly. "Rosie, where are you?"

Her head appeared above the rim of the wagon bed. "I'm here."

She was pale as a sheet, he realized as he hurried toward her. "Rosie, darlin', are you—"

"Bart, you mean, awful man!" Although hunched under the saddle blanket, her brown eyes spat fire. "You didn't have to knock his teeth out!"

"What?" Bart stopped, dumbfounded.

"That fellow didn't stand a chance after the first time you hit him. But you just kept on at him like some kind of wild animal. You could have killed him, and then where would you be?"

"I should have killed him. Do you know what that lowdown snake was planning to do to you?"

"He's probably going to die out there in the wilderness. Even if he doesn't, his brain will never work right again."

"His brain? Rosie, that fellow didn't have half a brain to start with."

"But you were so rough—you didn't know when to stop."

Confusion and anger racing through him, Bart shook his head. "I stopped when I was done with him. When I was sure he couldn't lift a finger against you, that was when I laid off him—and not a minute before."

Rosie sat scrunched up beneath the blanket, her eyes filled with tears. "But what if he dies? The sheriff will come for you."

Bart slammed his palm against the side of the wagon. "Blast it all, Rosie, what do you want out of me? I can't be a gentleman and a protector at the same time. I'm just what I am. Forget city duds and canes and pecan pie. I'm a man who uses his fists better than he uses his head, and that's never going to change."

Unable to stop trembling, Rosie stood beside an aspen tree as Bart began to gather the picnic supplies. Then he grabbed the shotgun, shouldered it, picked up the basket and returned to the wagon.

Oh, why had she snapped at him so? He had protected her in the only way he knew. The stranger had been planning to do terrible things. He might have taken it into his head to kill them both.

On the other hand, Bart had beaten the fellow into a bloody pulp. The memory of her gentle Bart slamming his fist into that man's mouth made Rosie shudder. This was the man she didn't want to acknowledge—this sledgehammer. If he could use his bare hands to take out a gun-toting thief, what couldn't Bart do? What wouldn't he do?

How could a woman feel at ease with someone who could explode like that? Yet Bart had done everything in his power to prove himself a gentleman. The memory of his fancy suit and cane, his picnic, his tender touch warmed Rosie's heart.

"Bart," she said as he stowed the basket. "I owe you an apology."

He lifted his head and with one finger tipped back the brim of his hat. "That's right."

It wasn't the response she had expected, but she continued. "I know you were trying to protect me. I'm very grateful."

"Yup." He slapped the wagon seat. "Get in."

She lifted her skirt. "Are you going to help me up?"

He stretched out an arm. Rosie frowned but took his wrist. As she hauled herself up into the wagon, her boots slipped on the bare wood and her skirt tangled in the wheel. Bart moved not a muscle to help her any more than holding out his arm.

When she had finally settled on the seat, she arranged her skirts, stuffed her loose hair under her bonnet and crossed her arms. But when Bart started the mare with a swift slap of the reins, she had to grab the sides of the wagon seat to keep from tumbling off.

They were almost back to Springer before he spoke. "I've done some thinking," he said. "Near onto a month now I've done my level best to be somebody I'm not. I told you outside the church the other night that new clothes can't change the color of a man's skin. Well, they can't change what's inside him, either."

"What's inside you, Bart?" Rosie asked.

He reached down, grabbed the shotgun and shook it in front of her. "This is what's inside me. It's what I'm made of, see? You can dress me up in a coat and tie, but underneath I'm still Bart Kingsley. I'm a half-breed, illegitimate no-good who's spent every year of his grown life on the wrong side of the law. I tried to be all you could want in a man, but I messed up today. I'm going to keep messing up real regular, because when push comes to shove, the citified dude steps out the door, and the gunslinger walks in. I don't imagine there's a thing in the world that can change that."

Rosie fiddled with the folds of her skirt. There were a thousand things she wanted to say to Bart. She wanted to tell him God could change his heart. He could be a different man if he gave God half a chance to work on him. And she wanted to say that she thought he was the bravest, strongest, handsomest man she'd ever seen.

But to be so bold would give him the idea that she cared about him too much. Rosie knew she couldn't let herself feel strongly about Bart. He *would* go back to his old ways. And if the sheriff caught him, Bart would be thrown in jail. More important, if Bart's outlaw past caught up with him, he'd leave town, and Rosie knew he would never be back.

No...she couldn't encourage him to try to change. Not when her heart was at risk.

"Well," she said finally. "Just do whatever you can to look like a good husband to me for the next few weeks. Then you can go off and be anything you want."

"You care more about that teaching job and that sidewinder's lost teeth than you ever cared about me."

"I sure never let anybody else be as forward with me as you were today," she countered. Unexpected tears filled her eyes. "Even that snake of a man I was supposed to marry in Kansas City kept his hands to himself after I set him straight."

Bart slowed the wagon as it rolled into town. "I meant this to be the best day of your life, Rosie. I meant it to be the start of something new between us."

"There can't be anything new between us," she said, brushing a tear from her cheek. "We started out wrong, and things have gone wrong ever since."

Bart was silent a moment. "If you don't think there's hope for us, if you don't believe I can change, then I reckon there's no chance at all. You were always my light, Rosie."

He eased the wagon to a stop at the Springer train depot. "If you can't see any light at the end of this tunnel of ours, if the only bright spot in your life is that teaching job, then I don't know what I'm doing."

"I don't know, either, Bart," Rosie said as she watched the three-thirty train pull into the station. "I don't know, either."

It took about five minutes for Rosie to lose her job as a Harvey Girl. She had just returned to the dormitory when Mrs. Jensen stormed into the pink bedroom and demanded to know where Rosie had been all day. When she announced that she had eloped with Buck Springfield, Mrs. Jensen turned on her heel and marched right down the stairs to tell Mr. Gable.

Tom Gable said he had half a mind to keep Rosie on if she wanted to work. He didn't know where he could get as reliable a waitress as her. But if she had set her heart on being a farmer's wife, there was nothing he could do.

Etta and the other girls flew into a flurry of questions, exclamations, giggles and sighs when Rosie told them about the train trip to Springer. Although she knew her hands were trembling as she packed her clothes, Rosie kept up a bright voice and a Harvey Girl smile.

Buck was wonderful, she avowed. The perfect husband. "I'll miss you all," she said as he drove his new wagon up to the Harvey House. "I'll come for ice cream soon."

"You better take good care of this little lady," Mr. Gable warned Bart. "She'll make you a fine wife."

"You're lucky to get her," Mrs. Jensen called out when Rosie was seated and the wagon began rolling away from the depot. "You just remember that, Mr. Springfield."

Rosie watched the familiar faces fade into the evening gloom. As the wagon rounded the corner, she heard Mr. Gable call out, "Back inside, everyone. We've got forty omelets comin' in on the seven o'clock from Denver!"

Rosie smiled as Bart turned the wagon toward the schoolhouse. As hard as it was to leave her friends at the Harvey House, it was exciting to think about the moment she would stand on Mr. Kilgore's doorstep and present her new husband.

"Be sure to tip your hat when you meet Mr. Kilgore," she reminded Bart. "He's very proper."

"Reckon I should kiss his hand?" Bart drawled.

"No!" Rosie laughed suddenly. "Bart, we've had a rough day, but once I have that teaching job, everything will be all right."

He pulled the wagon to a halt in front of the small house next to the one-room school, clambered out and rapped on the door. In a moment Mr. Kilgore opened it and stared agog at Rosie.

"Why, Miss Kingsley," he said. "I certainly didn't expect to see you at this time of evening. Do come in."

When he led the couple to a small front parlor, Rosie saw at once that she hadn't chosen the best time to apply for her new job. Mr. Kilgore had company—a man, a woman and three children hastily rose to greet the newcomers.

"Miss Kingsley," Mr. Kilgore began, "May I introduce—"

"I beg your pardon, Mr. Kilgore," Rosie interrupted, "but my name has changed since we last spoke. I am now Mrs. Springfield. This is my husband, Buck."

"Howdy," Bart said, tipping his hat.

"This is a surprise," Mr. Kilgore exclaimed. "I had no idea nuptials were in the offing."

"Oh, yes," Rosie affirmed.

"I've been planning to marry this gal for a long time," Bart put in. "And who are these folks?"

Mr. Kilgore cleared his throat. "Mr. and Mrs. Springfield, may I present Mr. and Mrs. Sneed and their children, Abigail, Tom and Lawrence."

"I'm so pleased to meet you." Rosie held out her hand.

"Indeed," Mrs. Sneed responded, stepping forward. "Congratulations on your marriage. I'm sure I'll be seeing a great deal of you once you begin your family."

"Oh?" Rosie replied.

"Yes, I'll be educating your children in the years to come. I've just been hired by Mr. Kilgore as the new teacher for his school."

Chapter Eleven

Bart could not get a word out of Rosie all the way from Mr. Kilgore's house to his homestead, a long wagon ride. The moment she had been able to exit the scene of her devastation gracefully, she had pulled her shawl over her bonnet and retreated into silence. Bart tried commenting on the full moon, the probability of rain, even the uneven gait of one of his horses. Rosie just sat.

He knew what she was thinking. A fine mess she'd gotten herself into: stuck with Bart Kingsley and no teaching job. Now she had lost her secure place and regular wages at the Harvey House, and the whole town believed she was married.

The worst was yet to come, Bart knew. When Rosie took one look at the barren hills, rocky streams and scrubby brush he owned, she would go plumb soggy. Already he could hear her sniffing under her shawl.

For all the world he wanted to take Rosie in his arms. But what did he have to offer? Outlaw manners and a sinful reputation. Oh, and a hole in the ground that was supposed to pass for a house.

Bart tugged his hat down over his brow. What he had to offer Rosie was pitiful—a fireplace made of river rocks, a bare plank floor and four plank walls, a bed with no mattress, a table with no chairs and two windows fitted with paper instead of glass panes.

He was a fair hand at carpentry, but horse work was his specialty. With the plowing, planting, digging and building he had to fit in around his job at the livery stable, Rosie was lucky to have a bed at all.

The more Bart thought about the bed with its hard board bottom and thin blankets, the more uneasy he felt. What would happen to a woman who, all in one day, had kissed a gentleman who turned out to be a wild animal, had seen her dream of teaching turn to ashes and had to start living like a mole in the ground?

Lord, he wished he'd had a better family to grow up in.

What was a man supposed to do with a crying woman? Most of the men who had lived with his mother—including the louse who eventually became Bart's stepfather—wouldn't have had a moment's patience with tears. More than once, Bart had seen his stepfather slap his mother's face for bawling about things.

Bart sure didn't want to slap Rosie. He wanted to hold her close and whisper in her ear that he'd take care of her. But maybe that wasn't the right thing to do. Maybe if he tried to comfort her, she'd cry all the harder. If he touched her, maybe she'd get scared of him again. Or mad.

The best thing to do was just not say anything, Bart decided. If he ignored Rosie, she couldn't think one way or the other about him. His hands grew damp on the reins as the horses pulled the wagon up the incline toward the clearing where he had dug the house. The track sure did feel rutted and stony. The pine trees seemed closer than he'd thought when he was clearing a road.

"All told I've got one hundred sixty acres," he ventured. "It's good land. Trees for lumber. Three streams with fresh water running all year. Once I've been living here for five years, I can go to Springer and file proof of my claim. Then the place will be mine."

Rosie said nothing. The wagon topped the hill and rattled toward the board-and-batten walls that rose a mere three feet above the ground. Bart tugged on the reins to pull his horses to a halt. For a moment he sat staring at the tar-papered roof and the two windows beside the front door.

"This is a far sight from Kansas City," he began. "Not what you were used to with your pappy."

"Help me down, Bart," Rosie said.

At least she was still alive. He clambered from the wagon and held out his hands. She had let her shawl slip down from her head. The full moon silvered her blue dress and washed her pale cheeks in alabaster.

"Thank you, Bart," she said when her feet were on firm ground.

"I'll fetch your trunk." To cover his uncertainty about the moments to come, Bart lifted her heavy trunk from the wagon bed and carried it toward the house. "This is a half dugout. Cheyenne Bill told me most homesteaders start off with one. It's warm in winter and cool in… Well, it's not much, to tell the truth…. I'm digging out a back room for storage."

"Is there a lock on the door, or do we just walk in?" Rosie asked.

"Not much point in a lock. Wait here while I light my lamps." Heart thumping, he descended the steps and pushed open the door.

Alone for a minute, Rosie lifted her head to the sky and sucked in a shaky breath. This was her home now, the place where she would be forced to live and toil until she could find a way to escape it. Her hope of freedom had come to nothing. She was more a slave now than she had ever been in her life.

This was her punishment for disobeying her father. For being deceitful to Dr. Lowell. For running away from her fiancé and her pappy. For letting Bart Kingsley kiss her under the cottonwood tree.

The half-buried house, the wilderness that promised backbreaking labor by day and the howls of wild animals by night, the husband she couldn't be sure of—all would be penance for her sins. In such a place as this, God was nowhere to be found.

"You can come down now, Rosie-girl." Bart held up a lamp, and Rosie could see the worried look in his green eyes.

"It's a good solid door," he said as she descended.

"You dug this yourself?"

"Well, sure, but it's not much." He stepped back as she entered the soddy.

At the first sight of the small room with its bare wood walls and floor, Rosie felt a lump form in her throat. But she had wept enough for one day. More than enough. This was her lot, and she would make the best of it.

"I don't have a cookstove yet," Bart was saying as he gestured toward the cold fireplace. "This'll have to do. I bought a pot and a skillet. They go a long way toward a decent meal. There's a pantry back here."

He slapped a wooden wall. "I'll cut the door between these rooms once I get things sealed good. I jump down in the hole when I need something."

Rosie pondered the notion of climbing in and out of a hole in the ground to fetch potatoes, sugar, flour and such. "Do you have a ladder?"

"I'll build you a set of steps." He hooked one thumb around a suspender. "Being as tomorrow's Sunday, I'm off work. Next week I'll work afternoons at the livery stable so I can do my spring planting. When you plant beets, you put out seed balls. When they sprout, you thin 'em. I'll rotate my sugar-beet crop with potatoes. If I can keep the blister beetles away and raise a healthy crop, Rosie, I can sell all I harvest. Beets bring five cents a pound, and I'll market the greens for cattle feed."

"Oh, I see," Rosie managed, trying to imagine how she would endure this desolate place. More troubling, how would she handle having Bart around? His green eyes, his teasing, his warm embrace and gentle smile would make it hard to maintain a prudent distance.

"How about some supper?" he was asking. "I've got oysters. Bought 'em last week just for you. The grocer said they're the rage with city folk."

Rosie tried to smile as she compared the lonely dugout to the luxurious oyster bar where she had attended parties in her previous life.

"Oysters would be nice," she said, drawing her

shawl from her shoulders. "Do you have a wardrobe or maybe a hook?"

"I've got a nail." Bart took her wool wrap and hung it on the single nail protruding from a plank.

"I'll take care of my things while you fix the oysters."

As Rosie sorted the clothing in her trunk, she wondered why Bart had no hooks. Would he have an ironing board? A washtub?

"Here's a stool, Rosie-girl." He presented the only seat in the house.

Rosie seated herself gingerly on the three-legged stool and made an attempt to arrange her skirt and bustle. Eyeing the pale gray oysters on his plate, Bart sat on the edge of the bed.

"Do they smell right to you?" He pulled his knife from the leather sheath on his belt and stabbed at an oyster. It shot off the plate and landed on the floor.

He looked up at Rosie. "Wilful little critters, aren't they?"

"I'll get spoons." She stepped to the mantel where three dusty, bent spoons lay among knives, chains and fishing lures. With two fingers, she lifted a spoon and wiped it on her skirt. She sat down in time to see Bart grab an oyster with his bare hand and pop it into his mouth.

An expression of vague discomfort spread over his face. He began to chew. He chewed a while longer. Then he chewed some more. Rosie watched, wondering why on earth she felt like laughing at a time like this.

"Is it good?" she asked him.

"Mighty fine," he answered around the mouthful of oyster.

While Bart continued to chew, Rosie slipped an oyster onto her spoon and swallowed it. Even though it was lukewarm and just out of a can rather than chilled on a bed of ice, the taste transported her to a time of gentility and refinement.

If a woman could dine on oysters in such a house, couldn't she make life here better?

"I don't know about your varmint," Bart spoke up, "but mine was as tough as an old shoe."

Rosie couldn't suppress a giggle. "Bart, you don't chew oysters! You swallow them whole."

As a grin lifted one corner of his mouth, he regarded his plate. "You sure about that? My mama taught us kids to chew our food before we downed it."

Rosie took her plate and sat down beside Bart. "Slide the oyster onto the spoon," she told him as she demonstrated. "Then put the oyster in your mouth and swallow."

"I'll give it a whirl." Taking her spoon, he chased an oyster around his plate before finally nabbing it. Then he followed Rosie's instructions and gulped the morsel whole.

"There!" she said with a laugh. "You did it!"

"Sure enough, Rosie-girl."

As he watched, she lifted another oyster and slipped it between her lips. Eyes closed, she savored the taste for a moment before swallowing.

"Mmm…" she purred. "Now it's your turn."

"How about if you snag me one?"

Rosie scooped up an oyster and slid it into Bart's mouth. "Now swallow."

He obeyed. By his expression, she suspected he was not acquiring a taste for them.

"In Kansas City, oyster restaurants are on every street," she told him. "After the theater, everyone goes out for oysters and champagne. They're said to be the food and drink of passion."

Bart took the spoon and served Rosie another oyster. After she swallowed, he bent and kissed the dampness from her lips. "Rosie-girl, you look so good to me right now. And I don't think those oysters have a thing to do with the way you make me feel."

"Oh, Bart, it was good between us this afternoon, wasn't it?"

She let out her breath as his mouth slipped down the side of her neck. "But that awful man scared me so much…and then I lashed out at you…and then Mr. Kilgore—"

"Hush now, darlin'. That mean-mouthed snake who tried to rob us is long gone. A good life is waiting for you—even without the teaching job. I'm not much of a gentleman, and this place is no Kansas City mansion, but if you'll have me, I'm yours."

She gazed at the intense light in Bart's green eyes. If only she could rely on him, if only she could be certain he wouldn't abandon her, if only she could be sure his past wouldn't catch up with him…

"It's going to take time," she said.

"I'm not going anywhere." He kissed her as if to silence her protest. "Tomorrow morning I'll build steps for the storeroom, just wait and see. Now come here, girl, and stop looking so sad."

He set the plates on the floor and took her into his arms. She shut her eyes, relaxing as his fingers stroked her cheek. Bart wanted to be the man to nurture and succor her, and it was time to accept that she had set her own course. His kisses were sweet and his touch stirred a flame to life inside her.

"Are you a betting woman, Rosie?" he whispered as he eased her onto the blankets that covered the bed.

"I did bet once on a game of whist," she recalled. "Then my father found out."

"Well, I'm willing to make you a bet I know I can't lose." He ran one finger down the side of her neck. "I'll bet that if you just relax and think about those oysters for a few minutes, things are going to look a whole lot better to you in the morning. What do you say, Rosie-girl? Do we have us a bet?"

"I just have to think about oysters?"

"That's all." He eased up on one elbow and began slipping her dress off her shoulders.

Rosie slept with sweet dreams…beautiful memories of Bart's love. It might be possible, she thought, to make a good life with Bart on his homestead. Yet even as she drifted in the contentment of a future as Bart's wife, she remembered that she would never be a mother. The doctors in Kansas City had declared her barren.

Nor would there be children singing songs and learning to count. No anthems. No recitations. She had lost the teaching job to another woman.

Even Bart was gone from their bed. Rosie slipped from beneath the blankets and went to one of the two windows. Although it was daytime, she could see almost nothing through the waxed paper that covered the openings. He had told her he would build steps into the pantry. But she could hear no hammer or saw.

Ashes in the fireplace, a dusty floor, chipped crockery were her lot. Life could not be filled with dreamy passion forever. Heavyhearted, Rosie dressed in a simple blue calico she had never liked—preferring her swishy silks instead. She had never enjoyed a silent room either. Rosie liked people, laughter, chatter.

Even as she mourned the past, she realized this tiny sod house now belonged to her to do with as she pleased. The land outside belonged to her, too. Was this what she had been after all along?

Every night on her knees, she had begged God for her freedom. Was this the way He had answered her prayers?

Bart's voice drifted into the house as he sang a hymn out in the yard. Rosie went to the door and peeked outside. Just beyond the house, he was chopping wood. She had to smile. Bart might be a terror at robbing banks and holding up trains. He might be the handsomest man this side of the Mississippi, and he made Rosie feel wonderful when he loved her. But Bart Kingsley couldn't carry a tune in a bucket.

Rosie shut the door and leaned against it. Bart hadn't gone away, as she'd feared. For this moment, at least, he was acting the reliable husband. In the weeks Rosie had known him again, he hadn't robbed a train or a bank, he hadn't murdered anyone, he'd worked at a decent job and started his own homestead.

If Bart could accomplish so much, couldn't she?

"Mornin', Rosie-girl," Bart called when he saw Rosie walking toward him. "You look good enough to eat."

She laughed as he caught her around the waist and swung her off her feet. "Morning, Bart."

"I've about got enough wood to start the fire." He set her back on the ground but didn't move his arms. "I should have done this before you came, but to tell you the truth, I didn't really believe I'd get you this far."

"Here I am." She shrugged one shoulder. "So what do you want me to do?"

"You could give me a kiss."

Emboldened, Rosie rose up on tiptoes, wrapped her arms around his neck and kissed him long and hard. "How's that?"

"Mercy, girl," Bart managed. "You're the best thing that ever happened to me."

She laughed. "But I don't think this is how people are supposed to act during the daytime."

"I don't think anyone cares how we act day or night. Do you?"

Resting her head on his shoulder, she gazed up at the brilliant blue sky. "We're all alone out here...just us and God."

"I imagine God allows a husband and wife a good amount of leeway, don't you reckon? Especially when they've found each other after six years apart."

"Yes, I expect so."

"Rosie, last night between you and me..." Bart held her head as he spoke. "Last night I knew things were going to be all right. Last night was like a promise."

"Oh, Bart." She ached for his words to be true.

"Don't you believe, Rosie-girl? Don't you think our loving was a seal? We're where we ought to be, with each other."

"For today we are," she said softly. "I guess for today we're right where we should be."

"And nothing—not one thing—is going to change that."

As Bart looked into her deep brown eyes, he vowed he would make Rosie love this place he'd built. He would teach her to see his vision of their future. He would woo her into trusting him. And one day, one fine day, he would find what he'd been seeking all these years.

One day he would win Rosie's love.

Chapter Twelve

Tossing a few logs onto the woodpile, Bart mused over what he had gotten himself into by bringing Rosie out to his homestead. It was a Sunday afternoon, only a week after they had settled into the soddy, and she was inside peeling potatoes. But enough time had passed to show him she was a city gal through and through, and she didn't have a lick of sense about frontier life.

Although Rosie had spent time on her pappy's farm outside Kansas City, it was nothing like this. She would peel those potatoes until they were nothing but nubs. He had offered to teach her, but she had insisted on doing the job her own way.

Bart's stepfather had beaten his wife for standing up to him. But as Bart buried the ax in the chopping block, he also buried any such instinct his stepfather might have instilled in him. Laura Rose Vermillion had always been Bart's light. And he would never snuff out that glow with the back of his hand.

Sitting near the window, Rosie tossed another potato into the pail. Etta and the others at the Harvey

House would be coming back from church, she realized. Rosie herself would have attended church if she'd been in Raton. Every other Sunday she was given the morning off to attend worship services. Although her schedule didn't permit her to teach Sunday school, she always sang in the sanctuary choir.

Now she tried to make herself sing a favorite hymn. After all, she should be grateful, shouldn't she? She was alive, safe and looked after by a man who cared for her.

But Rosie had neglected her nightly prayers of late. She hadn't read her Bible in days. With a sigh, Rosie picked up another potato. The truth was, she could hardly wait for Bart to come in from the fields each night. Everything about him filled her with joy—everything except his past.

"What are you doing sitting in the dark, Rosie?" Bart asked as he tossed his buckskin jacket onto the table. "Sun's going down."

"So much to do, I guess I hadn't noticed."

He lit a lamp. "When did you set these plates on the mantel?"

"Three days ago. They were coated with grime. Bart, your domestic habits are downright slothful."

"What did you expect from an outlaw?"

She shrugged. "Did it ever occur to you to sweep this place?"

"Sweep a dugout?" Bart took off his hat and ran his hand through his damp hair. "Rosie-girl, don't you know that tomorrow this place will be just as dirty as it was today?"

"Then I'll sweep it again, won't I?" She glanced at him. "And I'll have to wash those dusty britches.

If you're going to be a civilized husband, Bart Kingsley, you'll have to take regular baths and wear clean clothes."

"I don't know much about being civilized. But if you want me for a husband, darlin' you've got me."

Rosie picked up the potato pail. "I'm sorry I don't know more about being a wife. After my mother died, my father never remarried. You grew up without a father, and I grew up without a mother. We're in a fine pickle."

Bart studied the white foam gathering at the top of the pot. "You're a good wife, Rosie. The best. If all you want to do is sit around and eat Huffman's cream candies and pecan pie, it's all right by me."

Tears sprang into Rosie's eyes. "I don't want to eat cream candies, Bart. I want to clean your house and sew your shirts and…and…and be your wife."

In an instant he had caught her in his arms and was holding her close. "You don't know how bad I've wanted to hear you say that, darlin'."

"But I'm scared. I'm just so scared it won't work." She nestled her damp cheek against his shoulder.

"What's to stop us from making a wonderful life out here on our homestead?"

"That Pinkerton man could come after you. He could set a bomb for you like they did for Jesse James's mother. And what if my pappy tracks me to Raton? You did, so what's to stop him? You don't know Pappy like I do. If he ever decides to come for me, he'll use his money and his influence. Nothing will stop him. People are after us, Bart, both of us. We won't be able to hide here forever."

He set her back and looked into her troubled eyes. "What else has you all worked up, Rosie-girl?"

"I'm afraid to care about you, Bart...to care about you more than I do right now. What if you get yourself killed?" She touched the ridge of scarred flesh on his side. Then she kissed his neck. "What if you get hauled off to prison and they tie a rope around this neck?"

Bart nodded. "Keep talking, sweetheart. I know that's not all of it."

Rosie shut her eyes tight, trying to stem the flow of tears. "I wanted to teach school so I could be with children. But now I know I never will. And I'll never... never have any children of my own....We'll never have babies, Bart. Even if all the rest of it works out by some miracle, we'll never have children of our own."

He stroked her shoulder, pondering the significance of her words and wondering how deeply they would affect his life. "Listen here, now. I might like to have children with you, but I've gotten this far without them. So have you. If we don't have babies, we've got each other, Rosie-girl."

"Hold me tighter, Bart."

"I'll hold you for the rest of my life. I'll never let you go."

"Never, Bart?"

"Never, Rosie-girl. Not ever."

Rosie lived in an Eden of her own making. Once she finally accepted that Bart had indeed offered her freedom, she set about to create the little paradise of her dreams.

The fabric she had purchased for the schoolroom windows soon brightened the walls of the little dugout. Rosie fashioned the yards of chintz into billowing curtains and a tablecloth. Bart built her the framework of a changing screen, and she ruffled the cloth to fill in the panels. She used the remaining yardage to begin cutting triangles and squares to piece together a quilt for their bed.

The bed itself soon sported a new mattress filled with soft grass Bart brought in from his fields. Of course, the grass soon dried and grew brittle, but Rosie hardly cared. Their bed always felt soft and comfortable when she was nestled in her husband's arms.

Rosie caught herself reminiscing secretly about him at various times throughout each day, and always a smile crept over her lips. When Bart was in Raton working at his livery stable job, Rosie would think about him as she baked bread or weeded her kitchen garden or did the laundry.

Every afternoon while he was in the sugar-beet fields, she would fall into bed for a nap. Achingly tired, she would doze away the hottest hours. But by evening, when he came in for dinner, Rosie felt fresh and eager to be with him.

No matter how worn out he was from his labors, Bart's face always brightened at the sight of their table laden with freshly baked bread and thick beef stew, chicken and dumplings or shepherd's pie. Rosie discovered that observing Stefan and the other chefs at the Harvey House had given her a head start in cooking skills. With the help of a recipe book he bought for her at one of the mercantiles, she produced one hearty meal after another.

Soon after she began her life on the homestead, Rosie decided she would like to have fresh eggs on hand. Not only would this improve her baking, she reasoned, but she could send any extra eggs along to town with Bart when he went to work at the livery stable. With the money from fresh eggs and newly churned butter, Rosie planned to buy herself a real stove. Bart built a raised coop and fetched in a bunch of fluffy yellow chicks one day, and Rosie was off and running with her hen business.

After each day of tending to her chickens, milking the two cows, hoeing her garden, scrubbing laundry on the washboard, sweeping and mopping the ever-dusty dugout and cooking hearty meals, Rosie expected to feel drained and empty. Instead, the busy life sparked her desire to do more. She used some of her savings to buy fabric, and she fashioned several work shirts and two pairs of sturdy britches for Bart. She made herself two sensible dresses and a week's worth of white aprons.

Rosie decided to paint the inner walls of the dugout, and she sent Bart off to Raton with orders for a gallon of white milk-paint. He offered his opinion that white seemed like a pretty loco color for an underground house, but he obeyed. Within days, the house was sparkling clean. Bart declared the soddy looked bright as a new pin and bigger than it had before.

In fact, the beauty Rosie had brought to the little dugout led Bart to declare that he would not only finish building the pantry room, but he would also make plans for an upstairs—two fine rooms with big windows and a shingled roof. Bart figured that once the sugar-beet harvest came in, he'd have enough money to buy all the lumber needed to build the upstairs during the slow fall and winter months.

But now, the needs of his land consumed Bart. He hired young Manford Wade to help hoe sugar beets after school each day.

"She's as mean as a witch," Mannie confided to Rosie one afternoon when she was hanging laundry on the clothesline. "She's got red eyes."

"Red eyes!" Rosie laughed at Mannie's description of the new schoolmarm. "People don't have red eyes, Manford."

"No, they don't. But she does. Which goes to prove she's a witch, don't it?"

Chuckling, Rosie pushed a clothespin over the shoulder seam of a wet shirt that kept trying to slap her. "Mrs. Sneed is strict, and that's an essential attribute for a teacher, in my opinion."

"She whupped Lucy yesterday."

"Lucy? Oh, no!" Rosie clutched a dripping table-cloth as she pictured the responsible girl who had been left in charge of the recitation. "What on earth did Lucy do to deserve a whipping?"

"Didn't get her composition wrote. Lucy's grandpa up and died last week, and she loved him something fierce. Ever since, she ain't been the same. Ol' man Pete was a good feller. Cheyenne Bill gave a speech at the funeral. Tom and Griff came to the buryin', and you know if a dog'll come to a funeral, Pete must have been a fine man."

"I'm sorry to hear he passed away." Rosie fretted as she hung the last of the clothes. Whipping a child in mourning didn't sound like the act of a loving teacher. There must be more to the story.

"Did you hear about the charity ball last Monday night?" Manford asked. "Folks had them a fine dinner.

Leg of mutton, capers, mincemeat, roast beef, chicken, cake, oranges…"

He stopped speaking and glanced toward the trail. "Say, look who's coming up the road. It's Sheriff Bowman. Hey, sheriff!"

Manford waved and began trotting down toward him, but Rosie grabbed his sleeve and held him back. "Mannie, run tell my husband the sheriff is here. And make sure he understands it's Sheriff Bowman."

"Sure thing, ma'am."

Heart hammering, Rosie gave the boy a gentle push. Scanning the fields, she could just make out Bart's back as he bent to the plow. The sheriff was climbing down from his horse, rifle in hand and six-shooter slung on his hip. He took the reins with his free hand and started toward Rosie.

"Afternoon, Mrs. Springfield," he called.

"Sheriff Bowman. This is a surprise." Rosie wiped her hands on her apron as she greeted him. "What brings you out here?"

"I'll be plain with you, Mrs. Springfield," the sheriff said. "I've come out here with some news."

"Oh?" Rosie tried to remember her Harvey Girl smile. "I hope it's something happy."

"'Fraid not. There's trouble. Trouble with the law. And your husband is involved."

"My husband?" Rosie asked, lifting up a fervent prayer that God would allow Bart time to escape into the woods. "What can you mean by that? My husband is an honest man, Sheriff Bowman. I know for a fact that he registered our one-hundred-sixty acres in Springer. He showed me the homestead papers. The claim is legal."

"The homestead ain't the problem, Mrs. Springfield." He reached out and took Rosie's hands between his large callused palms. "It's a different sort of thing. Your husband's been accused of…well, of attempted murder."

Chapter Thirteen

"Howdy, sheriff," Bart called out as he approached the house. "Young Manford tells me you've come on business."

Bart observed Rosie's startled expression as he leaned an elbow on the dugout roof and adjusted his hat against the sun.

"'Fraid we've got a problem, Mr. Springfield," the sheriff said, straightening his cartridge belt.

"Call me Buck," Bart offered.

The moment Manford told him the sheriff had come, Bart knew he was through living life on the run. He also knew he would protect himself and Rosie. He didn't want to take up his outlaw ways again, but he didn't intend to have his neck stretched either.

"Well, Buck," the sheriff was saying, "I hate to cut short your plowing, but I've got trouble in town."

"What kind of trouble, sheriff?" Bart put an arm around Rosie's shoulders and drew her close.

"A feller came to see me at the courthouse yesterday. He claims you tried to kill him."

"Kill him?" Bart searched for memories of any number of men who might have tracked him down. Men from his past bent on vengeance. "How did he come up with that piece of hokum?"

"Says he was out for a ride a few weeks back, and he came upon you and the missus having a picnic. Says you took offense at something he said, busted up his face and knocked out five front teeth. Then you tied him on his horse and sent him out in the desert to die."

Relief pouring through him, Bart let out a low whistle. "All that, huh?"

"It's a fact he's missing most of his front teeth."

"Did this fellow say what got me riled?"

"He's a little vague on that. Says he thinks you'd been drinking and were cozying up to the lady. Says when he interrupted to ask directions, you jumped him."

"Directions, huh?" Bart laughed. "Sure, I remember that fellow. Short and raggedy with a mop of greasy hair?"

"That's him."

"He was trying to rob us!" Rosie exploded. "We had gone to Springer on the train to get married. Just ask Mr. Gable at the Harvey House."

"Already did, ma'am."

"We took a wagon out to have a picnic," she went on. "Then that awful man appeared. He put a shotgun to my head and threatened to shoot us both! He said he intended to tie up my husband and...and..."

"Mannie, run check on the horses for me," Bart cut in. As the wide-eyed boy hurried to obey, he lowered his voice. "My wife is telling the truth, sheriff. That low-down snake declared his intention of robbing us and having his way with my wife. When he was tying me up, I got the jump on him. I rearranged his face a little and tied him onto his horse. Any man worth his oats would protect the woman he loved."

The sheriff nodded. "I reckon so. All the same, the fellow's mighty hot under the collar. He checked the train records and found out who you were. He declares he's come to town to find you and make you pay."

"Pay?" Rosie retorted. "Look around, sheriff. My husband works at the livery six mornings a week, and every afternoon till dusk he's in his sugar beets. We're not rich!"

"Now, calm down, Mrs. Springfield." At that, the sheriff began coughing and couldn't speak for a moment.

Bart knew the man had been sick, but he was worried more about Rosie. The constant fear she lived with would do her in one of these days. She must be doubting her decision to trust that Bart could be a good husband. He had to do something to put an end to her worries.

"Buck, I want you to come back to town with me," the sheriff said after gaining his composure. "We'll get to the bottom of this. I'll send a wire to the law in Springer. I'll send another to your hometown. Get a few facts on your character. Where do you come from, by the way?"

"Mighty hard to say. I lived here and there until this pretty gal helped me make up my mind to settle down."

"Like a lot of men. Well, with you and the missus claiming the same thing, and with that rascal smelling so thick the lamps won't burn, I reckon any jury would let you off the hook. I hate to haul you in with your homestead up and going and the good work I hear you've been doing over at the livery." He paused and scratched his chin. "Besides that, you're Cheyenne Bill's cousin. That'll hold weight in a court of law."

Rosie shut her eyes and sagged against Bart. She looked like she was going to be sick. He knew the web of lies he had spun was just about to kill her.

"Mrs. Springfield," the sheriff said, "you'd better come with us. A woman's word won't hold much water, but you'll be safer in town. Bring the boy, too." He gave a quick laugh. "I almost forgot I came out here for another reason. There's somebody in town wants to see you, ma'am."

"Who is it?" she asked.

"Mr. Kilgore. Says he needs to talk to you about a teaching job. Seems Mrs. Sneed didn't work out so good after all."

Five times on the rutted track to Raton, Bart had to stop the wagon so Rosie could get off and throw up. He'd never seen anyone so sick. From the moment Sheriff Bowman had announced that Bart was accused of attempted murder, Rosie's skin had turned from its usual soft pink to a pale shade of green.

Not that the others in the party felt dandy either. Although Manford was asleep in the wagon, Sheriff Bowman rode just ahead and was about to cough up his lungs. It occurred to Bart that he could do the man in and leave his body on the trail. Folks would probably think he'd passed out and died from consumption.

But the minute the thought entered Bart's mind, he concluded it must have come from the devil and snuffed it out. He wasn't about to add another killing to his name, even if no one guessed he was the culprit.

Rosie would know. The Almighty would know, too. He didn't want to have to reckon with either of them.

Bart acknowledged he had sent more than one man to an early grave. But the killings had always been in self-defense. Not one time had he shot a man just for spite. In fact, he hadn't even witnessed the killings the James brothers committed during their infamous train robberies. A deadeye shot, Bart served as lookout— a role that kept him a fair distance from the doings.

After a goodly amount of time reckoning with God and his own conscience, Bart decided to keep the wagon headed for Raton. He would take his medicine and trust God to keep watch over Rosie.

As the wagon rolled into town that evening, she groaned. "Oh, Bart, I've never felt so awful."

He slipped his arm around her. "I've got you, darlin'. You just relax now."

She shut her eyes and rested her cheek against his arm. "I'm going to talk to Mr. Kilgore," she murmured. "I'm going to tell him I don't want that teaching position."

"Rosie…" Bart could hardly make the word come out of his throat. "Are you sure, Rosie? You've wanted that job for so long. You even married me so you could—"

"I'm married to you, and that's why I won't take the job." Her brown eyes searched his. "I may be sick, but I'm happy, Bart. Our homestead is good for me. You're good for me."

"I'm doing my best, Rosie-girl. I'm doing the best I can to be the kind of husband you want."

"I just… I just…oh, no!" Pushing him away, she held her stomach and moaned.

Bart pulled the wagon up to the Central Hotel and sent Mannie along home. After arranging for a room, he helped Rosie up the stairs, put her to bed and covered her with blankets. On his pillow he laid the small pistol he had hidden in the waistband of his britches. As he stood by the window and studied the shadowed street below, he decided he'd better do some more praying.

"Lord," he murmured, looking up at the moon so as to fix his focus on something visible, "I'm sorry about telling Sheriff Bowman my name was Buck. I should have 'fessed up, but You know what a passel of trouble that would have brought. Rosie didn't take it too good, and seeing as how You and I care so much about her, I need to ask You to work this thing out for us."

He fingered the twisted blue fringe on the curtain a moment before continuing. "Lord, I'm doing my dead level best to go straight, You know I am. And You know I wouldn't hurt Rosie for the world. I reckon I'd better turn all this mess over to You to fix up. Chances are, I'll tangle things up worse than they already are with that no-good snake who meant to hurt Rosie."

Bart watched a cloud drift across the blue face of the moon. "Anyhow...amen."

As he crossed to the bed, Bart wondered if God really listened to the prayers of sinful, wicked men like him. Seemed doubtful. But even as he pondered, an idea flickered to life in his mind. He would write a letter to his closest pal. The man who had taken him in. The man who had given him the best advice he'd ever gotten. Frank James, the older brother of Jesse James.

At ten o'clock the next morning, Rosie knocked on the front door of Mr. Kilgore's one-room schoolhouse.

She had managed to eat a dry biscuit and sip down a cup of hot tea. Feeling a little better, she had washed her face, knotted up her hair and dressed in a simple green gingham.

"Mrs. Springfield," Mr. Kilgore exclaimed when he saw his visitor on the stoop. "I'm so pleased to see you. Do come in."

Even though she had planned to take care of matters on the porch, Rosie couldn't resist stepping into the classroom.

"Good morning, Mrs. Springfield," the children chanted.

"Good morning, students." Rosie surveyed the garden of bright faces. "Lucy, I see you're leading the geography recitations today."

"Yes, ma'am," the little girl replied shyly. "Mr. Kilgore put me in charge."

"A very wise decision."

When Lucy's face broke into a brilliant smile, Mr. Kilgore took Rosie by the arm and escorted her to the front of the room.

"Students," he said, "Mrs. Springfield has spoken with me on several occasions about her desire to become your teacher. Not only has she passed her school board examination with distinction, but she's qualified to teach every subject we offer, and more besides. Although we have only a few weeks of school remaining, I'm pleased to inform you that until the summer break, Mrs. Springfield will fill our vacancy. This autumn, if she's willing, she'll become our full-time schoolteacher."

At that, the students clapped and stomped their feet on the wooden floor. Mr. Kilgore beamed at Rosie.

As the children got back to work, he addressed her in a low voice. "Mrs. Springfield, I am prepared to offer you four dollars and fifty cents per week until the summer. For the 1883-84 school year, I will pay you the grand total of two hundred and fifty-six dollars— a good deal more than you were earning at the Harvey House, I should think."

"Yes, but Mr. Kilgore—"

"I know," he said, holding up a hand to halt her protest. "I realize you received tips at the house along with room and board. I'm aware that you were entitled to free train rides. Of course I don't have those things to offer. My budget is determined by the school board, but I'm certain that, as a married woman, you will be housed and fed by Mr. Springfield."

"Mr. Kilgore, two hundred and fifty-six dollars—"

"And summers off, don't forget. Should you start your own family, my wife has agreed to take your baby into our home as part of her little flock during the day while you teach."

"Truly, that won't be necessary—"

"And as added incentive, I will allow you to manage the classroom exactly as you please, Mrs. Springfield. I'll rent McAuliffe and Ferguson's Hall for any performances you would like for the children to give. I'll even sponsor an end-of-the-year picnic as part of Raton's July Fourth festivities."

As weak as she was, Rosie felt a surge of excitement at the generous offer. Here was her dream, placed in the very palms of her hands! Yet she had told Bart she intended to spend her days at their homestead.

"I'm honored," she said when she could find the words. "Honored by your confidence in me."

"Then I'll see you tomorrow morning, Mrs. Springfield. Unless you'd like to start right now?"

Rosie inhaled the scent of chalk and old textbooks. "I'll have to speak with my husband."

"Of course, Mrs. Springfield. Loyalty to a spouse is highly commendable."

After the requisite farewells, Rosie shook his hand and stepped out onto the street. Leaning against the white picket fence that surrounded the school, she shut her eyes and tried to quell her excitement. The classroom could be hers after all! The slates and inkwells and chalk. And so many children! Even the fine salary. Would Bart want to deny her this dream?

But would she really be willing to change the life she had come to love? It wouldn't be long before Bart would need her in the fields. She thought of the soddy, her chickens, her pots and pans, the garden full of vegetables. If she taught all day, those would have to take second place in her life.

But how would she surrender the classroom? She could be a teacher! A real teacher!

As she made her way down the street, Rosie felt as if she were floating. The New Mexico morning sky was as blue as the pattern on a willowware plate, not a cloud to be seen, the mountains aglow in shades of olive, gray and violet. Wearing fresh coats of paint, the clapboard houses, hotels and saloons fairly strutted down the street. The adobe homes sported new layers of white *caliche* in preparation for the long, dry summer. The railroad had brought the bulbs and seeds of eastern flowers to town, and every yard was bursting with roses, peonies and hollyhocks.

"Good morning, Mrs. Springfield," Mr. Pace called from the post office as Rosie walked past.

"Morning, Mr. Pace." She gave him a little wave.

"Howdy, Mrs. Springfield." Raton's photographer tipped his hat as he hurried by with his dog, Tom, close at his heels.

"Hello, Laurie!" Mrs. Bayne tapped on the window of her dress shop, where she was setting up a display of calico fabrics.

Although she had been queasy that morning, Rosie felt positively perky as she stepped onto the depot platform outside the Harvey House. "Morning, Mr. Gable!" she called when she spotted the manager at the far end of the platform.

"Welcome back, Laurie! Go on into the lunchroom, and tell those girls to fix you a bowl of ice cream. On the house!"

"Thanks, Mr. Gable." Rosie hurried toward the front door, excited to see Etta and the other girls again. Her heart brimming with joy, Rosie almost breezed past a white poster tacked to the wall just inside the door.

Reward, it read in bold black print. Bart Kingsley. Rosie froze as she absorbed the message.

REWARD: Bart Kingsley $50, dead or alive. This armed and dangerous criminal is wanted by authorities in the state of Missouri for train robbery and murder. Vitals: black hair, green eyes, 200 lbs., 6'2". Half-breed Apache.

As the blood rushed from Rosie's cheeks, she read the list of offenses her husband was accused of committing:

* * *

Robberies:
October 7, l879—Glendale, Missouri, Chicago & Alton line
July 15, l88l—Winston, Missouri, Rock Island line
September 7, 188l—Blue Cut, Missouri, Chicago & Alton
line
Accomplice to murder:
July 15, l88l—Winston, Missouri Participated in the shoot-
ing deaths of William Westfall and Frank McMillan.

At the bottom of the poster, a notice in boldface
type read:

**Bart Kingsley was wounded in the territory of New
Mexico. Escaped. Believed to have been captured
by the authorities in Albuquerque, but it was the
wrong man. Last seen alive: Raton, New Mexico.**

Someone had drawn a circle around the last three
words. Rosie swallowed and touched the letters that
formed Bart's name. There was no picture but it hardly
mattered. How many men could fit that description?

Chapter Fourteen

Abandoning all thoughts of eating ice cream with her friends, Rosie fled the Harvey House. With the words of the poster fresh in her mind, she suddenly saw the sheet of white paper everywhere. One had been nailed to every post along the depot porch. Three more were glued to the windows of the saloon. Yet another fluttered from a pillar at McAuliffe and Ferguson's Hall.

Reward. Bart Kingsley, dead or alive.

"Dear God," Rosie repeated in a breathless prayer as she stumbled over a ridge of dried mud in the street. "Dear God, help...help!"

She didn't want Bart to die. If God didn't do something quick, the sheriff would arrest him and throw him in jail. He would be taken to Missouri, where the James gang had left an evil taste in the mouths of the lawmen. Surely they would hang him.

But what if Bart really had shot down those two men in cold blood? He had admitted to robbery. Why not murder?

Rosie stopped and grabbed a picket of the fence surrounding the sheriff's office. She ought to claim she never knew Bart's true history. Then she could teach, buy a little house and live the life she had planned.

No, she thought as she caught her breath. She must stand by the man she loved. She would tell Sheriff Bowman about their homestead and how Bart plowed and hoed until his muscles ached and how he tended his livestock. She would describe how he saved money and planned to expand their home. How good he was to her, and how kind to everyone.

Even though waves of nausea rolled through her again, Rosie knew she would face the sheriff and tell him Bart was a good man. He deserved forgiveness. He deserved a second chance.

Bart swung through the front door of the courthouse and called back over his shoulder. "Come on over for dinner sometime, sheriff. My wife makes a great apple pie."

"Sure thing, Buck." Sheriff Bowman stood in the doorway. "You need anything, just holler."

"Will do." Bart turned and spotted Rosie. "What are you doing out of bed, darlin'? You're as green as a new apple."

"I've been to see Mr. Kilgore." Rosie searched his eyes. "Did you see the poster?"

"The fool thing hung right over my head the whole time I was talking." He chuckled. "When I first spotted it, you could have knocked me over with a feather. I reckon people just see what they want to see."

He realized Rosie was still very weak, and the wanted poster had come near to doing her in. As he helped her down the street and onto the hotel porch, he tried to reassure her. "Sheriff Bowman has me set in his mind as a hardworking man, the cousin of Cheyenne Bill and as honest as the day is long. Shrewd as he is, I don't think it ever crossed his mind that I'm a half-breed green-eyed stranger who showed up in town right after Bart Kingsley ran out."

"Oh, Bart. It can't last long. Someone will guess."

He shouldered his way through the hotel door and settled her on a settee near the fire. In their room, he quickly packed their clothes, slung the bag over his shoulder and helped Rosie to the wagon.

Not until they had traveled some distance did she finally speak up. "What happened with that man who attacked us? Did he give up the fight?"

Bart pondered his answer for a moment. He didn't want Rosie to know how much trouble the old snake had actually been. Enough trouble that Bart kept his rifle on his thighs as he drove the wagon down the deserted trail.

"His name's Harwood, and he refused to give up," he told Rosie. "He wanted money for a new set of choppers. Ten dollars, to make amends."

"Ten dollars? We don't have that kind of money."

"Don't I know it." Bart shook his head. There had been times in his life when he'd had so much cash he hadn't known what to do with it all. But the money had been ill-gotten—easily gained and just as easily squandered.

"The more Harwood and I talked, the more the situation became clear to Sheriff Bowman. I pointed out there's only one road into Springer. Any fool could have made it to town without asking for directions."

"Of course," Rosie said with a sigh of relief. "Did he confess to trying to rob us?"

"Nah. When the sheriff was starting to put the picture together, the toothless devil claimed he needed to use the privy out back of the courthouse. Sure enough, off he skedaddled and never came back. Harwood didn't rob us or hurt you, and he lost his teeth to boot. That squares it for me."

"I guess so," Rosie sighed, snuggled down into the blankets and shut her eyes. "So it's all settled, then."

"Everything's going to be okay." He studied the rifle on his thighs for a long time. He sure didn't like what he had to say next, but he didn't want to keep anything from his wife, especially now, when her health was suffering so much from all this trouble.

Rosie had told him about the long illness she endured when he left her not long after their wedding—a sickness so bad it had rendered her barren. He sure hoped this incident wouldn't push her over the edge again. Women often had trouble with their nerves, he'd been told. Rosie's hearty spirit and gumption belied the fact that she was physically fragile. He had to tell her the truth, though, and he sure didn't like it.

"Well," he said finally, "there could be one hitch."

Rosie opened her eyes. "A hitch?"

"Sheriff Bowman sent telegrams to a couple of places to check up on me. I figured he'd come up blank looking for somebody named Buck Springfield."

"Did he wire Kansas City?"

"No." Bart took a breath. "But he did send a query to the Missouri law. With my description. A green-eyed Indian-looking fellow who stands six foot two and weighs two hundred pounds."

"Oh, Bart," Rosie murmured.

He gave her a long look. "Things could get interesting, if you know what I mean."

By the time the wagon arrived at the little soddy, Rosie was feeling better. But as her stomach settled, her head cleared, and she began to understand the import of what had happened.

Bart was again a hunted man. Not only were those awful posters everywhere, but Sheriff Bowman had sent a telegram to Missouri. It couldn't be long before someone figured out the truth.

Etta knew all about Rosie's past and the green-eyed man she once married. The livery stable owner saw Bart every day. How long would it be before he pondered the description on the wanted poster?

The only man in town who knew the full truth was Cheyenne Bill. But how had Bart persuaded the boxer to lie on his behalf? And what would it take to make Cheyenne Bill turn against him?

"You haven't said a word since we left town," Bart commented as he helped Rosie down from the wagon. He bent and lightly kissed her cheek before scooping her up in his arms and carrying her into the cool, sweet shadows of their home.

"I'm going to put you right here on the bed while I milk the cow and check on the chickens." After taking off her boots, he settled her beneath the sheets she had ironed so long ago—yet only the day before—when their life was golden.

Halfway to the door, Bart looked over his shoulder. "It'll be all right, Rosie-girl. Don't worry your pretty head about anything."

The moment he was gone, worry was all she could

do. Her prayers seemed to go nowhere—the words nothing but ashes in her mouth. The little house began to feel dank and cold, the unlit room filled with threatening shadows. Even the memory of her garden and budding roses did little to quell the dread inside her.

One thing alone gave her comfort—the image of small bright faces, well-worn desks, a chorus of voices reciting the alphabet. Thinking of the children, she slept and did not wake until almost dawn.

Tinges of pink and gold slanted between the open curtains of the two front windows when Rosie began to stir. A meadowlark sang out the promise of another sunny day. She snuggled close to Bart, drinking in the scent of his bare skin. He must have come home after she had fallen asleep. Was he dreaming of her now?

As she ran her hand over his massive shoulder and down his sculpted arm, he turned. His green eyes were misty emeralds in the early light as he gazed at her. "I love you, Rosie," he murmured. "I love you."

He did love her, she realized. He loved her so much.

"Bart, I want to keep what we have now. I want life to be this way forever."

"I can see the worry on your face." He stroked a finger down her cheek.

"I'm full of worries—full to the brim."

He shut his eyes and settled her cheek against his shoulder. "You always used to tell me that God is with us all the time, Rosie. Jesus told us not to worry, too. I was sitting on the church porch when the preacher read it out of the Bible, and I never forgot. Have you forgotten?"

"I know what the Bible says, but only Jesus could

be calm with this much trouble facing Him. Bart, you did so much wrong, and it's going to catch up to you."

He groaned. "If I could take away the past, you know I would. But I can't undo it. All I can do is ask you to forgive me for what I did and how I lived."

"I do forgive you, Bart. But who else will?"

"God will."

"But not those lawmen in Missouri. How long before they come for you?"

"I can handle it, Rosie. I've been on the run so long the trail feels like home. It won't be anything new for me to be churning up dust and riding for yucca country. Staying two jumps ahead of the law is the life I know best."

"What about me? Will you take me with you?"

"I wouldn't even if I could. You deserve a better life, Rosie."

"So you'll run off and leave me again?"

He was silent a moment. Then he released her and fell back on the pillow. "I can't let you live with so much fear that you're sick as a dog. It's wrong of me to keep you here in this bum dugout, raising chickens and milking cows when you were brought up to be a society lady. But no matter how wrong it is, the picture always changes when I think about giving you up. I did that once, Rosie. I'm not going to do it again—not unless you tell me to."

"I don't want to lose you either, Bart. But what will happen to us?"

"I've been doing a heap of thinking and even a little praying about all this. I think it's going to come out all right. The good Lord loves you just as much as I do. Maybe more, though I can't imagine it."

"He loves you, too, Bart."

"I don't know why." He sat up in bed and swung his legs to the floor. "Anybody who would love a varmint like me ought to have his head examined."

At that, Rosie giggled, wrapped her arms around him and kissed him good and long. The cow could just wait to be milked, she thought.

After breakfast, Bart hitched his horses to the wagon for the ride into Raton. He would be late for work at the stable, but he told Rosie he didn't give a hoot. Their time together that morning had restored his belief in their future.

"Don't work too hard, darlin'," he called from the wagon. "You still look a little green around the gills."

Rosie tried to smile as she watched him flick the reins and set the horses to pulling the wagon down the bumpy trail.

Hands still damp from washing the breakfast dishes, she studied Bart's broad back as the wagon neared the trees. How many days had she stood just so, waving him off? This should feel right...normal...good.

But it didn't. Not at all.

If he left, she might never see him again. He could be captured this very day—tossed into jail or killed. Worse yet, he might run. He would abandon her as he'd done before, heading out of town, hiding from the law, robbing trains for a living. She would be alone out here with no husband, no future, no money, nothing to even keep her alive. It could all happen in an instant.

"Bart!" Shouting, she ran down the trail after him. "Bart, wait!"

"Rosie?" The wagon had stopped at the bottom of

an incline. He climbed down and started toward her. "Rosie, what's wrong?"

"I'm going with you, Bart. Mr. Kilgore offered me that position at the school yesterday, and I'm going to take it. I wanted to live out here with you, but I just can't. I need… I need…oh, Bart, I need something I can count on."

He took off his hat as she came to a breathless halt before him. "And you can't count on me," he said.

"How can I?" she asked him. "I can't be sure of anything. But if I'm teaching, I'll have work and I'll have the money to survive when…if anything happens to you."

"Rosie, I promised to take care of you. Don't say you want to be a schoolmarm because you don't trust me."

"I do trust you, Bart, as far as I can. But I have to consider my own future. I'll take that job and…and maybe I'll buy a little house, too…just until things settle down. When I'm sure of you…of us…then I'll move back to the homestead again. Don't you see?"

"I see, all right. I see that you don't love me the way I love you. You don't have faith that I can look out for you and build us a good future. You haven't forgiven me either. Not the way I asked."

"I'm trying, Bart. My life hasn't been easy these past few years, and I've tried hard to make something better for myself. Don't ask me to give all of that up."

He nodded. "Maybe you're right. Maybe you ought to do exactly what you want and never mind what I'm trying to give you. The good Lord knows it's not much anyhow."

"Bart, please try to understand."

"Get in the wagon, Rosie. You go make yourself a

good life, and if you can ever see your way clear to pardon me for my past, then we'll see what comes of it."

She climbed onto the wooden seat and sat in silence through the long ride. Her impulsive run to the wagon had surprised her. Looking back on her own life, she realized how weak her faith in God really was. Despite prayers and Bible reading, she had little conviction that God would guide her along a path He had prepared just for her.

Instead, she had taken her destiny into her own hands again and again—impetuously marrying Bart once, and loving him again in the face of all that was rational. Running away from her father and Dr. Lowell. Pushing herself at Mr. Kilgore as though she was the only teacher worth having.

But what else could she have done? Just because she and Bart had started to build a life together, just because they loved each other and had taken that love to intimacy, she didn't have to commit her whole future to him. Did she? Was that what marriage meant?

No, it made good sense to distance herself from Bart a little and see how the situation turned out. Rosie was no naive, lovelorn schoolgirl. Certainly not. She'd seen too many of the harsh realities of life to count on a happily ever-after ending. People who did wrong in life eventually paid for it one way or another. It wouldn't be long before the law came after Bart. She might as well start preparing herself for that right now.

"You want me to let you off at the schoolhouse?" Bart asked when they rolled into Raton.

"Yes, please." Rosie wanted to look at him, but she was afraid she would lose her resolve to keep him at a distance. "I'd like you to bring a trunk of my clothes and toiletries to Mr. Kilgore's house."

"You'll be staying in town now?"

"For a while."

"A while? Buying a house sounds pretty glued down to me, Rosie."

"Bart, try to understand."

"I've been trying to understand you all the way here. I don't see how a woman and a man can do the things we did this morning and then chuck it out like an old cow chip."

"Our love isn't a cow chip!"

He pulled the wagon to a stop in front of the one-room school. "Then believe in me, Rosie. I won't do wrong by you, I promise."

She studied his green eyes beneath the shadow of his hat. "I won't do wrong by you, either, Bart. But I need this chance to give myself some roots, something I can hold on to when things go bad."

"Who says things will go bad?"

"Who says they won't?" She slid to the edge of the seat and climbed down from the wagon. "I'll send word to the livery stable when you can come for me again. It won't be long, Bart."

As she gazed up at him, he settled his hat lower over his brow. "I never had you figured for a hard-hearted woman, Rosie," he said. "But now I know different."

He flicked the reins and set off in the direction of the railway depot.

Rosie could not have imagined feeling worse than she did when she first set foot inside her new classroom. Not only had she driven Bart away, but she had given up something unbearably precious. To wake up each morning with her husband's big arms all warm and wrapped around her had become dear. To gaze out from their dugout and see his tall, strong figure laboring over the plow had filled her heart to overflowing. To stand in their cozy little home with stew bubbling over a snapping fire, curtains rustling in the windows, and the scent of wildflowers drifting through the open door had become heaven itself.

But she had fled that Eden, traded it for a few shekels worth of security.

"Mrs. Springfield!" Thomas Kilgore hurried between the rows of desks as she entered the room. "Welcome, welcome! Students, Mrs. Springfield is your new teacher."

Amid the clapping, he led her to the big wooden desk she had dreamed of for so long. Rosie had barely begun to accept what she had done—how swiftly she had reversed all her best plans for a life with Bart— when Mr. Kilgore began loading her arms with books, slates and tablets of lined paper.

"The school commissioners have selected Sheldon's English readers," he said, "Patterson's grammars and spellers, Robinson's arithmetic, Harper's geography and Spencerian penmanship books."

"Oh," Rosie managed as she gazed down at the well-worn books with their patched and tattered covers.

"Now, I've found that some of our students need supplemental work. Clark's Drugstore carries comprehensive geography books for a dollar and fifteen cents. I've been thinking of putting Minnie and Lucy to work in them—those two girls are so far ahead of the others. Manford and some of the boys may need the spelling books there that sell for two bits. The boys struggle to spell correctly, but I've had difficulty finding the right texts. You'd think parents would gladly buy books for their children. What with the price of whiskey at two bits these days, a schoolbook is not only cheap but a much more prudent purchase."

Rosie nodded, and hoped her numbed brain was absorbing at least some of what he was telling her.

"School begins promptly at seven," he continued. "Student tardiness is not tolerated. Break for morning recess at nine. Ring the lunch bell at noon, then start class again at twelve-thirty. Some, like Manford, must leave school after their midday meal and work at various occupations—mostly in the mines and fields—one or two days a week. Dismiss the rest of your students at four. You will give ample homework, won't you, Mrs. Springfield?"

"Yes, sir."

"It's vital that these children catch up with their city counterparts. Under your tutelage I expect them to be able to compete in any educational arena."

Rosie nodded, though she didn't see how. With their parents expecting them to do many chores other than schoolwork, the ragged homesteader children must certainly lag far behind city students.

"Discipline is a matter of the first order in my school, Mrs. Springfield," Mr. Kilgore went on. "Without limits and control, children cannot and will not learn."

"I agree completely," she told him.

"Good. Here is the switch." He pointed to a long, supple branch that had been stripped of twigs and leaves. Beside it hung a thick, smooth stick. "That is the cane, and in the corner is the stool and dunce cap.

Be frugal in their use, but do not hesitate to employ them to good benefit when needed."

"Yes, sir."

"I'll be next door instructing the high school students and tending to administrative duties. I shall be happy to take all disciplinary matters into my own capable hands. Any questions? Well, then, Mrs. Springfield, good luck."

With those parting words, he stepped out the front door leaving Rosie alone to face the fulfillment of her dreams.

Chapter Fifteen

Rosie dared to hope that Bart would drive his wagon past the school on his way out of town at noon, but he didn't.

As she sat on the front porch steps eating a lunch Mrs. Kilgore had fixed for her, she scanned the narrow, dusty streets for any sign of an ebony-haired, broad-chested man with his hat pulled low on his brow. Bart didn't come, and by the time Rosie rang the bell for afternoon classes, she had to accept that he had done just as he said he would and gone to work alone at their homestead.

Rosie had to learn thirty-seven names, figure out how to rotate the six grade levels and oversee recitations and slate work. By the end of the day, she felt like the director of a large orchestra of various and sometimes inharmonic instruments rather than the teacher in a one-room schoolhouse.

Exhausted, she rang the final bell and watched the students collect their homework and file out of the room. Manford Wade, who had not gone to Bart's homestead that day, lingered and gave Rosie his familiar red-cheeked grin.

"Bye, ma'am," he called from the row of coat hooks by the door.

"Goodbye, Manford. Practice your script tonight. Mr. Spencer would be rolling in his grave if he knew about the angles in your uppercase *B*."

"Aw, Mrs. Springfield, ain't a soul around these parts cares about my letter *B* but you and Mr. Kilgore."

Rosie brushed a wisp of loose hair from her cheek as she neared the boy. "Any young man who wants to make his way in this world must learn to write properly."

Manford stuffed his cap over his spiky red hair and gave a little shrug. "Us boys have got a game of picket going over in the alley twixt Walley's Saloon and Farley's Bakery. Then I got to go home and milk the cow and put up the chickens. If there's any time left before sundown, I'll do my letters."

"School should come before picket, Manford," Rosie admonished. "With a good education, you can become anything you want in this world—a doctor, lawyer, mercantile owner. But with picket, all you'll ever learn how to do is hide out and sneak around. Those skills will only serve if you want to be an outlaw."

"An outlaw? Naw, ma'am, I aim to grow up and be just like your husband—and I bet he can't write a Spencer *B* no better than me."

Tipping his cap the way Rosie had seen Bart do a hundred times, Manford took his leave. She stood silently in the doorway as Mr. Kilgore emerged from the classroom next door.

"How did things go today, Mrs. Springfield?" he asked.

Startled, she turned to face him. "Oh, everything was fine. I enjoyed the day very much."

"Would you like to come over to the house and take a cup of tea while you wait for Mr. Springfield to arrive? You're looking a little peaked."

"Thank you, Mr. Kilgore, but I won't be waiting for my husband today. We've agreed I'll stay here in town during the week. I plan to use my savings from the Harvey House to purchase a small town home."

"Oh?" His brow rumpling, Mr. Kilgore took off his spectacles and began cleaning them with a white cotton handkerchief he had pulled from his back pocket. "This is not an arrangement I had expected, Mrs. Springfield."

"Would you and Mrs. Kilgore be so good as to put me up tonight? Tomorrow afternoon I'll speak with Mr. Osfield about the house I'm hoping to buy."

"Already picked one out, have you?"

"Yes, sir. It seemed prudent."

"You're welcome to stay with us for as long as you like. I would prefer you invest your money in a horse and buggy so you can take yourself home to your husband each evening."

Rosie worked up a small smile. "We shall see. In the meantime I'd best collect my texts. I have a lot of preparing to do for tomorrow. I'd like to teach some songs for a spring musical program."

"Wonderful!" With the change in subject, Mr. Kilgore's attitude mellowed, and soon he was off and running with her idea. By the time Rosie stepped into the Kilgore home, he was positively giddy about the prospect of patriotic recitations, spring medleys, piano solos and even a small operatic play.

Mrs. Kilgore was quick to support the idea of Rosie

spending as much time as she wanted in their home, and she hurried to prepare the attic bedroom for their guest. After a quiet dinner, Rosie climbed up to the small gable room and worked on her lessons until the lamp wick burned low.

Her first day of teaching had been everything she had hoped. But she couldn't help weighing what she had given up against what she had gained. Finally she crawled into the cold, empty bed and fell asleep to dream of Bart.

A trunk filled with Rosie's clothes, shoes and other belongings appeared on the school porch the following day, but she never caught sight of Bart. As the week passed, she and the students settled into a schedule that began to chug along like a train on a well-greased track. Mrs. Springfield would tolerate no nonsense— no pigtails dipped in inkwells, no secret messages passed back and forth on slates. And most certainly no hidden tobacco.

Instead of the switch and cane, the new teacher found other methods of motivation. Within a week, the schoolhouse fence had been whitewashed by a pair of boys who couldn't refrain from chewing gum like a pair of old heifers. Three girls who had chosen to whisper rather than learn their geography lessons were stitching curtains from a bolt of blue fabric. A tardy Manford Wade scrubbed the classroom blackboard. Geraniums, planted by a group of playground fistfighters, flourished in window boxes built by a young man who dawdled in memorizing his Shakespeare soliloquy.

Mannie reported to her everything said about Rosie, complimentary or not. The new teacher's after-school punishments, it seemed, were the best thing going. She provided cold lemonade and sandwiches and regularly joined in the work. People wondered at Mr. Springfield, who never came to visit his wife, and they said she looked skinny and dark-eyed from sadness over it.

That first week, Rosie put down ten dollars on a small yellow clapboard house. The joy she had expected to feel never came. Instead, it was all she could do to keep from running to the livery stable, throwing her arms around Bart and begging him to take her home to their soddy.

She made it her crusade to remove every wanted poster in town. Needing paper to write a message, wipe a spot of mud from her shoe or mark a book she was reading, she tore down the posters one by one. She felt guilty for her gratitude that Sheriff Bowman had taken so ill with his coughing that he had no time to investigate Bart's background.

In fact, she began to wonder if everyone in Raton had taken ill. A bout of chickenpox felled the youngest students, while the others coughed and sneezed through their lessons. Rosie couldn't cure her bouts of nausea either. Finally she scheduled an appointment with Dr. Kohlhouser, whose dog Griff had made the school's front porch a favorite haunt.

One Saturday morning Rosie was sweeping that porch when Manford Wade and his chums sauntered by. "Hey, Mrs. Springfield," he called. "I just saw Buck over at the livery stable! He asked me out to work at your place this afternoon. We're gonna build a refrigerator!"

Rosie clutched the broom handle for support at the mention of Bart. "Refrigerator? Sounds like a big job."

"Not for Buck and me. We're gonna dig it wide and deep. It'll be so cool you can keep food in there for weeks without it spoilin'. Buck says it'll work by 'vaporation.'"

"Evaporation." Rosie took a breath. "So, how are things…on the homestead? The sugar beets, I mean."

"Buck says the beets are growin' like weeds, and come fall he's gonna have to quit his job at the stable to get 'em all harvested. He don't mind, though. With the kitchen garden abloom and the beets doin' so good, he thinks the two of you should do just dandy without the extra pay."

"That's what he said?"

"Ask him yourself if you don't believe me. Why don't you go see him, ma'am? Do the both of you good. If you think you're feelin' poorly, you should see Buck."

"Buck is sick? Mannie, why didn't you tell me!"

"He ain't sick the way you are. Buck is blue as an old hound dog day after day. He ain't hardly fun to be around. You better go see him, Mrs. Springfield. I reckon it'd cheer him up mightily."

"I may just do that. Yes, maybe I will."

By now, the other boys were shuffling their feet. "Come on, Mannie," one spoke up. "Let's get on over to the alley."

"Playing picket again, boys?" Rosie asked.

"Yes, ma'am. And we wanna watch the goin's-on at the shootin' gallery."

Rosie ruffled Mannie's sweat-dampened red hair. "On a Saturday, I can't think of anything better than a good game of picket. If I weren't all grown up, I'd join you myself."

This comment drew hoots of laughter from the group. "I reckon a schoolmarm playing picket would draw a bigger crowd than Charley Baker's shooting gallery," Mannie said.

"I expect you're right. Well, get along with you, then. And be careful around the guns, boys."

Manford waved as he ran off with his friends. The redhead was the only one of the older boys who didn't pack his own pistol. Rosie knew it was only because his mother was too poor to provide her son with that particular trapping of manhood.

Rosie swept the last dusty board on the porch, her thoughts on Bart. Was he really so sad? Could he have planned the refrigerator with her in mind? It was nearly noon. Should she hurry over to the livery stable and tell Bart she was ready to go home…at least for the weekend?

Rosie's worst fears had never materialized. Most of the posters in town had vanished. Harwood, the toothless troublemaker, had not returned. No one had a bad word to say about Bart. Filled with sudden determination, she propped the broom by the door and started across the street.

"Bart," she would say, "I've come about the refrigerator. I'd better go out to the homestead and make sure you dig it in the right place. I don't want it too far from my kitchen."

Her kitchen? Rosie shook her head. Why should she expect Bart to do anything for her? Oh, but she had missed him so much! The days without him seemed endless. The nights even worse.

"Bart," she would say, "I've come to tell you that I love teaching, I've put ten dollars down on a house and I'll do just fine without you. But I want you to know how lonesome I've been…and how much I want to go home…."

She stopped at the street corner by the livery stable and tried to swallow the lump in her throat. She couldn't cry in front of Bart. That would never do. But how was she ever going to hold back her tears when the thought of the man tore at her heart so?

Lifting up another of her futile prayers, Rosie walked up the hay-littered ramp into the livery stable. "Well, Bart," she would say in a perfectly casual voice, "So how have you been?"

"Rosie?" His deep voice came from somewhere in the shadows.

She stopped, unable to move. "Oh!"

"That you, Rosie?"

"If it's not a ghost, it's her," another voice spoke up—one Rosie realized as that of Cheyenne Bill.

"Rosie, what are you doing here?" Bart asked.

The two men emerged into a shaft of golden light. Bart was every bit as tall and strong and handsome as Rosie had remembered. His jet-black hair gleamed in the sunlit stable, and he wore no shirt. Ropes of muscle shone a coppery red across his chest and down the flat plane of his stomach to his leather-belted denims. His green eyes flickered.

"I…well, I…" Rosie fumbled, exactly as she feared she would. "I wanted you to know that…that my teaching job is wonderful. And… I hear you're building a refrigerator."

"Rosie?" Bart reached toward her, and she melted.

"Oh, Bart, I've been so lonely and—"

"A killin', a killin'!" someone screamed just outside the livery stable. "There's been a shootin'!"

Instinctively Bart grabbed Rosie and held her against his chest. The stocky Cheyenne Bill sprinted to a table near the stable window, grabbed a rifle lying there and bolted for the door.

"Stay here and guard your woman!" he barked. "I'll tend to this."

Bart whipped his six-shooter from the holster hung at his hip. "Bill, watch your back. No tellin' what kind of troublemakers are lurkin' out there."

The massive man swung around and gave Bart a lopsided grin. "Or lurkin' in here. See you later, Kingsley."

As Cheyenne Bill ran outside, one of the Harvey House kitchen boys sprinted past the livery. Rosie called out to him. "Jimmy, what's going on?"

"It's a shooting!" the youth called back as she and Bart headed for the door. "I heard tell a kid got killed over by Charley Baker's shootin' gallery. The men are threatening to lynch Baker for not taking better care of his business. They say Mrs. Wade's wild with grief!"

"Wade!" Rosie jerked out of Bart's arms. "Dear God, please not Mannie!"

Without waiting, she tore down the ramp and joined the crowd racing toward the alley between the bakery and the saloon. Heart aching, Rosie elbowed her way through the throng. "Not Mannie! Not Mannie!" she breathed.

But the moment she pushed through the ring of onlookers, she knew her prayers were in vain. Manford's mother huddled over the boy, her shrieks of grief piercing the air as Doctor Kohlhouser examined the small limp form.

Sheriff Bowman and a couple of deputies were attempting to hold back the crowd while at the same time keeping a close watch on the shooting gallery owner, Charley Baker. A group of men who had participated in the shooting gallery's games were studying the bullet holes in the board behind the target while Manford's young friends stood against the alley wall, their eyes wide with horror.

Rosie tried to push her way past the sheriff, but he caught her arm. "Not so fast, ma'am. It ain't a pretty sight."

"I'm his teacher, Sheriff Bowman," she pleaded. At that, he let her go. Falling to her knees beside Mrs. Wade, Rosie cradled the sobbing woman. Manford, eyes closed and body motionless, lay bloodied and lifeless in the dust. Then a pair of strong brown arms slipped beneath the figure as Bart lifted Mannie against his chest.

"I'll take the boy home," he said. "Doc Kohlhouser, if you'll follow me, you can look after him there."

As Bart started down the alley, the crowd parted. Mrs. Wade clung to her son's dangling hand, while the physician kept pace. Dizzy and weak, Rosie hurried after them, but when she reached the end of the alley, she felt a man's hand clamp around her arm.

"Come with me, Rosie," Cheyenne Bill ordered. "Kingsley won't want you to see it."

Rosie shook her head at the stocky man, whose crooked, flattened nose and lopsided mouth frightened her almost as much as the cartridge belts and holsters around his waist. But he left her no choice. "Now, come along, ma'am," he said. "You look puny as a wrung-out rag."

Taking her elbow, Cheyenne Bill ushered her down the street toward the edge of town where a small house stood alone. He pushed through a creaky front door and led her into a gloomy room with bare floors and a few sticks of furniture.

"Here, sit on this," he said, pushing a rickety stool at Rosie. Still rigid with shock and disbelief, she spread her skirts and perched on its edge.

"I'd give you some whiskey, but I quit paintin' my tonsils a while back." He laughed without mirth. "That coffin varnish sure is some powerful stuff. It'll eat its way plumb to yer bootheels."

He picked up an iron poker and prodded his fire back to life. "Charley Baker oughta hang for what he done."

"Mannie's not going to die," she whispered.

"The boy's dead already, ma'am, and you might as well get used to it. Somebody's bullet plowed clean through that target and the board behind it and put a window in the kid's skull."

"No!" Rosie jumped to her feet and paced across the sagging floorboards. "How dare you say such a thing? I saw Mannie barely fifteen minutes ago. He and Bart were going to dig a refrigerator out at the homestead this afternoon. He was laughing and looking forward to a game of hide-and-seek with his friends. He can't die just like that!"

Bill gave the fire a jab. "That's how it happens, Rosie. Just like that. Better he went quick than he lingered. I've seen folk linger. You don't want that for the boy."

Rosie shook her head as tears welled up. "I can't believe it. I just can't."

For a moment the big Indian stood awkwardly beside her, rubbing his meaty, callused palms together in consternation. Then he let out a breath. "Ah, blast it all, I never knew what to do with a leakin' female."

Rosie couldn't speak. Her mind denied it, but she knew Cheyenne Bill had spoken the truth. Mannie had been killed. Killed. Skinny Mannie with his red hair and broad grin, his winsome ways and mischievous smile.

"Why?" she blurted through her sobs.

"Ain't no good askin' why," Bill said. "You'll addle yer think box tryin' to figure it out."

"But I can't... I just can't accept it." She pulled her handkerchief from her pocket and blotted her cheeks. "Mannie told me...just a few minutes ago...to find Bart. He told me to go see Bart and talk to him."

"What fer?"

"Mannie said I could cheer Bart up because he'd been feeling blue of late. So I decided to go to the stable—"

"There you go! Don't ya see it? Young Manford was an angel of mercy sent to earth with a message. When he'd given it, the good Lord called him home."

"Oh, it's not that simple!" Rosie exploded. "Mannie's existence wasn't based on telling me to go to the stable and talk to Bart! He had so much potential. There was so much that boy could have done. He was a wonderful child and he would have made a fine man."

"All the same, you better heed his advice. You never know but what I said was true."

"What do you know about angels? You're a...a fighter. A boxer. Your whole life is glove contests, not religion."

"No doubt about it—Cheyenne Bill is a hard, hard man. But anybody with a lick of sense knows about angels. Here they be, all around us, fighting holy wars with the demons of evil."

Rosie groaned in disbelief, wondering how she could ever escape this obviously demented man. She studied a whiskey bottle on the fireplace mantel. He had said he didn't drink, but was Cheyenne Bill just liquored up or was he legitimately loco?

"Ain't you never seen a angel?" he was asking.

"No. Nor a demon for that matter."

"Maybe I got my brains scrambled in all them glove contests, but the fact is, I seen 'em plenty of times. Both kinds. Take the kid, Mannie, fer starters. You don't know nothin' about that young'un before he walks into yer life and makes a change in ya. Gives ya a message. Sets ya on the straight path when you was headin' off the trail. See what I mean?"

Rosie shook her head. She wondered where Bart was and if he had any idea she was here in this decrepit house with a man who belonged in an asylum.

"Angels is angels, and demons is demons," Cheyenne Bill was saying as he paced up and down the creaky floor. He grabbed the whiskey bottle and held it out. "This here is my own personal demon. Been fightin' him near all my life. Ol' Bart Kingsley, he let the devil's brood have their way with him fer a while, too. When your pappy told Bart he weren't no good fer ya, that he was just a dumb half breed who was never gonna amount to a pail of hot spit, that his family tree wasn't no better'n a shrub, that you deserved a rich life with swishin' silks and satins and a man who could keep you sitting in tall cotton, ol' Bart began to listen to them demons awhisperin' over his shoulder."

"What?" Rosie whispered. "Pappy told Bart all that?"

"It didn't matter to yer pappy that Bart loved you from the top of yer head to the soles of yer feet and woulda died fer you without blinkin' an eye. No, sir, all yer pappy could see was that Bart was half Injun and poor as a beggar."

"What?" Rosie said again.

"Fact is, Bart hightailed it outta yer life and began runnin' with the devil's brood. Sometimes it takes the good Lord a might of doin' to set a fellow like Bart back on the right trail. So God sent an angel to shoot him in the side."

"It wasn't an angel who shot Bart. It was Sheriff Bowman!"

"Don't split hairs with me, gal. Can't you understand this?"

"No, I can't," she answered bluntly. "You're speaking utter nonsense."

Giving her a look of pity, Cheyenne set the empty whiskey bottle back on the mantel. "Gal, ain't you never been to church?"

"I always go to church. I understand Reverend Cullen's been after you for quite some time."

"Now, there's a man who listens to the angels!"

"I'm sorry, but I have to go—"

"Wait a minute! I ain't done explainin' this. How're you gonna know what to do with yerself if you don't understand that Mannie Wade was an angel?" He gave a snort and began pacing again. "Here's the story. I'm awalkin' through the woods one day scoutin' me a rabbit fer my stew pan when I up and see this feller leaning against a tree lookin' like death warmed over. Lo and behold, I recognize right off he's a half breed like me. We jaw awhile and he tells me he's sufferin' from a gut shot and reckons he's fixin' to ride off to the great beyond, no matter that he just found the only woman he ever loved. On and on, this feller talks till before you know it I'm blubberin' like a newborned babe. Right then I begin to know that this feller is tryin' to set hisself on the right path. He's tryin' to listen to the angels, see?"

Rosie nodded, realizing that for the first time she actually understood his garbled speech.

"So, I aim to help this feller," Cheyenne Bill continued. "I haul him over to my house and we take up together, him and me. We cook up a story that he's my cousin, just come to town. We get him a job over at the livery stable, and we commence to takin' the folks by storm, ol' Buck Springfield and me."

He laughed so hard he could barely spit out his next words. "We was listenin' to the angels, see! So, everything works out perfect. Then you and him get together, and things is just pretty as peaches...till you up and move out on him. Don't you understand, missy, that you wasn't supposed to do that? That weren't part of the plan, see?"

Rosie stood. "No one ever told me there was a plan."

"Ain't you been heedin' the Reverend Cullen on Sunday mornings? *Of course* there's a plan. A grand and mighty plan. But you up and wandered right off it. You let all kinds of fears and worries take hold of you as strong as demon whiskey takes hold of me. Figurin' you could take care of yourself, you hitched up your britches and took off down the wrong road. So the good Lord sent an angel to set you straight. An angel by the name of Manford Wade."

"Are you saying that Mannie got killed because of me?"

"Now, why would I say a thing like that? I'm just tellin' you that Mannie gave you a message, and you better take note. Get on back to Bart where you belong. If that husband of yers is gonna be able to keep on listenin' to angels, he needs you by his side. Fact is, them demons has got loud voices, young lady. Mighty loud. But when Bart Kingsley looks at you, all he ever sees is the angels. Now get home to him, gal. You hear?"

"I'm no angel," Rosie said. "I never have been."

"Don't I know it. What I see when I look at you—well, what I see is a pretty woman—but fearful and ornery, too. But then I ain't in love with you. Bart Kingsley is."

"In love with me," she repeated the words.

"You don't think a man would trek across half the territory, get hisself shot, risk his neck movin' into a town where he's a wanted man, settle a homestead and plant sugar beets when he'd have a lot better luck robbin' a train—all that—if he weren't in love, do ya?"

"Well…" Rosie grabbed the door handle with a damp palm and gave a push. "Well…well, good afternoon, Mr.…Mr. Cheyenne Bill."

Grinning his lopsided grin, the Indian tipped his hat. "Evenin' to you, too, ma'am. It's been a real pleasure socializin' with you."

Chapter Sixteen

She had just arrived at the schoolhouse when Rosie saw Bart round the corner in his wagon. Lifting her skirts, she ran toward him as he pulled the horses to a halt, leaped down from the board and scooped her up in his arms.

"Oh, Rosie-girl," he whispered, his words almost a groan. "He's gone, Rosie. Our Mannie's truly gone."

"No, Bart," she cried. "Please, dear God, let this be a dream!"

They held each other, each wrapped in private grief, yet their tears mingled and their chests heaved as one with racking sobs.

"How can it be, Bart?"

He shook his head. "I don't know, Rosie. I just don't know."

As he spoke, Mrs. Kilgore hurried out of the house toward them. "We've packed you a bag, Mrs. Springfield. We've canceled school until after the funeral on Wednesday. Go on home with you now, honey. You need the rest."

Rosie gazed into the woman's red-rimmed eyes.

"Thank you, Mrs. Kilgore."

"Hurry now, before the sun goes down and the coyotes come out."

Her words moved Bart to action, and he lifted Rosie up into the wagon. Taking his place beside her, he flicked the reins and set the horses trotting down the street.

They were halfway to the homestead before either could speak. Rosie never knew she held so many tears, but the more she tried to stifle them, the faster they flowed. Her nose turned red and her eyes swelled almost shut. If she had been sick before, she felt ten times worse now. All she could think about was Mannie and his big grin. Every time she shut her eyes, she saw his cluttered school desk, his inkwell and tattered books, his spiky red hair, his ill-formed Spencerian *B* and his bright eyes.

"What did the doctor say?" she asked finally.

"There was nothing he could do. Mannie was gone before I got him home."

"Did he suffer?"

Bart shook his head. "The suffering is left to us. I swear I'd kill Charley Baker if I could get my hands on him. Don't look at me like that, Rosie. So would every other man in town. That sidewinder should have checked his target to make sure the board behind it was holding up. Any fool could have guessed it would get shot through. The board was only an inch thick. Baker should have known a .22-caliber rifle would soon cut holes in the board. If I'd been running a shooting gallery, I'd have put a sheet of iron behind the target. A pine board—no matter how thick—is going to give way in time. Turns out there were sixteen bullets lodged in the wall of the jewelry store at the end of the alley."

"Sixteen!" Rosie exclaimed. Then she sighed. "Oh, killing Charley Baker wouldn't bring Mannie back."

"No, but it would make me feel a whole lot better."

She sniffled and dabbed her handkerchief under her eyes. "Cheyenne Bill is angry, too. While you were with Mrs. Wade, he took me to his house."

Bart sat up straight. "His house? He didn't make you drink any of that home-brewed rotgut, did he?"

"The bottle was empty. He stopped drinking a while ago."

"*Tried* to stop. Ol' demon whiskey's got a mighty strong hold on Bill. I reckon he was talking to you about angels."

"How did you know?"

"Angels are Cheyenne Bill's favorite subject. Personally, I think he's been whacked on the noggin a few too many times."

"He believes Mannie was an angel sent to tell me to go home with you today."

"Does he, now? Well, maybe Bill is onto something there. I never knew a better kid than Mannie. If there ever was an angel on earth, it was Manford Wade."

"Cheyenne Bill said he found you in the woods after you left my dormitory room. He said the two of you cooked up the idea to tell everyone in Raton that you're cousins."

Bart gave the hint of a smile. "Bill's a good man, Rosie. A little off center on some things, but harmless as a fly. That's why the whole town loves him so, and he's why they've accepted me. Sure, he's so fierce he wins just about every glove contest in the area, yet folks invite him to all their birthday parties and neighborhood picnics. They made him leader of the hose company, and they write poems about him in the *Comet.* You mention his name, and everyone sings out his favorite boast, *Cheyenne Bill is a hard, hard man.* Fact is, I couldn't have a better pal."

Rosie fell silent. There were many things she wanted to clear up with Bart—especially Cheyenne Bill's revelation about the way her pappy had treated Bart many years before—but she couldn't summon up the energy to speak of it. Such things seemed so inconsequential now in light of Mannie's death.

What did it matter if the Ratonians found out about Bart's checkered past? Let them hem and haw about having a former outlaw in town. Bart was a good man now. Why had she ever thought she needed to run back to town and make her own life—setting off down the wrong road, as Cheyenne Bill had called it? The love between her and Bart was far more important in this world than having a teaching job or a clapboard house or a spotless reputation.

As the wagon topped the hill and Rosie could see the silhouette of the low dugout walls, she felt yet another pang of grief deep inside her heart. This farm had been one of Mannie's favorite places, and Bart had been his hero.

"Mannie thought the world of you, Bart," she said when he had pulled the wagon up to the barn. "He admired you so. I do believe he thought you were next to God Himself."

Bart gazed at the indigo mesas in the distance. "He told me once that he wished..." He stopped speaking and swallowed several times. "Mannie told me he wished I was his papa."

At that, Bart rolled his big shoulders forward and

covered his eyes with his hand. "Oh, God, oh, God, why did You let this happen? I could've made Mannie come out to the farm with me earlier today. I shouldn't have let him play picket. I could've... I wish..."

Rosie wrapped her arms around the broad expanse of his back and rested her head against his shoulder while he wept. The tenderness of Bart's heart suddenly came to her in a flood of remembrance. Cats sitting on his lap while he ate lunch, horses nickering with pleasure as he walked through the stables, the deep cuts of taunting children. Bart was a man like no other she had ever known.

He felt pain more deeply and he loved more fiercely. If her father truly had said the things Cheyenne Bill accused him of, no wonder Bart had fled from her. And if Cheyenne Bill insisted that Bart loved her, surely he really did.

"Bart," she whispered. "Oh, Bart." If it was possible to cradle a massive bullock of a man, Rosie managed it with her grieving husband. For a long time she held him, rocking slowly back and forth on the wagon seat while the horses grazed. She ran her fingers through the black hair at the back of his neck and stroked the taut muscles of his shoulders and arms. Gently she kissed his cheek and brushed away his tears.

"Don't go off again, Rosie," he murmured finally. "I want you here with me. Don't you see that? I took care of Mannie the best I could, and I'll take care of you."

"I know, Bart." She cuddled close against him as his arms came around her. "I shouldn't have stayed away. I shouldn't have been so scared."

"Nobody's going to get me. Nobody's going to tear us apart. You've got to believe that, Rosie. There's nothing, *nothing,* more important in this world than you and me and what we've built between us. Life's too short not to spend it with the one you love."

"Bart, do you love me? Do you truly love me?"

"Aw, girl, don't you know that by now?" He cupped her face and tilted it to the moonlight. "I love you so much, nothing can take me away from you again. Don't you see how it is? Once, I ran off because I thought it was for the best. Then you ran off because you thought it was best. It's not other people who come between us, Rosie. It's us. We keep tearing this thing apart. Why? Why do we do that?"

Rosie's shoulders sagged. "No, Bart, it's not you and me doing it. It's other folk. Cheyenne Bill told me what Pappy said to you that day after he found out we got married. That was why you left me, wasn't it? Pappy drove you off."

"I'll be jiggered," Bart muttered. "I told Bill to keep that business quiet."

"Well, he didn't, and now I know how it really came about. Pappy ran you off with all his talk about you being no good for me."

Bart kissed Rosie's cheek and rubbed his nose against the soft strands of brown hair that had tumbled down over her shoulder. "I don't want you ever to blame your pappy for what happened back then. He was doing what he thought best for you. Besides, he was right. I didn't have a single thing to offer you as a husband. You deserved better."

"What about your love? That was more than enough for me."

"I loved you back then, Rosie, and I love you now—

just as much and more." He kissed her lips. "Stick close, girl. Now and always."

"Oh, Bart, I will." Her heart full, Rosie met his ardent kisses with equal passion. She'd been so long absent from this man, it was all she could do to keep from crying aloud with need. As his mouth claimed hers, his hands caressed her shoulders and back as though to make certain she was real.

Just as hungry for him, she allowed her fingers to search out the warm skin beneath his collar and the broad, hard muscles of his chest. "Take me inside, Bart. I've been needing you so much."

His mouth moved over her neck and cheek as he lifted her out of the wagon and carried her across the moonlit yard to their front door. Inside the dugout, he set her on their bed and stretched out beside her. Oh, he was a beautiful man. His green eyes caressed her as he reached for the buttons at her neck.

"Rosie-girl," he murmured. "I love you better than life itself."

She smiled, wrapped her arms around his chest and allowed her eyelids to drift shut.

It had once seemed impossible to Bart that he would ever have his Rosie so near his heart again. But as time passed he began to believe that he had been wrong.

Rosie let her option on the house elapse. She took Mr. Kilgore's advice and used her savings to buy a small buggy and a gentle horse. Early each morning she drove her rig to town while Bart rode just ahead. At the school she continued to teach the children she had come to love as if they were her own. The death of Manford Wade had affected everyone deeply, and it took time for the students to resume their carefree behavior. But eventually they went back to their usual antics, and their teacher was obliged to cook up a new round of her very popular after-school punishments.

Bart's sugar-beet crop promised a good income. Thanks to his careful thinning, good irrigation and diligent measures against blister beetles, leaf spot, black root, root rot and curly top, the plants had flourished. During the cool nights and warm days of the New Mexico summer, the long, silver-white taproots were growing toward a prime weight of two pounds or more each. Their crowns sent out brilliantly rich greens, each leaf a good two feet long. Bart planned to sell the leaves and crowns for livestock feed. The farm demanded so much of his time and energy that he knew he soon would have to quit his livery stable job just to keep up with his own fields.

With Rosie's earnings, they bought another milk cow and the lumber to build a two-bedroom addition onto the top of their soddy. Bart finished digging the refrigerator alone, and he gradually filled it with venison, wild turkey, quail and rabbit. The kitchen garden began to yield a bountiful harvest, and the eggs Rosie sold in town brought in enough extra income to fence off the garden from hungry varmints.

Rosie started to grow healthier almost right away. With Bart's teasing and her own comforting home so close at hand, she perked right up. As she felt better, her worries about Bart being carted off to jail subsided for the most part, and they began to attend a few of the Gate City's social functions.

May brought frequent rain, but they drove into town on the twenty-first for the grand charity ball at McAuliffe and Ferguson's Hall. The New Mexico Livestock Association hosted a ranch dinner four days later, and the *Comet* announced the building of a new Atchison, Topeka and Santa Fe Railway passenger depot. To everyone's sorrow, on the fifth day of June, Sheriff Bowman died suddenly of a lung hemorrhage. He had been married just two years and was but thirty-six years old. The town mourned the county lawman, but Rosie couldn't deny her relief that any investigation of Bart's background surely would cease.

By mid-June three men had tossed in their hats for the vacant position of county sheriff. As Bart's sugar beets grew and Rosie's students learned their parts for the recital, the town scheduled a big hunt, formed a football club and made plans for the coming Fourth of July celebrations.

With all these public events to attend, Rosie decided it was high time for Bart to work on his manners. She sewed new shirts, trousers and ties, and taught him to wear them properly. As she learned to cook, she taught him how to pronounce English pea soup au gratin, roast sirloin of beef au jus and salmi of duck.

At night in bed they rehearsed polite conversations about the weather, current local and national news and the state of political affairs—anything to keep Bart from regaling polite company with his favorite jokes, as he had been known to do on more than one occasion. Usually, however, Rosie's nightly lessons on morals and manners deteriorated into teasing, laughter and eventually such sweet passion that she forgot anything else.

On Sundays they went to church, sometimes taking a nervous Cheyenne Bill along with them. Rosie taught

Sunday school, and Bart volunteered to help landscape the church property.

In fact, Rosie realized one noon as she was driving her horse and buggy away from the schoolhouse, she and Bart had settled into a life so full of contentment and peace that it almost frightened her. Every day held more promise than she'd ever known in her life. Each night in Bart's arms she felt more and more at ease with the world they were building.

The only wrinkle in the whole picture was her health. Though it had improved considerably, she still felt that something might be seriously wrong. Mourning Mannie, she had missed an appointment with Dr. Kohlhouser, but as time passed, she scheduled a quick lunchtime visit while the children played tag and picket under the supervision of Mr. Kilgore.

Rosie drove her buggy to the doctor's office and pulled it up outside the small frame building. After lapping the reins over the hitching post, she bent to give Griff a pat on his massive head, then stepped over the dog and entered the building.

"Afternoon, Mrs. Springfield," the physician greeted her.

"Good day, doctor." She gave the burly man a smile as he escorted her into his examining room. He gestured to a chair, and she seated herself demurely, hands in her lap.

"Now, how would you describe this problem of yours, Mrs. Springfield?" Taking a notebook, he adjusted his spectacles and stared at her.

"It's a…a feminine problem, sir."

"I see. Of what nature?"

"Well," Rosie said with a flush, "I was ill some time

ago, and since then my monthly flow seems to have stopped altogether."

"What sort of illness did you suffer?"

"A violent stomach ailment. I was nauseated for several weeks. That subsided finally, but my cycles never resumed."

He lifted his head and gave her a tender smile. "I'm assuming, therefore, that you believe you may be with child."

"What?" Rosie sat up, startled. "Oh, no, that's impossible. I can't have children."

"You can't? How do you know?"

Rosie fiddled with the folds of her skirts. She had known this was going to be difficult, but she hadn't expected this turn of conversation.

Finally she cleared her throat. "I was married before, you see. To my husband."

"Your husband?" He made a note in his book. "May I ask, Mrs. Springfield, when your husband passed away?"

"Oh, he didn't. Pass away, I mean."

The doctor was staring at her with a new look on his face, a look of disapproval. "So, you are a divorced woman?"

"No, the first husband is the same one I have now. But he left me, you see. Back then." Rosie began to wish mightily for a fan. "I trust this is a confidential conversation, Dr. Kohlhouser."

"Of course."

"I am a married woman—and have been for the last six years. Mr. Springfield is my husband. But past events rendered me unable to conceive. So, will you please tell me what's wrong with me?"

The doctor placed his notebook on his leg and tapped the tip of his pen against it. "I'm going to have to ask you some more questions, Mrs. Springfield—about your marriage."

She bristled. "I don't see why. That is none of your business."

"It certainly is if I'm to learn why your monthly cycles have ceased."

Rosie sank back into the chair. "All right," she said glumly. "If you must know, my husband left me two weeks after our wedding."

"And I'm assuming you had a normal marital relationship with him during those two weeks."

"No." She wrung her hands. "We were very young, you see. I lived at home until my father found out what we'd done."

"Ah. But as you didn't have a true marriage relationship with your husband, you could not have conceived. So how do you know that you're unable to have a baby? Were you with another man during the years before you reunited with Mr. Springfield?"

"Another man? Oh, of course not!" She shook her head. "No, I loved him. I loved him so much, in fact, that I became very ill after he left me. I was sick all the time for more than a year—unable to sleep, unable to eat. My cycle completely stopped, Dr. Kohlhouser. My father is a physician, you see, and he took me to be examined by several doctors, friends of his. They all said the same thing—I'm barren."

"Will you permit me to send to these physicians for your medical records, Mrs. Springfield?"

"Absolutely not." Just the thought of contacting men

who would rush to her pappy and tell him where she was sent a chill into Rosie's bones. "That's all in the past."

"Do you now have a normal marriage relationship with Mr. Springfield?"

"Yes, I do. But why won't you simply take what I say as fact, Dr. Kohlhouser, and tell me what else could be wrong with me?"

He shrugged. "I'll try my best. But a healthy young married woman with your symptoms certainly would seem to call for a diagnosis of pregnancy."

"I'm not going to have a baby," Rosie whispered. "I can't. Please don't mention it again."

At the look on her face, the doctor's own visage fell into tender lines, and he patted Rosie's knotted fingers. "There now, I know how much you love little ones, Mrs. Springfield. Your work at the school has been exemplary. I'll see what I can do for you."

Rosie bared herself to the humiliation of a thorough exam. All the while, the doctor questioned her about every imaginable awkward thing. Had this or that changed? Was she always so emotional? Had her husband noticed anything different about her? She wondered how a woman doctor might be different, but of course such a possibility was remote.

Finally Dr. Kohlhouser allowed her to dress. "Mrs. Springfield," he said when she was seated in yet another chair, "I can arrive at only one diagnosis, and it's based on twenty-five years of medical practice. You are with child."

A tingle washed down Rosie's spine as she stared at him. "With child. But that's impossible."

"Mrs. Springfield, after your husband left you and your cycles ceased, did they ever begin again?"

"Well, yes, after a couple of years."

"Sometimes emotional collapse combined with a lack of proper nourishment can cause a woman's monthly cycle to be interrupted. Your cycle righted itself after time, and when you renewed your marriage with Mr. Springfield, you conceived."

"Are you sure?"

"As certain as I can possibly be. You have every symptom. Based on what you've told me, I would say you're about two months along. Maybe more. If I'm correct, you'll deliver sometime around…oh, next January."

Rosie couldn't speak.

"Now, I could be wrong."

"Yes," Rosie breathed, certain he must be and fearful he might.

"I could be mistaken, and you'll deliver in December. Or February. We'll know better as you progress. But if I were a betting man, Mrs. Springfield, I'd wager you're going to have yourself a baby in a few months. I've been wrong only twice in my career, and I've delivered nigh onto three hundred babies."

"A baby…" she whispered.

"Congratulations. I hope you're happy."

"Happy! Of course—oh, a baby!" Rosie jumped out of her chair and ran to the window. She felt lightheaded, fairly dancing with joy. But when she looked out at the reality of the bustling street, she had to turn again to the doctor.

"How?" she asked. "How can I possibly have conceived, Dr. Kohlhouser? All those doctors examined me, and they were good men, too. Friends of my father."

Dr. Kohlhouser shrugged. "As much as I'd like to claim that modern medicine is perfect and physicians never err, I'm sure you know that is not true. Your dear father, as you must have discovered by now, is merely mortal. He makes mistakes. We all do."

Rosie thought of the speech her pappy had given Bart—about his worthlessness, about the failure he would be as a husband, about the terrible life he would give his young wife. Pappy had been wrong. Very wrong.

"Yes, Dr. Kohlhouser," she said. "My father made a mistake. And…and I need to forgive him."

"A wise decision, especially under the circumstances. He'll want to know he's a grandfather." The physician adjusted his spectacles again. "Now, I am going to record my assumption that your husband suffers no difficulty whatsoever with his reproductive system. And you, Mrs. Springfield, are as fertile as the good springtime earth."

Rosie's hands slipped down over her belly. For a long moment she stood in silence, trying to absorb the doctor's words. She was with child. Through their loving, she and Bart had created a new life. Even now the baby was growing inside her body—developing, strengthening, forming into a beautiful child, the essence of each of its parents.

"A baby," she murmured again. "A baby!"

Dr. Kohlhouser laughed. "Or maybe two. Now, Mrs. Springfield, here's what you are to do."

She listened in a fog as he explained how important it was that she rest, eat properly and take in plenty of fresh air during the months to come. She mustn't tire herself or corset herself too tightly. The baby needed room to grow after all. She mustn't be left alone much, and toward the end she should move into town to be close to the doctor when her time came.

"Yes," Rosie replied to everything he said. "Yes, yes, of course."

But as she walked out the front door, her head might as well have been a blank slate. She was going to have a baby! Forgetting all about her horse and carriage, her afternoon classes and the doctor's admonitions, she began running down the street toward the stables. *Bart!* She must tell him right away. How happy he'd be! Oh, she couldn't wait to see the expression on his face when she told him they were going to have a child of their very own!

"Bart," she murmured aloud as she rounded the corner of the depot. "Bart, a baby!"

She whispered the refrain as she ran across the platform in front of the Harvey House, oblivious to the late-lunch train and the arrival of passengers who were startled at the sight of a woman dashing past them, her blue dress flying around her knees.

"Bart!" she shouted as she ran up the ramp into the livery stable. "Bart, where are you?"

"Rosie!" He emerged from the shadows and caught her before she could slam into him. "Rosie, what are you doing here?" His voice was harsh, as cold as steel. "You're supposed to be at the schoolhouse!"

She blinked at him and tried to fathom the look on his face. At the same time, it dawned on her that he was hiding something. Something he didn't want her to know about.

"Bart?" she asked, flashes of fear darting through her mind. "Bart? What's going on?"

"So, this is the little woman you've been telling me about," a man announced, striding out into the middle of the stable, his pistol drawn. "Rosie, is it?"

She stared at a face worn into crags, at blue eyes hard and glittering. "Who are you?"

"Ain't you told her about me, Injun?" the man asked, jabbing Bart in the side with his gun. "You better introduce us, pal."

Breathing hard, Bart pushed the barrel of the six-shooter away from his injured side. "Rosie, this is a pal of mine from a long time back. We used to ride together in the old days. His name's Bob Ford."

"Robert Ford," she mouthed. "Robert Ford...the man who killed Jesse James."

"That's me. Not only that, but I saved young Bart from a bullet a time or two." As he spoke, two more men emerged from the shadows. "And now me and my buddies have come to town to pay you folks a friendly visit. For old times' sake, if you know what I mean."

As Rosie turned to Bart, Bob Ford began to laugh.

Chapter Seventeen

"Rosie, get on back to the schoolhouse," Bart barked. "Stay with the Kilgores tonight. We'll talk about this tomorrow."

"You mean we rode all this way and we ain't gonna get us a home-cooked meal?" Ford complained. "Now listen here, Miz Kingsley, don't pay your husband no heed. You head on home tonight and whip us up somethin' dandy to eat. We been livin' on beans for almost a month now."

Rosie glanced at Bart. To the best of her knowledge, she'd never seen him truly angry until this moment. Now she remembered, by the stance of his body, what became of men like that toothless Harwood fellow who tried to cross him. His bare biceps were bunched and knotted. Big fists clenched, his knuckles had gone white as bone. The muscle in his square jaw worked as he gritted his teeth, and his eyes sparked with a burning green flame.

"I told my wife to go back to work, Ford, and she'll do as I say." His head snapped toward Rosie, but his eyes stayed on the intruder. "Get out of here, woman!"

Her hand covering her stomach, Rosie started for the door. But when she crossed into the shaft of afternoon sunlight, she stopped and swung around. "Tell me one thing," she demanded of Bob Ford. "I want to know how you found Bart."

"That's easy. Injun writ a letter to Frank James a while back. Frank mentioned it to some of the boys, and word leaked out. Everybody knows where he's been hidin' out."

Rosie stopped breathing. "Everybody?"

"Didn't I just say that? Are you deaf or something?"

"Watch how you talk to my woman, Ford," Bart snarled. "She's no lowlife like you."

"I ain't a lowlife, Injun. I'm famous, don't ya know?"

"Yeah, you pulled the trigger on Jesse. That sets you real high in some people's books."

Bob frowned. "For your information, Injun, I *am* famous. I'm makin' a name for myself as the man who shot the most wanted outlaw in the United States of America. Once I get rollin', folks will line up and pay good money just to get a gander at me. I'm fixin' to get plumb rich off my reputation."

"Well, why don't you get your famous hide out of Raton and take it someplace where people care."

"Now, watch how you talk in front of the lady, Injun." At this, Bob guffawed, and his two companions joined in the laughter. Sobering after a moment, the outlaw nodded at Rosie. "Don't worry, Miz Kingsley. We ain't gonna cause you no trouble. We just got tired of Las Vegas and thought we'd head over your way to visit a spell. Ain't that right, boys?"

"Tired of gettin' run out of places on account of your famous reputation, Ford," one of them countered.

Then he tipped his grimy hat at Rosie. "They call me Snort, and this here's Fancy. Pleased to meet ya, Miz Kingsley."

Rosie gave the two men a quick scrutiny. Snort, a skinny, brown-haired fellow with a big nose and an enormous walrus mustache, wore a pair of six-shooters strapped to his thighs and cradled a rifle in his arms. Fancy, the dirtiest, greasiest, smelliest man Rosie had ever laid eyes on, had a mane of thick black hair and a stomach twice the size of his hips.

"Good afternoon, gentlemen," she greeted them in as polite a tone as she could muster. "Bart, I'd like to speak with you a moment, please."

"Better do what the lady says, Injun," Bob admonished.

Accompanied by derisive laughter, Bart took Rosie by the elbow. As soon as he had propelled her outside, he placed his big hands on her shoulders.

"I want you to stay away from the homestead, Rosie," he said firmly. "Don't even think about going anywhere near it. Ford's not having much success at cashing in on killing Jesse, and he may be on the dodge from the law. I suspect the boys want to hide out at our place a few days, but I'll run 'em off as quick as I can."

"Bart, that man could ruin you!"

"My reputation's the least of it, girl. No telling what these fellows have up their sleeves."

"But what if the law finds you? They'll take you away to Missouri and they'll hang you."

"Rosie, don't you remember what we said about Jesus? He said we're not to worry. Now I want you to stop frettin'. I know how Ford operates, so let me handle this. Go back to the school and act like nothing's going on. I'll let the boys ride out to the home-

stead and stay with me for a couple of days. I'll feed
'em and let 'em rest, and then I'll send 'em packing.
It'll be all right. But I don't want you around, hear?
They're rough men. Killers."

"Oh, Bart!"

"They're not going to kill *me,* Rosie. I'm their pal."
He shook his head and studied the cloudless sky for a
moment. "God help me, I'm their *pal.*"

"Bart, there are things I need to talk to you about.
Important things. I need to tell you—"

"We'll talk later, darlin'. Now go on, before Ford
and his sidewinder buddies get itchy feet."

He gave her a little push that sent her down the
ramp. On the platform she turned to call him, but he
had vanished back inside the stable. Breathless, she
stood immobilized for a moment as passengers and
baggage boys scurried around her. As she stepped onto
the street, the stable's side door slid open, and four
men on horseback thundered down the ramp. As they
galloped out of town in a cloud of dust, Rosie realized
that one of them was Bart.

Having blamed her tardy return on the doctor visit,
Rosie managed to get through the rest of the school
day. She claimed an illness she truly felt, and the Kilgores were more than happy to put her up for the night.
The next few days, however, were an endless torment.

Rosie couldn't concentrate on the lessons she was
teaching. Bart promised to come for her, but he didn't,
and she feared the cause of his absence. Each day,
Rosie went to the livery to see if Bart had been at work
there. The stable owner told her he hadn't seen or heard

from her husband. As much as the man hated to lose Bart, he'd been forced to hire a replacement.

If Rosie had briefly dreamed of a happy family— herself, Bart and their baby—she squelched that image the moment she realized the seriousness of her situation. The men who had invaded her life were outlaws. Killers, Bart had said.

And although Bart had denied it, Bob Ford *was* famous. There wasn't a soul in the territory who hadn't heard of the killing of Jesse James by a member of his own gang. If Bob Ford made Bart's true identity known in town, that would be the end of everything the two of them had worked so hard to build.

Sick at heart, Rosie drew the curtains in her classroom on a hot Friday afternoon after the children had gone home for the weekend. The blue light dampened the usual cheer that seemed to settle in the quiet room at the end of every day. After putting away her texts, she drew her summer shawl around her shoulders and tried once again to figure out what Bart was doing and why he had not come for her.

Had he been too worried about exposing himself to return to town? She knew he wouldn't easily give up the livery stable job that had supported them so well, not when the sugar beets were still so many weeks from harvest. What if he had been kidnapped by those outlaws and forced to participate in some heinous crime— a bank robbery or train holdup? What if he'd been obliged to shoot someone? Straightening desks as she circled the room, Rosie made her way to the door.

What if Bart wasn't even at their homestead anymore? Maybe the lure of the old life had drawn him

away. What if he'd gone off and left the cows swollen
with milk and the chickens unfed?

Bart wouldn't do a thing like that...would he? As
she locked the schoolroom door, Rosie tried to swallow
down her greatest fear. What if Bob Ford had killed
Bart? He might have shot Bart to get the money they'd
buried beneath the cottonwood tree by the stream...
or lynched him for refusing to go along with him and
his boys on some outlaw scheme...or stabbed him in
an argument.

If Bob Ford would shoot Jesse James in the back
of the head for reward money, what would keep him
from doing the same to Bart? Dead or alive, Bart was
worth fifty dollars!

"Dear God, please don't let him be dead," Rosie
prayed as she left the school yard. "Please keep him
alive, and show me how to reach him. And please help
me to stop worrying!"

She had been so preoccupied—with the baby, the
effort to conduct her lessons with some semblance of
normalcy and her anxiety about Bart—that she hadn't
sorted through everything clearly. Now as she stepped
onto the porch of the Kilgores' home, Rosie felt a sudden certainty stab her heart.

Bart was dead—killed for the fifty-dollar reward!

Propelled by dread, she rushed into the kitchen and
grabbed Mr. Kilgore's rifle from the top of the cupboard. Just as Mrs. Kilgore was descending the stairs,
Rosie ran out the back door. In minutes, she hitched up
her buggy, climbed onto the seat and urged the horse
into a trot.

"Mrs. Springfield!" Mrs. Kilgore called from the
kitchen door. "What's the matter? Where are you going?"

Rosie turned briefly and gave the kind woman a wave. "I'm going home, Mrs. Kilgore! If I'm not back Monday morning, send a deputy out to the homestead."

"A deputy? Oh, my!"

But Rosie's buggy was already rounding the corner and rolling out of town. The mild-mannered mare couldn't know what had gotten into her mistress as Rosie worked the reins like a madwoman along the rutted trail. The buggy bounced and jounced into ruts and over hummocks. Rosie's hair tumbled from its knot, fell around her shoulders and slid down her back. Her stomach began to ache, tighten and cramp.

Unwilling to slow her pace, she urged the horse up the bumpy track. The buggy seat swayed, its springs tossing her this way and that. Perspiration streamed down Rosie's temples. Her dress dampened and her corset poked her ribs and pelvis. The cramping in her stomach increased, but she couldn't stop.

"Bart," she cried as she guided the mare up the last hill toward the dugout. "Bart, please, please don't be dead!"

When the buggy crested the rise, she could see lamplight through the paper window panes. The sight calmed her a little, but she kept the horse at a canter until the buggy was almost to the dugout.

At the sound of the wagon and the mare's hooves, the front door swung open and three men emerged.

"Rosie!"

She recognized him right away, although the slanting late-evening sunlight revealed only his silhouette. "Bart, thank God! You're alive!"

Pulling back on the reins, she drew the buggy to a halt and set the brake.

"Rosie, why are you here? I told you to stay away."

Even though his words admonished her, Bart's voice was soft with relief. He held out his arms, and Rosie slipped down into them.

"I was so worried about you, Bart," she said as she hugged him close. "You told me you would come back to town, but you didn't. Your boss gave your job away to somebody else. I've been sick with fear."

"Aw, Rosie." He held her away and studied her face. "I told you not to worry. Everything's going to be all right."

"How can you say that? Those men are still here. You've lost your job. And I'm... I'm..." Convulsing with a sudden sharp pain, she bent over double.

"Rosie? What is it?"

"Bart, I'm sick. I... I need to lie down. Take me inside."

"Oh, darlin', not again." He picked her up in his arms and pushed past Fancy and Snort, who had been gawking. "Get your lousy hides down there and put a clean blanket on the bed," Bart barked at the two men, who shuffled into the house.

"Well, if it ain't the missus." Bob Ford rose from the little table Bart had built. Swaying, he held up a half-empty whiskey bottle. "'Bout time we had a woman to entertain us."

"Shut up, Ford," Bart growled. "Rosie's sick."

"Sick? How're we gonna have a fandango with a sick woman? I'm in the mood to kick up my heels and I sure ain't gonna do it with you, Injun."

Bart ignored him and laid Rosie gently on the rumpled blanket. He knelt beside her and took her hand in his. "What's ailing you, Rosie?"

"Oh, Bart," she whispered. "My stomach hurts. It really hurts. You may have to fetch Dr. Kohlhouser."

His green eyes narrowed. "Fetch the doc? Rosie, what's wrong?"

Biting her lip against the pain, she looked away. How could she tell him about their baby in the midst of such chaos? In the past three days, their tidy little home had been turned upside down. The table was littered with empty whiskey bottles. The floor was buried under an inch of dust and trash. The room smelled of rotting food, liquor and unwashed men.

"Rosie?" Bart repeated as he laid a hand on her shoulder.

When she looked at him again, what she saw startled her. Gone was the clean-shaven man whose broad shoulders haunted her dreams. Bart looked almost as bad as he had the day he'd crawled out from under her bed at the Harvey House dormitory. His chambray shirt and denims were stained. His hair hadn't been washed or combed, and he couldn't have had a bath in days.

"Bart, what's happened to you?"

"Me? I'm fine. It's you I'm worried about." He rubbed the backs of her hands with his thumbs. "Listen, you just rest now. I'll brew you a pot of tea. How's that?"

"I don't want tea, Bart. Why haven't you shaved?"

He frowned. "I haven't been thinking about shaving, Rosie. That's the last thing on my mind."

"How many of those empty bottles are you responsible for?"

He turned his head, as if seeing the mess for the first time. "None. The boys have been here three days, and they...well, this is how it always is. This is how we live."

"But not you," she murmured. "Not anymore. Right? Have you milked the cows and fed my chickens?"

"Yes, Rosie."

"What about the sugar beets?"

Smoothing a hand over her damp brow, he gazed down at her. "Why don't you get some rest, darlin'? It's plain you're overwrought."

"I am not overwrought!" She rose up on her elbows. "Just look at my house. You and those criminals have made a pigsty of it."

"Now, Rosie," he whispered, attempting to calm her. "I've been working as hard as I can to…um…get along with Bob and the fellers. Would you just settle back until they're ready to leave?"

"I'll run them off myself. Hand me that rifle."

Before she could climb out of bed, Bart took her shoulders and pressed her back onto the pillow. "Rest, Rosie," he commanded. "We'll work things out in the morning."

Cramping again, she curled up into a ball of pain as he returned to the table where the others were engaged in a hand of poker. Rosie buried her face in the pillow to keep from crying out. What if she lost the baby? How awful to feel the tiny life torn from her body!

Forcing herself to breathe deeply, Rosie tried to find peace in her misery. Bart was alive, she reminded herself. The house was still standing. The crops were in the field, and the stock had been cared for. Maybe things weren't so bad.

But just look at her home. Rosie gave the room another quick study before shutting her eyes again in dismay. If the house was disturbing, the conversation that drifted her way was worse.

"I reckon we're about two jumps ahead of that low-down Las Vegas sheriff," Bob Ford was saying. "Whatcha think, Snort?"

"That posse was campin' on our trail till we had saddle sores." He took a swig of whiskey, then struck a match on his boot and lit up a cheroot. "Anyhow, I suspect we lost 'em. Nobody's gonna guess we came thisaway."

"Who'd ever want to wet his whistle in this rat's nest?"

"Hey, watch what you say about my abode," Bart put in as he slapped a card onto the table. "Raton may have been named for a varmint with yellow teeth and a hankering for cheese, but it's been comfort to me."

"Sure," Fancy said with a laugh. "You got yerself a female to warm yer blanket. I'd settle down for a while, too, if I had me some purty lips to kiss at the end of the day."

The men chuckled, and Bart glanced over his shoulder. "That little gal is as sweet as barnyard milk, if you want the truth, boys. We're making a home here, and I aim to live the rest of my life inside the law."

"Aw, sure you are," Bob chuckled. "Injun, you wouldn't know the law if it hit you upside the head. Your name don't exactly tally with the Bible, and I reckon you're just wastin' the talents the Devil gave you, sittin' out here on this mesa."

"Quit your jawing, Ford." Scowling, Bart glanced at Rosie again, then lowered his voice. "Anybody ever told you you're mouthy?"

"I reckon Jesse might have, and look what it got him."

The room fell silent. As the pain in her stomach gradually subsided, Rosie listened to the sound of cards being flipped onto the table and the swish of liquor in the bottles as the men swilled it. Finally Fancy gave a loud, gusty belch as if to announce that he was ready to change the subject.

"So, what about the Sante Fe line, Injun?" he asked. "You reckon we could pull us off a good one?"

"What? You're joshing me."

"No, I ain't. The minute Bob heard you was in Raton, he says, 'Injun'll have what we need to know about the Atchison, Topeka and Santa Fe, and we'll make us some *dineros*. Let's head on over there and find Injun and have us a good time.' Ain't that right, Bob?"

"Now that you mention it, I did say something like that. So why don't you tell us what you know, Injun? With the trains hauling passenger cars up the pass, we ought to have an easy time pulling off a job on one of them slow movers."

Rosie watched through a cloud of gray smoke as Bart tossed his cards on the table and leaned back in his chair. "I'm not a train robber anymore, fellers. You might as well get that set in your noggins right off. I'm not going to get myself strung up for aiding and abetting neither."

"You gone yeller on us, Injun?" Snort jeered.

"I'm no coward. I just made up my mind to go straight."

"Straight as a snake in a cactus patch. What's the matter? You plannin' a deal on yer own, Injun? Don't you want to cut us in?"

"I'm telling you, Snort. I'm not interested."

"You tryin' to say yer plannin' to dig sugar beets till yer gray and wrinkled?"

"Naw, he's just airin' his lungs," Fancy said. "Come

on, Injun. Yer the best gunman this side of the Mississippi. What you got up yer sleeve?"

Bart gave a yawn and scooted his chair back from the table. "What I got up my sleeve is a good woman and one hundred sixty acres of land so quiet I can hear daylight coming."

"Can't hardly beat that," Snort said.

"To add to it, I got decent food to eat, a sturdy horse and enough religion to set my soul at ease. No sheriff's breathing down my back, no posse's licking at my trail and my tail's not saddle sore from churning up the dust for weeks at a time. I got honest work, honest pay and a warm bed to come home to at night. And if you boys will excuse me, I'm aiming to settle myself in with my lady right now."

"I'll be cussed if I don't think he means it," Fancy declared as he watched Bart head for the dressing screen.

"He's a little addlepated is all," Ford said, gathering up the playing cards. "A female will ruin a good man ever' time if she gets half a chance. Leave it to me to set him straight. Come on, fellers, let's roll out and get some sleep."

Rosie watched as the men kicked aside whiskey bottles and tossed saddle blankets on the bare floor. In a moment Bart pulled back the edge of the quilt, slipped into the bed beside her and drew his hands up her arms and over her shoulders.

"I missed you, Rosie-girl," he whispered in her ear. "If you're still awake, I want you to know I'm sorry you got scared and rushed out here looking for me. I couldn't come back to town. I couldn't get away from them, see?" He let out a deep sigh. "I wish you weren't so sick over things all the time. You've got to trust God that it'll turn out okay, hear?"

She shut her eyes. No, she didn't want to hear Bart. She couldn't listen to his gentle words, and she couldn't let herself be swept away by his touch. She had more to think about now than ever before. It wasn't just her own future and her own hard-fought freedom that were at stake. It was the life of an unborn child.

"Rosie, can you hear me?" he was asking against her cheek.

She waited a moment before nodding.

"The boys have drunk up the liquor they brought, and they've spent their loose change. I know they're starting to think about moving on now, and I reckon they'll be heading out tomorrow or the next day."

"To rob a train?" she whispered, still turned away from him.

"What they do doesn't matter to us. They'll be gone. Long gone. It'll just be us again here at home."

"Until the next outlaws come hunting down their old pal."

Bart was silent, his breath stirring the strands of hair around her neck. "Maybe so, Rosie," he said finally. "Are you going to give me up because of it? Or do you love me enough to stay with me, whatever comes our way?"

"Do you love me enough to put the past behind you, Bart? That's what I want to know."

"I can't just run Bob Ford out of my house. He saved my life. Ornery as the man is, if it wasn't for him I wouldn't be here today. I'd be dead as a can of corned beef. I owe him, Rosie. A man stands by his pals, and that's just the way it is."

"I know that," Rosie whispered. "But sometimes… sometimes a man has to choose between his friends and his family. And Bart, you have a family now."

She waited, breathless, as he absorbed her words. Did he know what she meant? Could he see the changes in her that she already felt? Could he sense the soft weight in her belly? Did he know by the tears in her eyes that she was not the woman he had married, that she was different now? Different and new and blossoming inside? *Oh, please, Bart! Please understand.*

"Rosie," he murmured, turning her to face him, "you're all the family and friends I'll ever need or want. I've promised to take care of you and protect you with my life, and I aim to do just that. Now I want you to quit your fretting and snuggle up here in my arms. Get yourself a good night's sleep, and things will look better in the morning. I swear it."

Before she could speak again, he tucked her head against his shoulder, let out a deep breath and fell sound asleep.

It hadn't taken four nights in the same house for Bart to figure out how Snort had gotten his nickname. If the roof of the dugout hadn't been nailed down, Snort would have sent it a mile high with every one of his thunderous snores. When Bart rolled out of bed Saturday morning, he could have sworn the walls were shaking.

He studied Rosie's sleeping form for a long time as he stood pulling on his buckskin jacket. She sure looked innocent and frail. Her skin was as white as the underbelly of a rabbit, and just as soft. Long brown hair fell in thick, shining ropes over her shoulders and across the pillow. Her fingers lay spread across the quilt, relaxed as though they hadn't worked as hard as Bart knew they always did.

But it was her parted lips and dark lashes that stirred his soul. *Lord, I love the woman,* he prayed in silence. *You know I'd give every inch of ground I own, every sugar beet I've planted, everything I possess just to make sure she stays with me, content and as peaceful as she looks right now. But, Lord, how am I going to get rid of Bob Ford and his pair of no-good saddle tramps?*

Bart had mentioned several times that they might want to head on out, but they'd just made themselves more at home. None of them lifted a finger to tidy up the place. Instead, they had made a filthy mess out of Rosie's beautiful little home.

If politeness hadn't worked, Bart was sure force would never do the trick. Trying to order Bob Ford off his land would bring a hailstorm of bullets at the worst. At the very least, the men would rob him, tear up everything they could get their hands on and ride off with his horses and cows. There was no telling what they might do to Rosie, woman-starved as they were, and Bart knew he would have to keep an eye on her every minute.

Rubbing the back of his neck, he thought of the time she'd given him a haircut. He had to smile. In those days, he hadn't been much better put together than the fellows snoring on the floor. But there had been one difference between Bart Kingsley and Bob Ford: Bart wanted to make a respectable life for himself, and he had. Bob was still footloose and bent on making trouble.

Well, he thought, if politeness wouldn't get rid of the

three moochers, and if forcing their hand would cause more trouble than it was worth, he'd just have to think of another way to run them off. Quick.

"Get yourself up and quit shaking down my house, Snort," Bart said, giving the sleeping outlaw a swift kick in the hindquarters. "You know anything about milking cows, boy?"

Snort rolled over and began rubbing his eyes. "What you wakin' me up fer, Injun?"

"We got a woman in the house now, Snort. Time to shape up."

He nudged Fancy with the toe of his boot. "Rise and shine, cowboy. If you want breakfast, you better fetch some eggs."

"Breakfast?" Fancy worked his dry tongue around the inside of his mouth. "All I want is another shot of rotgut. I got a headache as big as Lincoln County."

"And your breath is strong enough to bust a mirror. Come on, I'll boil you some strong black coffee, and you can get to work sweeping."

"Sweeping?" Fancy glanced at Bob, who was just stirring. "That's woman's work. Put yer wife to the job, why don't ya?"

Bart looked at the bed. Rosie had sat up and was staring at her disheveled house with a look of shock.

"Rosie, darlin', settle back now and rest a spell," he told her. "Us boys'll take care of you, won't we, fellers?"

"Not me," Fancy groused. "I'm headin' outside to water the daisies."

Before Bart could say another word, Fancy and Snort had fairly run to the door and flung themselves through it. Bob sat up on his haunches and laughed.

"Got rid of them two, didn't you? Just mention honest work, and they hightail it out of here."

Bart hunkered down beside the man who had once saved his life. "Bob, I've got to speak plain with you," he said. "It's time you boys hit the trail. We've had some good laughs jawing over the past, but I meant what I told you about my new life. I've gone straight. That means I've got to tend my crops and my livestock. I've got weeding and irrigating and hoeing to do, and unless you boys want to join me, I'm going to have to ask that you head out."

"Some thanks you show to a man who saved your life," Ford spat. "I reckon you owe me more than a few days in yer hideout, Injun. And I aim to collect."

Bart eyed Rosie, who had risen and was stepping over whiskey bottles on her way to the dressing screen. "What is it you want, Bob?" he asked in a low voice. "Speak plain."

"I want the Atchison, Topeka and Santa Fe, *hombre*. I want me a nice, fat bankroll. You don't think I came all this way just to catch up on old times, do you? No, sir, I tracked you down for one reason, Injun. With Jesse gone and Frank living the clean life, you're the best there is at setting up a train heist, and I aim to put you back in the business."

"I'm not robbing any trains, Ford," Bart growled. "Not a one. I made that clear last night."

"Now, don't get riled. You just put that brain of yours to work figuring out a plan of action. Me and the boys'll skedaddle into town for some more whiskey. When we get back, we'll set ourselves down and put the details in place. It'll be just like old times, don't you know? Remember Jesse, Frank, me, you—all the boys in together? Pals."

"Yeah, and you shot Jesse in the back. Some pal."

Ford jumped up and grabbed Bart's collar. "Jesse had it comin', and you know it! Every one of us considered plugging him for the reward. I was the only one man enough to do it!"

"You were the only one low enough to do it," Bart said, knocking Ford's hand away.

"Sure I was, you yellow-bellied half breed. Now get to work planning that train job before I blast you to kingdom come."

Bart had no doubt that Ford meant what he said. He also knew Ford wouldn't stand a chance if it came to a shootout between them. Bart could outdraw all the boys in the James gang, and Ford had never been much of a deadeye in the first place. He'd managed to plug Jesse only because the outlaw had been hanging up a picture and had his back to his killer. And if it came to a fistfight, Bart could fold Ford up like an empty wallet.

But there was more to consider than the present conflict between the two men. First, there was the undeniable fact that Bart did owe Ford his life. Such a debt could never be looked at lightly. Second, there was Rosie, who had to be taken out of the situation before it blew sky high. Third, there were Snort and Fancy, both of whom would stick by Ford. With three men against him, the battle would be tougher, and Bart sure was hoping it wouldn't come to that.

"We'll talk over your loco train robbery," Bart stated bluntly, "after I take care of what's important."

"You do that," Ford responded as he walked toward

the door. "Meantime I'll join my pals in that outhouse of a garden you got out there."

"Stay out of my wife's vegetables!" Bart hollered.

Laughing, Bob Ford climbed the stairs and banged the door shut behind him.

Chapter Eighteen

While Bart did his morning chores, Rosie worked to put her home back in order. To her relief, she discovered that the cramps she experienced the night before had not led to any spotting, and she still carried the tiny life inside her. Fierce with determination to protect her unborn baby, she made up her mind to do whatever it took to keep the child safe.

After all, how well could the baby grow if its mother was constantly fretting and scared to death? Bart kept telling her to trust Jesus and stop worrying. It was about time she learned how to do just that.

With this outlook firmly established in her mind, Rosie ran Bob and Snort out of the house the minute they tried to come back in. When Fancy elected to disobey her orders, she took her broom to his backside until he sprinted howling through the door. Sweeping didn't take as long as she had expected, but setting the house to rights required far more than a lick and a promise.

Bart's shirts and britches lay in a heap by the dressing screen. Not a single dish, cup or spoon had been washed in days. A ring of some undetermined scum encrusted her fine black iron pot, and she couldn't bring herself to ask what it was. Worst of all, the house stank of stale cigarette smoke and whiskey. If she hadn't known better, Rosie would have thought she was walking around in a low-class saloon.

She had just filled the cookpot with boiling soapy water when she heard the front door open. Thinking it was Fancy again, she grabbed her broom and swung around.

"It's time to go," Bart announced. "I'm taking you back to town."

Rosie stiffened and propped the broom up against the table. "I'm not going back to town until Monday morning. If you want to run somebody off, get rid of your pals."

"This isn't something to argue about, Rosie. While I was out tending the stock, I made up my mind."

Planting her hands on her hips, she lifted her chin. "You made up your mind? Don't I have a mind to make up, Bart Kingsley?"

"In this case I've made the decision for you. I've thought it all through, and it's for the best."

"What's best is me living with you in our house— by ourselves. I've done some thinking, too, Bart. There was a time when just the thought of your outlaw days scared me so much I wanted to run away from you. The very notion of Sheriff Bowman searching the Missouri law records sent me scampering off to Raton to hide out with the Kilgores."

"I remember. That was a plumb crazy notion you took into your head, girl. I knew the sheriff couldn't track me down on the little information I'd given him.

But this is different. Bob, Snort and Fancy are real mean men, Rosie. They've got a bad streak in them a mile wide, and I want you to stay clear of this place until they're gone."

"You don't seem to understand that I'm not afraid anymore, Bart." She wiped her hands on her apron and came to stand before him. "You told me to put my faith in Jesus, so I am doing just that. More than a year ago I decided I wanted a different life than the one my pappy had planned out for me. I left Kansas City to find my new path. I gave up marriage to a wealthy man to go after my dream. I left my good job at the Harvey House so I could keep the dream alive. I've been scared. I've been poor. I've worked my fingers to the bone—all for that dream, Bart. And just when I thought I'd lost it forever, I realized I had found it right here in this little dugout with you. So don't tell me to start running away again. I'm through with that. This is my house. Those are my chickens out in the yard. That's my kitchen garden those outlaws are defiling. And you're my husband. It's my dream. It's what I believe God planned for me all along. I'm not turning my back on it. Do you understand me, Bart Kingsley?"

"Plain as day. But the fact is, that little dream of yours is in danger of getting blown to pieces if you don't do what I say. You're coming with me to Raton if I have to hogtie you, Rosie."

He reached out to take her hand, but she jerked away. "Bart! Don't do this!"

"I don't have a choice," he said, grabbing her around the waist and slinging her over one shoulder. "You've got a city-girl way of looking at things, but dreams don't always work out as neat and pretty as you paint them."

As he spoke, he carried her into the sunshine and deposited her on the seat of the wagon.

"Bart!" she cried as he circled in front of the horses to take his own place. "Please, Bart, let me stay here."

"Better gag her!" Snort hooted. "We don't want no female squallin' all the way to town."

"Just shut up and get in the wagon," Bart snapped.

Rosie sat in utter shock as her husband pulled his hat low on his brow and gave the reins a quick flick. Ford and his boys scrambled onto the moving wagon bed, but Bart hardly seemed aware of them. Glowering, he grabbed his rifle and set it across his thighs.

She couldn't believe he actually had carried her over his shoulder to the wagon! Despite her fine speech about her dreams and God's plans, he had tossed her around like a sack of potatoes. To think that the man could be so rough—never mind that he had no idea of her delicate condition.

She glared at him from the corner of her eye. Maybe he was worried about the outlaws, but that gave him no right to treat her worse than he treated his cows and horses. She crossed her arms and set her jaw as the wagon bounced down the track. Once those men had gone, she would give Bart Kingsley what for!

If he truly loved her as he said he did, he would have listened more closely to what she was saying. He would have taken her feelings into account. Most of all, he would have run off those pals of his a long time ago.

"So tell us about the Atchison, Topeka and Santa Fe, Injun," Bob Ford said from the back of the wagon.

"I'm busy," Bart growled.

"You said you'd talk once you got them chores done. So talk."

Bart gave the reins another flick. "I said I'm busy."

"You want us to ask little Rosie? She used to work at the Harvey House, didn't she?"

"Leave her out of this. We'll talk later."

"How're us boys gonna rob a train if we don't plan it, Injun? You know better'n anybody how important it is to lay out a good scheme. Now, when does the richest train roll through town?"

Bart had clamped his jaw shut, and Rosie had never seen him look so dark. Was he angry with her? Was he mad at Ford and his boys? Or was Bart actually considering robbing one of the trains that passed through town? A chill washed into her bones when she heard him begin to speak.

"Any one of 'em could be loaded," he began. "You've got three or four a day pulling up from Albuquerque and Lamy. They go through Las Vegas, Wagon Mound and Springer picking up passengers and freight on their way east. Then you've got the trains down from Denver. They've come all the way from Kansas City loaded with goods and settlers."

"You reckon we could take a bigger haul off the westbound traffic?"

"Probably. Hard telling, though. There's some good money going east these days. Gold and silver coming out of the territories. Rich cattlemen taking their profits to banks in Missouri."

"Sounds like a pretty good flow both ways."

Bart nodded. Rosie could hardly believe her ears. Was he just trying to pacify these outlaws, or was he actually discussing which train to rob? For all she could tell, he was helping them plan an armed holdup. Was he going to join them? Had her worst fears come true, that Bart had been lured back to his old ways by the temptation of easy money?

For a moment she considered grabbing the rifle off his lap and peppering all three of those filthy criminals in the wagon bed. How awful to think of needing to escape from Bart. Tears of anger and dismay filled her eyes at the injustice. Just when they had begun to build a normal life, a life more fulfilling and passionate than she'd ever dreamed possible, everything had come crashing down.

Bart had slid back into the role he'd worked so hard to leave behind him. When Rosie took a closer look at the man she loved so deeply, the sight of him sent a curl of panic shooting through her stomach.

His black hair blew away from the angles and planes of his face. The high Indian cheekbones, his father's legacy, had bronzed to deep mahogany. Instead of the clean, starched white shirts she had sewn for him, Bart wore his rugged buckskin jacket. His faded denims and boots, the holsters on his thighs and the ammunition belt around his waist forced her to see what she wanted so much to deny: Bart looked every bit the gunman he was.

Even if he didn't really intend to rob one of the inbound trains, he wouldn't stand a chance in town if he showed up looking like this. Sheriff Bowman was no longer around to identify him, but there were three deputies who would.

Besides, a whole town full of people no doubt had read the wanted posters describing a green-eyed Indian. To top it off, Bart was in league with a man who loved to boast that he'd shot Jesse James. That would seal Bart's fate.

"We want to stop a train that's pulling into town, don't we, Injun?" Ford was asking. "Ain't I right about 'em bein' slower comin' in? There's that switchback and all."

"The switchback isn't used these days," Bart responded. "The train used to have to climb to the summit with all those steep grades and sharp curves. That was an eight-thousand-foot pull. But there's a tunnel now, so the trains aren't so slow coming in, but they're not so fast going out either."

"So either way might work?"

"Might."

"Any bridges?"

"There's a trestle at Raton Pass. It's pretty shaky."

"Hey, boys, how about that? We could stop the engine while it's on the trestle. It'd only take one of us to keep it in line while the rest of us could work the safe and the passengers."

"Sounds good to me," Snort said. "Whatever Injun thinks."

"What do you say, Injun?"

"I say we just hit the city limits, and you boys better shut your gates if you don't want the whole town in on this."

Rosie wanted to shrink into her boots as the wagon jolted down the street past stores and restaurants filled with people she had come to love and respect. How would they react if they knew of the conversation she had just heard?

Oh, there had been a time when she was just as pristine and pious as any of them. But now, thanks to Bart Kingsley and his pals, she was party to a crime. Just for having listened to their plans she could be brought before a jury! Especially if she didn't run straight to the sheriff's office and tell the deputies everything she knew. Yet, if she did, she'd be turning Bart in, too.

She studied his handsome profile as he pulled the wagon up to the hitching post in front of the Central Hotel. How grim he looked. The light had died in his green eyes. His face was as dark as she'd ever seen it.

As he came around the wagon to help her out, she remembered what he'd once told her. He said that his life had become black—as black as a tunnel with no end in sight. And she was the only light he'd been able to remember. Rosie was Bart's shining light. Now he seemed ready to snuff it all out again.

"Bart," she whispered as she slipped into his arms. "Bart please—"

"Stay here at the hotel, Rosie," he cut in. "You'll be safer where there are lots of folks around you."

"Safer?"

"Don't go to the law, Rosie. I don't want to complicate things, you hear?"

She stared at him as he lowered her to the ground. "Bart, what's become of you?"

"Just do what I say and don't ask questions."

"Oh, Bart."

"C'mon, Injun," Snort called. "Time's awastin'. Let's head over to the Bank Exchange Saloon and bend our elbows a spell."

"Rosie, get inside the hotel quick," Bart said in a low voice. "Take this and keep it hidden so no one sees." He thrust a small revolver into her hands. "I'll come back for you when I can."

Clutching the gun, she watched him stride away and swing up into the wagon. Without a backward glance, he drove the wagon from the hotel and steered it toward the nearest saloon.

Rosie stayed up in her little room all the rest of the day. She didn't feel up to going downstairs for lunch, and she knew she didn't stand a chance of putting on a cheerful demeanor for the hotel's owners and guests. Instead she sat in a rocking chair by the window and watched the trains pull in and out of town.

All the while she rocked, she held her hands over her stomach as if to protect the tiny life within her body. Visions of small hand-smocked linen dresses, knitted booties tied with white ribbons, quilted flannel coverlets and lacy crocheted blankets flitted through her thoughts and mingled with memories of whiskey bottles strewn about, coarse language and the cold steel of a six-shooter.

Maybe Manford Wade had been sent by God to tell Rosie to stick by Bart. But why did she have to bring a child into the world of outlaws with their foul smell and rough demeanor? A baby, no matter what its heritage, deserved the very best life had to offer.

She wanted picture books and sun-gilded tea parties, puppies and tender gardens for her baby. She wanted the child to go to school and to learn manners and decorum. She wanted fine clothes and good healthy food and clean skin. Most of all, she wanted loving parents to nurture and guard the baby until the time was ripe for opening windows and setting the child free.

If she told Bart about their baby, would that make the difference for him? Would it pull him back from the brink on which he now balanced? Or would a child even matter to him?

How well Rosie knew that Bart had never experienced the love of a father. His mother certainly hadn't given him the affection and gentleness he needed. So why should she think Bart would suddenly be filled with glowing images of fatherhood, as she was?

With a sigh, Rosie stood and went to the mirror over the washstand. As the dinner bell rang from the floor below her room, she brushed back strands of loose hair around her neck. What hope was left for her and the seed of life inside her? Even now Bart might be completing the plans that would destroy any dreams for happiness they had ever cherished.

With a weight of sadness heavy on her shoulders, Rosie left her room and made her way down the carpeted hall to the stairs. In the foyer, she followed the rest of the hotel guests into the dining room. Seated at a table by a window, she tried to make herself read the menu, but the words were a blur. She had just settled on chicken soup when a shout from a nearby table startled her.

"Laura Rose? Is that you?" In the dining room, not ten feet away, Rosie's father had risen from his chair and was crossing toward her. "At last I've found you! And it's about time."

Stunned, for a moment Rosie couldn't speak. "Oh, Pappy," she finally managed. "Hello."

"Stand up, young lady."

Rosie's urge to bolt was quelled by the sharp command. Accustomed to obeying her father's every word, she jumped to her feet.

"Laura Rose," he said, "you will accompany me out of this room at once, and I shall speak with you in my private quarters."

Dr. Vermillion took Rosie's hand and drew her away from the table. All but dragging her up the stairs, he unlocked the door to his suite and prodded his daughter through it.

"I want you to know, Laura Rose," he began, "I have been searching for you for six months. I engaged the Pinkerton National Detective Agency from New York City, and their men scoured the entire state of Missouri. Believe me, I've spared no expense in tracking you to this forsaken outpost. My dread was that you had been abducted for foul purposes. Far worse, I feared you might have run away as you stated in the cruel note you left behind when you vanished. Am I to assume that you did flee the man who loves you and—even yet—stands ready to make you his wife and take you into his fine home?"

Rosie wished the floor would open up and swallow her. "My note was accurate. I left on my own accord."

"Why?" he demanded. "Why in the name of all that is decent would you do such a thing? Have you any earthly idea the ramifications of your actions? Never mind the expense you've caused me, do you know what I've been subjected to personally?"

"No, sir. I don't."

"Why, it's taken every ounce of fortitude I possess to hold up my head in public. Your rash and thoughtless behavior threatened not only my standing in polite society, but my professional reputation as well."

"I'm so sorry, Pappy," Rosie murmured. "I didn't mean to cause you any harm."

"When I finally learned you had been observed laboring as a common waitress in this pitiful town, I could hardly believe my ears. Why? Why, Laura

Rose?" her father repeated. "What led you to do such a despicable thing?"

She cupped her hands over her stomach. "Oh, Pappy, it's because…because… I don't love him," she fumbled. "I don't love Dr. Lowell and I never have. He doesn't love me, either."

"Love?" the physician exploded. "What does love have to do with anything? We arranged a marriage, if you recall."

"You arranged it."

"And you agreed to it. Your life was beautifully laid out for you—tending a lovely home, managing more servants than I've ever kept, making the proper social calls and seeing that your husband's calendar of events was adequately filled."

"Yes, Pappy, but I didn't want that life."

"A life of leisure and luxury? Dr. Lowell stands ready to provide you with everything your heart could desire."

"Not everything," she said. "I want more than a husband. I want a real family—one in which the parents truly care for each other. Pappy, I know I've been heedless and willful, and I hope you can forgive me. But I do believe God directed me here. I've always wanted to be a teacher. And now that's what I am."

"A teacher? Laura Rose, you can't be serious."

"I certainly am serious. On obtaining my certification, I took a position at a school here in town. I earn a good salary, and in a few weeks I shall sign a contract for the 1883–84 school year."

"You most certainly will not," her father stated.

"Yes, I shall, sir. You know almost nothing about my dreams and hopes. You never have because you didn't ask me. You don't even know me well enough to guess the sort of life I long for. I've always wanted to teach school and I'm good at it. I won't let you take that away from me."

"I'm your father, young lady. I'll do with you exactly as I please."

Rosie squared her shoulders. "I'm a grown woman, not a child. You'll do nothing of the sort."

Dr. Vermillion let out a breath and rubbed his temples. "Oh, Laura Rose, you have been so difficult at times. You have no idea the trials you've brought me since your mother died. Your running away from me is a most ungrateful act."

"Please forgive me, Pappy. I truly didn't mean to hurt you in any way."

Dr. Vermillion shook his head. "Laura Rose, I can only assume that your desire to remain in this town as a teacher is a passing fancy—one from which you will recover in time. Now, if you'll allow me to escort you to your room, I shall settle the matter of our travel arrangements by return train to Kansas City tomorrow."

Dr. Vermillion hurried Rosie down the hall to her room. Though she protested, he took the key from her hand, unlocked the door and pressed her inside.

"You will stay in this room until morning," he said, "at which time I'll come for you and escort you to the train. You will return with me to our home in Kansas City where you will resume your life as if nothing scandalous had happened."

Trembling with anger and frustration, Rosie stared at him.

"I shall make it known," he continued, "that you left Kansas City and traveled to New York, where you have been fitted for your wedding trousseau and been trained for your future role as Dr. Lowell's wife."

"That will be a lie."

"Yes, but it will garner understanding for you from the women in our society. They, in turn, will pass that information to their husbands. You will then simply carry on as before. Do you understand?"

"Of course I do, Pappy."

"I had begun to wonder if you were even listening." He regarded her a moment longer. "At least your adventure in the west has had some benefit. You are looking quite lovely, Laura Rose. I believe once Dr. Lowell has seen you again, he will find it more than acceptable to resume our family's connection with his. Good evening, my dear."

Her father shut the door behind him, and then Rosie heard the key turn in the lock.

"Oh, God, oh, God!" Rosie prayed aloud, falling to her knees at the side of her bed. After hearing her father's footsteps fade away down the hall, she had drawn her curtains and turned down her bedding. Unable to make herself perform the most common tasks of washing her face and unwinding her hair, she could think only of rushing to her bedside to implore the Almighty.

"Dear Lord, if You ever loved me," she cried, "if You ever cared for me at all, help me now! Pappy has come for me. He's going to take me to that…that… odious man…."

Unable to go on, she gave in to the tears that had begun to flow. Against her cheeks, her hands grew wet, and sobs tore from her chest.

"Dear God, I can't…can't do this! I'm so confused.

So scared! Pappy wants to take me back to Kansas City, but…" She broke into tears again. "Oh, I want Bart so much. I don't know what to do, dear Lord. I want everything to be the way it was. What shall I do? Will I ever see Bart again? Where is he?"

"Now, don't put up holler, Rosie," a muffled voice said. "I'm under the bed."

Clapping her hand over her mouth, she gave a strangled squeal as a familiar pair of legs appeared, followed by a broad chest and massive shoulders. Finally, with a last grunt, Bart's head slid out from under the bed frame.

"Bart, you'll be the death of me yet. What on earth are you doing here?"

"Answering your prayers, I reckon." With a smile, he rolled onto his knees and took her in his arms. "I love you, girl. I wanted you to know I'm here for you— to protect you and keep you close. I'll always be yours."

"But…but how…?"

"I climbed through your window to bring you these." He held up a small brown sack.

"Huffman's cream candies!"

"Here, Rosie, have one."

How could she possibly think about sweets at a time like this? But in spite of everything, his kind gesture made her want to smile. "Bart—"

As she said his name, he popped a tiny candy into her open mouth.

"When I heard the key in the lock," he said as she chewed, "I scouted out the best hiding place I could find in a hurry before you and your pappy could walk through the door."

"Pappy is very unhappy with me," Rosie said.

He paused and regarded her evenly. "Is he still planning to marry you off to that Kansas City fellow?"

She nodded. "Dr. William Lowell."

"He tracked you down, did he?"

Nodding, she got up off her knees and sat on the bed. "He hired the Pinkertons, too."

Frowning, Bart eased up beside her. "Did he say anything about me?"

"No. But it won't be long before he finds out."

"Well, if this ain't a pickle."

She glanced at him as she swallowed the last of her candy. "At least you smell better than you did the last time you were under my bed."

Laughing, he threw one arm around her shoulders and gave her a hug. "Me and the boys got into a tangle with some fellows at the saloon, and I wound up in the horse trough. Good way to get a quick bath, I found out."

"You were fighting?"

"Just a friendly scuffle. Seems Bob's reputation as the killer of Jesse James doesn't make him as popular as he'd hoped. I tried to warn him about that, but he never was one to listen to good advice."

"So, the whole town knows who he is now? That means they know about you. Bart, you'll be arrested. Is that why you came to hide in my room? Are you running from the law again?"

"Rosie, you're as jumpy as a speckle-legged frog. Did you know that? I've never seen a woman who could worry as much as you."

"I'm trying to give everything to God," she said. "But I have good reason to fret. Pappy is planning to haul me back to Kansas City tomorrow to marry

Dr. Lowell. Bob Ford, Fancy and Snort are stirring up all sorts of trouble. The Pinkerton detectives and the deputy sheriffs are sniffing everywhere for you. And there's more…other things you don't even know about."

He drew her close. "I know all I need to know. I heard your prayer about us when I was under this bed, Rosie. You said you wanted me, and that's all that matters. God's going to take care of us, don't you know that? After all these years of going to church and teaching Sunday school, don't you trust the Lord, girl?"

"I trust God, Bart, but I don't know if I trust you."

"If you don't trust me now, I don't reckon you ever will. I promised to take care of you. I promised to work things out for us, and I aim to do just that."

She shook her head, wanting to believe him but so uncertain. His hand on her shoulder felt big and warm, so comforting that the memories of their happy days together on the little homestead flooded into her heart. Yet despite sun-filled images of sweet pies baking in the fireplace, fragrant peonies in a pitcher on the table, damp sheets flapping in the mountain breeze, Rosie couldn't shut away the threatening clouds that had gathered overhead.

"I want to trust you, Bart," she whispered. "It is as I said in my prayer—I want things to be the way they were before. But life isn't like one of the slates in my schoolroom. I can't just erase the parts I don't want."

He bent and kissed her cheek, his touch soft and endearing. "I hope you don't want to erase me, Rosie-girl. I told you once, you're the light of my life, the bright spot in all the dark years of my past. That still holds true—truer than ever. You've got to believe that I won't do anything to risk snuffing out that light."

"Oh, Bart, I need light, too! Things are crowding in on me and I can't... I just can't seem to..."

"Come here, darlin'. You've done enough crying for fifty folks lately." He took her up in his arms, drew her close and kissed the tears that had started down her cheeks. "Don't cry, Rosie. It's going to be all right, I promise."

"Don't, Bart," she said in a muffled voice. "I can't endure any more broken promises."

"I haven't broken a single promise since I found you here in Raton," he answered, but as he spoke the words, he shook his head. "Aw, Rosie, I know darkness hangs like a thunderstorm around us. I'm trying to comfort you, but things look about as bad as they can. I've done all I can to run off Ford and his pals, but they're still in town."

"Plotting a holdup? If you help them rob a train, Bart, your life is over."

He shrugged. "Folks know Jesse James's killer is in town."

"Do they know you've joined him?"

"They know Buck Springfield is an acquaintance."

"How long before one of the deputies remembers those wanted posters?"

"I'm not worried about that. I'm wondering how long it'll be before one of Ford's boys calls me by my real name."

"If the Pinkerton men tracked me down," Rosie said, "how long can it be before they follow the trail straight to you?"

Bart was silent a moment. "What about this feller who aims to become your husband? Your pappy locked you up in this room with every intent of taking you back to Kansas City tomorrow to marry you off to that doctor."

Rosie brushed the tears from her cheeks. "What else can I do? What future can we ever have together?"

With a muffled cry, he pulled her close. "I love you, Rosie. You're my wife, and I'm not going to let anything come between us. Nothing!"

"How can you say that? What hope do we have?"

"Rosie," he said, taking her head in his hands and lifting her face to meet his. "Rosie, say you love me. Give me that tonight."

A wayward tear trickled out of the corner of her eye. "I do love you, Bart. I love you with all my heart. If the darkness comes, Bart, remember that."

With a groan of anguish, Bart hugged Rosie close. She slipped her arms around his shoulders and kissed him. Oh, his breath was warm and sweet, and his skin smelled of rainwater! She tangled her fingers in his hair as he pulled the pins from the soft knot at the nape of her neck.

As the long hours of the night drifted away, they loved each other in the expression of promise and hope that only a husband and wife can know.

Chapter Nineteen

"Laura Rose." The rattle of a key in the lock sent Rosie bolt upright in bed.

"Oh, no!" she cried in a hoarse whisper.

"What is it, darlin'?" Bart asked, sitting up in a tangle of sheets.

"Hush! It's my pappy!" Rosie pushed him with all her strength. Bart rolled to the floor and began scrambling under her bed yet again.

"Laura Rose? I expected you to be up and packed by now." Dr. Vermillion walked into the room just as Bart's head disappeared below the edge of the bed.

She jerked her sheet up to her neck. "Pappy, you have entered my room without my permission."

"I beg your pardon," her father said. "I forget you're no longer my little Rosie."

"I'm far from that. I'm twenty, now."

"Two or twenty, you'll always be a child to me. Only a parent can understand that."

"I do understand," she said, thinking of the baby who even now moved inside her. "More than you know."

With a chuckle, he shook his head. "We'll see what

comes of your marriage to Dr. Lowell, my dear. Now be dressed in fifteen minutes or we'll miss the train."

As he shut the door, Rosie hurried across the room and set a chair beneath the knob. "And stay out," she added as a final note.

"Rosie, darlin'," Bart said as he clambered out from under the bed. "That was a close one. I wonder what your pappy would've said to finding a man under your bed."

"Better than in it anyhow." She couldn't help smiling, but as quickly as it had started, her smile fell away. "Oh, Bart, my pappy has my life all planned out."

"Only God can map out a life, Rosie-girl. You stood up to your pappy pretty good if you ask me. It won't be long before you convince him you're no longer his little baby. You're mine."

"I won't be if Dr. Lowell marries me. I've seen the man. I know his reputation. If he ever gets me alone—"

"No!" Bart caught her by the shoulders. "He's not ever going to have you to himself, Rosie. No man but me will share your bed. I swear it. Now, get yourself dressed and keep that chair under the doorknob. I've got to take care of a few things with the boys, and then—"

"The boys! Bart, you aren't going back to Bob Ford, are you?"

"Rosie, I've got to square things with him. What I have in mind won't take more than an hour, and then I'll come back here for you."

"My father will get the hotel to tear down this door, Bart. Once he makes up his mind to do something, he does it. He searched half the continent for me, and he's bound and determined to take me home. I can't hold him off for an hour."

"You have to. Use that gun I gave you if nothing else works."

"But why can't you take me with you? What are you going to do?"

He put a finger over her lips. "Don't ask. If you don't know what I'm up to, you won't worry. And you won't tell your pappy. This business is between me and Bob Ford. I'm going to take care of our future, Rosie—in every which way."

"But what are you going to do?"

As images of Bart robbing a train flooded through her, Rosie tried to grab him while he pulled on his buckskin jacket and his denim britches. But he was already making for the window, and by the time she reached him, he was halfway out.

"Let me go, Rosie," he said, taking her hand from his jacket. "It's got to be this way."

After kissing the back of her hand, he climbed through the window and skittered down the sloping roof. As she watched him leap down and disappear into a tangle of honeysuckle, she felt a thick lump form in her throat.

"Oh, Bart," Rosie whispered. "You don't know what you've just asked of me."

She pushed down the window, and for a long time she stood gazing out at the mesas that ringed the town of Raton. This first day of July, a Sunday, would be blistering hot.

After morning church, children would play marbles and hopscotch in the cool shadows of their homes. Mothers would read from the Bible until their young ones napped. Fathers would drip with sweat as they tended their stock. Dogs would lie panting under wagons, and rattlesnakes would bask on burning stones.

Would this be the day Bart Kingsley robbed a train? Was that how he intended to settle his future with Rosie—in a flurry of bullets, a life on the run and easy money taken from others who had earned it the honest way? Did he think that her love would bind her to him, no matter what he did?

Gazing down at the opened box of cream candies, Rosie tried to picture herself living in such a world. Plenty of other women did, she knew. There was nothing so unusual about falling in love with an outlaw and following him on the trail until the law caught up with him.

Could she do it? Did she love Bart enough? She certainly did love him. There was no question in her mind about that. She certainly didn't want to go back to Kansas City with her father.

If word about Bob Ford's schemes got out, and if people learned about Bart's past, Rosie would lose her teaching position. Traveling with an outlaw gang might be her only choice.

When she considered all the options, one thing took precedence. Her child.

Never, never would she bring a baby into a world of guns and fists, a life of tobacco smoke and whiskey, a home filled with cussing, quarreling and threats. Bart had not been brought up with a father and mother who loved and nurtured him. She was raised by a man who treated his daughter little better than some of his possessions.

But this baby, this innocent life inside her body, deserved the best she had to offer.

As Rosie stood by the window, she knew what her choice must be. There was only one place where this child could receive love, security, nourishment, clothing, education—a future.

Clamping her jaw tight against threatening tears, Rosie began to dress. "Let me go," Bart had begged. Although he vowed he loved her, he couldn't escape the truth about himself. He wanted to be set free. He wanted his old ways, the life he knew best—*Let me go.*

"Yes, Bart," she whispered as she drew her shawl around her shoulders and pulled the chair out from under the doorknob. "Because I love you so, I'll let you go."

At seven forty-five the Atchison, Topeka and Santa Fe engine pulled out of Raton station. Steam blanketed the windows, and chunks of burning coal shot from the firebox as the train gathered speed on its way to Denver. The whistle blew, and the turning of the wheels settled into a rhythmic click on the tracks.

Rosie sat wedged in the corner of a seat in a passenger car, her eyes shut and her throat working hard to swallow the thick lump lodged in it. As hard as she tried to block all sound, all sight and every sense in her body, she couldn't help but hear the voices of the men who sat nearby.

"Railroad stocks are up, you know," a passenger told her father. "I'm thinking of investing some capital myself, and the Atchison, Topeka and Santa Fe line has impressed me greatly."

"With round-trip tickets to Kansas City at twenty-five dollars, she'll be bringing in a pretty penny." Rosie's father tapped the newspaper in his hand. "You should speak with Mr. W. F. White. He's the general passenger agent and a good friend of mine. He could give you the inside story."

"What about this Harvey fellow? I hear he's taking over restaurants all along the line. Clever idea, if you ask me."

"Indeed. He used to hire men to service his eating houses, but it seems they haven't worked out as well as the women he's using now. Mr. Davis, the hotel proprietor, told me that Raton is where Fred Harvey first hired women. It seems he was having a difficult time keeping his male employees in line. The changeover worked so well, he's converting all his staff to women."

"Makes sense, of course," the other man concluded. "Women belong in roles of servitude. It suits their God-given nature best."

"Naturally. Of course, Harvey will want to retain his male chefs. I'm told he imports them from the continent."

"The continent! Maybe the Harvey Houses would make a good investment. You can't deny he's positioned to expand."

Rosie wished she could fade into the upholstery of her seat. It was obvious the men hardly noticed she was there. Having accomplished his aim of rounding her up like a lost cow, her father had switched his focus back to business.

He didn't even seem to remember that she herself had worked for Fred Harvey and would have an insider's view of his operation.

Oh, she felt ill again! Though she longed to look

outside, she couldn't bring herself to sit up. It had been terribly difficult to see for the last time the townspeople she loved so dearly.

The hotelkeeper had intercepted her in the foyer with word that a message had come for "Buck." Rosie had forced a smile and said she'd let him know. But of course she couldn't. She would never see Bart again. Even if he returned to Kansas City, she couldn't let him near. Her heart was too fragile and their child's life too precious.

How difficult it had been to leave the hotel and stand on the railway platform for the last time. Etta had waved at Rosie from inside the dining room, where she was serving breakfast. The baggage boys called her name as they scurried to load the train with trunks and parcels. The owner of the livery stable inquired as to Buck's health. She gave him a brief greeting as he hurried on.

They were all behind her now—Raton and the people who had brought her the only freedom she'd ever known. Somewhere behind her, Mr. Kilgore and his wife were dressing for church. They would check in on the classroom before climbing into their buggy. Reverend Cullen would be studying his sermon notes.

Cheyenne Bill, now a regular at church, would button on his new white collar and comb his hair the way Rosie had taught him. Mrs. Wade would visit her son Manford's flower-strewn grave. Tom and Griff would sniff the ground around one of the saloons, then dig beds in the bare dirt and settle in for a long snooze.

It had been a good time, hadn't it? Rosie thought. In spite of the ups and downs, the uncertainties and worries, she had been happy in Raton. Very happy.

The best and most poignant memories were of her days with Bart Kingsley. She thought of their little homestead. Were the chickens up and scratching in the dirt? Had the morning glories bloomed on the tree by the river? Were jackrabbits peeking through the fencing around her kitchen garden as dew evaporated from the heads of lettuce?

"Butchers' cattle are scarce this summer," Dr. Vermillion told the passenger in their car. "Thirty-five to forty dollars, I hear. Milk cows run from thirty to sixty according to quality, and yearlings are going for eighteen to twenty-two. My stock will be up—well up. As a matter of fact, I'm finding myself constantly on the lookout for new investments. I'm considering the purchase of some fine art pieces for the house. I may make an excursion to New York or possibly Paris. I imagine I can solicit any number of suitable traveling companions from my club. The only problem I'll have is taking time away from my office."

"I see your visit out west has whetted your appetite for adventure, Dr. Vermillion."

"A trifle." The man laughed and Rosie realized what a contrast it was to Bart's deep chuckle.

They'd had had such fun, teasing each other and laughing—never mind that they were adults and led a responsible life on their farm.

Oh, those sun-sprinkled days! What would Rosie ever do without them? What would she ever do without Bart? And the child...never to know a good father, one who tickled and romped and played.

Of course she would never marry Dr. Lowell. Rosie's pregnancy and the ensuing baby would take care of that problem. The esteemed physician with a rumored reputation as a bully would doubtless refuse to consider honoring their arrangement. That alone eased Rosie's heart.

She squeezed her eyes shut and laid a warm hand on her stomach. Bart would have made a good father, no matter if he had gone back to his outlaw ways. He was a tender and kind man, and he knew just how to ease a troubled spirit. It was true, too, what Bart had promised Rosie. He had protected her. He had provided for her. And he'd kept her secure. He would do the same for a child—she had no doubt about that.

"Hams are running eighteen to twenty cents a pound out here in the territory," Dr. Vermillion was saying, "and dressed pork is at ten."

"No!"

"I should say so. If I had my books here, what I couldn't do! The love of money may be the root of all evil, but it keeps a man climbing to the top, you know."

"Yes, indeed."

Rosie's father joined the other man in laughter as the train chugged into a tunnel and darkness fell over the car. It was a long tunnel, and the intensity of the gloom silenced the passengers and made Rosie open her eyes.

Utter, utter blackness. A shade of ebony she could not recall in the darkest of her dreams. And this was how Bart had described his life without her.

Oh, Bart…

What did it really matter that he had unsavory pals or a wicked past? She recalled Dr. Kohlhouser's reminder that no one was perfect, not even her pappy. Without Bart, Rosie knew her life would be as bleak and empty as this dark tunnel. Surely God's hand hadn't brought them together again only to tear them apart. In Kansas City, she and her baby might be safe, but what joy would there be in a world without Bart? Without love?

"Pappy," she said, opening her mouth for the first time since the train left the station. "Pappy, I must speak with you."

"Laura Rose, what is it? This is only a tunnel. Are you afraid?"

She stood, swaying in the darkness. "I'm not afraid. Not at all. And I've come to a decision. When the train stops at the next station, I will get off. I'm going back to Raton where I belong."

"I beg your pardon?" Her father's hand clamped over her wrist, but she shook it off. "There are things you don't know about me, Pappy. Things you can't understand and never will. For six years you've denied the truth that I was already married when Dr. Lowell spoke for me."

"Laura Rose!" the physician exclaimed as the train emerged from the tunnel. "You are imagining things."

Rosie saw his face as light filled the car. "I married Bart Kingsley six years ago, and you know it," she stated firmly. "I'm a married woman, and what's more I am now carrying his—"

"A holdup!" someone screamed from the front of the car. "It's a holdup! We're being robbed!"

"Robbed!" Cries of dismay flooded the car as the passengers scrambled to the windows. The train began to squeal to a halt, and great clouds of steam billowed from beneath the engine.

As it lurched to a sudden stop, the passengers in the crowded car were tossed back and forth, jerked and shaken like rag dolls.

"A holdup! Look—gunmen!" Rosie elbowed her father aside and stuck her head out the window. Sure enough, three men on horses had surrounded the engine. The engineer was climbing down from his station, and the fireman had leaped from the box. Expecting strangers with bandanna-covered faces and armloads of weaponry, Rosie was dismayed to see men she recognized instantly.

"Bob Ford!" she gasped. "And Snort and Fancy! Oh, no—not *this* train, Bart! Not *this* train!"

But her hopes died as the door to her car banged open and Bart Kingsley climbed aboard, his six-shooter drawn. Striding past the cowering passengers, he doffed his hat.

"Morning, folks," he said, handling the gun with an absent air. "Sorry to trouble you. Hey, there, Rosie-girl."

"Bart!" Wide-eyed she watched him walk toward her, his towering form a startling contrast with the smaller men who hovered protectively around their wives and children. "Bart, don't do this!"

"Don't do what?" He stopped, a puzzled expression on his face. "We've come to save you, darlin'. Don't you want to be rescued?"

"Save me?" She glanced at her father, who was trembling like an aspen leaf in autumn, his face florid. "From what?"

"You don't mean you went willingly with your pappy, do you?" he asked as he took off his hat in bewilderment.

"Well I... I..."

"Of course she came with me willingly," Dr. Vermillion sputtered. "And who are you?"

"Don't you know me, doc? I used to work for you out at your country house. I'm Bart Kingsley. I'm Rosie's husband."

"Her husband? You certainly are not! My daughter is unmarried, and her future husband awaits her in Kansas City."

"Is that so?" Bart flipped back the edge of his buckskin jacket and drew a folded sheet of paper from his britches pocket. "I've carried this certificate every day of my life. A true and verified marriage license from the state of Missouri."

"A marriage license?" Dr. Vermillion exploded. "Laura Rose never told me anything about a legal license."

"You were so angry, Pappy. You wouldn't listen to a thing I said."

"It's legal, all right," Bart assured him. "Dr. Vermillion, I'm your son-in-law and have been for six years."

Rosie glanced at her father, who had gone as white as a sheet.

"It's true, Pappy," she told him. "Bart and I are married, and we have been all these years. I've loved him every day of every one of those years, and I love him now more than ever."

She turned to the passengers on the train who stood gawking. "Bart and I were wrong to deceive the good people of Raton, but we didn't do it out of malice."

"I mean to make a good life for both of us," Bart concurred. "And I mean to keep on loving my wife and making her happy as long as…as, well, forever."

"Laura Rose," her father spoke in a low voice. "You're standing there ruining every chance I ever gave you in life."

"No, Pappy." She moved to stand at Bart's side. "What God has joined together, no man should tear apart. I belong with Bart, no matter what comes our way. I trust him…" She caught herself for a moment. Then certainty flooded her. "Yes, I do—I trust Bart to protect me and keep me safe. I trust him to see to my livelihood and my happiness."

Glancing up at the tall man whose green eyes shone, she placed her hands over the soft curve of her belly before adding, "And I trust him to provide a good home for our baby."

"Baby?" Bart grabbed Rosie's shoulders and swung her around. "Baby?"

She laughed. "If God's willing, Bart Kingsley, I'll make you a papa in January."

"Hallelujah!" He swung her up in his arms and planted a big kiss on her lips.

"What's going on here?" a voice said behind Bart's shoulder. "You still holding up this train, Mr. Kingsley?"

As Bart turned, Rosie saw two of Raton's deputy sheriffs striding down the aisle. But before the chill of fear had a chance to wash through her, the man clapped Bart on the back.

"Gonna be a papa, huh?" one of them said. "Well, good thing. You can set that kid on the right track so he don't steer off it like you did."

"Sure enough." Bart laughed again and gave Rosie another hug. "Come on, girl, we've held this train up long enough, don't you reckon?"

"You're not…robbing it?" she whispered.

"Now, why would I do a thing like that? Beets selling for five cents a pound, chickens laying so fast you can't keep up with them, cows so fat they're practically giving buttermilk and…and a baby on the way! I'm the richest man in the world, Rosie-girl."

As he turned to escort his wife down the aisle, Bart gave her father a backward glance. "So long, Dr. Vermillion. Don't you worry yourself now. I'll take care of Rosie. I always said I would, you know. And don't be a stranger—I want my babies to know their grandpappy."

The morning sunshine hit Rosie full in the face as she and Bart left the shelter of the passenger car.

"Hey, boys, I got me a young'un coming!" he called to Ford and the others. "How about that?"

"Yahoo!" Snort shouted and fired off two rounds as the train whistle blew and the engine began to build up steam.

Bart leaned close and whispered to Rosie on his way to his horse. "Were you ever going to tell me about the baby?"

She gave a happy shrug. "Not unless you straightened yourself up. And I guess you did."

"I didn't change myself, Rosie. A man can only do so much. God changed me. He's the only way I got out of the mess I was tangled up in for so long. It took an act of God to straighten me up and help me walk straight."

"God *and* a loving wife." She gave him a sideways glance and then giggled. "But how did you manage to sweet-talk the deputies and get Bob Ford to help you stop the train? Bart, what's going on?"

He set her on her feet by the stallion he had ridden into a lather all the way from the livery stable. Patting the horse on the neck, he waved and hollered his thanks as Ford, Snort, Fancy and the deputies started back down the track toward Raton.

"When I left you this morning," he explained when they were alone at last, "I went to the boys and laid out the straight line. I told them they could do whatever they wanted, but I wasn't going to be party to holding up any more trains. Ford was mad as a rattler on a hot skillet. He kept jawing at me while I walked back to the hotel to fetch you, but I just kept telling him he had no choice but to go straight. Before I knew it, he'd up and decided he would do just that. When we got into the lobby, the manager handed me a letter that had come in the mail a few days back. It was from Frank James."

"Jesse's brother?"

"Sure enough. He allowed as how after he got my letter, he talked to his pals in Missouri—and he's got friends in high places, you know. Seems the law decided to check out what little hand I had in those train robberies, and Frank volunteered to vouch for me. It didn't take too long before they'd cleared my record off the books."

"Really? Oh, Bart, that's wonderful!"

"Only thing—they don't particularly want me back in Missouri. Fact is, they said if I set foot in the state, they'd arrest me."

"That's fine with me," Rosie said with relief.

"I reckoned you wouldn't care too awful much. Me and the boys had started up the stairs after you, when lo and behold, the manager said you'd gone off to the depot with the man who'd marched you out of the dining room the night before. I'll be jiggered if it wasn't Bob Ford who came up with the notion to round up the deputies, hold up the train and haul you off."

"But you didn't know I left Raton on purpose," Rosie said.

"Why did you do that, darlin'? Why'd you leave me again, after all we've been through?"

She sighed. "It was the baby, Bart. I want a good life for this child, and I could only think how awful it would be to bring up our little one in an outlaw's world. But once I'd gone a short distance on the train, I knew I'd been crazy to leave. We were inside the tunnel when I made up my mind to get off at the next station and come home to you, no matter what kind of life we had to live."

Bart softly kissed her cheek. "I promised you a good life, Rosie," he said. "When will you trust me to give you that?"

She gazed up into his green eyes. "Now, Bart. I'll trust you right now."

"Then hop on this horse, girl, and let's head for home. Those poor milk cows are probably about to bust their britches."

Laughing, Rosie set her foot in the stirrup. Bart cupped her waist with his hands and helped her up into the saddle.

He climbed on behind her, took the reins and spurred the horse down the hill toward Raton.

As they rode along, Rosie leaned her head back on his shoulder and shut her eyes in the warmth of the golden morning sun. "It's a bright day, Bart Kingsley," she whispered. "A bright day after a long, dark night."

Placing his hand over her stomach, he kissed her lips. "A bright, clear, shining day, and not a cloud in sight, Rosie-girl."

* * * * *

Author's Note

The mesa-rimmed town of Raton, New Mexico, saw many prosperous years to come with farming, livestock, railroading and coal mining as profitable industries. According to *The Raton Comet* and other publications, the historical characters in *The Gunman's Bride* went on to lead peaceful lives.

Mr. Thomas Kilgore's students began attending school in a brand-new building in fall 1884. Charles Adams sold the Comet in 1886, and the newspaper was renamed *The Raton Range*. It continues to publish today. The Reverend J. A. Cullen resigned his pastorate in 1883, and his position was filled by the Reverend J. W. Sinnock. Dr. Kohlhouser's beautiful home on Third Street was converted into St. Patrick's Academy. His dog, Griff, no doubt joined the rest of Raton at the funeral of W. A. White's beloved canine, Tom, who was laid to rest beneath a beautifully carved tombstone in March 1885.

Cheyenne Bill, the popular boxer, bolstered his reputation as "a hard, hard man" by winning so many bouts that he came to be called the Terror of the Wicked West. He rigged himself up in fine new clothes, got a haircut, went regularly to church and continued to be the subject of humorous but good-natured poetry published in the local newspaper.

Mathias Broyles Stockton became the new sheriff of Raton in June 1883. That same year, Charly Baker was found guilty of criminal negligence in the shooting death of eleven-year-old Manford Wade.

Robert Ford ran into trouble with Raton's deputy sheriff, Jack Miller, and challenged him to a gunfight. Ford failed to appear, was branded a coward and was run out of town. After roaming the west in a failed attempt to capitalize on the killing of Jesse James, he was gunned down in a saloon in Creed, Colorado, in 1892.

In Missouri, Frank James succeeded in his goal of living a quiet life with a home, wife and children. The brother of Jesse James died a natural death in 1915.

It should be recorded that on the evening of January 10, 1884, Mr. and Mrs. Bart Kingsley became the proud parents of a healthy nine-pound boy whom they named Buck. And, of course, they all lived happily ever after.

To learn more about the factual basis for *The Gunman's Bride*, the author suggests the following:

Conway, Jay T. *A Brief Community History of Raton, New Mexico: 1880–1930*. Raton: Smith's Printing & Stationery, 1991.

New Mexico Magazine (various articles). Sante Fe, New Mexico.

Poling-Kempes, Lesley. *The Harvey Girls: Women Who Opened the West*. New York: Paragon House, 1989.

The Raton Comet (all issues from 1883). Raton, New Mexico.

Stanley, F. *Raton Chronicle*. Raton Historical Society.

**WE HOPE YOU ENJOYED
THIS BOOK FROM**

LOVE INSPIRED

INSPIRATIONAL ROMANCE

 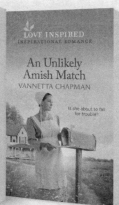

Uplifting stories of faith, forgiveness and hope.

Fall in love with stories where faith helps
guide you through life's challenges, and discover
the promise of a new beginning.

6 NEW BOOKS AVAILABLE EVERY MONTH!

SPECIAL EXCERPT FROM

LOVE INSPIRED
INSPIRATIONAL ROMANCE

Temporarily in her Amish community to help with her sick brother's business, nurse Rachel Blank can't wait to get back to the Englisch *world...and far away from Arden Esh. Her brother's headstrong carpentry partner challenges her at every turn. But when a family crisis redefines their relationship, will Rachel realize the life she really wants is right here...with Arden?*

Read on for a sneak preview of
The Amish Nurse's Suitor *by Carrie Lighte,*
available April 2020 from Love Inspired.

The soup scalded Arden's tongue and gave him something to distract himself from the topsy-turvy way he was feeling. As he chugged down half a glass of milk, Rachel remarked how tired Ivan still seemed.

"*Jah*, he practically dozed off midsentence in his room."

"I'll have to wake him soon for his medication. And to check for a fever. They said to watch for that. A relapse of pneumonia can be even worse than the initial bout."

"You're going to need endurance, too."

"What?"

"You prayed I'd have endurance. You're going to need it, too," Arden explained. "There were a lot of nurses in the hospital, but here you're on your own."

"Don't you think I'm qualified to take care of him by myself?"

That wasn't what he'd meant at all. Arden was surprised by the plea for reassurance in Rachel's question. Usually, she seemed so confident. "I can't think of anyone better qualified to take care of him. But he's got a long road to recovery ahead, and you're going to need help so you don't wear yourself out."

"I told Hadassah I'd *wilkom* her help, but I don't think I can count on her. Joyce and Albert won't return from Canada for a couple more weeks, according to Ivan."

"In addition to Grace, there are others in the community who will be *hallich* to help."

"I don't know about that. I'm worried they'll stay away because of my presence. Maybe Ivan would have been better off without me here. Maybe my coming here was a mistake."

"*Neh.* It wasn't a mistake." Upon seeing the fragile vulnerability in Rachel's eyes, Arden's heart ballooned with compassion. "Trust me, the community will *kumme* to help."

"In that case, I'd better keep dessert and tea on hand," Rachel said, smiling once again.

"Does that mean we can't have a slice of that pie over there?"

"Of course it doesn't. And since Ivan has no appetite, you and I might as well have large pieces."

Supping with Rachel after a hard day's work, encouraging her and discussing Ivan's care as if he were…not a child, but *like* a child, felt… Well, it felt like how Arden always imagined it would feel if he had a family of his own. Which was probably why, half an hour later as he directed his horse toward home, Arden's stomach was full, but he couldn't shake the aching emptiness he felt inside.

She is going back, so I'd better not get too accustomed to her company, as pleasant as it's turning out to be.

Don't miss
The Amish Nurse's Suitor *by Carrie Lighte,*
available April 2020 wherever
Love Inspired books and ebooks are sold.

LoveInspired.com

Daisy went over to the bassinet and lifted out Tony,
cradling him against her. "Of course. There's lots
more video, but another time. The footage of what the
ranch looked like before Noah started rebuilding to the
day I helped put up the grand reopening banner—it's
amazing."

Harrison wasn't sure he wanted to see any of that. No,
he knew he didn't. This was all too much. "Well, I'll be
in touch about that tour."

*That's it. Keep it nice and impersonal. "Be in touch"
was a sure distance maker.*

She eyed him and lifted her chin. "Oh—I almost
forgot! I have a favor to ask, Harrison."

Gulp. How was he supposed to emotionally distance
himself by doing her a favor?

She smiled that dazzling smile. The one that drew him like nothing else could. "If you're not busy around five o'clock or so, I'd love your help in putting together the rocking cradle my brother Rex ordered for Tony. It arrived yesterday, and I tried to put it together, but it has directions a mile long that I can't make heads or tails of. Don't tell my brother Axel I said this—he's a wizard at GPS, maps and terrain—but give him instructions and he holds the paper upside down."

Ah. This was almost a relief. He'd put together the cradle alone. No chitchat. No old family movies. Just him, a set of instructions and five thousand various pieces of cradle. "I'm actually pretty handy. Sure, I can help you."

"Perfect," she said. "See you at fiveish."

A few minutes later, as he stood on the porch watching her walk back up the path, he had a feeling he was at a serious disadvantage in this deal.

Because the farther away she got, the more he wanted to chase after her and just keep talking. Which sent off serious warning bells. That Harrison might actually more than just like Daisy Dawson already—and it was only day one of the deal.